At Love's
Bidding

Books by Regina Jennings

LADIES OF CALDWELL COUNTY

Sixty Acres and a Bride

Love in the Balance

Caught in the Middle

A Most Inconvenient Marriage

At Love's Bidding

*An Unforeseen Match**

*featured in the novella collection *A Match Made in Texas*

AT LOVE'S BIDDING

REGINA JENNINGS

F
JEN

BETHANYHOUSE

a division of Baker Publishing Group
Minneapolis, Minnesota

© 2015 by Regina Jennings

Published by Bethany House Publishers
11400 Hampshire Avenue South
Bloomington, Minnesota 55438
www.bethanyhouse.com

Bethany House Publishers is a division of
Baker Publishing Group, Grand Rapids, Michigan

Printed in the United States of America

Library of Congress Cataloging-in-Publication Data

Jennings, Regina (Regina Lea)
    At love's bidding / Regina Jennings.
      pages cm
    Summary: "In 1873, when Boston native Miranda Wimplegate mistakenly auctions off a prized portrait, her grandfather purchases the entire Missouri Ozarks auction house where it was sent. After traveling to the Ozarks to recover it, they make surprising discoveries about their new business"— Provided by publisher.
    ISBN 978-0-7642-1141-6 (softcover)
    1. Man-woman relationships—Fiction. 2. Missouri—Social life and customs—19th century—Fiction. 3. Ozark Mountains—Social life and customs—19th century—Fiction. I. Title.
PS3610.E5614A95 2015
813'.6—dc23   2015015392

Scripture quotations are from the King James Version of the Bible.

Cover design by John Hamilton

Author is represented by Books & Such Literary Agency

15 16 17 18 19 20 21   7 6 5 4 3 2 1

CHAPTER 1

Boston, Massachusetts
May 1873

Behind the massive marble building where even in May the crisp sea air never chased away the odors ground into the cobblestones, the newsboys and shoe-shiners gathered, waiting on her. They didn't have much time. Every moment away from their posts meant missed customers, but Miranda Wimplegate was under similar constraints. The auction only paused briefly at noon, just enough time for her to snatch a tray of apricot tarts and French meringues and sneak out before Grandfather took the platform and the bidding resumed. The silver platter dug into Miranda's side as she made her way down the narrow steps of the servants' entrance. She wished for something more substantial to feed them, but the dirty scamps of Boston—unlike the French *citoyens*—preferred cake, so her head was safe, at least until her mother learned of her largesse.

Little Ralphie sat at the foot of the steps, but he hopped up quick enough when she opened the door. He was nearly trampled as the boys wrestled for the sweets on the tray, but she held back a choice few for him. After they settled down,

Miranda took her perch on the top step, Ralphie sitting next to her French kid boots. They weren't really kid leather, probably just cow, but Ralphie didn't know the difference. He was content nibbling the edge of the tart, holding it in hands as grubby as the bottom of the trash bin beside him.

"Well, are you gonna tell one of your stories or not?" That was Connor. Quick to express his impatience but always listening, always thinking. He wouldn't work the corner in front of the Wimplegate Auction House much longer. Already his shoulders were broadening. Soon he'd catch the eye of one of the dock foremen and would give up hawking papers for a better paying job—a job that would begin to bow his back before it ever had a chance to reach its full height.

Miranda balanced the empty silver tray on her lap, careful to keep it from getting scratched against the rough ground. "We'll continue the story about Joseph. You remember what I told you yesterday?"

"Aye."

"Sure."

Two boys tussled as boys do when one wants to savor a treat and the other has already consumed his. With a quick thump to their heads, Connor quieted them.

He was trying to help, but Miranda saw an opportunity for improvement. "Connor, I'd rather be interrupted than have you inflict pain on someone. Remember that, please. Turn the other cheek . . . and our story today is a perfect example." She tried to smooth Ralphie's stiff red hair as she began. "Joseph was sold as a slave by his brothers, but God didn't forget him. . . ."

How she wished they still had the neat classroom leased across the alley, but since Grandmother died, Grandfather had let his work with the street children wane. He was all business now, but she couldn't give it up, even if Mother didn't approve of her feeding their expensive sweets to the urchins. As she talked, Miranda glanced between the buildings for a glimpse of the church clock on Park Street. She was running out of time.

But someone else was in a hurry, too. The sound of hooves clacking on the cobblestone street preceded the jet black buggy careening around the corner. What was this? No one made their arrival in this alley, especially not someone riding in a conveyance like that. The horses expelled a burst of moisture as the buggy rolled to a stop at the corner. Was this another buyer, rushing in from some gilded minor palace of Europe? If he was in search of a particular piece of art, he should have taken an earlier boat.

Ralphie shifted to get a better look as the door opened and a modestly dressed man emerged. Clothes nicer than a clerk's, but only just. Black suit, nondescript features. He closed the door of the carriage and leaned back into the window. A velvet curtain was pushed aside. Nodding, he seemed to accept some secret commission with the intensity of a matador. A lady's gloved hand emerged to grip the door frame. Longing crossed his plain face as he took the final instructions, transforming his features into more noble lines. Finally, with a gallant tip of his hat to the woman inside the carriage, he sprang from the step and strolled determinedly around the corner to the front of the building.

A mission. There was no other way to describe his attitude. His chances would've been better had he arrived promptly, but why walk through the rotting potato skins of the alley when he could have been delivered directly to the impressive double doors in front?

But had he bothered to look Miranda's direction, he'd probably wonder why a lady decked out in silk was kneeling among the street kids in a back alley. If only she had the courage to insist that Father lease a place for their lessons to continue. . . .

Before Miranda could get back to the lesson, shouts were heard from the opposite direction. Another of her newspaper boys skidded around the corner with two big youths at his heels. It was Franklin, and judging by the bullies chasing after him, he was in trouble. Catching him by the collar of his threadbare shirt, one of the thugs threw him against the wall.

"I said, give me your money. I'm hungry and you already had something to eat."

"It's my money. I have to take it home."

Not wanting her youngsters to get involved, it was up to Miranda to intervene. She only wished the two bullies weren't quite so big. Then again, who wasn't taller than she?

"Stay here," she ordered the boys. Forgetting the silver tray in her hand, she picked her way over her seated audience.

"Excuse me?" She gripped her wrist with her empty hand to hide its trembling and approached in her most winsome manner. "Excuse me? Is there something I can help you with?" But she might as well have been invisible.

Miranda winced at Franklin's whimper as he was lifted from the ground. The sound of ripping cloth sped her approach. "Now, gentlemen, there's no need to tear his clothing. What good does that do?"

"It's not in his pocket," one youth growled. "He's hiding it."

Franklin's feet dangled in midair. His face bloomed tomato red as the boy's clutch on his twisted collar tightened. Miranda looked behind her to the back door of the auction house. Could she run inside and find help?

Before she could decide, Franklin's head hit the brick wall. *Thud.* "If you don't hand the money over, I'll beat it out of you." *Thud*. "You won't be able to eat anything tonight." *Thud*. "Tell your mother—"

Franklin's little skull ricocheted off the wall with each thrust. The only fighting he was doing was fighting for air.

Miranda felt her own face warming. Her jaw clenched and then somehow the heavy tray was making a huge arc through the air and slamming the thug upside the head. The handle dug into her soft palm as she continued to swing her silver weapon and land some impressive blows that rattled her teeth.

"What's wrong with you, lady?" the bully yelled, his arms shielding his face.

"She's crazy!" the other shouted.

"You will not mistreat this child!" Miranda swung with every word, most of her strikes landing on the solid young men. One missed swing connected with the brick wall and made her see stars, but it didn't slow her down. "Depart, and don't let me catch you or . . ."

They dropped Franklin and took off. The holey soles of their boots flashed as they ran away. Miranda blinked. She hadn't even finished her threat, which was good because she really didn't know what she was planning. The roaring in her ears subsided until she could hear the street sounds again. She lowered the tray, afraid to turn around and face her young friends. She'd always congratulated herself on the example of refined womanhood, genteel manners, and Christian love that she displayed for the disadvantaged youth. How much damage had she done in an instant?

Judging by the boys' cheers and laughter, she'd just reinforced the very behavior she was trying to eradicate. Lovely.

Surrounded by his peers, Franklin was on his feet and enjoying the attention as the boys gathered their wares and prepared to return to their stations. Their eyes shined as they waved good-bye to her, not the least bit embarrassed for her unladylike display. Living in the slums, they probably witnessed such behavior regularly. Miranda shuddered. Deep down was she no better than a common washerwoman?

The clock struck the half hour. She smoothed her hair, then looked at the tray. It would never again lie flat on the buffet. Maybe Cornelius was right. Better for her to remain silent than to make a fool of herself.

The last to depart, Connor ambled over with his hands in his pockets. Could she repair the damage she'd done?

"I must apologize," she said. "I comported myself very poorly just then. Turn the other cheek, I told you."

"Naw." The raw skin of his face flushed. "You shoulda seen your grand-mamma when I was little. She rescued me once just like that, but I think she used a broom."

Grandmother? But before Miranda could question him further, he hurried away, bawling an Irish ballad at the top of his lungs.

She was late, but she could hardly go inside looking like a brawler. Miranda paused at the door to compose herself as she transitioned between the two very different worlds. On the other side of that door were no hungry boys, only well-fed, well-heeled buyers looking to amass a menagerie of art for their homes, or to find an undervalued item that could be sold for a profit elsewhere. Not that making a profit was wrong—some buyers were extremely charitable—but while their money might reach across the divide, those boys never would.

And Miranda and her family were stuck somewhere in the middle, catering to the elite but working for a living.

Better put the incident behind her. Miranda tugged her short jacket into place and turned for the door. Already skipping through the sales order and preparing to answer questions about the next offering, she'd forgotten the black buggy. Only then did she realize that she was still being observed. Beneath a stylish hat, a veiled woman peered out of the buggy window. Her scarf draped from her bonnet and across her mouth and nose, leaving only a pair of startling green eyes visible, eyes that pinned Miranda with curiosity.

Miranda halted with the dented tray dangling from her hand. The lady had seen Miranda's unladylike display and most definitely did not approve.

To earn the trust of the wealthy, the Wimplegates had to mimic the careful manners of their clientele. But occasionally Miranda came face-to-face with someone who saw through her ruse. Someone who reminded her that while she might wear velvet and silk, she was working for her living just the same as the fishmongers at Quincy Market—minus the odor. The lady daintily tugged her veil higher—with a real kid glove, no doubt—then with a smart rap of a parasol on the roof of her carriage, the horses sprang to life, and the driver spirited her away.

Feeling chastened, Miranda ducked inside. She eased the tray onto the buffet unnoticed, although there'd be questions aplenty later. Perhaps the lady was bidding against a competitor and wanted her identity hidden. That wasn't unusual, but in the same way Miranda could spot the hand of a master craftsman, she suspected there was more to the story. Cornelius might know who they were, but she hated to ask him. Lately, every conversation with him involved some plea to answer his proposal.

"Miranda." Her father's diamond cravat pin flashed in the light as he motioned her to him. "Mr. Wakefield has some questions about the Hepplewhite desk. Are you free?"

"Of course." As far as customers went, Mr. Wakefield was bearable. He asked intelligent questions and didn't expect her to stand around while he calculated how much he was willing to spend. "Follow me, please."

She retrieved a copy of her catalog from a brass stand as they passed along the silk Oriental rug. Today's offering of fine furniture and unappreciated heirlooms came courtesy of the once mighty LeBlanc family. Perhaps they were mighty still, but if the liquidation of their valuables was any indication, the new heir would burn through the carefully hoarded riches before his older brother settled into the family mausoleum. Thank heavens for dissolute younger sons. Without them, her family's auction house would stand empty.

Miranda smoothed the sale catalog, her eyes darting down the list and descriptions she'd composed and taken to the printer herself. How she'd loved the Chippendale settee with its elegant lines and flawless upholstery. She'd miss the Revere tea service that was selling today, but with Paul's silversmith mark clearly discernible, they'd make a nice commission on it. The priceless artifacts that passed through her hands amazed her. The beauty, the craftsmanship, the history—she sighed. If only she could spend more time alone with the treasures and less time with the pretentious buyers. But her descriptions clearly expressed her appreciation for the fine pieces, and that's what made her valuable on sale day. That's why Father wanted her to escort bidder after bidder down the endless aisles of their warehouse. That's why Mother expected her to smile prettily and tell them what important piece was being offered. That's why she wanted just a moment away from the suffocating masses crammed inside the salon—a moment she'd instead used to savagely assault a couple of young men.

What had come over her?

Her grandfather's voice echoed through the hall as he called for the next offering. What were they selling now? As she led Mr. Wakefield through the back of the salon, Miranda happened to glance at the easel on the stage as Grandfather read the catalog description. Her steps slowed. There must be some mistake.

Forgetting Mr. Wakefield, she stopped and flipped open her copy of the catalog. Page four . . . no, five. The card on the auction table read *Item #109*, but the large portrait on the easel wasn't the Copley that was listed. It was no painting she'd ever seen before. In a daze, Miranda walked closer but stopped at the last row of chairs. The bidders exchanged glances as her grandfather finished reading the catalog description she'd composed. True, it was a portrait of a man wearing a satin waistcoat and lace cravat of the late eighteenth century, but it appeared to be a family portrait, not a masterpiece. Even their clients realized the mistake, as their throat clearing and wagging beards attested.

Miranda's throat tightened. Someone should say something. She looked for her father, but he wasn't in the salon. With a nod of his head and the smack of his gavel, Grandfather opened the bidding. She squinted again at the painting. Could the family have submitted it after the catalog had been published? As much as she wanted to know what was happening, she wouldn't interrupt. Miranda had already humiliated herself enough for one day. The catalog crumpled in her fist. Hopefully there'd be no harm done, because she could not contradict Grandfather before a room full of clients

The gavel fell and her grandfather called out the winning bidder's number. She released a painful breath. This time she hadn't made a spectacle of herself. She'd passed the test. Mr. Wakefield waited at her heels. She had a job to do. With a quick smile thrown over her shoulder by way of apology, Miranda passed to the other gallery where the Hepplewhite waited.

With her last view of the salon, she spotted the mysterious man from the carriage tucking his number into his waistcoat pocket and departing with a satisfied smile.

CHAPTER 2

Amid the rows of high shelves squatted three tables, positioned to catch the first light of morning. Between sale days the Wimplegate family gathered here to inspect and assess the offerings for future auctions. Besides her meetings with the paper boys, it was Miranda's favorite place to be. Except for today.

"You are in trouble."

Miranda lifted her head along with her magnifying glass and saw the distorted face of Cousin Cornelius frowning at her through the lens. One monocled eye studied her with the same quizzical intensity she'd expended on the jeweled brooch. She wished he wouldn't fuss over her. Honestly, she wished he didn't think of her at all, especially since he'd started talking marriage.

She lowered the magnifying glass. "The LeBlanc estate?"

Cornelius folded into the empty chair between her and Grandfather. His neck creased against his high starched collar. "The LeBlancs' lawyer is on his way. Monty King claims the portrait was a priceless family heirloom, and LeBlanc had no intention of selling it."

Grandfather snorted as he finished recording the details of

the saber before him. "He's carting up and selling everything of value that belongs to the LeBlancs—not that I'm complaining at six percent commission, mind you."

"But how did it get to the block?" Miranda asked. "I never came across it during inventory." And why hadn't Grandfather realized the mistake? He'd built this business with a razor-sharp memory and a keen eye for detail. How could he have suffered such a lapse in judgment? And on a sale day, of all days?

With steady, blue-veined hands, Grandfather slid the saber into its scabbard. "Someone in the family must have sent it over. I don't see how they can hold us responsible."

Cornelius's gaze met hers, and he had every reason to be concerned. Grandfather was his great-uncle, and as a phrenologist, Cornelius took particular interest in family traits. Through his monocle he studied Grandfather's bowed head, which was bare except for a fringe of graying hair wrapped like a thick equator around a shiny globe. Miranda could only imagine how he wanted to get his hands on it and feel for any new protrusions that might explain Grandfather's blunder. If one could really determine a person's character by the bumps on his or her head, as Cornelius claimed, Grandfather would be an easy study.

But no time for study now. The glassed door at the end of the warehouse swung open to admit her father, followed by two men, both of whom appeared to have been mistreating foodstuffs for quite some time. Grandfather and Cornelius rose to their feet.

"This is Mr. Monty King and his assistant—"

"McSwain." The man's face was shaped like a pyramid with dulled edges. His walrus whiskers twitched with uncertainty as his boss, Mr. King, barreled toward Grandfather.

"You are going to get that portrait back. You had no right to sell it." Mr. King's small bald head was of a level with Grandfather's equator, but he leaned forward as if speaking down to him. The profligate folds of his cravat reminded Miranda of a still life she'd seen at the Athenaeum—an apple sitting on a pillow. Only his smooth head had no stem protruding upward.

"We will do what we can," Grandfather said, "but the LeBlancs share the responsibility. They brought it to us."

"Did you use the words *LeBlanc* and *responsibility* in the same breath?" Mr. King's jowls continued to shimmy after his head had stopped. "Frederic LeBlanc couldn't name his ships, his wharf, or his captains without help. All he knows is that his picture of dear old Grandpère is missing off the wall. As his solicitor, I insist you return it. You have a month. After that, I'll bring suit against you."

McSwain produced a small notepad and pencil stub. Holding it at arm's length, his pencil moved. "Take Wimplegates to court," he said. Then squinting upward asked, "Can you spell *Wimplegate?*"

Mr. King's eyes grew hard. "Leave the note-taking to me." But instead of cowering, the man bit his fleshy tongue and continued to make letters.

Seeing their rudeness toward Grandfather made Miranda wish for her silver tray. But Grandfather could defend himself.

"Sue us for selling something you brought us? Bah," Grandfather spat. "You won't win."

"So what? Just the spectacle of poor Mr. LeBlanc on the stand pining for his family treasure will be enough to ruin you. No one will trust the Wimplegate Auction House after that."

"Ruin . . . the . . . auction . . ." McSwain flipped his pencil over to erase a mistake.

"Outside," Mr. King ordered, his apple head growing red.

With a shrug, McSwain stepped out the door and closed it behind him, his pyramid silhouette easily discernible through the frosted glass insert as he struggled with his note-taking.

"Now, listen." Mr. King rested his knuckles on the table next to the jeweled scabbard. "I know you have records. You'll hunt this down, and I can tell Frederic how helpful you were, but just in case you're thinking that you'd rather the buyer keep his prize, I'm here to tell you that wouldn't be a good idea. Do you understand?"

"We will do what we can," Father said, "but why threaten us? This was not our responsibility."

Or was it? Miranda ducked her chin. She'd known it was a mistake. She knew that painting wasn't in the catalog, that Grandfather was confused, and she'd let it sell anyway. If the piece was truly a family heirloom, she couldn't blame them for being upset.

"I don't care whose fault it was," Mr. King said. "Mr. LeBlanc appreciates me because I get things done without bothering him. Cornelius can tell you that I'm a fair man, and if you do your part, then we'll have no problems."

She'd never seen her father so angry. He didn't blink, didn't move, but disdain poured out his cold eyes.

Mr. King rapped his knuckles, causing the sword to clatter against the table. "No problems, right?"

From outside the door a hearty "Right, boss" was heard.

"Imbecile," Mr. King muttered. He straightened. "If we understand each other, I'll take my leave. Truly, I don't want to see this fine establishment go out of business. What would be the point? Just get the painting back." His small, hard eyes covered each of them in turn. Satisfied that his message had hit the mark, he turned around—a gradual maneuver that took him three feet—then he flung the door open and hit the feckless McSwain on the head with his hat before they sauntered out of sight.

Miranda ran her fingers over the rubies in the brooch before her. Between her father and grandfather, they could fix this. No one was more capable than they, but even the clever Wimplegate men needed a moment to catch their breath. Cornelius was the first to recover.

"I'll talk to him. Father and Monty were childhood friends. Maybe he can convince them not to prosecute our relatives."

"We aren't that close of relatives," Father growled.

"We could be closer." Cornelius nudged her foot beneath the table.

Miranda pulled away, irritated as always whenever their possible union was discussed. "Now is not the time."

"When is?" He leaned across the table, blocking her view of her father and grandfather. "Taking care of this little mistake could be my wedding present to you. Even if Father isn't thrilled about Mother's poor relations, he wouldn't hesitate to speak up for my fiancée."

Poor relations? There had to be another way.

"We must get it corrected before word gets out." Grandfather took up the sword again and bounced it in his palm. "Do you really think your father could get somewhere with them?"

Cornelius beamed. "He wouldn't let anything happen that would mar the joy of my nuptials."

Before he could touch her again, Miranda choked out, "Have we looked at the register? If the bidder had a number, he had to have a name."

"The bidder's ticket led nowhere," Father said. "False name, false information. Only the money was real."

The black carriage. Miranda's chair squawked as she spun it

around. "But I saw the man who bought the painting. He wore a black suit, had a trimmed beard, and a hat . . ."

Her cousin shook his head. "You just described every man on the streets of Boston."

"But he came with a woman. I would recognize her. Maybe not her features, but her attitude, the way she made me feel. She was warning me, censuring me . . ." Come to think of it, perhaps Miranda should consider before going any further. What danger could the woman have foreseen?

"Write down what you remember," Grandfather said. "Perhaps she'll reappear at tomorrow's sale. We'll be on the lookout for her."

"She doesn't have the painting. Not anymore." Miranda's father pulled an envelope out of his pocket. "Mr. Wakefield happened to overhear our mystery buyer at the cargo desk after the sale finished. He shipped one moderately-sized crate on the westbound."

"To New York?" Cornelius asked.

"Even farther. Hart County, Missouri."

Grandfather whistled. "Never heard of it."

"Neither had the shipping agent. It'll change rail lines in New York and then again in St. Louis. After that is anyone's guess."

"Then it's gone." Miranda fingers curled around the bauble. How she wished she'd had the courage to speak up. After staying at Grandfather's side throughout Grandmother's illness and death, why had she let him down now?

"Why didn't you tell Mr. King your information?" Cornelius asked.

"Because I don't trust him," Father said.

"He's one of my patients," Cornelius said, "and has an obvious excrescence in both agreeableness and conscientiousness."

"Have you found those traits displayed beyond the lumps on his skull?" Father asked.

Cornelius elevated his thin nostrils. "As I said, my father and Mr. King frequent the same clubs. Given the right circumstances . . ."

Miranda's nails dug into her palms. She'd always assumed she would marry Cornelius—so busy was she with the family business that she hardly knew any other young men—but as she got to the age that it was actually possible, she'd begun to resist. As far as his threatening to withhold help, that was the wrong tactic. She might hate making a choice, but she resented having them made for her.

"Do we know where in Hart County it's going?" Grandfather asked.

"Maybe we do." Her father opened the envelope and fished out a slip of paper. "I've had the telegraph wires buzzing this morning, and my efforts have been rewarded. It appears there's an auction house in Hart County. At least it's a place to start." He slid the paper across the table.

"Do they have it or not?" Cornelius asked.

"They wouldn't have it yet, but we mustn't tell them what we're looking for," Father explained. "It's an auction house. If they know we're desperate to get the piece, they'll make us pay dearly. Better to act uninterested in that particular item and buy it back unopposed."

Even a novice knew better than to disclose one's intent at an auction, but Cornelius rarely dirtied his hands at their place.

"Where is Hart County?" Miranda asked. "Could there be many antiques there? Enough to keep an auction house in business?"

Her father shrugged. "Fine estates have lined the Mississippi

23

for years, especially around St. Louis. And not only is there an auction house in Hart County, but it's also for sale. The owner telegraphed me to give me a bid."

"We could buy the whole auction house?" Her grandfather clapped his hands together. "How much?"

"I don't think it's necessary," Father said, "but the price was surprisingly low." Absently, he stuck a finger in his ear and twisted as he thought.

"I'm responsible for the sale, so I should be the one to recover it," Grandfather said.

"You won't be able to find it," Cornelius said. "And how can you afford an expensive trip west? Especially if word gets out and no estates will hire you?"

"I'll have Patrick prepare my bags." Bless Grandfather and his ability to ignore Cornelius. Leaving his sword and scabbard on the table of items for the next sale, Grandfather strode away.

"If he's determined to go," Cornelius said, "then I suppose Miranda and I will do what we can from here to smooth things over." He trailed his fingers along her arm. "Maybe this unfortunate mistake will finally convince you how much you stand to gain."

The brooch skittered out of her fingers. "I'm going, too." She shoved her chair backwards and pinched her skirt narrow to fit around Cornelius and reach her father. Her words spilled out in desperate eloquence. "Grandfather hasn't been himself. Under normal circumstances he could out-bargain and out-deal anyone, but recently his thinking has been impaired." She searched Father's face, looking for any sign that her words were hitting their mark. "I could check on the details—timetables, tickets—and make sure he remembers to take his meals."

After a searing look toward Cornelius, her father nodded like the sage he was.

"Not a bad idea. Your mother and I think you spend too much time at the auction house. Maybe a little travel would bolster your confidence."

"I think she's perfect in every way," Cornelius said. Miranda could only guess that confidence was one attribute he thought she could do without. "And what if things don't go as planned? She could come back even more fearful. Don't forget, I've done a complete phrenological examination of Miranda, and from the way her skull is shaped, she has an overlarge capacity for caution and a cavity in the self-esteem area. We're proceeding against nature to try to cultivate—"

"Poppycock." Charles Wimplegate pinched his daughter's chin. "We all know she is smart and capable, but maybe she needs to prove it to herself. Four weeks, Miranda. You and Grandfather will have a grand adventure and return with the LeBlancs' troublesome portrait. Then we'll put these rumors of our incompetency to rest. You can do this."

Probably not. More than likely Cornelius was right, but it was her fault the painting hadn't been saved. If she couldn't recover it this way, then Cornelius's suggestion might be the only solution.

A train ride. No public performances, no uncomfortable confrontations. Merely making sure Grandfather's cravat was clean and he didn't eat too much rich food. She'd behave herself, bite her tongue, and come home with the painting. What could go wrong? With Miranda's morbid imagination, she could think of thousands of horrifying outcomes, but she should have stopped Grandfather from selling the portrait in the first place. She had to do this. Her family needed her.

CHAPTER 3

Pine Gap, Missouri

Pine Gap. That was the name of the town, but all Miranda could picture were President Washington's ill-fitting wooden dentures. Keeping her eyes glued to the window, she waited for the endless trees to thin and reveal their destination. According to the conductor they should arrive soon, but how could a town of any size exist in such an isolated area? Naked rocks jutted out on both sides of the train, where the railroad had blasted through the mountains—menacing, sharp overhangs that hadn't healed from their recent injury. Had Mother known about the miles of wilderness they would cross, she never would've let Miranda go.

Miranda had barely been able to pry herself out of Mother's arms as it was. On second thought, she was giving herself too much credit. Father was the one who'd ultimately separated the two. Without his firm insistence, she would've climbed back into the hired hack and sulked home to where she'd feel safe and sound—until Cousin Cornelius called again.

"I wonder if our auction house is close to the depot." Grand-father rested both hands atop his cane. Since they'd left Boston, he'd been a fidgety bundle of excitement. Striking up conversations at random, exploring the shabby depots, anxiously rocking, as if his efforts could speed the train along the tracks. "Our first priority is to recover the LeBlanc portrait, but I don't deny that I'm excited to see what other treasures our purchase has netted us."

Miranda studied the seams on her gloves. Once her father had located the auction house owner, her grandfather had taken over the correspondence. Thinking it not prudent to ask outright about the portrait, he merely expressed interest in the auction house itself, and before her father could stop him, he'd purchased the entire business—lock, stock, and barrel, as they said. Their weekly receipts weren't much, but the number of items for sale and the number of bidders was impressive, leaving Miranda to suspect, and her grandfather convinced, that they'd stumbled upon a goldmine. Here was a place where antiques, furnishings, and jewelry went for pennies on the dollar. All they needed to do was to box up the inventory, ship it home, and they'd not only have the LeBlanc picture, but a tidy profit besides.

"You're certain the owner hasn't sold anything?" Miranda asked.

"He gave me his word. As of the twenty-eighth of May, he hasn't sold a thing, but waits for us to arrive. That painting should be safe in his warehouse."

"I hope so," Miranda said. "I hate to think of being away from home any longer. Grandmother always fretted if you weren't home for dinner. I can only imagine what she'd think of this adventure."

He fidgeted before answering. "Your grandmother was a dear woman but a bit of a worrywart."

"How could she help it, with your antics to trouble her?" Miranda tucked her hand beneath her grandfather's arm. His eyes dimmed with memory. Grandmother's passing had changed him. He used to be so open, so approachable, to even the lowliest laborer. Now he used a blustery whirlwind of activity to chase people away and perhaps to dispel thoughts of his own mortality.

The steam whistle blew. The wheels screeched. Still nothing but trees outside the window. Miranda checked her fob watch, a souvenir her father had purchased from the first sale she'd cataloged. Just past noon. They should arrive . . .

A log building appeared. A stubby rock chimney, a short platform, and a massive pile of firewood met her eye. Confused, Miranda scanned the railcar. Unlike other stops, no one seemed to notice that the train had halted. No gathering packages, no adjusting hats and buttoning overcoats. Was this their stop?

Her grandfather's mouth tightened. Standing, he flagged down the porter. "Excuse me. Is this Pine Gap?"

"Yes, sir. They'll unload your bags to the platform. Good luck to ya."

Grandfather widened his stance. The unlucky porter was blocked in. "But I don't see the town," Grandfather said. "We're in the middle of a wilderness."

"The town is just around the hill, or so they say. Follow the wagon path, and you can't miss it."

Grandfather's white eyebrows lowered. Miranda snatched her shawl, her parasol, and her handbag from the seat beside her and waited for Grandfather to clear the way, but he remained immovable. The porter cleared his throat. Embarrassed, he turned to Miranda. "Does he need further assistance, or . . ."

Or do I need to physically remove your grandfather from my path? Unfortunately she was becoming more and more used to

28

his strange episodes. Miranda tugged on his sleeve. "Come on, Grandfather. This is our stop."

His whiskers twitched, and with a last look at the forest, he propelled himself forward and out of the passenger car. Their bags emerged from the baggage car at the end of the train. The porter hopped back on board and saluted them as he rolled away, chipper now that the onerous responsibility of Elmer Wimplegate was no longer his to bear.

The countryside was beautiful. Hills folded and tucked into each other, covered by trees and the fresh colors of spring. The area didn't look to be inhabited at all, but perhaps it was a resort area where the rich and mighty brought their families to escape the pollution of the city. No limit to the number of mansions that could be hidden away in the valley. Or that's what Miranda was going to believe until she had proof otherwise.

High overhead an eagle circled. Or was it a vulture? Miranda took a step closer to Grandfather. Either way, they needed to find accommodations. Although Grandfather burned bright all day, by evening Miranda could spot the signs of fatigue. The travel was taking its toll on the elderly man.

From the log depot stepped a man with his dusty coat swinging open, and the laces of his high boots untied. He grunted a greeting and then turned to lock the door behind him.

"Excuse me, young man." Grandfather strode with his cane flashing. "We've just arrived from Boston and were wondering if you've received any luggage or packages from there recently?"

His face bristled in annoyance as he took quick measure of them. "Are you missing something?"

"Yes, we are. I'm afraid we had a package sent ahead of us, but it was misaddressed. If anything arrives from Boston, could you please notify us? I'm not sure where we'll be staying or how we'll get to town—"

"You won't be hard to track down, but I ain't seen nothing from Boston." He whistled, and a dog with lanky legs and a scarred coat jogged out of the woods.

Grandfather cleared his throat, although his voice already trumpeted strong. "But we need assistance. We must have accommodations for the night."

"I reckon everyone does, but be careful who you share a roof with. There's them in these hills that don't cotton to strangers. The town is just over the hill yonder. Head up that road there . . ."

At the pointing end of his gesture, they spotted a wagon rolling toward them. Miranda sighed. Not a carriage, just a bundle of boards nailed together over some wheels. The driver of the wagon had his sleeves rolled up and his striped shirttails tucked in . . . a stylistic choice not all Missouri men favored, Miranda had noticed. When the stationmaster waved, the driver swung his team of mules to the platform.

"Isaac, lad," the stationmaster called. "You think you could give these folks a ride to town?"

Ride with a stranger? They hadn't been introduced. Miranda wished Grandfather was as wide as the columns on the portico in the back of the auction house, but since she couldn't hide behind him, she was forced to face Isaac-Lad. He was older than she'd first thought, with sad, dark eyes that seemed filled with uncertainty like her own. He pulled the brake and climbed down the wheel spokes with an unexpected grace. "If I can be of assistance."

"Awfully kind of you." Grandfather aimed his cane at the bags, as if this man's sole purpose in life was to do his bidding. "Those are our only cases."

The stationmaster had already melted into the forest, leaving the three of them alone. So adept at hiding was Miranda, that only then did the man from the wagon really see her. At first he merely smiled politely, but then his head snapped to do that horrible second glance she so hated. She could never decide what was more insulting—that she'd initially been dismissed so easily or that the looker found something that required further inspection.

"Beg your pardon, ma'am. Isaac Ballentine, at your service." He swung his hat off and bowed deeply.

Miranda's cheeks warmed at the attention. "Nice to meet you," she mumbled and lifted her bag.

"Allow me." Mr. Ballentine took the handle of her satchel. Quickly she released her grip and hid her hand behind her. He wasn't a railroad employee, so she wasn't sure where he fit into the social hierarchy that was so clearly defined in Boston. He hopped off the platform and then turned to help Grandfather descend. When it was Miranda's turn, she gingerly took his hand. Even through her gloves she noticed that Mr. Ballentine didn't have the work-roughened hands she'd expected. His hands were as pale and delicate as a poet's. With ease, he swung the bags behind the seat. Miranda looked away as he lifted her trunk, not sure how to treat the man. They were in his debt—an unusual circumstance.

"Do you think you'll be comfortable on the bench, Miranda?" Grandfather pointed at the front of the wagon. "It will seat three, or I'll ride in the back if it'll muss your dress."

The thought of Grandfather riding into town in the back of a wagon nearly choked her. She started to answer, cleared her throat, and started again. "We'll fit."

"It's big enough," Isaac-Lad, er, Mr. Ballentine said. "I wouldn't want to embarrass you'uns on your first day here."

31

"We appreciate you interrupting your plans on our behalf," Grandfather answered.

"No bother. I'm tickled I can help." The mules rattled their harnesses restlessly. Mr. Ballentine turned just as pounding hooves were heard through the trees. The wagon shifted with the animals' nervous movement. Miranda shaded her eyes to see into the shadows.

A lone rider broke into the clearing, leaning over his horse's neck as he raced forward. Clouds of dirt burst into the air with every stride. His bearded face was hard, while his body bristled with energy. His well-worn cotton shirt stretched across his shoulders and arms, defining muscles that even Titian had never put on a canvas. The man's eyes narrowed as he spotted them standing below the platform. This time Miranda really did hide behind Grandfather, but Isaac Ballentine didn't flinch. Instead, he climbed into the wagon and sat stubbornly waiting for the newcomer.

Sweat-dampened hair clung to the young man's neck. "Are you going to get out of that wagon, or do I have to pull you down myself?"

Aghast, Miranda silently pleaded with Isaac to give the man what he wanted, but from the obstinate set of his shoulders he seemed determined to refuse. Isaac turned so she could appreciate the full force of his defiance. "I'm not afraid of you, Wyatt."

Maybe Gentleman Isaac was brave, but he certainly wasn't very intelligent.

"I was hoping you'd say that," this Wyatt growled. He swung off his horse and made a rush for the wagon.

"Can't you do anything?" Miranda clawed at her grandfather's elbow.

Although he didn't cower, Grandfather shook his head. "Maybe years ago, my dear, but not now. Our friend is on his own."

With one boot in the spokes of the wheel, the attacker hoisted himself up, grabbed Isaac by the collar, and pulled him to the ground. Landing on his feet, Isaac attempted to shove out of his grasp, but he was no match for the brute. Miranda covered her mouth. This was no boy to be frightened away by a woman, even if she did have a silver tray. She couldn't get involved, but how could she just watch?

Grandfather clamped her arm in a death grip. "Don't you dare," he said. "You're too much like your grandmother."

Wyatt's fist smashed into Isaac's cheek and dropped him with a thud in the dirt. Standing over Isaac, his chest heaved as he fought for a breath. Wiping his knuckles on his pant leg, he poked Isaac with his boot until he rolled over.

"Do you feel better now?" Isaac touched his cheekbone and checked his fingers for blood. "Does hurting me make you feel better?"

"Now that you mention it, I reckon it does." With a purposeful swagger he grabbed his horse's reins and tied them to the back of the wagon, then swung himself into the wagon's seat. A low grunt startled the mules, and the wagon labored up the hill, carrying Miranda's bags along with it.

Miranda clutched her chest, certain her heart was about to escape from her rib cage. Pulling out of Grandfather's grasp, she ran on shaking legs to Isaac's side and knelt in the dust. "Are you all right? What can we do?"

With a groan, Isaac slid his jaw from side to side. "I'll be fine."

"But he stole your wagon. Shouldn't we find a police officer?"

"The sheriff finds it safer not to get involved." He smiled

drowsily. "Don't fret over me. I'm more worried about your trunks."

Miranda balled her hands into fists. That Mr. Wyatt deserved a stern rebuke. That's what he needed. And poor Isaac. If only she could make him forget his injury with a tray of pastries.

"We must notify the authorities," Grandfather said.

"You'll get your bags back, and when you do, just know I kept my word," Isaac said.

Miranda's heart swelled. Who was this generous soul who went to such lengths to protect them?

Isaac rocked to his knees, then found his feet. The wistfulness reflected in his eyes found its mark in her compassionate nature. Here was a man she could look up to. Actually, she *was* looking up to him because she was still kneeling. Isaac held out his hand and this time she took it purposefully as she stood.

"I'm sorry to expose you to such downright meanness," he said, "but seeing how you have no bags to carry, I think you might be better traveling to town on your own. My company seems to have brought you trouble." But before she could protest, he'd turned to Grandfather. "And, sir, I don't reckon I ever did catch your name."

"Elmer Wimplegate, and this is my granddaughter, Miss Wimplegate. We intend to be in town for a few days. If I can be of service, please let me know."

"I will, sir. Again, I'm sorry I couldn't help you get to town, but now that I'm afoot, it's going to take me twice as long to reach my destination. If you'll excuse me."

He found his hat and beat it against his leg, stirring up a cloud of dust in the still afternoon. With another near-bow he said, "Mr. Wimplegate. Miss Wimplegate," his shoulders every inch as proud as when he'd found Miranda and Grandfather pacing the platform. He started out with a limp, but before he'd crossed the railroad tracks, it'd disappeared.

"What a charming young man," Grandfather said.

But he wasn't watching Mr. Ballentine, he was watching Miranda watch Mr. Ballentine.

She straightened the ribbon beneath her chin. "I hope they catch that brute before we leave." And before he had time to go through her trunk. The thought of him emptying out her more delicate wardrobe items . . . She used her bag to fan herself.

"With this sort of welcome, I hardly know what to expect from our auction house," Grandfather said.

"If the portrait is there, we won't worry about anything else." But maybe she could spare a smidgen of concern for the friendly man who'd lost his wagon in their service. Once they'd secured their fortune, she'd see what she could do to restore his.

CHAPTER 4

She was the prettiest woman he'd ever seen.

Wyatt guided the mules up the dirt road toward town. When he'd first caught sight of his wagon, he hadn't stopped to see who was watching. His feud was with Isaac, but what in tarnation had a lady like her been doing at the depot? The old gentleman he'd noticed right off and kept an eye on him, not wanting to involve him in their scuffle, but the lady . . .

Her dress was decked in more ribbons and lace than Walters' Dry Goods sold in a decade. Even though they'd all been dyed the drab color of pinto beans, they couldn't disguise her womanly curves or her striking beauty. Her dark eyes were probably gorgeous when they weren't angry. And over her round little chin the daintiest lips pouted, or maybe that was only because she was furious. Wyatt's shoulders slumped. How long had Isaac been there? Long enough to make an impression, no doubt. Just the thought of her falling for Isaac's charms made him want to punch his brother again.

The mules trotted toward the feed mill. They were already running late, but try as he might he couldn't ignore Widow

Sanders kneeling in her flower bed. Mostly because she popped up and bounded through her irises when she heard him coming.

"Are you on your way to the sale?" With her dirty gardening gloves, Widow Sanders pushed back her slat bonnet. Wisps of hair—a few of them gray—waved around her unlined face.

"Yes, ma'am, but we aren't selling anything today."

"Well, fiddlesticks." Her smile was quick and confident. "Then lucky you will get my rhubarb pie without having to bid on it."

Lucky him. "I've barely finished the last one. Why don't you keep it this time?"

"No, no." She smacked her gloves together, sending clumps of fertile soil flying. "You might as well have it. I'll bring it by this afternoon."

"I'll be watching for it." And so would his pigs. They gobbled up her pies in nothing flat. At least they'd have a good supper. Between the trouble at the auction house, beating the snot out of his brother, and the pretty miss at the train station, this day couldn't get any worse. His only consolation was that no matter how poorly he'd behaved, he'd never have to see the fine lady again.

"Have you given my idea any more thought?" Widow Sanders asked.

Idea? All Wyatt could think of was how tiny the city lady's waist looked compared to that big mess of a skirt. "What idea would that be?"

"The garden club, silly. I need just one more person before I can make the garden club official."

"How many do you have signed up already?"

Widow Sanders scratched beneath her bonnet strap. "Just me. You'd make two, but that would be perfect. We could take turns winning the Garden of the Month award."

"Why not make it Garden of the Year and we won't have to award it as often?"

"I thought of that, but to win for a whole year sounds down-right pretentious. I'd rather win it twelve times a year . . . six, I mean, because you'd win it half the time."

Wyatt sighed. "I've got to get to the barn. Those animals will be chewing on each other if I don't hurry."

"Think it over. No sense in making a final decision right now."

Wyatt hawed, the mules pulled in their traces, and they were off. Widow Sanders lived at the edge of town, the last house before the feed mill and sale barn. Sensing they were almost to their destination, his horse whinnied behind him. He turned to check on the tethered animal when his eye caught a most loathsome sight. With a groan, Wyatt swung himself around, afraid to look behind him again. He would see the lady, most definitely, because he'd stolen her luggage.

The two traveling bags and the trunk could only belong to her and the old man. That's what he got for bursting in with both barrels blazing. When would he learn to slow down and think things through? Even if his brother had deserved his comeup-pance, there might have been a more handy time to deliver it.

He pulled the wagon up to the feed mill where his order was already waiting on him. Late. He hated being late. He tossed the feed sacks into the wagon bed as easily as if they were parlor pillows and then headed out for the sale barn.

The smell of large animals in tight quarters reached him before he rode into the clearing. One farmer's barn smelled strong enough. Multiply that odor by fifty, and it was enough to make your eyes water. Especially when they weren't selling anything. Why had Ol' Pritchard allowed the livestock to ac-cumulate? Wyatt didn't like it. Didn't make sense to take stock in and hold them. The animals had to be fed, and that dug into profit. Besides, Pritchard knew that Wyatt had been saving up to buy the barn from him, so why was he shutting down operations? Something stunk about the deal, and not just the crowded livestock.

The pens wrapping around the west side of the red building teemed with bottled-up energy. Surrounded by unfamiliar smells and challenged by the males from rival herds, no one was happy. And the feed? Wyatt spent half of each day making sure every animal had feed and water available. Another reason Isaac deserved the whooping. It was one thing for him to idle around town, but when he stole Wyatt's wagon to go sparking, he jeopardized Wyatt's job.

Pulling the wagon up against the nearest fence, Wyatt set the brake and hopped in the back. He flipped open his jackknife and stabbed the bag, ripping a gash in the top. Heaving the bag to his shoulder, he leaned across the high fence and shook out the kernels on the teeming swine below. The hogs fought over the spilling corn as it bounced off their backs and was trampled beneath them. Once that pen was fed, he stepped over the bench seat, pulled the wagon up ten feet, and repeated the chore for the next pen.

"Wyatt!" Pritchard himself stepped out of the wide front doors of the sale barn. "Still feeding? You're running late today."

"Yeah. Well, my wagon took off without me. Had to hunt it down."

Pritchard tucked a dirty strand of his long hair behind his ear. "Isaac again?"

Wyatt nodded. He tossed the empty feed sack into the back of the wagon. "It's not good to have these animals crowded like this. Are we having a sale tomorrow or not?" Pritchard might be his boss, but Wyatt felt no obligation to hide his frustration. "You haven't sold a single hoof in the last two weeks. Farmers want their money. Butchers need the meat. What's going on?"

Pritchard shuffled his feet. Whatever he was getting ready to say, he fully regretted having to say it. "I didn't mean to wait this long to tell you, but I sold out . . ."

He kept talking, but the rest of his words ricocheted off Wyatt's ears like bird shot against a horse trough. He'd sold out? Wyatt dropped out of the wagon. He'd worked here since he was big enough to carry a bucket of feed and help his pa. Owning it had always been their dream. When Pa died Wyatt hadn't changed a thing, even used the old wooden gavel on the auction block just like Pa, but now some stranger would set up shop here? Pritchard hadn't even given him a chance.

" . . . demanded that I stop sales until they came to take over."

Wyatt paced the length of the pen, then spun and returned. "It's gone? Just like that? You know I wanted to buy it." Because that was what he was supposed to do. Pa had already planned it out.

"Calm down, Wyatt. You'll get your chance. This fellow don't know the first thing about running the place, but he threw a wad of cash at me. Wait two months, three at the longest, and then get it for a pittance. He'll be glad to be rid of it by then."

To be honest, Wyatt didn't have the money. Not yet, and he wasn't keen on getting a bank loan. He tugged on his beard. "How much longer do we hold the livestock? Those cattle will bust the pens—"

"He's coming in today from Boston. Mr. Elmer Wimplegate was supposed to arrive on the noon train."

"I was there before I went to the mill, and I didn't see—" Wyatt's teeth snapped together so hard that bright stars shot across his vision. His belly clabbered. A new boss, from Boston of all places? "Why didn't you tell me?"

"Well, you're too late to give him a ride now. Someone will point him in the right direction. You'd better get inside and get your books in order. Your new boss won't be in a good mood after walking all the way from the station."

And he'd be that much more incensed when he learned that the man who filched his luggage was the manager of his sale barn. So much for first impressions.

Chapter 5

They'd walked a half a mile up a rocky road and still no estates were visible. True, the thick forests and mountains on both sides could hide Bunker Hill, but Miranda had thought to see some impressive iron gates or manicured drives. Something besides trees and rocks.

"No cause for concern." Grandfather mopped his brow with a monogrammed handkerchief. "We can't be far."

"It's not the distance that concerns me. I'm more worried about being accosted by some ruffian in this isolated stretch." She peered into the thick undergrowth but couldn't see farther than she could throw a marble bust. Then suddenly, after the next rise, there lay a rough little village before them.

"Pine Gap." Grandfather pushed his handkerchief into his breast pocket. "A gap in the pines, and there it is."

Or part of it, anyway. A line of white homes and log cabins nestled between the cedars, then disappeared into a dip before showing up again on the rise on the other side of the valley. Brown roofs could be spotted between the leafy cover to the right, giving evidence of another street, but beyond that was uninterrupted wilderness.

"This isn't what I was expecting," Grandfather said at length.

Miranda tucked her gloved hand into the crook of his arm. Get the painting, and then they could leave. "Someone will have information. Let's press onward."

He smiled at her enthusiasm and continued forward. Miranda's heavily fringed skirt swung erratically as she picked her way over the uneven ground. Had someone purposefully sown the road with boulders, they couldn't have made it any bumpier. And she'd always thought the cobblestones of Boston too rough.

In the nearest yard, a peony bush waved drunkenly at them. Miranda drew back as a sprightly woman emerged, wearing a faded sunbonnet. Behind her stood a small shed—probably made to store her gardening tools in. With a filthy glove she pushed a strand of hair off her wrinkled nose and looked them over.

"Well, hello. I ain't never seen you'uns before."

Grandfather touched the brim of his hat by way of introduction. "Elmer Wimplegate at your service, ma'am. We just arrived from Boston and are looking for the auction house."

At this she pushed up her sleeves and set her hands against her narrow hips. "Boston? You don't say. I'm Mrs. Sanders—folks around here call me Widow Sanders—and I don't know that I've ever met anyone from so far away. That's a far piece, to be sure. You're looking for the sale barn?" A fly buzzed around the brim of her bonnet. With lightning precision the woman swatted it down.

"Perhaps we are talking about the same place," Grandfather said. "Are you referring to a place that auctions off valuables?"

"Why, sure. You can buy just about anything at the sale barn. You just follow this road"—here she gestured and Miranda nearly ducked, remembering the fate of the fly—"and see if it don't take you straight there. Course there hasn't been any sales this week, and don't ask me how come. That Pritchard's got something up his sleeve."

"Thank you for your information. I hope our paths cross again." Grandfather was responding well to this woman's energy.

"There ain't that many paths out here," she said. "You're bound to see me sooner or later."

Miranda smiled politely as they passed by. The gardener didn't go back to her work but continued to stare the entire time Miranda and Grandfather were in sight.

"Well, well, well," Grandfather said once they were out of earshot. "So the whole town is abuzz with what is going on at the auction? Little do they know we just snatched their treasures for a ridiculously low price."

Miranda kept her head ducked. Far be it for her to question her grandfather's judgment, but she'd be surprised if this town brimmed with fine art and priceless jewelry. Didn't he see that woman's clothing? Even if the inhabitants of Pine Gap were the caretakers for the local estates, her simple speech and rough manners would exclude her from service in all but the most humble of establishments. Not since they'd left St. Louis had they seen any community remotely capable of supporting an auction house like theirs. She bit her lip. If they didn't find the painting, how were they going to afford to pay for their trip, much less the expense of a new auction house?

The road seemed to dead end at a large red monstrosity constructed with no thought of aesthetics or even decency. The hulking building sported walls blown wide at odd angles as if some interior pressure had warped it out of symmetry.

"Why would anyone do that to this poor town?" Miranda asked. And then the smell hit her. It was too late. Her opened mouth had captured the taste, so thick she needed to scrape it off her tongue with a butter knife. Grandfather's handkerchief made another appearance and swiftly covered his nose. Miranda almost crammed her reticule into her mouth but managed to fish out her own handkerchief despite watering eyes.

"What is it?" she asked. Even the livery stables in town didn't smell as strong. The giant red barn had stove pipes jutting out at maniacal intervals. Too many stoves for a barn, and of course she'd seen much bigger houses, but none thrown together so haphazardly.

"Maybe we took a wrong turn." He lifted his cane toward the open doors, wide enough for a carriage to drive through. "Let's inquire inside. Or would you like to wait here?"

What she'd like was to run back home and lock herself in the inventory closet with the oil paintings and Chinese vases. Careful not to breathe any more than necessary, she shook her head. "As long as that outlaw is on the loose, I'm staying with you."

They covered the gravel clearing and stepped inside the cavernous passageway. High, fly-specked windows flooded the building with light and illuminated a gated arena set beneath a high platform. "It looks like a sacrificial altar," Miranda said.

"I believe the occultists are more sanitary," Grandfather whispered.

"Mr. Wimplegate?" A hatless man with unfashionably long hair hurried out of an office.

"How does he know your name?" Miranda asked, but the man was already pumping her grandfather's hand by way of greeting. Only courtesy forced her handkerchief from her face.

"Mr. Pritchard here. So sorry we didn't have someone to

pick you up, but here you are. Now, I did just as you asked and haven't sold a thing ever since you wired the money. We just took everything the folks brought in, but didn't let none of it go."

Grandfather sputtered. "You're the owner of the auction house?"

Mr. Pritchard slid his hands into his pockets and rocked from heel to toe. "I was until last week."

"But where is it?"

The rocking stopped. He tilted his head. "Where is what?"

"The auction house."

Mr. Pritchard glanced nervously at Miranda, an occurrence that was happening more frequently as Grandfather lost clarity. "This *is* the auction house, Mr. Wimplegate. And it's all yours."

Miranda stumbled backwards. Again her eyes traveled the grimy heights of the room to the yellowed windows. They had bought this place? This Gehenna? Oh, Cornelius was right. She should've called her mother into their meeting and started planning a wedding instead of packing for this trip.

"You hold auctions here?" Grandfather asked. "In this filth?"

"Animals are like to make a mess, sir. And I would've never kept them penned up for so long if it weren't for your instructions. Normally we clean the pens between sale days, but with them full we haven't had a chance."

Pens? What was he talking about? Why would he allow animals inside?

Grandfather covered his eyes. His fitted gloves couldn't hide the tremble in his hands. "You're telling me that I purchased a livestock auction?"

"Yes, sir, and the only one in the county. Guaranteed to bring a crowd every week." Mr. Pitchard's suspenders parted as he thrust his chest forward.

Miranda could stand silent no longer, not while this man spoke in circles. "But don't you sell furniture, antiques, and jewelry?" she asked.

"Sure we do. We sell anything a person wants to be rid of. Widow Sanders even brings her rhubarb pies every week. Now, between you and me, there's not much market for them, but that doesn't mean . . . "

If Miranda's greatest fear hadn't been drawing attention to herself, she'd seriously consider a fit of hysteria about now.

"I don't believe this." Grandfather blinked slowly, as if he'd suddenly been given sight for the first time. "You mean to say this is the business I purchased?"

He swayed slightly. Miranda must intervene before he lost his focus. Since leaving home, she'd witnessed these bouts more and more frequently. She took him by the arm, stood on her tiptoes, and whispered into his neck, "Grandfather, all is not lost. Remember why we are here."

His eyes sharpened and he scanned the hallway. As unlikely as it seemed, someone in the area had the portrait they were looking for. Maybe it wasn't at the auction as they'd hoped, but they still needed to recover it. Whatever dreams he'd held for this auction house, nothing was more important than finding the painting and saving their business back home.

"I know nothing about the management of a livestock auction," Grandfather said. "What am I to do?"

"Well, that's a pickle, isn't it? But you have Mr. Ballentine. He's our auctioneer and practically runs the place."

"Mr. Ballentine?" Miranda asked. Finally a good turn. A man with some manners and decency to aid them. Modulating her voice so she wouldn't sound too eager, she tightened her grip on Grandfather's arm. "We met him at the train station. Remember?"

"You met him?" Pritchard's batwing eyebrows lowered as he gazed toward an opened door in a hallway. "If you want to wait in the office, he'll keep you company while I show your grandpa around."

Miranda skimmed her hand over the dark fringe of bangs that covered her forehead. How had Isaac-Lad made it here so quickly? Last they'd seen of him, he was headed up the other side of the mountain. And yes, she'd rather ponder the man's transportation than why she felt suddenly eager to see him again. Maybe it was because he might be the only person on earth who could help them survive this disaster. Or maybe it was because he wasn't Cousin Cornelius.

Grandfather's handkerchief made another appearance as he followed Mr. Pritchard outside. Miranda lifted her chin and composed herself. Although she wasn't accustomed to dealing directly with men beneath her station, this was business. Nothing she could do to avoid it.

The door to the office stood open. She eased around the corner and saw him bent over a ledger making tally marks on a pad of paper. She rapped lightly on the door frame, standing half hidden by the entryway. Mr. Ballentine lifted his head. His hair shone lighter than she remembered and he'd grown . . . a . . . beard.

"You!" she gasped.

He stood, rippling with the strength of an unspoken threat.

What was he doing here? Robbing the auction? She squeaked, darted out of the office and ran, shooting a look over her shoulder to make sure she wasn't being followed.

But she was.

"Wait." His shadow stretched across the dirty floor, closing the distance between them. "Where are you going?"

Good question. Before her was the arena, and she didn't see a way through the circular pen enclosed by iron bars. She turned a full circle, head tilted up to the highest row of benches, stretching to the roof. She refused to be the next sacrifice. There had to be a way out.

And that man blocked it.

She squared her shoulders. "What did you do with Mr. Ballentine? He's supposed to be in the office."

"Maybe I can help you."

Was he laughing at her? What kind of sadistic, cruel . . .

Courage. No matter how her humors were balanced, she had some and needed to use it.

"I want my grandfather. I . . . I demand that you tell me how to reach him."

He shrugged. "You could use the livestock door in the arena. I don't know that you want to walk through the pens, but—"

She'd walk through anything rather than spend another moment in his company. With all the dignity she could muster, she heaved open the wide, wooden door.

CHAPTER 6

Wyatt latched the gate closed behind him and let her get a head start. He wouldn't allow these people to just walk in and avail themselves of his sale barn. That dandy wouldn't know nothing about the animals, for starters. He wouldn't know a heifer from a cow, a steer from a bull, a piggy sow from a water-belly. He wouldn't recognize spavins or mastitis. And he wouldn't know the people. He wouldn't know that the Parrows liked to buy all the long-haired goats, and that Leland Moore's checks were no good. He wouldn't know that Mr. Finley always lied about his horses' ages and that Mrs. Rankin needed help driving her livestock home. He wouldn't know that the 1870 calendar hanging in the office covered a bullet hole from when Fowler and Walters had a falling out, and any mention of the date when the two of them were in the office would spark the feud back to life quicker than a flea could jump off a hot skillet.

The rough wooden fence rasped against his hand. Running this place didn't come easy for him, but he wouldn't let it go. Not without a tussle. Pritchard was right. If he could clamp ahold for a few months, they'd see that they'd gotten themselves in over their heads. He just needed to humor them until they gave up. And try not to steal any more of their belongings.

He pulled the lever to open the wooden gate and scanned the yards. The stiff breeze stirred up the smells of the overcrowded pens. Wyatt squinted as a gust spat a cloud of dirt into his eyes. Where had she gone? There, by the horses. Wyatt crammed his hat down until the band dug into his forehead, and set his feet moving in her direction. She clutched the old fellow's sleeve, eyes wide just like at the train station, but this time she was talking up a storm.

"And then I caught him at the desk. I didn't see him with any money, but . . ." She closed her mouth as he came near. Her gloves stretched over her knuckles like a second skin, but she didn't look away. Was that a touch of defiance in her stare?

He hoped so.

"Howdy, ma'am." Wyatt removed his hat and actually did a bow, like he was fixing to start off a reel. "I didn't mean to scare you."

"That's him," she whispered. How her eyes sparked.

Poor old Pritchard frowned. "Wyatt? Wyatt wouldn't rob me."

Now the old gent spouted off. "He . . . he stole our belongings at the train station. He accosted our escort in broad daylight and rode off with the train . . . with the wagon, as shameless as Jezebel."

Jezebel? Wyatt's chest expanded—a very manly chest below his thick beard, thank you. "I didn't steal your bags. You left them in the back of my wagon."

"Your wagon?" The old gentleman didn't seem to have his eyes under control. They roved wild, and while his anger came across loud and clear, his words slurred. "I don't know whether to pity your lack of virtue or your lack of intelligence, young man. Cross me again and when I'm done, no captain will allow you on board even if you were John Paul Jones himself."

What was the old fool talking about? Wyatt could feel his hackles rising, but then he took another look at the girl. Her forehead wrinkled, and the sorrow in her deep brown eyes washed the starch clean out of him. She loved this old goat, no matter how batty he was. Wyatt had best stop and think before tearing into him again. Sometimes beneath the dirt and grime, there was a man worthy of respect, so possibly beneath that gold watch fob and silk waistcoat there could be someone tolerable, too. He shouldn't vilify him just yet, but diplomacy and cash money—Wyatt had always run short on both.

"We're getting off to a sorry start, sir." He pulled his mouth back in what he hoped would pass as a smile. "My name is Wyatt Ballentine. The man you met at the train station was my brother, Isaac. We had ourselves a little family dispute. That's all."

"Boys will be boys," Pritchard interjected, dusting off his hands. "I've got to be going, but you have Wyatt. You'uns should get along just fine. Just fine." Then with a slap to Wyatt's back, he lit out toward home.

The chain on the gate beside Wyatt rattled as a calf rubbed against it. The three of them stood as still as cornstalks. Mr. Wimplegate stared at something in the distance, and the young lady remained firmly at his arm, keeping as far away from Wyatt as possible.

Wyatt slipped his hand through the slats of the fence and scratched the bristly back of the calf. "How about—"

"Where can—"

Wyatt stopped. So did she. She turned pale beneath the brim of her hat as if the sound of her own voice scared her. "Go on," he offered.

She pressed her lips closely together, and her head did a tight little shake that wobbled her hat ribbons. "You, please."

"I was going to suggest that we go inside. We have a lot of work to do, and your . . . ah . . ."

"Grandfather."

"Your grandfather doesn't need to get blistered by this heat. Not after the walk from the depot. Once we get in the office—"

But she wasn't listening to him. Her attention was focused on her grandpa.

Sweat trickled down Mr. Wimplegate's cheek, leaving a shiny line like a slug trail. "Animals," he muttered. "They sell animals, Miranda."

Miranda. Wyatt tucked her name away to be appreciated later. Right now his first concern was to get them out of the sun before they wilted. He knew better than to take Miranda's arm. She'd probably claw him up good if he came anywhere near her. On the other hand, her grandfather had already lost a hinge on his gate and was swinging cattywampus.

"Excuse me." Her lips barely moved, as if afeared he might take offense. "Certainly we need your help, but first I'd like assurance that we aren't in danger of being accosted."

Now she had his attention. "Not by me, sister."

Her eyelashes fluttered as she dared a glance up at him, then settled low again. "My grandfather and I have not procured lodgings. Considering all we've been through, I think it best to get him someplace where he can recuperate and gather his wits. Could you convey us to the nearest inn . . . if the wagon hasn't been returned to its rightful owner, that is."

Maybe he'd best look for another job immediately.

"*My* wagon and your bags are at the hitching post. If you'd be so kind as to follow me."

This had all the makings for a disaster, but he couldn't walk away. He and his father had given too much building this. Back when times were contentious, it'd stood as neutral ground where his neighbors could set aside their feuds to conduct business. It meant a lot to the area. He couldn't let it fall apart, even if he had to help these meddlers.

And hopefully he'd help them right back on the train to wherever it was that they belonged.

<hr/>

A man's good judgment was a thing easily overcome by the most frivolous aptitude—sit a horse well, possess hunting land in the country, or know where the best lobster is served. Any of those talents could cause a male to endure—nay, cherish—a coldhearted blackguard. Miranda gripped the iron side rail of the wagon's bench and wondered again what skill the thieving brawler possessed that convinced Mr. Pritchard to let him handle his money box and financial records. She tugged on the strings of her reticule, checking that it couldn't be spirited away without her knowledge. If this man committed some mischief against her and Grandfather, what recourse did they have?

Isaac-Lad. He was her only hope. The only person who might care enough to challenge his brother.

The curved rail of the bench crushed her skirt, but she'd refused to sit in the middle, smashed against Mr. Ballentine. Grandfather was unwell, and they couldn't have him pitching headfirst out of the wagon at the next steep curve. No, he must be protected at all costs. Grandfather's vague answers and repeated questions worried her. Had the shock been too much for him? Would he be better tomorrow? If not, they'd get right back on the train and head home—portrait or none. Right back to Cornelius.

She shuddered. Any dreams she'd had of finding the painting in a velvet-draped showroom had vanished—along with her hopes for a nice hotel. They'd have to settle for a boardinghouse, or anywhere away from the awful smells of the sale barn.

Although the avid gardener no longer knelt beneath the peony bushes, Miranda recognized the gardening shack. Were they stopping for directions?

"Get down. We're here," Mr. Ballentine said.

This wasn't a tool shed? Miranda tasted the acid that crawled up her throat. The narrow cabin looked like it had been squeezed through a railroad car. Barely room for the front door to swing open without hitting one of the two windows on the side. "This is a boardinghouse?"

"Sometimes." Mr. Ballentine held Grandfather's arm as he helped him down from the wagon. "We don't get visitors often, but when we do, Widow Sanders puts them up."

Rather than exit on Mr. Ballentine's side, Miranda decided to take her chances on her own. There were no steps, only the wide wagon wheels whose slanting spokes took the place of ladder rungs. She turned, gripped the side of the bench, and slowly lowered one foot. Hooking her heel on the only horizontal spoke, she knew the next step down had to hit soil. With pointed toe she fished, jabbed, waved. Where was the ground? She couldn't lean much farther backward and maintain her balance. The ground should be there. Really, it was ridiculous. The men had already walked around the wagon, and she was still fighting gravity. The weight of her skirts and bustle finally tilted the scales against her. With one foot still on the spoke, she released her hands expecting to find terra firma immediately. Instead, she found air.

And Mr. Ballentine.

She crashed backward into his chest. Her arms flung out.

He caught her beneath her arms, his hands coming shockingly close to her . . .

"Bust your ankle and you'll be sorry," he said.

She swirled around, but finding herself facing him was even worse. His nearness discombobulated her. Thankfully she didn't have to respond before he stepped to the side.

"We're on a mountain," he said. "You have to account for the slant, or you'll go rolling down the hill, curls a'tangling and petticoats flashing."

"My petticoats are none of your business," she managed.

He grinned. "Then I'll let you handle the trunk in the back of the wagon while I try to convince Widow Sanders to keep you."

"She doesn't have room for us," Grandfather said. "She barely has room for a front door."

"Wyatt!" A man's voice rang out. Miranda spun to see Isaac Ballentine coming up the hill, swinging his arms easily and smiling through a fat eye. "Keep your hands off that lady. If you want to rough someone up, have another go at me, but you leave her be."

Miranda could've cried in relief.

Wyatt's face hardened to marble. "Didn't expect you back so soon."

"There was no need for you to confiscate the wagon, after all." Isaac swung his arm up to rest on the side of the wagon bed.

"No need at all, besides two hundred head of hungry animals."

"But these fine people haven't done you any harm. Why act so hostile to the lady?"

Wyatt's eye twitched as he glared at her. Miranda wanted to duck behind Grandfather, but she didn't need to bother. Wyatt had no interest in looking at her any longer.

"Mr. Wimplegate," Wyatt said. "Are you planning to have a sale tomorrow?"

Grandfather wrung his damp handkerchief. "We haven't made a sale catalog yet, and I don't have the first clue how to describe our merchandise. Usually Miranda writes the descriptive copy—"

"Sale catalog?" Wyatt crossed his arms over his chest. "Are people in Boston so thick-skulled they have to read about what they are seeing before them?"

Miranda couldn't catch the gasp that escaped. This buffoon had no idea how a well-written description could raise the price of an item. "Obviously you don't know the first thing about running an auction," she said.

"Excuse me?" His brow lowered.

Grandfather's voice boomed beneath the spreading oak branches. "Tomorrow we'll determine our course and whether or not your services will be required. Until then, I'd advise you not to touch a single carat."

Isaac choked on a laugh. Maybe carat wasn't the appropriate word, but Wyatt seemed to understand. The house behind him wavered in the light, but whether the heat waves were from the sun reflecting off the shingles or from steam coming out of his ears, Miranda couldn't tell.

"If you need something," Wyatt said, "my house is up the mountain. Just turn in on the path next to the old dash churn."

"Wyatt keeps promising to haul it off," Isaac muttered for Miranda's ears alone, "but he never will. Too sentimental."

"Bring the wagon home," Wyatt growled as he punched Isaac in the arm, but Miranda had seen him strike before, and this hit lacked conviction. Then he and his stinking boots scuffed up the road to the barn.

CHAPTER 7

Miranda had slept well despite the screeching locusts and bellowing bullfrogs. The windows had no glass, thus explaining the volume. It also explained why Widow Sanders could slap down a flying insect with such precision. She'd had ample opportunity for practice.

Finally finished with her hair, Miranda jerked on her boots and shoved the buttons into their loops. Through the door she heard Grandfather's hard soles slap the stairs as he headed down to breakfast. The night before, Isaac had stayed long enough to see them settled. Would he make an appearance today, or would they be stuck with his moody brother? With her boots fastened securely, Miranda shook out her skirts and descended the staircase.

She paused before entering the kitchen, allowing the setting to form a complete impression. The yellow curtains over the sink lifted on a breeze that danced over the table, teasing the peonies that twisted in the canning jar full of water. Outside, the birds competed with one another, their songs gaily clashing as they floated in the cheery morning sunshine.

Widow Sanders hummed as she clattered her pots and pans

over a simple stove, while Grandfather anchored the scene in his severe black suit with his Bible spread atop the white tablecloth.

He spotted her and raised an eyebrow. Miranda came forward. "Just appreciating the striking figure you cut this beautiful morning." She dropped a kiss on his forehead before taking a seat herself.

"But it can only be improved by the addition of a stunning young lady."

"I disagree. Another figure would dilute the impact and upset the balance."

They both grinned. Arguing art was one of their favorite pastimes, and Miranda was relieved to find her grandfather lucid enough to play along. Since they had no galleries to visit today, no procurements at the auction house worth appreciating, they'd have to evaluate the setting they found themselves in.

"I'm tickled to have you here." Widow Sanders turned and slid two steaming bowls on the table before them. "I've always wanted to have room to board guests."

"And maybe someday you will." Grandfather closed his Bible and set it aside.

Miranda bit her lip as she tried to remember if she'd ever seen this bubbling white goop before. She picked up her spoon and stirred. Not oatmeal.

"It's grits." Widow Sanders took her seat. "Ten times better than any you'd eat in Boston, I'd wager."

Grandfather didn't wait to be asked but blessed the food before Miranda could question Widow Sanders' claim. She allowed his words to blend with the birdsong and lovely breeze. She thanked God that He was here, even if the circumstances weren't ideal and the accommodations were primitive. And where would they be without Widow Sanders? Although Jesus had slept in a manger, Miranda was grateful He hadn't required that sacrifice of her . . . yet.

The grits were warm on her throat and the milk cool. Simple flavors but sustaining and comforting. Grandfather asked Widow Sanders about the area, the population, the presence of the local gentry . . . to which the woman chuckled and replied, "You're looking at them." But even that couldn't dim the eagerness from his eyes.

"You know, Miranda, I've had some time to think about that auction house, and I don't consider it a total loss. As long as we're here, we might as well try our hand at turning a profit. I've worked in an auction house most of my life. What's the difference between livestock and fine furnishings? They will sell just the same."

"What's the difference? Besides the fact that our new employees are covered in filth instead of broadcloth? And that they are surly, rude creatures instead of genteel and—"

"Now, Granddaughter, we must give Mr. Ballentine another chance. I'll see how he does today, and we'll go from there. He does seem knowledgeable about our investment, so I'd rather not terminate him."

"Terminate him?" With a hand to her thin chest, Widow Sanders whooshed out a laugh. "I'm not sure what you're talking about, but in this part of the country, that means something entirely different."

While Widow Sanders chuckled over her misunderstanding, Miranda felt the helplessness of her situation closing in around her. Grandfather wanted to stay and work at the auction house? With the animals and that . . . that man? Was it possible to drown at the breakfast table? Her lungs felt full of water.

But she had to be careful what she said. No discreet servants here, pretending not to listen. For all they knew, their every conversation would be announced on the town square at noon—if there was a town square.

Thud! The kitchen door shook. Miranda's spoon splashed into the goopy grits. Widow Sanders clamped her mouth shut, then grimaced. The doorknob rattled violently, making the seedlings in the tin cans by the window tremble.

"That girl." Widow Sanders rose, pulled the door open, and allowed a blond streak of braids and skirts to tumble inside. Landing hard on one knee, the girl scrambled up, pulling against the sink.

"Eb Shipman came to town a'gunning for Moore. Something to do with a missing coon hound. Said he'd string him up iffen he catches him. Sheriff Taney won't do nothing on account of his wife being blood kin to Eb. Uncle Fred won't say naught in the paper 'cause they'll come gunning for him, sure as the world, and that's not all. There's also an old man and his granddaughter come to town yesterday. Be watchful . . ."

Grandfather cleared his throat. The young girl threw a braid over her shoulder and turned slowly to look at them. "I declare, Widow Sanders"—she blinked large—"you got company." She treated them to a sly smile that Da Vinci would've killed to paint.

The feisty whirlwind delighted Grandfather. He beamed at her and enunciated each word. "We are the new owners of the auction house. We've come all the way from Boston."

The child crossed her arms over her chest, and her smile hardened into a challenge. "Is that so? How come Mr. Pritchard would sell it to you when he knew Wyatt's been hankering to buy it for years? Seems downright unfair, if you ask me."

Grandfather whipped back as though he'd been slapped. Miranda pulled her lips in tight to keep from laughing. Her experience with the street boys had prepared her well, although this urchin might be more lively than the lot of them. "How old are you?"

"Twelve. Well . . . nearly."

"You take it easy on these folks, Betsy," Widow Sanders said. "They're my guests."

"Well, surely they don't mind answering some questions. Did you bribe Pritchard? Throw buckets of money at him? Who is the criminal here? You or Pritchard?"

"No one's a criminal." Widow Sanders pushed the kitchen door closed with her sturdy shoe.

Betsy took a piece of toast and tore off a corner. Still chewing, she continued, "And how did you even hear about Pine Gap and the sale barn? Pritchard didn't run an ad, and you don't even subscribe to the paper. My uncle is the editor, and I checked."

Her too-large pinafore sagged off one shoulder, and her faded dress hung on her, waiting for the day when the bony girl would grow to fill it. Her large, expressive eyes animated every one of the dozen or so moods she'd displayed since she'd burst into the kitchen.

Grandfather sputtered. "We came because we're searching for . . . for—"

"Investment opportunities," Miranda supplied, hoping that he'd forgive her for interrupting, but they couldn't share the purpose of their journey with this volatile child, whose uncle owned the newspaper, no less.

"In Pine Gap?" Her eyes darted from Miranda to Grandfather, as if searching for signs of intelligence. Finding none, she ripped another bite of toast. "Things must be pitiful in Boston for you to come here, and that's a fact. Now, how about we get started out to the sale barn? You say you're here to make a buck. Best get to working. Wyatt is waiting on us."

An empty feed sack blew in front of Wyatt. He stabbed it with his bootheel, then bent to pick it up, cursing his luck at being caught between angry customers and an unreasonable owner . . . an unreasonable owner with a snooty, prissy grand-daughter, who also happened to be beautiful. But of course she was. Wyatt had never had any luck.

Three alleys meant thirty pens of thirsty animals. They were so dry he could drain the Gasconade River down to the rocks before they'd be satisfied, so he'd better get started. With the animals being held for so long, tempers were bound to be short. Let a farmer find his cattle with a dry trough, and there'd be trouble. The last thing these mountains needed was another out-break of feuds. So far, the Ballentines had managed to straddle the fence when it came to local hostilities. The sale barn was a safe place for trade, and it seemed everyone wanted to keep it that way. Good thing. Neutral ground in Hart County was rarer than flat land.

Wyatt had the pump singing, water splashing into the barrels in the back of the wagon. His mules brayed, alerting Wyatt to the company coming over the hill. The whole crew? What had he done to deserve this? From the beguiling smile on Betsy's face and the way Miss Wimplegate was watching her, his girl had already been at work. If he needed to know anything, Betsy would get it out of them.

If he could only get the barrels full before they interrupted him. Water splashed against his mostly clean shirt. He forced the tension from his chest at the welcome sensation. He had to keep his temper. Simmer down. Nothing good could come from upsetting these folks. He continued pumping and tried to see the barn through fresh eyes.

Before the barn, Wyatt had gone around with his pa to conduct sales wherever people were apt to gather. Once he was good enough with his writing and arithmetic, or at least better than Isaac, he stood by his father at the auctioneer's stand and kept notes of the buyers and the prices. Then came the barn. Wyatt had helped the men raise it, but too soon his pa's strength began to fade. That's when Wyatt began to chant the lulling rhythms of the auctioneer's song himself. There'd been a time when he dreamed of greater things, but he'd grown up, seen how the world really worked. He was destined to run the sale barn—if he could keep out of trouble with his new boss. With the barrels full, he hopped down and went to meet the spry gentleman next to the pens.

"Wyatt Ballentine." Elmer Wimplegate planted his cane into the ground and nearly posed. "I've made a decision. You're going to continue working for me, and my first order of business is to get you in a suit. We can't run an auction with you looking like a common laborer."

Where had this man concocted his ideas about auctions? Wyatt pulled his wet shirt away from his chest. "I don't have a suit, and if I did, I'd be saving it for my own burying, not ruining it by hopping gates, herding cattle, and driving pigs."

"And regarding that beard . . ." Wimplegate's eyes turned steely.

Well, horsefeathers. Wyatt would have to try another angle. "I can't get a suit by . . . when do you want to start the auction?"

"That'll depend on how quickly your printer can print a catalog."

"We don't need a catalog," Wyatt said.

"How do you know if you've never used one? Miranda is quite talented with her descriptions. She really adds value to the items."

Wyatt studied that spun-sugar granddaughter of his, dressed in another drab shade somewhere between brown and dirt brown. Talented with descriptions? So she could tell a whopper. That's what that meant. And she probably didn't cotton to bearded men, either.

Betsy piped up, "Are we going to have a sale on Monday or not?"

"We couldn't be ready by Monday, could we?" Elmer tilted his head until his flat hat brim was parallel with the slanting roof of the barn. He waved a pesky fly away from his mouth.

"These animals have been ready for weeks." Wyatt propped a leg up on the fence, hoping Mr. Wimplegate would forget about his duds. "The longer we keep them, the more we lose in feed and the less healthy they are. Today is Thursday. By Monday you'll be ready to be rid of them."

Elmer squinted through the plank fence at a pen of lambs. "Won't they bring more if you wash them up a bit? You know, give them a spit and polish to bring a few more dollars?"

Betsy giggled. If Wyatt thought for one second that Mr. Wimplegate would wash all these critters himself, he'd be tempted to play along, but he knew only too well who'd be standing in ankle-deep manure with a bucket and sponge and bathing goats.

"Clean animals don't sell any better than dirty ones, Mr. Wimplegate. People want them healthy, though, and the longer they sit here, the weaker they're getting."

Wimplegate nodded. "I suppose that makes sense. A goose

won't sit on a bureau and appreciate in value like a Gainsborough painting. It does appear that Miranda was right. I don't have the foggiest notion of what I've gotten myself into."

Wyatt dared a look at her. Jaw set, eyes mistrustful. She didn't want to be there. He didn't want her there. Maybe they could work together?

For a moment Wyatt tried to imagine a Boston auction of art and fancy furniture. He wouldn't know where to start there, either. "Don't you worry. Let me get this place to rolling, and you won't have any regrets. Everything will be just fine."

"But I'm not going to shirk my duties. I play a vital role in the auction back home, and this venture will be no different. Let no one say I played the fop while others did my work. I intend to set an example."

Of how to drive a teetotaler to whiskey? But he did agree to having a sale Monday, didn't he? Wyatt could shout hallelujah for that.

"Let's go inside and you can walk me through the process." Wimplegate dusted a cottonwood puff off his shoulder. "Show me the bidder's numbers, the catalogs, the sales receipts, and how we can best get through Monday. Then once we're done, we'll go to town and see if there's not an idle tailor looking for something to keep his Saturday evening busy—and a barber."

How far was he willing to go to keep this dream alive? Wyatt motioned them ahead of him. Without the auction house, where would the people of Hart County meet to conduct their business? What else would force them to be civil to one another? But he knew working for Mr. Wimplegate wasn't going to be easy. How the fellas would jeer at him sitting up at the auctioneer's table while stuffed into a sausage casing of a suit. And what would the fancy Miss Wimplegate think?

He'd look like a buffoon compared to the rich, barbered gents she was used to.

Boston. He'd never been there, but the name of the city chilled his innards. Shame. That's what he felt when he heard it, although he'd done nothing wrong. He knew it was a town so big that you could live there your whole life and never get to know all your neighbors. But he had to wonder if Miss Wimplegate and her grandpa had ever bumped elbows with anyone who might know of him. Probably not. He couldn't imagine the refined Wimplegates having anything to do with the likes of that kind of people. With the likes of his kind of people.

"I'll unlock the office," he said, "but I'm bound to get these animals watered before it gets any hotter."

Mr. Wimplegate didn't quarrel with him, but once inside he took to the account books like they were pulled taffy.

Looking at the fancy gent got Wyatt pondering what his life would've been like had the stories been true. But they weren't, and there wasn't no sense in stewing over it. He'd do the best he could with what he had, but without his job at the sale barn, he had nothing.

CHAPTER 8

"If you're serious about having a sale here," Miranda said, "then while you look at the books, I'll see if I can tidy the salon."

Betsy's freckles bunched up in confusion. "The salon?"

"She means the grand room where you sell everything." Grandfather remained bent over the ledger.

"It's already clean." Betsy shoved her hand into the pocket of what she probably considered a clean pinafore.

Poor thing. What would the scamp be doing if she lived in Boston? Living in a disease-ridden tenement? Working in a textile factory all hours of the day? As much as Miranda needed to look for the painting, she didn't have the heart to send Betsy away.

Betsy followed her out of the office. "I reckon I'm supposed to come. Wyatt told me to keep an eye on you."

"What's he afraid of?"

"For starters, he thinks Isaac might be sweet on you and told me to tell him if Isaac came within a mile of you."

Miranda lowered her eyes. Isaac found her interesting? Her lips curled of their own accord. It shouldn't matter. She couldn't imagine having a beau from these parts. Then again, besides

Cornelius, she'd never had a beau anywhere. She stayed too busy working with Father and Grandfather. Mother would occasionally wrangle an invitation for Miranda to some musical evening or social event among their peers, but more often than not she found herself hiding—preferring to observe than be observed.

But what if Isaac was one of the gentlemen merchants in her set? The thought of him with his melancholy eyes gazing at her over a candlelit table at the Tremont Hotel did have merit. He'd place his open palm on the linen tablecloth, and Miranda would slip her hand into his . . .

And then his brother would burst through the dining room, lunge at his throat, and upend the table. China would explode, crystal would shatter, and once again innocent Isaac would bear the brunt of Wyatt's uncontrolled fury. Miranda's lips tightened.

She stood at the edge of the cavernous arena. What could be done? Dirt and other natural substances she'd rather not identify were all that kept the room from austerity. Flies swarmed everywhere. The worn wooden seats doubled as stairs. Put cushions on them and they'd only be stepped on. That left the table in the front. A cloth maybe to cover the primitive board? A lamp? Some candlesticks to dress up the work area? After all, their customers would spend hours staring at the auctioneer. They might as well give them something to look at besides Wyatt Ballentine.

Her ears warmed. The thought of looking at him all day was decidedly disconcerting.

"You're going to spruce this place up, huh?" Betsy's bone-china complexion gave her an angelic appearance, an impression that was criminally misleading. "I'm not sure you're the right person for the job. If you were going through all the trouble of getting a fancy dress with ribbons and bows, why would you pick colors that only an earthworm could love?"

"The color is called cinnamon, and you are not exhibiting proper manners."

"But you ruined what would otherwise be a humdinger of a dress."

"The dress is understated and classy. It shows reserve and it's . . . it's—"

"Boring." Betsy flopped on the first step and rested her chin in her hand. "The color is boring."

"It's respectable. I'll not array myself like a strumpet—" The door leading from the pens in back swung open. Miranda stopped herself just in time.

But Betsy wouldn't let it go. "Wyatt," she asked. "What's a strumpet?"

Miranda's eyes burned, they stretched so wide. "What are you doing?" she whispered. "You know good and well—"

"Betsy," he warned, "where did you hear that word?"

Helpless. Miranda was helpless and at the mercy of a wickedly clever eleven-year-old. Her eyes went from piercing to pleading. Betsy lifted her chin in victory. "I heard it here at the sale barn. I just wanted to see what it meant."

At least Wyatt didn't look fooled. "Watch your mouth, Betsy Huckabee. You don't talk that way in front of a lady."

She dimpled, clearly unafraid of his bluster. Evidently, she'd never seen him rough up his brother.

Feeling minutely justified by Wyatt's defense, Miranda waited until he made it inside the office before she asked, "What'd I ever do to you?"

"You took Wyatt's sale barn. That's what." Betsy drummed her heels against the hard seat beneath her.

Enough arguing with a child. Miranda Wimplegate couldn't set herself against this unruly brat, even if sorely provoked. Instead, she'd do what she could to improve the girl's prospects. It might be the only thing she accomplished on this journey.

Carefully picking her way around the dirty arena to the auctioneer's table she called over her shoulder, "Your uncle owns the newspaper? Is there that much news here?"

"Not often. Mostly he sells the papers from the city, but we print our own when there's a call for it."

"Is he raising you?"

"Yep. When my aunt died, I came to town to help with my little cousins. Three boys in all. My ma and pa live away from town."

Miranda didn't have the first clue where to procure knick-knacks for the table, but surely with the tireless Widow Sanders' help she could at least have a vase of fresh flowers by sale day. If she could only move the ugly equipment out of the way.

A large metal frame extended from beneath the floor and spanned the front of the table. She leaned on it and it gave a bit, sinking a few inches into the ground. When Betsy climbed the rungs of the pen, the beam shuddered beneath Miranda's fingers. What a hazard. It was neither steady nor attractive. Short hooks descended from it on which were hung heavy metal disks—possibly an attempt to stabilize the structure and keep it from swaying so. Whatever could they have been thinking to leave this eyesore sprouting right before the focal point of the room?

Betsy took a seat at the table and tossed the gavel from hand to hand, imitating a carnival performer.

"Do you miss your family?" Miranda asked. To her surprise, the metal disks were easily removed from the hooks. She would

71

hide them beneath the table. Once she found a drape to put over it, no one could see them there.

"I do miss them, but they come to town right often. Especially my brother Josiah. He works here on sale day."

And they hadn't had a sale day for quite some time.

"Besides," Betsy continued, "Ma says I can learn more city ways here than at home. Someday I'll be a sophisticated lady like Abigail Calhoun."

City ways? Here in Pine Gap? Miranda couldn't imagine how backward those in the hills must be.

She'd successfully dismantled the discs and hooks from the beam. The steel beam itself was too heavy for her to lift. She considered pushing it out of the braces where it balanced, but a quick look below the table assured her that she didn't want to have to pick it up off the dirty floor. Turning her attention to the table, she measured it with an eye used to determining the length of sideboards, bureaus, and the like. With a crisp nod she smiled at Betsy. "You'll help me find some fabric, won't you? By Monday I can have this table adorned more appropriately. Widow Sanders might even have a vase I could use for some fresh-cut flowers."

"You think Wyatt is going to sit in a mess of flowers?"

"Just wait until you see him dressed up. We'll get that nasty beard shaved off and get him out of his old stinky clothes, and he'll look as handsome . . . as . . . as . . ."

Only one thing could make Betsy look so happy, and that would be if Wyatt had returned and was standing behind Miranda at that moment.

"What did you do to my scale?"

Thankful that he'd chosen to ignore her plans for him, she answered, "I don't have it." Besides the steel frame, the table was empty.

He rushed around the arena pen with remarkable speed. "This." He grabbed the metal frame with both hands. "You disassembled my scales."

Her eyes flickered over the beam, once balancing on the supports but now resting heavily on the struts. "I've never seen a scale that big." Not really an excuse, but in such circumstances one should say something.

"You've never weighed five tons of cattle before, either."

Her face burned. The last thing she wanted was a lecture from this ruffian, but he was right . . . and she hated that she must admit it.

"I'm sorry." She fiddled with the silver charms on her bracelet. "I was trying to help."

He didn't move. His fists were still on his hips and his legs were planted wide, but somehow she could sense the anger had gone. Instead, he was studying her, just like she might study a painting. But she was no masterpiece, and she didn't appreciate the attention.

"I'll help you put it back together." She squatted and began gathering the various disks and hooks.

"I'd do better on my own." His chest sunk as he surveyed the mess. "It has to be perfectly balanced. No room for inaccuracy."

She'd messed it up, and she couldn't fix it. Just like losing the LeBlancs' painting. The metal pieces clanged out of Miranda's grasp as she deposited them on the table. Stepping away, Miranda clasped her hands behind her back. "I'm going to get a tablecloth for this table and a vase of fresh flowers. It'll add a touch of class to the place."

Did his eyelids weigh five tons, too? Because he seemed to have trouble keeping them from drooping. "It's your place. Do what you want. Your grandpa will be looking for me, so I'd best go." Another look at the pile of the disassembled hardware, and he turned to march to the office.

Betsy whistled. "You sure ain't much help around here."

True, but unfair. She wasn't supposed to be adorning a livestock barn. She was supposed to find a painting and get home before the LeBlancs took them to court. Time was running out.

Widow Sanders' peony bush buzzed with evening guests. Wasps dallied from bloom to bloom, tracing their scalloped paths in the air. The sun hovered on the crest of the western mountain, just waiting to dip beneath. A calming setting if one could forget what had brought them to it.

"How did you get rid of that girl?" Grandfather reclined in a wicker chair, his jar of sweet tea drawing an occasional wasp to be swatted away.

Miranda readjusted her tree-stump seat in an attempt to find level ground. "She went home to fix dinner for her uncle and nephews. Maybe I can get away tomorrow to search for the painting without her."

"Painting?"

Miranda smiled at his joke, then realized he wasn't jesting. A chill raised bumps on her arms. *Dear Lord*, she prayed, *has he forgotten already?* "The LeBlancs' painting. Remember?"

"Oh, that. You know, I don't see it as critical as I did once. This place is a bonanza of opportunity. Even if we don't find it, we might make our fortune here."

Was this more than a memory lapse? The farther from home they traveled, the more his personality changed, and right now Miranda felt very, very far from home.

"Grandfather, one aisle of our auction house is worth more

74

than this sale barn, the cattle, and all the land it's on. Buying the barn was a mistake."

"You're awfully free with your opinion," he snapped. Miranda dropped her gaze to her dirty fingernails and cringed at his tone. "Buying that barn has opened doors for us. While I was at the bank, I met a Mr. Rinehart who receives regular shipments of art from the outside world. We're going calling on him tomorrow. He wouldn't have been so friendly if he didn't appreciate the investment we are making to the local tradesmen."

"Then the LeBlancs' painting wasn't sent to the barn after all?"

"How would I know?" He shook his head. "Instead of questioning my every decision, Miranda, why don't you go search the barn now that we're free from our escorts?" He straightened in his chair and dug in his waistcoat pocket. "Here's the key to the padlock. I wish you luck."

Miranda's eyes stung. A timid child, she hadn't occasioned many reprimands—and never one from Grandfather. She missed the key he tossed and had to retrieve it from the soil. "It'll be dark by the time I get back . . ."

"The mill has already closed, and there's nothing else between here and the barn. You won't see a soul."

She should refuse. It wasn't safe. All Betsy's warnings about the hostility of the hills played in excruciating detail. Should Miranda assert her opinion that going alone was foolhardy, or was her reluctance further proof of her cowardice? Yet it might be the best chance to investigate without the grumpy Mr. Ballentine looking over her shoulder. Bravery. Her cranium ached at being stretched in the unfamiliar area.

"If I'm not back in a half hour . . ."

Ignoring her concern, Grandfather rocked his chair and hummed. Maybe having Betsy around wasn't so bad, after all.

The sun-dappled road passed beneath tangled branches. It was impossible to tell which tree spawned the limbs. Soon all would be dark and the canopied walk would go from shaded to menacing. She hurried across the wagon yard toward the hulking barn, afraid to pause, afraid to check over her shoulder. The rusty padlock creaked at her twisting of the key, then with a click sprang open.

After removing the padlock and loosening the chain, Miranda tried to pull the giant door open. She'd forgotten her gloves, but her fingernails already carried a thimbleful of dirt beneath them. No room for more. She dug her heels into the gravel walkway and tugged, her skirt brushing in the dirt behind her. When the door finally decided to give way, she had to hurry to keep ahead and not have a foot caught beneath it. Catching her breath, she dusted off her hands and gingerly set forth into the shadowy building. Yellowed sunlight filtered through fly-speckled windows, but at least she could see in the office well enough. The calendar on the wall swayed as she rifled through a collection of empty crates. She remembered the size of the frame. Where could it hide?

She checked behind a desk—cobwebs, some scraps of paper, and cigarettes burned to the nub. Every other desk faced the door. One cabinet might provide results, but upon opening it, she found the space sliced up by shelving. Besides the door she entered, there was one other that beckoned. It was full-sized, but nothing suggested that it'd been opened regularly. Pushing her fear behind her, she turned the knob. A wall of pitch black greeted her. Her nose twitched, prompting a fit of sneezes. Grandfather wouldn't expect her to go in there, but if she didn't, who would? A quick search through the desk drawer uncovered some matches. She took the wire handle of the lantern, struck a blaze, and with a jut of her chin, entered the dark corridor.

And she wasn't surprised when the door closed behind her.

This was just like her warehouse back home—a big room that echoed. The lantern wavered with her trembling. Nothing to be afraid of, she told herself. She was all alone and things couldn't hurt her. Holding the lantern aloft, she recognized the tiered ceiling. This storage space ran beneath the seating above her. The evening breeze nudged against the barn's wood siding, and she could hear the shuffling of the small rodents that were sharing her space.

The room stretched toward the center of the arena, with the ceiling stepping lower and lower, the inverse of the seating above it. Beneath the bottom step was only space for a breadbox. The lantern light didn't quite reach the farthest corners, but she suspected they were as empty as the rest, if you didn't count the cobwebs and rat droppings. The narrow cavern curved as it wrapped around the arena, following the contours of the seating. Ahead, Miranda spotted bulky items. A broken gate leaned against the wall. Empty feed bags had drifted beneath the seats, and a rusted-out water trough lay gasping on its side. Nothing of value. Nothing that had been moved in years. Her task was halfway finished, but she was still not successful.

At the end of the passage, Miranda exited to find herself where she'd expected—in the arena. She only had the other side to go. Symmetrical. It shouldn't take long.

Already familiar with the inverted stair-step shape of the room, Miranda forged ahead. Must get back before dark. Already the crickets were chirping outside. The moldy scent told her there must be a leak on this side of the building. Hopefully it wasn't a dead animal. She swung the lantern low, allowing its beams to shine into the farthest reaches of the center of the room. All the time she had to watch her step, carefully making her way over the wooden braces and a pair of dirty work boots.

Miranda froze. Her heart stopped. Someone was wearing those boots. Slowly she lifted the lantern up, praying the vision would disappear, but no. A man stood in her way, blocking the exit. His red beard jutted from his face like a chisel. He was compact, stronger than she was, and he was hiding in the sale barn.

Not one of those things was good.

Lord, let my death be swift and painless was her only thought. Did that make her brave or a coward? If she were brave, she'd turn around and run, but her feet were glued to the floor.

"Didn't mean to startle you, ma'am." His voice had the uneven, musical draw that she'd heard more frequently the farther into the mountains they traveled. "Thought you might need some help."

"Who . . . who are you?"

He held her gaze, weighing her just as surely as if she was sitting on the scales. "Just passing through and saw the door open."

Passing through? Even Miranda knew the sale barn was at the end of the road. Behind it was nothing but a cliff. But it'd be rude to mention his mistake, not to mention probably fatal.

"I don't need any help." Each word felt like sandpaper passing through her throat. Thinking of her fearless grandmother, she took a giant breath and uttered the two words that might be her last. "You're trespassing."

His eyebrow rose. His mouth twitched. "I'll be heading out, then." One last look around the room, and he left, disappearing into the dark shadows that curved with the bend of the arena.

Miranda fell against a support beam. She had to get home. Now. Deciding not to follow him, Miranda retraced her steps to the open arena. No time to recover her composure. She would run all the way back to Widow Sanders'. Just try to stop her.

She burst through the door and was immediately grabbed. Dropping the lantern, she swung at the man's face with an untrained fist, amazed how much it hurt when she hit his cheek. Another scuffle, and her arms were pinned to her sides. She kicked, only then realizing that the shins she was thrashing were covered with a different pair of boots.

"Miranda!" It was Wyatt. The light of the unleashed flame distorted his features into something more sinister than usual. "What are you doing?"

Good thing he was holding her arms down, or she might just hug him. "There's a man in there, under the stairs."

His brow lowered. With a long reach, he grabbed the gavel off the table and tested its weight before opening the door beneath the bleachers. "Don't go anywhere," he said.

How about back to Boston? But seeing there wasn't a train at that second, she complied. He disappeared, leaving her to right the lantern and sweep the broken glass from the hurricane globe into her hand. Broken glass. Not the most effective weapon, but she'd use it if she must.

Lord, please protect me from the wicked, she prayed, leaving it up to God to judge which man best fit that description. Wyatt was gone an awfully long time considering the space beneath the seating was limited. Still peering into the darkness, Miranda heard footsteps coming into the room through the main hallway. With a shaky puff she blew out the lantern and brandished her shard of glass. Not much light came in, but enough to make out the outline of a man. Too tall to be the redhead. Did she want it to be Wyatt?

"Miranda? Where'd you go?"

She lowered her weapon. "I heard you coming, so I blew out the light."

"I already knew you were in here."

"But I didn't know if it was you, or . . . oh, nevermind." She didn't care what he thought. Only that she wasn't alone. She worked her way to the entrance, carefully avoiding the rows of seating. "How did that man get beneath the stairs?"

Instead of answering, Wyatt caught her wrist as she passed. He held her arm up in the waning light and scowled at the key dangling there. The shadows hid most of his face, but they couldn't hide the warmth of his grip.

"He got in the same way you did. You left the front door open. There's a broom closet just opposite the office. It's the only other access to that side of the arena."

Miranda jerked out of his grasp. What did he mean laying hands on her like that? No workman had ever touched her before.

"You don't know who he was? No suspicions?" she asked.

"I don't abide folks nosing around here after dark, including you. Why are you here, anyway?"

"That's none of your business." For some reason she could never reproduce the haughty Boston tone when she needed to. This time she only succeeded in sounding breathless.

"I reckon my business is chasing down strange men who scare you?"

She really wished she could see him, because despite his mountain drawl, the authority in his voice made her forget his ragged beard and homemade clothes. Hard to remember her superiority when it was only the two of them.

"Look," he said. "I don't think you want to be here in Pine Gap, and it's no secret my life would be a sight easier if you weren't. Why can't we help each other out?"

Miranda sniffed, unsure that this wasn't a trick. "I have to stay here for Grandfather."

"What will it take to get Grandfather back home?"

Father had told her to keep their quest a secret. Otherwise they'd have to pay . . . and pay dearly. "We won't stay a day longer than necessary," she said. "On that you have my word."

She couldn't see his face, but he seemed to be weighing her proclamation. Finally he made his own offer. "If there's anything I can do to hurry you on home . . . you have my word." Promising to do anything it took to get rid of her? How charming. "But if you're going to be out carousing at night," he said, "you'd better be prepared to defend yourself. These hills are crawling with outlaws and ne'er-do-wells."

"Thank you for the warning." Maybe she couldn't do haughty, but she had sarcastic in her repertoire. "I'll return to my abode now, before the light fails."

"I can't let you go alone." He took the broken lamp from her, left it in the office, then waved her outside. Swinging the heavy door closed, he wrapped the chain in the handles and held out his hand to her. "Give me your key."

Miranda slid it off her wrist, but not until he'd palmed it did she realize her mistake. "You don't need a key to lock a padlock."

He dropped the key into his pocket. "But I need this key to keep you out of trouble." He snapped the padlock closed. "Now, let's both be pondering on how to get you back where you belong."

81

CHAPTER 9

Why, when he had pens plumb overflowing, did Elmer Wimplegate decide to go calling on the neighbors? Wyatt stepped outside the modest clapboard house and looked out over the valley that ran just below his property. The morning sun reflected in the river that ribboned its way through the bottom of his land and on into town. Stretched out vertically, they owned acres of wooded ground, but standing at the top of the hill, he could throw a good-sized rock and come pert near to hitting the boundary river. Maybe he could now. He hadn't tried since he was a boy.

How he missed his parents. Ma leaving wet kisses on his cheek, even when he was so tall she had to pull him down to do it. Pa letting him fight his own battles but standing nearby, ready to rush in with a broom handle if his older brothers ganged up on him. They were all gone now. All but Isaac. When the railroad had come through looking for strong backs to conquer the Ozarks, Pete and Clifford had moved on. Once they'd got a taste for the larger world, none of Ma or Pa's pleas could bring them back home. Had Isaac stayed for any sentimental reason, Wyatt would've been grateful. He hated being alone. But he'd been gifted with Isaac's company on two accounts—first being that Isaac couldn't take the chance that Wyatt might succeed at something, and second, Isaac didn't have the ambition to do anything else. Lacking his own dreams, Isaac was content to sit back and shoot down Wyatt's.

Wyatt felt sorry for Isaac at times, because it did seem that Isaac's one purpose in life was to oppose anything Wyatt attempted. If Wyatt resolved to save money, Isaac came home with a new pocket watch. The day Wyatt would beat out a rug was the day Isaac would shell peanuts on it. Sometimes Wyatt wondered if he shouldn't just leave and start somewhere new. What would it be like to not operate under the begrudging oversight of a big brother?

But something new was coming. God was at work here. His soul told him to prepare. Good or bad, change was ahead. He turned from the peaceful vista before him and headed to the barn to harness the mules.

By the time he arrived at Widow Sanders', they were waiting. Elmer paced a circle around her oak tree while Miranda sat on a tree stump in a sad gray dress that probably cost more than a whole pen of cattle. If he had a woman as fine looking as Miranda, he wouldn't let her dress so somber. Then he hopped down from the wagon and got a look at his own canvas britches. Maybe he could do better, too.

"We're coming," Mr. Wimplegate called.

Miranda pulled on some smooth gloves that were as bland as the rest of her getup. But when he handed her up, he couldn't believe the softness of the fabric. As soft as a downy chick. He shook his head. No wonder Isaac got all the ladies. No woman wanted to hear thoughts like that.

Releasing her hand, he hauled himself up next to her. At least he didn't have to ride crammed against Elmer this time. A flap of reins and the mules strained forward. They'd ride through town on their way to Rinehart's place—a decent stretch, nearly halfway to Saint George.

In the alley between the newspaper office and the dry goods store, they caught a glimpse of Betsy pushing a wheelbarrow of vegetables to town. Her ever-ready smile flashed, and then she was gone.

"It seems she floats about without much supervision," Miranda said. "Who's watching out for her?"

"Be on guard, Wyatt," Elmer said. "Miranda's yet to meet a street urchin she could turn away from."

He hadn't expected the high-and-mighty Miss Wimplegate to think twice about little Betsy, but that she did was to her credit. "Betsy's not neglected. Maybe she doesn't have a nursemaid following after her with a clean handkerchief, but her uncle's a decent fellow, and the whole town keeps an eye out for her. And she still has her folks. They come to see her when they're on this side of the river." How could anyone pity Betsy? She had what he wanted most.

They rolled out of town following the narrow pass through the green mountains. He felt Miranda relax against him, no longer fighting the contact of his body against hers as they swayed up and down the gullies. Something about her smelled like Widow Sanders' roses. On the next rough washout he let himself rock toward her to see if he could figure out whether it was her hair or her perfume, but no matter how he sniffed, he couldn't quite decide.

Sneaking a glance, he found her face alight with pleasure as she took in the valley spread before them. Wyatt wanted to ask if she thought the hills as beautiful as he did, but with her grandfather—his boss—along for the ride, he decided against it. So the wheels creaked along, leaving him to imagine that conversation and many others he'd like to have with her.

The sounds of the wilderness changed. Wyatt pulled the mules to a halt. No birdsong, only a constant rustling. More than one man. More than a couple of men. Miranda was watching him, waiting for him to explain. He saw fear in her eyes and for once she wasn't afraid of him. He brushed his hand over her soft glove by way of comfort. They couldn't avoid whatever was ahead. No place to turn off in a wagon, so he'd just pray that this group wasn't up to any mischief.

Around the bend came men mounted on horses and mules. Wyatt knew them but didn't like what he saw. Clive Fowler raised his giant fist and halted the group.

"Don't pay us any mind, Wyatt. We don't aim to bother you'uns none."

Wyatt scanned the group. Customers of his, decent fellows who didn't look like they were enjoying themselves, but there was one man he didn't recognize. This man was on foot with his hands tied in front of him. His face was lowered, and the knees to his britches were caked in mud.

Wyatt really shouldn't get involved, but these were his woods, too. "You catch yourselves a bandit?"

Fowler readjusted the rifle that rode on his lap. "Looks like it. Mr. Rinehart caught him poking around his place. Thought we'd give him a few lashes to teach him some manners, then send him on his way."

Now Miranda's hand sought him. She tugged on his sleeve. "The barn," she whispered. "That's him."

His neck tightened as he considered his options. One wrong word and this fellow's future could be changed forever. Hopefully, Miranda would understand if he didn't add fuel to the fire.

"What's Sheriff Taney say?"

Wyatt's question was met with grunts of disgust. "Sheriff who?" Fowler mocked. "You know good and well there's no sheriff around here. Not when you need him. Don't you fret, Wyatt. We aim to be fair. These boys answer to me."

And to tell the truth, they seemed controlled. Wyatt pitied the man for what lay ahead, but then again, what business did he have nosing around the sale barn and the Rineharts'? Better drive him out of the county now before he did any real damage.

They filed past the wagon. Even though the prisoner never raised his head, Miranda shuddered as he stumbled by. Wyatt was struck by the uncontrollable urge to wrap an arm around the frightened lady. Almost uncontrollable, because he did manage, but it troubled him fiercely. Soon they were gone. Wyatt leaned around Miranda to check on Elmer, who was dozing in his seat, chin dropped to his chest.

"Why didn't you tell them?" she asked.

Good question. When he considered what might have happened to Miranda had he not shown up at the barn when he did, it was Wyatt's turn to shudder. "He didn't break no laws that we can prove. He'll get what's coming to him and maybe something extry."

"Will he be back?"

"Do you do much praying, Miss Miranda?"

Her mouth turned a frown and she picked at her gloves. "Of course I do."

"Then maybe that's why I showed up when I did at the barn. God is watching out for you."

Silently she lifted her eyes to gaze at her sleeping grandfather. Once again, Wyatt was struck by her care for the gent. It couldn't be easy on her, coming out here, being at the mercy of the old coot's broken logic. She needed help. She needed to get back home.

———————❦———————

The road broke out into a clearing. Atop a gentle rise sat the Rineharts' fine house. The morning sun illuminated the white building, throwing it into sharp contrast with the emerald lawn where a dozen or so sheep grazed placidly. The house looked promising the way it perched on the hill like the top tier of a bride's cake.

How Mother would enjoy seeing this place. From Father's anguished telegram that morning, Miranda knew they were worried about her—both her safety and her success. That they hadn't immediately located the painting within the auction house had the whole family concerned. Not a day went by that Monty King didn't inquire about their progress, and Father was running out of excuses.

As they neared, Grandfather began polishing his cuff links. Every time he was preparing to meet a wealthy client he had to make sure his cuff links were spotless. Miranda wormed her hand through the crook of his arm. As if anyone ever caught him looking less than pristine. Grandfather always presented himself as if he were preparing to sit for one of the many portraits they dealt with.

A cat bolted from beneath the porch as they pulled up in front of the house. Giant baskets full of the variegated leaves of wandering Jew hung from the veranda ceiling. This could be the place they were looking for. According to Betsy, Mr. Rinehart had come from old money in Tennessee, and his wife received shipments from back East every week. Miranda rattled her silver bracelet, then wondered if she, like

Grandfather, did that every time she prepared to meet an influential client.

The heavy oak door swung open and Mr. Rinehart escorted a rounded-nosed lady outside. Once past the threshold, she arranged her overskirt to show off the flounces and didn't forget to point her toe so that a satin shoe peeked from beneath her pleated underskirt. Definitely not sewn by a Parisian designer, but then Miranda's were only basted together by an Irish woman who had a good eye for imitation. The tilt of her head, the way she looked Miranda down from head to toe, as if measuring her for a better dress, made Miranda feel uncomfortably at home. Surely they would find the LeBlancs' painting here. Mrs. Rinehart had the same ability to discredit a woman that many of their esteemed customers possessed.

Putting on her brave face, Miranda allowed Grandfather to escort her to the door, where she followed Mrs. Rinehart's lead by merely ducking her chin instead of a more formal curtsy. Finally meeting her eyes, Miranda studied the mass of tight curls Mrs. Rinehart had gathered behind her left ear. Miranda didn't trust any woman who styled her hair asymmetrically. It seemed off-kilter, as if her judgment was unbalanced. Still, she would hope for the best.

They passed inside while the men discussed the lone intruder that Rinehart had found. Mr. Rinehart expressed remorse at turning the man over to the vigilantes, but one couldn't be too careful. Once through the threshold, they entered a long, narrow foyer with empty crates stacked on the wool runner. Grandfather cleared his throat. Miranda hid a smile. Betsy hadn't been mistaken about the shipments. But they were quickly encouraged to pass through the crowded entryway into an even more cluttered parlor.

Miranda was well acquainted with every style of curio likely to appear in a fine home, but she'd never seen an example of each in the same room.

"We shipped most of our furniture from Tennessee, where his family is from," Mrs. Rinehart said. "Are you familiar with the Rineharts of Nashville?"

"I regret I haven't had the privilege." Now refreshed from his morning nap, Grandfather accepted a steaming cup of tea and smiled his thanks as Mrs. Rinehart handed Miranda a cup and settled on the sofa next to her husband.

Wyatt seemed unsure what to do with his hands, folding them in his lap, and then with a lurch, sitting up straight in the chair and grasping the arms. Only then did Miranda realize he hadn't been offered a drink. Were his boots clean? When he crossed his ankles and tucked them beneath the chair, Miranda realized he had the same worries. For being married to a plantation owner, Mrs. Rinehart didn't seem as if she'd be forgiving of stains on her thick red carpet.

"You are impressed with our furnishings." Mrs. Rinehart rocked from side to side as if creating a nest for herself in the sofa cushions.

"Er . . . yes, ma'am," Miranda answered.

Grandfather came to Miranda's rescue. "I don't know if Mr. Rinehart has informed you, Mrs. Rinehart, but I'm the proprietor of the Wimplegate Auction House in Boston. We deal in fine antiques, estate sales, and works of art, so it's only natural that we'd note your many fine pieces."

Miranda had to drop her gaze to her bracelet. Some of their furniture was passable, but the way it was lined up wall-to-wall made the room feel more like a warehouse than a living area. Unfortunately, the various items cluttering the table were similar only in their newness and their lack of value.

Mrs. Rinehart rose and made her way to the smaller walnut secretary. She dropped the lid down and came back with a paper-bound book with a woodcut print on the cover. Mr. Rinehart's mouth twisted in rueful patience as she returned to her seat.

"When did you come into town?" she asked.

"Last Friday," Grandfather answered.

"You may have arrived with one of my shipments. Nearly every week something I've purchased is delivered."

Never show your interest when making an offer, Miranda reminded herself. If Mrs. Rinehart had indeed organized a purchase from the auction, they mustn't act as if they were interested. If she knew they'd come all this way to retrieve a portrait, she'd ask an inordinate amount for it. Miranda settled her teacup into the saucer and arranged it on the crowded end table.

"Have you recently purchased something from Boston?" Grandfather took another sip, as calm as the harbor on Sabbath.

"No. Not Boston." She raised the booklet and waved it. "I purchase my treasures from Montgomery Ward in Chicago."

Miranda sighed. Her shoulders slumped. With a minuscule jerk of his chin, Grandfather telegraphed courage to her. "What manner of treasures would those be?" he asked.

Mrs. Rinehart straightened her head, defeating the considerable weight of the off-centered hair. The paper crinkled as she flapped the cover open and flew through a few pages. Turning it upside down, she extended it toward them. Miranda leaned forward to see the page blotted with circles, stars, and strikes.

"My goal is to work through the Carpets, Curtains, and Linens section this month. In July, I'll start on the Cutlery section."

"A mail-order catalog?" Miranda asked.

"It's the newest thing. Every item you can imagine is at

90

your fingertips if you but have the funds. And we do, don't we Charles?"

He took a sudden fascination with the length of his fingernails. "The farm back in Tennessee has done well this year. My brother is very generous. . . ."

"Um-hmm. And I'm picking the best items from each page, but sometimes I just have to order one of each, because you can't have too many damask towels, you know. How could you decide between bleached or half-bleached linen? Hemmed borders or knotted fringe? And the colors? Well, as you can see here, the pictures show the designs but not the colors. You have to see the colors." She pointed to a sideboard whose drawers stood slightly ajar, crammed full with red and orange linens. "It's nice to have spares, don't you think?"

"If you have room," Miranda replied.

"We do," Mrs. Rinehart answered. She rocked back into the sofa. "So where is the supplier for your business located?"

"We deal in estate sales and antiques," Miranda said.

"Oh? All used furniture, then?" She frowned. "You could get new things if you wanted. They might be more at the onset, but people are willing to pay for quality."

Quality? Like these shoddy sticks of furniture? Miranda's teacup rattled on the saucer as she retrieved it.

"Miss Wimplegate is particularly interested in art," Wyatt blurted. "You can't buy that from a catalog."

Miranda turned to stare at the scruffy man, wondering what could have prompted that admission. How he even knew? But more surprising than his defense of her was the sight of him. Sitting in the red velvet chair in front of the bay window, his arms stretched out with the light streaming over his shoulder, he resembled nothing so much as a Russian tsar on his throne. Wrap an ermine mantle over his shoulders and she and Grandfather would swear they'd seen his portrait on display. A commanding presence is how she'd describe his pose if she were writing about him in the catalog.

Mrs. Rinehart interrupted her thoughts. "Oh, you can buy art from the catalog. They have some lovely landscapes that would look just the thing."

Grandfather honed in. "Have you ordered any art or had any shipped in lately?"

Good thing Grandfather remembered their quest, because Miranda couldn't stop imagining Wyatt in various, more noble settings.

"No." Mrs. Rinehart flipped through the pages before turning it to show them. "Framed pictures have an area on page seventeen, so I haven't reached them yet."

A quick scan of the walls showed a few family pieces in expensive frames but nothing that looked particularly collectible. Miranda scrunched her nose. Another day gone by and they were no closer to finding the missing piece. What was happening back home today? Had Cornelius tried to help, or was he waiting for her to do her part?

Again she felt Wyatt's gaze. Quickly she blanked her expression. *Never let them know what you're after*. Better to appear unconcerned, bored, and aloof than to tip your hand. Besides, the less interesting she was, the fewer reasons he'd have for watching her. And he still was.

The tea in her cup had cooled and so had their hopes of the Rineharts having the missing painting. Grandfather and Mr. Rinehart had fallen into a conversation about the particulars of healthy livestock with frequent questions to Wyatt for verification. Unease crept across her like the fog from the harbor. Why did Grandfather need to know anything more about livestock? If they sold all they had Monday, then, please God, she and Grandfather would be gone by next sale day. The thought that Grandfather enjoyed a discussion about livestock concerned her. Maybe Cornelius needed to get another phrenological reading from his skull. Something had changed.

The visit wrapped up cordially. Mr. Rinehart observed manners she hadn't thought to find in this area, especially from one whose pastime involved amassing a small fortune in junk. Wyatt brought up the wagon for them as the Rineharts made promises of seeing them at the church raising. Although she and Grandfather hadn't heard of it before, it sounded like the logical place to go if one wanted to meet people. After helping her to her seat, Wyatt climbed up next to her while Grandfather finished his conversation with Mr. Rinehart.

"Sorry you didn't find what you were looking for." Wyatt's arm bumped against hers.

Miranda's skin prickled. What had Grandfather told him? She kept her voice even. "What gave you that idea?"

He rubbed the smooth leather rein with his thumb. "You're not the only one who's quietly observant."

He had been watching her, and if it weren't for the importance of their mission, she might have wondered if he liked what he saw. But this was Wyatt Ballentine, the barn manager, not a European noble, not even a banker. She mustn't let her imagination lead her astray. She and Wyatt had nothing in common.

Grandfather climbed in next to her and adjusted his hat against the sun. "That was a fun visit, wasn't it? Mr. Rinehart's a man of diverse interests, which I didn't expect. And what did you think of Mrs. Rinehart?"

"I don't like her hair all pushed up on one side of her head,"

Wyatt answered. "Makes her look off-balanced . . . like she's fixing to fall over."

"I was speaking to my granddaughter," Grandfather said.

And his granddaughter couldn't stop staring at the bearded man next to her. They at least shared one thing in common. Miranda stuttered, "She . . . she's methodical."

"I could use her to clerk at the auction house, but I'd hate to hear her disdain for our *used* art and furniture," Grandfather laughed. "You did well, Miranda. The manners your mother taught served you admirably."

Perhaps, but they didn't fool the intriguing man at her side. Had she been careless or had Grandfather dropped his guard? Either way, sharing company with Wyatt Ballentine was proving risky. Best do as little of it as possible.

CHAPTER 10

Constructing a church didn't sound like much of a party, but Widow Sanders insisted that it was the only diversion available on a Saturday. She'd cooked all day while they were visiting the Rineharts and was convinced there'd be some prize given for the best dessert. Miranda wouldn't put it past the woman to invent a competition just so she could claim to win.

Grandfather and Miranda left a bit later than their hostess, but they wouldn't have any trouble finding the church site in the tiny town. Already the sound of hammers echoed off the hills. The clanging reminded her of the shipbuilders in the navy yard just across the river from Boston. Boston reminded her of Mother and Father. Mother and Father reminded her of all that was at stake.

"Did you telegraph Father yesterday?" Miranda took Grandfather's arm as they rounded the corner of the Walters' Dry Goods Store.

"I told him it might take longer than we hoped to find our treasure, but not to despair. What we have here might be worth more than all our contacts on the East Coast."

Miranda's heart sank. She should've sent the message herself. "You keep saying that, but I don't understand."

"Miranda, remember the old wardrobe we hauled off from the abandoned apartment? Had that wardrobe been polished up and unscratched, they never would've asked us to move it. Because of its ugliness, we were the ones to discover the hidden panel and the cache of jewels inside."

"There aren't any jewels hidden in that stinking building. I looked."

"But there's potential, and no one else is trying to tap it. Just think of the artisans here who have never had a market where they could sell their wares. Think of the potential if all these people decided to trade their furniture as often as they trade their animals."

Cram one more piece of furniture into Mrs. Rinehart's house and you wouldn't have room to change your mind. "But animals are different," she said. "People can't eat their furniture." They'd made their way past the business district, such as it was, and found themselves once again in a residential park consisting of cabins crammed between large trees. Residential park? Goodness, Miranda's skill at exaggerating the charms of an item were asserting themselves.

"The poor man is just as vain as the rich. I have plans to expand the offerings at this sale barn, and it promises to be wildly successful. You'll see. Soon we'll be shipping rare and precious collectibles out of here by the crate, but first we'll see how the auction progresses. Sale day is the day after tomorrow, Miranda. All our work will pay off."

His eyes sparkled with religious fervor and they hadn't even built the church yet.

Lord, help him, Miranda prayed. *Help us*. She'd worked in their auction house since she could remember and knew a fair bit about the business. Nothing in this situation looked promising to her. She must be alert, for Grandfather's judgment was slipping. Father and the rest of the family were counting on them. They couldn't return empty-handed.

Miranda and Grandfather hadn't missed anything at the church site. People were still walking up, wagons rolling to a stop. She even saw a family of three on the same mule—mother, father, and a boy almost old enough for school sitting in the front.

And there was Isaac, looking dapper in his black waistcoat and white shirt-sleeves. Miranda bit her lip. She'd been away from home for less than a week and here she was thinking a man looked dressed up even without a suit coat. Well, Isaac was the exception. Fortunately, she'd chosen to wear her lightest gown. In the right light, a smidgen of pink would lift off the tan, but it definitely wasn't shaded like an earthworm.

She hadn't meant to interrupt the conversation Isaac was having with the pretty brunette, but when he saw her he ended it. The lady seemed surprised by Miranda's appearance—she thought everyone in town knew about her and Grandfather—but with a troubled look went to join the other girls.

"Who's that?"

"Just a girl from around here," he said, continuing to shoot worried glances over his shoulder. "I was asking her if she'd seen Wyatt. Being around these church folk might do him some good, but I don't know if he'll dare show his face."

Hadn't Wyatt given her a word of encouragement about God's care the day before? Before she could ask Isaac to explain, Widow Sanders reached them.

"Isaac, imagine seeing you here on church grounds. Next

thing we know you might come on a Sunday and stay for meeting." Then she leaned toward Miranda. "This new building will be dandy. I've not missed a meeting since we started assembling at the school in '58. Varina Helspeth hadn't missed, either, but last winter she'd heard that the snow had kept our circuit-riding preacher from making it across the valley. Well, turned out that he did make it and Varina stayed home. Now I'm the only one with perfect attendance." She turned to hurry away, then spun again. "Well, here comes Wyatt. The reverend was looking for him."

Wyatt strode through the crowd in his worn trousers and faded blue shirt. As usual, he was dressed for work, and as Miranda scanned the crowd, she realized that Isaac was the exception. He was also the only man besides Grandfather not bent over the wooden framework of the walls that would soon go up. Instead he was talking to the ladies.

One by one the frames were completed and men gathered in anticipation of the raising. The reverend removed his hat, wiped his shiny forehead with his handkerchief, and then motioned someone forward to pray over their endeavor.

It was Wyatt.

Astonished, Miranda turned to Isaac, but he'd already bowed his head and closed his eyes. Miranda's eyes refused to close. Wyatt leading a public prayer? What kind of church was this? But no one else reacted with shock. Just a hearty *Amen!* when he was finished.

Had Grandfather seen that? Miranda turned to look for him, but instead she saw Mr. Fowler, the leader of the vigilantes.

"That Ballentine boy—you keep your eye on him." He swung his sledgehammer absently as one might swing a pocket watch on a chain.

"Why, what's he done?"

The man fixed her with a withering stare. "I'm not accusing Wyatt, I'm bragging on him. He works hard. He's trustworthy. I'm a sure judge of character, and I'm telling you Wyatt Ballentine is going to be someone."

Miranda watched as Wyatt bent and grasped the frame on the ground. At the count he strained with the other men and heaved the heavy skeleton upright. He was strong, but they had strong men back home. You could find muscle for hire in any rotting alley. But Mr. Fowler wasn't entirely wrong. Something about Wyatt set him apart. He had the respect of these people, but they weren't completely at ease with him. Besides Betsy, did he have any friends?

Isaac stopped at her side and followed her gaze to his brother. "Wyatt always gets fawned over at church. That's why he likes it so much. When we were little his favorite story was about Joseph. I think he imagined that all his dreams of grandeur and superiority were God-ordained."

Miranda eyed the man with the ragged beard and dirty work clothes. What was the matter with these two? Must she contradict Isaac and defend Wyatt now? Couldn't they leave her out of their bickering? "I haven't noticed him being too proud," she murmured.

"Did you know we're not brothers? He's adopted."

"Adopted?" Her eyes traveled swiftly over Isaac, looking for a resemblance.

"Yep. Ma and Pa told him how his parents died on a wagon train in Kansas. That's how they got him when we were young. But he turned it into some epic saga and liked to pretend he was the son of some rich man from a powerful family."

Wyatt? Miranda really shouldn't laugh, but the thought

was ludicrous. She shook her head in disbelief. Not rough and tumble Wyatt with his burly shoulders, his raw expressions, and his passionate, barely-controlled temper. Although there was that moment at the Rineharts', sitting in the velvet chair . . .

She tossed her head to dispel the image. "What did your parents say?"

"They encouraged him—speculated on how important he might be, and then they'd hold him up as an example when he did something good. '*Why can't you work as hard as Wyatt? Why don't you say, "Yes, ma'am," like Wyatt?*' My brothers couldn't stand it. They left as soon as they were able."

"So what happened? What brought him down?"

"The truth." Isaac motioned her toward the water bucket. He took out the dipper and offered her the first cool drink, but Miranda wasn't that thirsty—had never been that thirsty in her life. "Ma had some information about his uncle. They'd tried to contact him right away when Wyatt's folks had died, but they didn't get anywhere. Later, when Ma and Pa were getting on in years, they told Wyatt they'd try again. They did, and this time he got a reply. You should have seen how excited Wyatt was when word came back. He walked into the kitchen and handed Ma the letter, shaking too much to open it himself. Well, she read it, turned white as an egg, folded it up, and tossed it into the kitchen stove."

"Why? What did it say?"

Isaac crossed his arms and looked over his shoulder at the walls going up behind him before answering. "For all of Wyatt's airs, he was lower than the poorest child in Pine Gap. Illegitimate. Driven from his home. Without my family he was nothing."

For his smug glee, she nearly dumped the water bucket over

him. Instead, she tucked her hands under her arms, feeling guilty for encouraging Isaac. She'd expected a lighthearted story from their childhood—Wyatt had been bested in a race, embarrassed at school, something to amuse herself with when he was giving her that disapproving look. But there was nothing funny here. And to laugh at Wyatt's horrible discovery? Miranda's good humor vanished. She valued her family enough that she couldn't laugh to hear that someone had lost theirs.

———⟨∞⟩———

Uncertainty. That's what played across her face. Miranda stood with arms crossed and studied the ground. What had Isaac said about him that made her unable to meet his gaze? Wyatt leaned against the post of the frame, holding it steady as they rammed rocks into the hole around the footing. She didn't seem afraid of him yesterday, so what had changed? As much as she irritated him at first, he was finally seeing the sincere woman hidden beneath her highfalutin ways. And that worried him. As long as she was high and mighty, he knew Isaac didn't stand a chance, but Miranda was letting her guard down—not a safe thing to do when Isaac was around. Isaac's two weaknesses were pretty women and finding ways to avoid work. Marry a rich girl like Miss Wimplegate and he might be able to indulge both failings at once.

And Wyatt wasn't just whistling Dixie about her looks, either. He'd seen her plenty of times over the last week, and still she knocked the breath out of him. Today she had on the finest gown he'd seen yet. The pale pink gave her olive complexion a glow while the wide neckline framed her delicate collarbone and hinted of what lay south of there.

The rocks had been fitted, and here came Josiah Huckabee with a wheelbarrow of cement. "Howdy, Wyatt." He smiled as he tilted the wheelbarrow and dumped the contents into the hole. "Betsy's been telling me about that new gal in town. I reckon that's her over there?"

Wyatt glared at the sixteen-year-old. "She's a lady, Josiah, not a new gal. You be on your best manners. You hear?"

Josiah's eyes twinkled. "I hear ya, chief. Gonna go over to that Katie Ellen and try to spark myself a gal, too."

Wyatt rattled the post, tamping it to make certain the cement had settled in the bottom. "I don't know what sparking has to do with it," he said. "I'm building the church."

Fowler approached, his powerful forearms bared and already smudged with toil. "Wyatt, been meaning to tell you that we lost that fellow who'd been poking around Rinehart's place."

"You lost him?" Wyatt picked up a shovel to clean where Josiah had spilled. "How in the world?"

Fowler shot a juicy stream of tobaccy to the ground. "It's a sight when a dozen men can't keep an eye on one outlaw. We got thinned out going through Watson's pass, and when we regrouped on the other side, there wasn't hide nor hair of him. Just the rope. Goes to show we need to get ourselves organized, especially if the law don't do their job."

Wyatt's skin crawled. As far as anyone knew, the man hadn't harmed anyone, but what had he been doing at the sale barn that night?

"I'll be watching for him," he said.

"If the man has any sense, he's put Hart County behind him. He's got to know we take care of our own." Fowler's spine stiffened. "Lookee there. Caesar Parrow came to town. I've got a word to speak with him about his coon dog. Hear tell it's getting into Mrs. Rankin's chickens, and we can't have that." And he strode off to do his unassigned duty.

The four walls were up and set, along with one of the interior support walls. Three more to go when they called for dinner. The church ladies had put out a hearty spread. Wyatt helped himself to chicken and dumplings and went to join the workers in the shade.

With her skirt blowing behind her, Miranda stood into the wind, shading her eyes as she peered down the road. It didn't take a genius to figure out she was looking for her grandpa. Cutting across picnic blankets and baskets, Wyatt took the short path to join her, plate in hand.

"He took out?"

Miranda blinked into the wind and nodded. "I worry about him so. He's changed since Grandmother died, and it's gotten worse since we left."

"Should we go fetch him?"

Miranda lowered her hand. "If I find him, I can't make him come back." The lace around her collar flipped up and brushed against her neck.

"You're very patient with him."

"I love him. Taking care of him is part of the deal."

Wyatt rubbed a sore spot over his heart. "I don't think you realize how special you are." Seeing her startled reaction, he wished he could swallow the words back down his throat. Instead, he motioned to the table. "Food's over there."

"Isaac," Fowler cried out. Seated by the Moore girl, Isaac's shirt was still clean and white. "Why don't you favor us with one of your poetry recitals?"

Isaac leaned toward Miss Moore, and whatever he whispered in her ear made her blush. He got to his feet. "I'd be glad to entertain you, seeing how you've been working so hard, but since this here is holy ground, maybe I should quote something from the Bible."

103

The women nodded in unison with their fans as they stretched their feet on the ground before them. Miranda had her plate now and Wyatt followed her to the shade. Isaac stepped into the open space, boxed in by the empty frame of a church behind him, and began.

"Though I speak with the tongues of men and of angels, and have not charity, I am become as sounding brass, or a tinkling cymbal. And though I have the gift of prophecy, and understand all mysteries, and all knowledge; and though I have all faith, so that I could remove mountains, and have not charity, I am nothing."

Wyatt remained standing, transfixed by the simple words his mother had insisted they learn. Isaac's voice was as smooth as corn silk. He did a fine job of elocuting, for sure.

"And though I bestow all my goods to feed the poor, and though I give my body to be burned, and have not charity, it profiteth me nothing. Charity suffereth long, and is kind."

Wasn't that what Miranda was exhibiting?

Isaac continued, but then there was a pause. " 'Charity envieth not; nor does it . . . it doesn't . . .' " He floundered.

Before Wyatt thought, he heard his own deep voice taking over.

"Charity vaunteth not itself, is not puffed up, doth not behave itself unseemly, seeketh not her own . . ."

He hadn't realized what he'd done until he saw the surprised looks around him. Behaving unseemly? The very words stabbed

---

his conscience. He halted. "Go on, Isaac," he said. "You know the rest."

Isaac flapped his hand in a helpless gesture. "No, you go on, little brother. You've bested me again. Go on and show them how good you are."

"I didn't mean to stop you."

But Isaac was done. With a perfect blend of resignation and nonchalance, he gathered his plate and Miss Moore and meandered away from the church yard.

"Don't worry about him," Fowler said. "He's a sore loser. You'd think he'd be used to it by now."

Used to having a little brother who would never let him win? Isaac and their two older brothers were a family. They'd merely picked up Wyatt along the way like a stray dog allowed to follow them home. If it weren't for Pa and Ma, their pa and ma, he would've run away many years ago, but his parents tried to cover for their sons' resentment. And maybe that made it worse. Maybe they covered too well and brought more attention to him.

Wyatt dropped to the ground next to Miranda as she murmured some polite words of praise for his performance, but he took no joy in her comments.

She sacrificed for her family, while he couldn't stop competing with his. What must she think of him?

She'd met nearly every woman at the barn raising . . . or church raising, rather. Betsy had been most helpful in dragging ladies over to meet her, although her introductions were usually awkward at best. But still, Miranda had no clue where the painting could be. Who bought it in Boston and to whom did they send it? Scanning the yard, she didn't see one person likely to appreciate an oil painting of a French American from the last century. Not one. Now, if it'd been a thick quilt or a pair of sturdy boots, there'd be no end to her suspects.

And then there was Wyatt, whom she'd completely misjudged. On top of the building he lay stretched out on a beam, reaching down to nail the wooden peg into the support at the corner. She'd thought him unsocial, proud, but now she understood. He didn't think he'd be accepted. He had to prove himself. She knew what it was like to be the lowest ranked person in the room, and while she usually elected to hide, he tried to compete.

Wyatt's mallet clattered among the rocks below him.

"Wyatt dropped his mallet," Betsy's brother sang as he hopped from beam to beam.

Tired of standing by, observing, Miranda stepped forward. "I'll get it." Snatching the mallet, she raised it above her head, but didn't come near to reaching Wyatt.

He rested his head on the beam. "I'll come down."

"No need," she said. "I'll get a ladder."

With Betsy's help she leaned one against the corner post. Wyatt held it steady above her. She climbed up, juggling the mallet while holding on to the rungs. Miranda wanted to do this for him, but she hadn't counted on it being so far up. She also hadn't counted on the way the ladder leaned right into where Wyatt lay. He let loose of the ladder to reach for the mallet and it swayed. Miranda's eyes widened. Wyatt made a mad grab and caught the top rung with his left hand.

"I guess you're going to have to come closer."

That's what she was afraid of. Another step brought her to his shoulder. He waved with his right hand on the other side of the beam. That was her goal. Another step lifted her level to him. Face to face. She'd never noticed how green his eyes were, or how strong the cheekbones emerging above his beard were. They stood there before the whole town, waiting . . . on what?

"Your mallet." The rungs pressed into her chest as she reached around to place it into Wyatt's empty hand.

"Thank you."

Josiah Huckabee shimmied across the beams. "Ain't you gonna give her a kiss, Wyatt? She came all the way up here."

Wyatt's eyes turned a shade darker. Miranda couldn't move away, for lying there she saw the young man who was rejected by his family and picked on by his older brothers. She didn't mean to sway toward him. She should just refuse. . . .

With a clang, Wyatt dropped the mallet again. Miranda straightened as it dashed against the rocks.

"Josiah, you get my mallet this time," Wyatt ordered. "Miss Wimplegate has already done me a favor. I can't ask for more."

His eyes held hers, but she had no reason to stay. Jerking out of her trance to start down, she bounced the ladder off its resting place against the post. Wyatt pulled it back again. "This ladder has got a bad case of the wobbles," he said.

So did her knees. Without another word, Miranda descended while silently chastising herself. The unfortunate children of Boston had found their way into her heart, but Wyatt Ballentine wasn't a child. He was a laborer, a working man, and as such he needed neither her pity nor her charity.

Beyond that she had nothing to offer him.

Chapter 11

Monday had finally come. The wagon broke through a tight spot in the trail. Wyatt leaned to the side to keep from getting whacked by a branch that jutted into the road. Mustn't get his spanking new duds snagged before the boss man saw him. On second thought, the sooner his clothes were ruined, the sooner he could return to dressing like a reasonably intelligent man. He directed the mules to Widow Sanders' house, threw the brake, hopped down, and jogged through the scattered bushes to the door. Before he could knock, the door swung open and Elmer Wimplegate stepped outside with hat in hand and cane on his arm.

"Glad to see you early." The man consulted his watch, closed it with a click, and dropped it into his pocket.

"It's sale day." Wyatt tugged on his waistcoat, eager to start the day well with his boss. "I've been waiting for weeks to get this mess cleaned out."

The door cracked open and Miranda eased out. Wyatt removed his new hat. Her skin still bore the softness of early morning. Her hair had been freshly combed and styled. He reckoned she still smelled like soap, or even something fancier. Roses, maybe?

"You look nice today," he said. If only she'd give him half a chance.

She looked down as if she didn't remember that she wore a pale green dress. "It's nothing special."

"It's nice," he persisted.

"And look at you." She gestured to his fancy suit, but before he could respond she'd gone all pink and turned away. "Grandfather, what will we do for lunch? I don't have one packed." Her dark eyes shone warmly on her grandfather.

Wyatt rolled a button on his new coat between his fingers. Why did her gentle concern make him sad? Was it because he had no one who made it their business to fuss over him?

"No need to bring food," Wyatt said. "The ladies bring vittles to sell."

Elmer poked at Wyatt with his cane. "Widow Sanders is cooling your rhubarb pie even now. She said to tell you she'd have it to the ring in plenty of time."

His rhubarb pie. The only part of the sale day he didn't mind missing.

"What time will we be back?" Miranda asked, her eyes falling somewhere lower than his chin. Yes, he still had the beard. Elmer might buy him a new suit, but no one was going to tell him when to shave.

"That depends. We keep selling until the last item has been auctioned or until it's too dark to see the arena. And then we have to write up all the bills and settle up with the bidders. It's not unusual for it to go into the night."

She bit her lip and his heart did a funny dropping thing. "I don't want Grandfather to become overspent."

"Nonsense, girl!" Elmer dismissed her with a wave of his hand. "You know Cornelius says I have permanent stamina. It's dictated by the bone structure of my skull."

"Cornelius?" Wyatt tilted his head. "Who's Cornelius?"

The question must have tickled Elmer, for he strolled away to the wagon chuckling.

"He . . . well, it's not official," she said, "but he's . . . he's my cousin."

"You have an unofficial cousin?"

"If you must know, Cornelius and I are to marry." She tucked her chin, her mouth tightened. "At least that's what he wants."

Wyatt found he couldn't swallow. He'd never considered that she might have a beau back home, but the thought made him boil. "What do you want?"

"I want my family to be taken care of, but I might not be able to do that on my own."

"But why Cornelius? What makes him so special?" Wyatt had already taken a dislike to the man and only wanted more reasons to hate him.

"He's nice. Respectable. He's a doctor. A phrenologist."

"I've never heard of any such thing."

"He's a specialist. He measures the size and shape of his patients' heads to discern their character, personality, and mental state."

Wyatt's eyes rolled heavenward. "What kind of monkeyshine has he been selling you?"

"His readings are very helpful. It does one good to know his or her natural mental strengths and limitations."

"Has your cousin Cornelius taken a gander at your grandpa's head?"

Miranda's eyes wandered to the wagon where Elmer was waiting. "Of course he has. Why?"

Elmer's cane beat against the wagon's floorboards. "The sale," he called.

The sale. The sale! "Yes, sir. We'd best get going."

They loaded up and no further words were spoken until they reached the sale barn. People were already congregating in the yard. Shouts of greetings filled the air, as well as cold looks of hostility. Friends who'd missed their weekly meeting had finally perambulated over the hills, giving the sale as an excuse to leave their farms and talk to someone besides their wives and their mules. Enemies availed themselves of the chance to find new offenses. Either way, there were buyers and sellers aplenty. His overstocked pens would be empty by day's end, and Wyatt's troubles would be nigh to solved.

He would've been in high cotton had he not been wearing a fancy suit.

Eyes widened as he passed. Women tittered. Men chewed their cigars slowly and grinned like possums at his foolishness. And all Wyatt could do was tip his new stovepipe hat and pretend he didn't look like a St. Louis politician.

No one wanted to sit before the sale started, but once the bell sounded they would rush to the arena. Elmer had continued to fret over the lack of a catalog, and Wyatt had run out of explanations. Elmer would understand once he saw the sale in action. Wyatt didn't need a book to tell him the attributes of the animals before him.

He'd introduced Miranda to Fred Murphy—Betsy's uncle and the newspaper man who helped in the office on sale day—and left her there, presumably to help with the accounts. Then he took Elmer into the arena and positioned him at the auctioneer's

111

table before the animals entered. One less chance for the old coot to get injured. He handed him the receipt book, having already gone over where to fill in the seller's name, the buyer's name, the head count, weight, and price of each lot. True to his word, Elmer seemed to understand the importance of keeping all the particulars straight. And knowing that Wyatt had reliable help in the office and out back in the pens, he was set to sell, and sell fast. They'd never had so many animals waiting, and who knew what household goods and miscellany would arrive before the day was over? Efficiency was the key.

He walked around the arena, greeting people as usual, even though he looked like a grinder's monkey. When he finally reached the auctioneer's platform, the catcalls and whistles had to be acknowledged. Pushing back his suit coat, Wyatt hooked his thumbs into his waistcoat and walked the length of the platform and back before taking his seat. The audience howled in appreciation before quieting down for him to begin.

At his signal, the south door to the arena opened and five milk cows jogged inside. Betsy's brother Josiah followed them. With his cattle prod he chased them around, allowing everyone to view the offering before he stepped out of the ring, allowing Wyatt to swing the rider of the scale down the arm until it swayed into balance. He announced the weight, casting a glance to make sure Elmer had all the pertinent information recorded, and Wyatt reached for his gavel to open the bidding, but it wasn't there. He bent to peer under the table, but the wooden gavel had vanished.

Knock! Knock! Knock! He sat up quickly, narrowly avoiding hitting his head on the table. There it was. His father's gavel in Mr. Wimplegate's hands. Elmer stood.

"Welcome to the Wimplegate Auction House." His pompous

voice rang out over the shocked gathering. A woman pulled her shawl closer around her shoulders. A man spat into the empty coffee can on the stairs. "Today's sale includes priceless offerings from estates throughout the area. Anyone who has procured a bidding number at the office will be allowed to participate. If you'd like to use credit we will finance any buyer who has applied—"

Every eye was on him. Feeling like a child, Wyatt tapped his arm. "Excuse me, sir."

Elmer stopped cold. He glanced down at Wyatt, still seated. "This better be important."

"The people don't have buyers' numbers. I just write down who bought what."

"But how do you know who they are?"

"I just know. And we don't offer credit. They have to have cash on the day of the sale."

Elmer's mouth tightened. As much as Wyatt hated to correct him in front of the crowd, they had to do this right. Once the auction began you couldn't undo all the sales. You'd never have the same group, the same opportunity to get the same price. One shot, that's all you ever had.

Elmer cleared his throat. "My assistant tells me that for this week the bidding cards are unnecessary, but in the future be prepared to register at the office."

Wyatt tried not to notice the snickers. He tried not to feel as stupid as he undoubtedly looked.

"So let's begin now with these fine bulls."

"Cows," Wyatt whispered.

"There are five bulls in the arena. Who would like to open the bidding?"

Wyatt rubbed his forehead. At least everyone else knew the

difference between a milk cow and a bull. Surely he wouldn't
have to void the sale based on Elmer's mistaken description,
but was he not going to get to auctioneer at all? Did Elmer plan
to do the actual selling, too?

"Seven cents," Caesar Parrow called out.

Elmer dropped the gavel against the table. "Seven cents, my
man? You must think me ignorant. Even I know that bulls don't
sell for a penny each."

Wyatt spun to face him. "They are sold by the pound, Mr.
Wimplegate. By the pound."

Slowly Elmer lowered to his seat. Finally Wyatt had his full attention. "But how can they figure what they're worth? They have
to multiply the weight by the price to see what they'll bring."

"They have a good idea what they're worth by the pound,
and we have charts in the office that give us the exact amount.
It's not complicated." But he couldn't take his eyes off the white
veined hand holding his gavel.

Elmer straightened the cuff of his shirt. "I think I understand." He stood again. By now, the farmers had kicked back,
leaned against the step behind them, and prepared to enjoy
the show. And Wyatt was about to throw his tie away and
join them.

"So seven cents. The bidding starts at seven cents." Elmer
paused. Only the animals disturbed the silence. Outside, pigs
squealed and the yard boys hollered as they loaded up the alleys with the next animals. Josiah peeked through the window,
wondering why he hadn't been given the call to open the north
gate and remove the animals yet.

Wyatt's hopes for a quick sale were dead.

Elmer turned to him. "Why aren't they bidding?"

"You aren't doing it the way they're used to."

Mr. Watson stood and waved his coonskin hat. "Turn Wyatt loose. He'll show you how it's done."

Elmer sputtered a protest, but as the shouts increased, he sank into his chair, defeated. The loose skin on his neck waggled. He pushed the gavel in Wyatt's direction. "You win. Go on."

Here he was again, humiliating someone publicly, but what else could Wyatt do? The sale had to continue. Getting these animals sold was more important than saving Mr. Wimplegate's pride. Wyatt wrapped his fingers around the familiar handle. The flat indention on the gold band fit against the pad of his thumb. Like a fish dropped into the stream, like a pigeon released from the cage, he stood, even forgetting that he was dressed like a Parisian peddler, and bellowed in a deep baritone.

"We're right glad you came out today and we apologize for the late start. But since we're all accounted for and have some cows awaiting us, let's get right into it. Seven cents will start the sale for these cows straight from Turnbull's dairy." And from there the musical cadence began to roll. "Who'll give me seven . . . seven . . . who'llgivemeseven . . . There. . . . misterparrowonthefrontbench . . . now. . . . sevenandahalf . . . sevenandahalf . . . doIhearahalffromanyone . . . Yes . . . misterwatsonbidssevenandahalf . . . we'reuptoeightnow . . . onlyeightforthesegoodcows . . . lotsofmilk . . . enoughforyourneighbors."

If he forgot that Elmer was the boss and that Elmer was sitting at his side, it was for the best. Wyatt had been waiting for weeks to get rid of these animals. The customers were ready to buy, the owners had been ready to sell for days, and Wyatt was ready to prove himself once again.

CHAPTER 12

Did animals know how bad they smelled? Even inside the office, the odor was as thick as clam chowder. Miranda rolled her pencil between her fingers, wishing she knew how to help. The line of impatient people stretched out the door into the midday heat, but all she could do was lean over the desk and watch Mr. Murphy. He traced a horizontal line across the page, squinted through his spectacles, then transferred the number to an account book.

"You owe twenty-two dollars and thirty-seven cents." He craned his neck upward to the farmer standing before him.

The farmer already held a wad of bills and counted out the amount. From experience Miranda knew that most of that money would go to the one who brought the animal in, but a portion would stay with the auction house—their fee for brokering the deal. She wondered if this place got the same six percent that they did in Boston. Difficult to eke out a living on the slim margin. The more profitable opportunity was in snatching up the artwork that was underselling. Of course the auctioneer couldn't take his own bid, but a representative for the house could. Her father played this role. If their job was to get the best price for their customer, then their bids were appreciated and those undervalued works might bring a pretty penny in the warehouse.

An open window admitted a hot breeze into the room, fluttering the pages of an out-of-date calendar hanging on the wall. Unlike their auction house, the Pine Gap barn didn't bother much with embellishments. How differently she'd imagined this place when Father first mentioned it. Ridiculous to think that someone had sent an heirloom portrait here. Maybe they'd made a mistake. Maybe the painting hadn't been shipped to Missouri at all. She only had a few more houses left to visit, and they didn't sound like the type to harbor the missing plutocrat.

"What are you doing in here?" The woman's round shoulders melted into breasts that were supported by the apron tied around her waist.

Miranda had never seen her before and didn't know what her offense was, but began apologizing anyway. "I'm sorry. My grandfather owns this auction house. I really don't mean to be any trouble."

The woman tugged her apron higher and sneered. "Because you've been no trouble at all. Not even when I had to wait two weeks to sell my chickens."

"And your grandfather harassed my wife," a young man wearing overalls piped up. "He trespassed on our property claiming to be looking for some artist. A likely story, if you ask me."

So that's where he went after leaving the churchyard? He'd refused to tell her.

"What do you mean our tickets aren't ready?" a cowboy growled to the cattleman behind him. "It's that old man. That's who's holding up the show."

Miranda wanted to melt into the desk when a mountaineer

gnawing on a cob of corn spoke up. "What's that? They don't have the tickets yet? Should've known that uppity fellar didn't know what he was doing."

"Maybe Mr. Ballentine needs some help in the salon . . . I mean the arena," Miranda suggested.

The woman sneered. "You go on and ask what the holdup is. Wyatt will appreciate it."

Of course he wouldn't, but it was either go, or stay and listen as Grandfather took the blame for the delay. But how could Grandfather be to blame when he was standing in the doorway of the auction house doing business of his own?

"Have you stopped selling?" But even as she asked, she realized that she could hear Wyatt calling the bids from the arena.

"Miranda, may I introduce you to Mr. Leland Moore? He's been telling me about the opportunities he sees abounding here. Evidently, there are some very lucrative deals."

Red rimmed the man's watery blue eyes. Tufts of blond whiskers spotted his jaw, making an uneven fringe. Miranda stepped closer to the wall. "What kinds of deals are those?" she asked.

"I'll let you know when it's time. Can't have you fretting over nothing." Then Grandfather motioned Moore outside in an obvious attempt to leave Miranda behind, but after a moment of internal debate, she followed him. She passed through the spacious hallway, stomach rumbling at the savory aromas seeping out of every basket hanging from a woman's arm. Stopping in the yard, Miranda was hailed by Betsy. The woman Betsy was bringing to her walked with grace and a sense of balance that Miranda only then realized she'd missed seeing. Here everyone walked bending forward or leaning back as if perpetually accounting for the hills they traversed. This lady stood upright—sea legs, as Miranda's captain uncle would've deemed them.

"Miranda, this here is Miss Abigail." Betsy reached backward to catch her hand and hurry her forward.

"Abigail Calhoun." She wore a blue riding dress that perfectly suited her fair complexion. Curvy Miranda envied her elegant lines. "Betsy tells me that you're visiting from Boston."

"Yes, ma'am. My grandfather and I."

"And her grandfather is batty as all get out," Betsy added cheerfully. "Miranda has her hands plumb full keeping him out of trouble."

"Betsy!" Abigail grimaced by way of apology. "Please excuse the girl. As much as we've tried, we can't beat any manners into her."

Betsy only grinned.

"I'm afraid there's some truth to it," Miranda admitted. "He's gone off with Mr. Moore to discuss a business venture. I'm not sure whether I should intervene or not."

Abigail Calhoun shaded her eyes and scanned the amassing of wagons, mules, horses, and buggies. "There's poor company, and then there's Leland Moore."

"He'd rob a squirrel of its last nut," Betsy added wide-eyed. Then she pointed. "Over there."

Truly Miranda had planned to do this on her own, but having two companions gave her weak skull some extra protrusions. Seeing their approach, the weasely man crammed some bills into his pocket. He spoke out of the corner of his mouth and Grandfather spun to face them.

"Is there a problem?" Once, back in Boston when Grandfather was selling a painting, a bidder called out from the audience that it was a fake. That was the only other time Miranda had seen him puff up like he was now. Not a good sign.

"Wyatt needs your help inside," Miranda said.

"I've got more important things to do."

Abigail stepped forward with a gentle smile. "How are you feeling, Leland? I do hope this isn't moonshine money you're collecting."

"I've got business dealings with Mr. Wimplegate, and they ain't none of your concern," Moore said.

"The only business you know is the business side of a jug," Betsy said.

"You know Doctor Hopkins said you'd feel much better once you've kicked that nasty habit." Abigail said it as compassionately as a saint.

"Come on, Grandfather. Let's discuss things before you make any big decisions." Miranda took him by the arm, but he shook her off.

"I've been trading and selling since before you or your father were born. I refuse to acquire your permission before I invest my own money. Forgive my granddaughter, Moore. She's forgetting her place."

He took the man by his threadbare sleeve and turned to march away from them.

"Moore," Abigail called, "Jeremiah has been looking forward to having a discussion with you over the corn seed you borrowed last spring. Expect him to call on you soon." But Moore already had his ear bent to Grandfather's grandiose plans.

What new mischief was this? But she appreciated the kindness of the woman who'd tried to intervene. "Well, thank you, anyway," Miranda said. "I'm grateful."

"I'm afraid your grandfather is putting his faith in the wrong man," Abigail said. "Wyatt would be able to help, but after seeing how he treated Wyatt this morning, I doubt your grandfather would appreciate his interference." Abigail's sincere face furrowed with concern. "Why doesn't he trust Wyatt? Wyatt wouldn't do him any wrong."

Betsy smiled at the woman she clearly adored. "Mr. Wimplegate and Miranda don't think much of Wyatt."

Miranda gasped. "That's not true," even if it had been until recently. "I'm just getting acquainted with him."

Abigail shifted her lunch basket to her other hand, sliding her arm through the hoops. "Most of the people here won't think much of you, being an outsider, but they'll get used to you . . . unless you get on the wrong side of a feud, that is. But give Wyatt some time. These mountain men begin to grow on you."

Had it not been for the collective dislike of Mr. Wimplegate, Wyatt might have had a lynch mob on his hands. As it were, everyone seemed to pity him, and rather than add to his woes, the crowd swallowed their ire until he finished correcting the mistakes made by his boss that morning. Now it was noon and time to sell the baked goods, nevermind that they still had livestock to work up before anyone would leave.

Abigail Calhoun had just entered from the outside. Wyatt motioned to her, and she smoothed her tidy traveling dress and came forward. As if on cue, other women got to their feet and wove through the men as they made their way down to ground floor. While Josiah was driving the last of the livestock out of the arena, Abigail came across and ran her fingers over the prissy tablecloth on his auction stand.

"This is new," she said.

Wyatt stretched his arms forward and felt the pull of the tailored coat across his back. "A lot's new around here."

The ladies crossed the arena and deposited their goods on the auction table. Peeking into the dinner pail, Wyatt inhaled the toasty scent of fried chicken. He poked around the cloth covering until he was certain he hadn't missed any vittles and then moved aside to let the ladies sell their wares without his interference.

Some of the crowd moseyed outside, where they had their dinner pails already waiting, but others stayed to barter for the best meal. Should he go find Elmer? He didn't want the man—or his granddaughter—to go hungry. Only a few platters or pails remained when Mrs. Turnbull hurried inside bearing a disturbingly familiar pie tin.

"Wait, Wyatt. Widow Sanders didn't have time to come today, but she sent her rhubarb pie."

Elmer had already turned down Widow Sanders' pie, or Wyatt would've claimed it for him. As it were, he was forced to put on the same performance he did every week.

"All right then, we'll auction off Widow Sanders' delicious rhubarb pie. It's still warm, boys, so get your bids ready." He gripped his gavel and started at two bits, praying that time passed would have clouded someone's memory of the weekly Sanders pie, but no one bid. Beneath his melodic calling, Wyatt groaned. Two bits and that was all. Here he went again, faking bids just to save Widow Sanders' pride. With a yelp, he pointed somewhere toward the east of the room, never making eye contact with a supposed bidder and raised the price to three bits. After a few more pleas he pointed near the bottom of the seats and raised the price to four. When no one stirred to bid on the pie, he interrupted his cadence. "I can't let this go for fifty cents, fellas. You know I'm going to have to bid it up to five bits. Come on. Who's hungry for the best pie in the Ozarks?"

His acting skills depleted, Wyatt ended the bidding and wrote himself up for five bits. He faked a smile—the same smile he produced every week when Mrs. Sanders made her pie especially for him—and slid the pan to the edge of the table.

The last of the food had been spoken for. They still had some cows, plus sheep, goats, and poultry to sell before they got to housewares, but from here they would make good time. Water jugs passed from man to man. The ladies grouped in a corner, fanning the sleepy children on their lap. Nothing brought the town together like sale day. They might feud and bicker on the streets and in the hills, but come sale day everyone swallowed their bile and came together for their mutual benefit. At the auction, everyone was treated equally. No one could charge you more just because you fought on the wrong side of the war or because you were uglier than the warts on a hackberry tree. The prize went to whoever wanted it the baddest, no discrimination. Even young Josiah had managed to buy a sow now and then, which, considering how many outhouses he'd tipped over, was remarkable.

What if Wyatt gave up on this? Would someone take his place? This gathering was too important to the community to close down.

Yesterday, Wyatt had given the whole situation to God. Again. Repeatedly he confessed his desire—that he get to buy the sale barn himself. And he admitted that if God wanted to keep him from that goal, then he'd accept it, but staying put surely felt like the easiest thing to do. Else he'd spend every day thinking about how he'd failed his pa.

And again his other Father—the one in heaven, not the one who died before he knew him—his heavenly Father reminded him that He had a plan and that the forming of Wyatt's character meant more to God than whether he succeeded in his ambition.

Frankly, God's plan scared Wyatt something fierce. Thinking back through the Bible, those people God loved, well, He put them through the wringer. They didn't have life easy. And there might be a great reward at the end, but in the meantime you'd best get your slingshot ready, because likely there was a giant or two coming after you.

Or there might be a beautiful woman come to watch you call the sale.

He started up the bidding again but found it difficult to get going with her standing in the entry. Did anyone notice when he skipped from five cents a pound to five and three-quarters? Were they frustrated at the way he couldn't scan the crowd for bids without lingering in Miranda's direction? Wyatt ran his hand down the long horizontal beam of the scales, then turned the dial to the precise weight. It was almost a relief when she rose and made her way toward him. Giving up on steadying the scales when he was so out of balance, he contented himself with admiring her beauty as she crossed the room. Her eyes claimed most of her face, but once you got past them . . . if you could . . . there were also some nice full lips beneath a cute nose and . . .

He cleared his throat. "Can I help you?"

"Actually, I was coming to see if I could help. The customers in the office are getting restless."

He held out a ticket for her. "Your grandfather didn't record the information we needed. We had to go back and correct them."

"And I'm afraid Grandfather won't be back to help. He's scheming a new business opportunity with Leland Moore."

"Of course it'd be Moore." Wyatt rubbed his eyes. "He'd be the first person I'd expect to take advantage of your grandpa."

"That's what Abigail Calhoun said."

"Always has a hard-luck story, always has a pot of gold beneath the next rainbow. He'll rob you blind. You must warn your grandfather."

Miranda wrinkled her nose. "In case you haven't noticed, my grandfather doesn't take orders very well, but if you need help, maybe I can learn."

He couldn't deny the hole he was in, but could the uppity young miss who kept his head spinning be the answer he was looking for?

CHAPTER 13

Seemed like every eye was trained on her as she made her way around to the business side of the table. Wyatt scooted his chair forward as she squeezed her skirts past him. Once seated, she arranged her skirts primly, aware that her elevated position put her knees at eye level for some of the bidders.

Wyatt wrapped his arm around the back of her chair and leaned in. "Josiah will tell you the name of the farmer selling the animals. Write that here. I'll give you a description of what's selling and how much it weighs. Write that here." He pointed to the box on the form, his arm sliding against her as he reached across. She gripped the seat of her chair and held on as he continued. "And be sure to get the weight. That's absolutely necessary."

She had to look away. She needed something to dilute his effect on her. Lifting her eyes, the first person she saw was Abigail, whose gentle smile offered sympathy for her predicament. Resisting the urge to fan her warm cheeks, she ducked her head, and the form before her came into focus again.

"When the bidding is over, you write the winning amount here and the buyer's name here. Do you understand?"

She nodded. Even though the form was different, the information was the same. She grasped the pen in the inkpot and tapped off the excess. "I'm ready." She was ready for him to stop leaning against her and put some space between the two of them. She was ready for Josiah to drive the animals around so everyone would study the sheep instead of her.

Wyatt removed his arm from the back of her chair. He grasped the gavel and banged it against the table. Josiah stepped out of the pen and allowed him to weigh the sheep. Miranda watched his hand skim the metal beam, tapping the rider until the beam swung free, perfectly balanced.

"Five hundred and sixty-five pounds."

His black coat sleeve had a brown swipe of dust on it, but what had she expected working here?

"Five hundred and sixty-five pounds," he repeated.

Miranda followed the sleeve up to his expressive face. Oh. She was supposed to write it down. She dipped the pen into the inkwell and scratched the number into the box. It was going to be a long afternoon. But just before he started on the next animal, Mr. Moore entered, and standing behind Abigail's tall husband didn't hide him from Wyatt's notice.

"Give me a minute," Wyatt announced, and left her at the table alone.

At least everyone watched him now as his discussion with Moore grew more and more heated.

"What's that to you?" Moore's voice rose above the crowd. "If you're dead set on getting in everyone's business, why don't you tell that smooth-talking brother of yours to stay away from my daughter?"

Was he talking about Isaac? Wyatt had other brothers, but . . . The roar of laughter notified Miranda that the conversation had ended and Wyatt was dragging Moore out the door by his shirt collar. Not knowing what to do with her hands, Miranda took the gavel and lowered it to her lap. The wooden mallet had seen much use. The head was scarred, although the handle was worn smooth. And most curious was the gold metal band worked into it. She'd never seen a gavel with a band on the handle before, although Grandfather's back home had gold leaf painted on the rises.

Wyatt had returned from his ruffian errand. Mr. Fowler puffed excitedly on his pipe and slapped him on the back as he passed. Would they have responded the same way if they'd seen him treat Isaac thus? Somehow Miranda thought they just might. Still bristling, Wyatt took his seat.

"Where's Grandfather?" she asked.

"Moore wouldn't tell me. Said I'm going to reap the whirlwind when he tells Elmer how I treated him."

Miranda was growing a strong dislike for this Moore character. "Nonsense. Grandfather knows good counsel when he hears it."

They'd just resumed the sale when the crowds parted and Grandfather came barreling toward them like an out-of-control fire wagon. Stumbling through the gates of the arena, he marched up to the table and projected loud enough for the whole town to hear.

"You will not go behind my back to discuss my dealings," he ordered Wyatt. "If you wish to maintain your employment, you will not interfere with my business. Do you understand?"

Miranda cast a horrified look at Wyatt. His lips turned white and his eyes widened as Grandfather's voice rose to a shout.

"Your only task is to keep this auction house going. My other dealings are confidential and do not require your approval."

Grandfather's face burned red and his spittle sprayed across the table, hitting Miranda as well as his target. "Do not interfere with my partner. Am I clear?"

Wyatt's back was rigid, but he looked just as shocked as the rest of the crowd, who found their auction interrupted by a raving lunatic. Miranda would give anything to be able to crawl into the dark anonymity beneath the table, but she couldn't do that. She couldn't leave Wyatt defenseless, and she couldn't allow Grandfather to further alienate the townspeople. Trying to ignore her shocked audience, Miranda focused on her grandfather.

"Let's go outside and talk about this," she whispered.

"In all my years I have never observed such insolence. . . ." Grandfather continued to rail, leaning over as if he were about to drag Wyatt across the table by his new lapels and throw him in with the sheep.

She scanned the room, but no one was moving. No one knew quite what to do with them. "Grandfather," she pleaded, "you're causing a scene."

"I want to cause a scene. Mr. Ballentine will never treat me like this again. He needs to remember it for the rest of his life."

Guaranteed. The whole town would remember.

"Think, Grandfather," she said. "Would you do this at home? Would you denigrate an employee on the stage in our auction house? Remember our auction house? The blue velvet drapes? The red padded chairs for the bidders?" She allowed her voice to go wistful, hoping she was drawing him into a calmer state of mind. "Remember how dignified you are? Remember your reputation for quality and respectability?"

Grandfather wiped his mouth. With unsteady feet, he took his first step back. He rotated to face her and grabbed her arm with desperate hands.

"I remember, Miranda. I remember it all, and that's what I'm trying to save." His bottom lip quivered. "He doesn't understand what we have to lose. He doesn't understand why I have to take the gambles I take."

No longer aware of the people surrounding them, Miranda patted his arm. "I understand. You can trust me, because I remember all of it." His grip lessened as she continued. "And you can trust Wyatt, too."

Grandfather's mouth turned down. His chin hardened. Slowly he shook his head, then more fiercely. "He's got you fooled, Miranda. I love you, but you are gullible where he's concerned." He pulled out of her grasp. "I'm going with Moore. I'm leaving you in charge, but watch him."

With a last glare at Wyatt, he left. His shiny shoes flashed as he strode through the crowd. Men stepped out of his way and women held their skirts aside as he passed. Miranda twisted her hands. She couldn't stop him, could do nothing to help him, but maybe she could help the man who'd borne the brunt of his outburst.

"Ten minutes," Wyatt announced. "Give me ten minutes, then we'll get to rolling again." The gavel rapped before he tossed it on the table and stormed out the back.

He'd borne it valiantly—the man she'd accused of being incapable of controlling his temper. He'd refused to return Grandfather's unfounded accusations or even to defend himself before a town full of people who'd known him his whole life.

Conversation resumed inside the room, and it was no mystery what they were talking about. Miranda couldn't leave him outside alone, not when her grandfather was responsible for his embarrassment. She worked her way around the ring to the door that led to the pens. Bursting outside, the dust of something stronger than soil filled her nostrils. A dry cough and she spotted Wyatt, elbows resting on the top of the fence. Remembering to watch her step, Miranda lifted her skirt and eased carefully to his side.

"Are you all right?" She dropped her hem and wrapped her hands atop the highest plank.

His shoulders raised and his head dropped. "I should've known better than to get involved, but I can't stand to watch Moore take advantage of him."

"Grandfather didn't mean what he said—"

"He certainly did. He meant every word of it, and I don't blame him. If a man stepped into my business, I'd be riled up, too." He straightened, removed his hat, and ran his fingers through his hair. "I know why he's mad, but I'll do it again if I have to."

She shaded her eyes to look up at him. "You didn't volunteer for this. Dealing with him . . . he's different now."

Wyatt's eyes were sad. "How long has your Grandfather been like this?"

"That depends. Sometimes he's brilliant. Sometimes he explains his actions and they make perfect sense. Other times I think he has a reason for his behavior, but when I talk to him, his reasoning is flawed. That's why I came with him in the first place. We were worried about his making the trip alone." That and avoiding marriage to Cornelius.

"What are you supposed to do about it?"

"I watch that he's getting enough to eat and rest. That's about all the help I'm worth. He won't listen to me as far as business is concerned."

"You'll never recover any money he gives to Moore. You can kiss it good-bye."

Money they could ill afford to lose. Especially if the LeBlancs ran off their other accounts. "I don't know what to do."

Wyatt counted off his advice on his fingers. "First off, you need to find out how much cash money he's carrying. These roads aren't safe, especially if word gets out that he's got pockets full of double eagles. Second, we can go to the bank and encourage them not to loan him more money—"

"What?" Miranda cast nervous eyes to the sky above her. "I couldn't tell the bank to refuse Grandfather. He'd be livid."

The fence creaked as Wyatt leaned across. "Listen, honey, unless you have so much money you need to make room in the coffers, you'd better shut him down. I've been with him a week and have seen him make ridiculous offers. He thinks animals are worth twice what they'll bring. He carries on like junk is treasure. It won't take long for the ne'er-do-wells around here to take advantage of him."

"I'll telegraph Father. He'll tell us to come home."

He seemed to digest this information. "What will happen to the sale barn? Will he keep it open?"

One would have to be pretty obtuse to miss the importance of his question. He waited, breathless. In his handsome face she saw the young man hearing for the first time that his family was ashamed of him and wanted nothing to do with him. Here he was again, waiting to see if his dreams would be crushed.

"I don't know what will happen. We can't manage it from Boston."

"Then you'd sell it, of course. And if you give me some more time, I might be able to put together a decent offer. I don't know what your grandpa paid—"

"You know I can't make any plans for him. I don't want to get your hopes up."

He settled back against the fence, his eagerness fading. "Of course not." With a last swipe at his hair, he pulled his hat on and bumped her elbow with his. "Come on. If we're going to finish before sundown, we'd better get going."

"How often do you have these sales?" she asked.

"Once a week. Why?"

Because Miranda would do everything she could to see they were on the train before next Monday rolled around so the poor man could conduct his business in peace.

CHAPTER 14

Who would've guessed that sitting next to Wyatt would completely erase her unease of being the center of attention? Having every eye on her didn't bother her nearly as much as the man at her elbow. His shoulder brushed hers. The stiff fabric of his coat rubbed against her arm as he pointed out a blank spot on the paper. He lowered his voice from his public calling to share a wry observation. Once she got the gist of the instructions, once she caught Wyatt's rhythm and could make sense of his chant, she enjoyed working with him. Enjoyed the camaraderie and enjoyed the feeling that she was contributing. She didn't know how to help Grandfather, but after the horrible scene Wyatt endured, anything she could do to ease his job gave her pleasure. Was that wrong of her?

And he was still at her elbow, walking her home before he returned to the barn that night to help Betsy's uncle Fred settle up with the last customer. Take away the barnyard smells that clung to both of them, and she could imagine that they were on a promenade through Boston Common, especially the way he walked with the easy gait of a man with the world at his feet. Ever since seeing him in that suit, Miranda couldn't erase the thought that he held some inborn quality that set him apart. Although Isaac's gentle manners were more pleasing, Wyatt possessed an air that wasn't learned. He might work with his hands, he might sport a scruffy beard, but he had a nobility about him. It was evident in the way he faced adversity, the way he treated everyone, and by the way they adored him. Obviously, he was capable of rising to the very heights of his particular social class.

Had the thin mountain air affected her reasoning, too?

As they rounded the corner to Widow Sanders' house, Betsy rose from the porch step where she'd been sitting. Miranda smiled, happy to see the girl, but she only had eyes for Wyatt.

Betsy picked up a Mason jar of tea off the porch and rushed to hand it to him. "A new pot is steeping, but this is the last that's cool."

Miranda wetted her lips, suddenly realizing how parched she was. With a start she also realized how closely Wyatt was watching. He took the jar from Betsy and held it out to Miranda.

"Ladies first."

Miranda took the jar in both hands, her fingers covering his. "Thank you." She'd almost forgotten how to swallow, and he must've forgotten how to work his fingers, because he stood there, fingers entwined, until Betsy snorted. His eyebrow gave a little hop, and he released the jar. Miranda refused to think how she looked slurping out of a canning jar and instead enjoyed the cool, slightly bitter liquid washing down her throat. She lowered it and had to force herself not to swipe at her face with her sleeve as Betsy was wont to do.

"Is Grandfather inside?" she asked Betsy as she offered the jar to Wyatt.

Betsy tugged on her blond braid. "I saw him and Moore

drive by the house a few hours ago. I hollered for him, but he didn't stop."

Wyatt gulped the rest of the tea down, then handed the empty jar back to Betsy. "That man needs a keeper."

Just then Miranda turned to see Grandfather waving merrily from the wagon as it made its way up the hill toward them. Moore wasn't with him. He was alone, unless you counted the piece of sculpture riding in the back.

"You won't believe what I've acquired." He pulled the wagon alongside the house and gestured to the log standing on end in the back of the wagon.

The tree must've been impressive, because the trunk was a full yard in diameter, but it'd been carved into a figure, the honey-colored wood taking on a golden skin color. Above the shoulders where the head should've been was a narrow neck, headless and smooth, but beneath that—

Miranda stepped up to the edge of the wagon. Grandfather came around back. Beaming with pride, he dropped the tailgate and gestured. "Isn't she a beauty?"

Every ounce of blood in Miranda's body must have made a mad dash for her face. No Baroque artist had ever been more enamored with the voluptuous female form as the backwoodsman who'd carved the rough likeness, heavy of breast and generous of buttocks. In fact, the artist had hardly bothered worrying about a waist at all, but merely gave an impression of space between the two areas upon which he wished to concentrate his efforts. That was her professional opinion. Her opinion as a maiden having to face the obnoxious figure in broad daylight was even more harsh.

Betsy whistled. "Wonder who he used as a model." She looked down at her undeveloped chest and then assessed Miranda's rather healthy form. "I don't think even Miss Miranda—"

"Betsy!" Wyatt lifted the tailgate and dropped the pin into the staple, all without looking up.

"You cannot ship this to Boston," Miranda said.

"Of course not," Grandfather laughed. "I won't be parted with Lady Godiva. That's what I named her. I thought we'd keep her in Widow Sanders' garden to enjoy."

"I don't know who Lady Godiva is," Betsy said, "but Mr. Godiva is one lucky man."

"Go sit on the porch, Betsy." Wyatt could sure be bossy when the mood struck.

Miranda crossed her arms over her chest, suddenly feeling exposed herself. "Widow Sanders does not want this in her garden, Grandfather. It's vulgar."

"Nonsense. It's no different from Venus de Milo."

Wyatt cleared his throat. "That might be fine and dandy for some foreigners, but no one in this part of the woods would put this outside. That's all I'm saying."

"Well, it's about time you met with some culture." Grandfather unhooked the tailgate again. "Are you going to help me unload this, or do you want Lady Godiva to ride in the back of your wagon all week?"

Wyatt took his time weighing his options, but really, did he have any? Elmer had bought this monstrosity—just wait until he got his hands on Moore—and he didn't want to leave his wagon behind. Hopefully the widow would forgive him.

He leaned into the wagon bed and stretched out his hands, but then stopped. Exactly where could he grab? He drew back and scratched his head. Somehow it didn't feel right handling the woman, even if she had no modesty. He quirked his mouth to the side and went in cautiously. It was just a tree trunk, he reminded himself as he wrapped his arms around the stout waist of the figure and hefted Lady Godiva out of the wagon.

"Where do you want it?" he grunted.

"In a bonfire," Miranda said, but Elmer led the way to an empty space in Widow Sanders' rose garden. He deposited the statue with a thud and turned to find Widow Sanders, fists against her hips, mouth ajar, and eyes bugging.

"What in tarnation is that?"

Wyatt ambled past her. "C'mon, Betsy. I'll take you home."

Betsy hopped off the porch and ran to the wagon, where Miranda stood, still too shocked to move.

"What am I going to do?" she asked.

Wyatt stood at her side and watched the widow bickering with Elmer. She jabbed her finger at him, but Elmer only had eyes for the controversial lady. "You're going to take care of your grandfather as best as you can. God hasn't forgotten you."

She nodded, her chin quivering. For crying aloud, did she know how badly he wished he had an answer? Did she have any idea how he wanted to take care of this for her?

With a tightness in his chest, he reached for her. One hand on her shoulder, a squeeze. Her chin dropped. "I'm not doing very well."

"Don't give up. Help will come when you need it." His big old hand was probably crushing her. If only he knew what to do, but his position wasn't the best. As unstable as the old man was, he couldn't cross him. One wrong move and Elmer could ruin everything Wyatt and his father had worked for.

"I've got to go back and make sure everyone leaves with the animals they bought, but if you need me I'll be here in a jiffy.

And tomorrow I'll keep him with me. If nothing else, we'll keep him so busy he won't have time to buy any more . . . art."

She flashed him a watery smile. "I underestimated the strength of the muse in these hills."

He wasn't sure what that was supposed to mean, but the way her warm shoulder compared with the cool wood statue . . . he shouldn't make any more comparisons. He cleared his throat, then hightailed it to the wagon where Betsy waited.

Betsy smiled innocently, which meant she was thinking thoughts that were anything but.

"I know that look. You're up to no good, so you might as well tell me."

Betsy held on to the seat as the wagon rocked to life. "I don't know how you're going to take this, Mr. Wyatt, but I expect you won't be appreciating my observation."

"I expect you're going to tell me anyway."

"Sure enough." Betsy nearly sang her next words. "You love her."

Wyatt's neck tightened. "Hogwash. A fancy city lady like her? I might as well poke myself in the eye as fall in love with her. She ain't looking for an auctioneer for a husband."

"I didn't say she was in love with you, you big oaf. I said you loved her. All the signs are there. The way you get real quiet when she's around. How you'd just as soon put a whooping on Isaac as let him breathe the same air as her. And how just then, it took you a full two minutes to decide whether or not to touch her shoulder. I nearly split a gut laughing at you."

Wyatt tried to stare her down, but Betsy's pert, lightly freckled face registered no remorse. "Don't look so scared," she said. "She's a nice lady and I won't tell her."

"There's nothing to tell. You're out of your ever-lovin' mind."

139

He leaned forward, rested his elbows on his knees, and watched the mules' backs as they plodded toward the sale barn. The nervousness, the hesitation that Betsy saw wasn't love. It was uncertainty. Wyatt didn't trust Miranda, and he had to be on guard because he was too vulnerable where she was concerned. No one had ever made him question his plans like she had. All these years he thought he knew who he was, what he wanted, and then, from the moment she hopped off the train, he began to wonder if there was something more. Maybe this life he'd so carefully planned for wasn't what he desired. Maybe he'd only settled for it because the pain of his family's rejection kept him from trying anything grander. But knowing that Miranda existed led him to want things that had never seemed possible before.

Was that love? He didn't think so. He pulled up to the barn as Betsy sprang from the wagon and skipped into the building. If not love, then infatuation maybe, but Wyatt wasn't a fool. He wouldn't wager his heart on someone who wanted to leave, who had nothing in common with him.

Nothing in common besides a love of family. Besides a sense of duty to those she cared for. Besides faith. And besides an abhorrence for naked tree-stump women.

CHAPTER 15

The next few days found them traveling through the mountains to make visits on people who had no interest in seeing them. Wyatt expected Elmer to pull these shenanigans, but even Miranda seemed to be hankering after something specific. Although she did her part at the auction, she seemed to have something else on her mind.

"Who exactly are you trying to meet this time?" Betsy asked.

Try as he might, Wyatt couldn't keep his attention from straying when Miranda was in the back of his wagon, but between the crooked mountain road and Elmer's ramblings, he needed to focus if he didn't want to dump the lot of them into a gully.

Betsy continued, "If you're looking for ladies your age to visit, most of them are married. We do have a few bachelors about, though. We could start with old Widower Robbins and work down to Cross-Eyed Carl."

Funny that she didn't mention him in her list of bachelors. Wyatt's back straightened. Did Betsy think him less interesting than Carl?

"Is that your uncle?" Miranda asked.

"You've met my uncle," Betsy said. "He ain't cross-eyed, but he is a widower. Of course, that would make you my aunt. . . ."

"No—riding toward us. Is that your uncle?"

Wyatt turned to look behind them, and sure enough, there was Fred Murphy. He pulled the mules to a stop as Betsy hopped up in the wagon bed and waved him over. "I thought you were staying home with the boys today."

"I'm going to see your pa. It's been eight years since those bushwhackers jumped him. Just wanted to report on how things were on his side of the mountain. Do you want to go with me?"

Betsy twisted her mouth around. "I did want to visit Miss Laurel and Doctor Hopkins. That's where we're headed."

"It's on the way." He tipped his hat to Wyatt and Miranda, while pretending to miss Elmer. Was there bad blood between them already? "Lead on. I'll follow."

They didn't have far to go. Before they knew it, they were being entertained just outside of the charmingly shabby cabin of Laurel Hopkins.

With one bare foot propped against the pile of firewood, Laurel carefully skimmed her knife across the surface of a green apple. The peel softly thudded in the dirt. Two more days of making visits with the Wimplegates, and Wyatt wasn't sure who was the looniest—Elmer for buying their junk, or himself for toting them hither and yon. The only treasure they'd found today was a good place to sit in the shade and sip sassafras tea while waiting for the afternoon sun to weaken. Betsy drowsed against the tree, her golden head nodding slightly, while he played peekaboo with the Hopkinses' oldest girl peering around the corner of the house at him.

"There you go." Laurel held up the peeled product for inspection. "That's how I make the face. Now I'll let it soak in some watered-down lemon juice to keep it from wrinkling too soon."

She tossed the apple and it landed in the bucket with a splash. Laurel wiped her hands on her apron. "Phoebe is playing with the final product. Come here, sweetie. Let them see."

Wyatt couldn't help but marvel at the rosy-cheeked girl with the pint-sized prairie bonnet. Although the child's dark hair resembled her mother's, he could easily imagine a child of Miranda's with similar coloring. He caught Miranda watching him and suddenly felt like stretching his legs. Excusing himself, he stood and moved beside the woodpile where he could stand a bit while still keeping an eye on the goings-on.

Phoebe brought her doll to Elmer and presented it proudly. The clothes were simple calico, matching what all the women around there wore. Elmer turned it over in his hands, inspecting it as carefully as he would a precious gem. His head twitched in surprise, then he laughed.

"Look at the face, Miranda. Remind you of anyone?"

Miranda shifted on the tree stump stool to get a better look. The doll's darkened, flesh-colored face had wrinkled into an exact replica of geriatric skin. Even the hands curled into gnarled paws that were surprisingly lifelike. The sunken mouth beneath the hooked nose curved in comic disapproval.

Miranda smiled fondly. "It's the Great Dame, Mrs. Winthrop."

Nothing about the doll looked that great to him, but what did he know?

"Precisely," Elmer said as he took the doll from Miranda. "She's enchanting, Mrs. Hopkins. How much would you sell her for?"

"Oh, I don't know. It's just a doll, but Phoebe is partial to her."

"Then keep that doll, but would you be interested in making more? Perhaps hundreds more? I think our customers in Boston would find them charming bits of artisan handiwork. Would you make them for two dollars each?"

Laurel's eyes bugged and Wyatt felt giddy himself. Two dollars? They couldn't sell a wrinkled apple doll for two dollars, could they? This was even worse than Elmer's offer for the homemade soap they'd seen yesterday. He didn't know how much money these city people had, but they surely didn't treat it as something very precious.

But maybe he wasn't the only one to think that. "It's time to go." Miranda nudged Betsy awake. Betsy yawned and rubbed her eyes.

"Let's say good-bye to Doc Hopkins first," she said. With a hand on her knee, she pushed up into standing position—he swore that girl got taller every time he saw her—and led Miranda to the backyard.

They were getting nowhere. Those apple dolls might amuse little Ralphie and the younger newsies, but no one was going to buy one. As far as the search for the painting, Widow Sanders had promised that Laurel Hopkins possessed artistic skills of note but hadn't mentioned that her medium was withered apples.

So far their leads had brought them no luck. Maybe they should be checking businesses instead of residences. Although she hadn't seen anything that vaguely resembled the shops of Boston, she knew that somewhere in this town they had proper clothing for sale. At least good enough for Mr. Wyatt to cut an impressive figure. For whatever his education lacked, the man did know how to fill out a suit. The fitted lines of his coat followed his powerful build and the proud tilt of his head. . . . Well, she supposed he'd been born with that. And even today in his working clothes he had that easy energy that was so attractively male.

Still drowsy, Betsy dragged her feet through the clover as they rounded the house. Clucking ahead alerted Miranda to the presence of the chicken coop before she made out what the wire cage was. She recognized Dr. Hopkins from the sale barn, but he remained bent over a thick tree stump inside the flimsy wire pen.

"Let's go in," Betsy said, now fully awake.

The thin wire dug into her hand as she lifted it over the post and swung open the light gate. "I hope I'm not interrupting." The soggy ground sponged beneath her boots as she stepped forward.

"Shut the gate," the doctor called. From his hand dangled a bouquet of feathers. Squirming feathers. Was that a chicken?

Miranda stretched the wire over the post to secure the coop. The thud of a hatchet on wood drummed against her ears. She spun. A flash of metal and then the ball of feathers came alive.

It couldn't be a chicken because it had no head. Only a bloody stump of a neck remained. And then Dr. Hopkins released it. With hurricane force, it bounced, flopped, and whirled directly at Miranda. She fell back into the chicken wire, but her feet were as heavy as granite. She couldn't move. The maniacal beast was doing all the moving for both of them. It knew neither up nor down. With flapping wings it hurled itself into the air and into her face.

Shrieking, Miranda covered her head with her arms. "Get it away!" she yelled and got a mouthful of feathers. She fell backward. The thin chicken wire gave way, and she crashed through the frame of the gate. Lying on her back and swatting at the spinning bundle of bloody feathers, she repelled it again and again, terrified of the unworldly beast. Then as suddenly as it'd begun its attack, the monster succumbed to exhaustion and dropped next to her. Miranda rolled away from the horrid twitching lump. On hands and knees, she scrambled over the fallen chicken wire to get some distance between her and the monster before collapsing on her backside.

Miranda swiped the hair off her face, only then noticing how dirty her gloves were. Her hat covered one eye. A strand of hair had lashed across her mouth and tasted nothing like her shampoo. She shoved her hat into its rightful territory as the world beyond the flurry of feathers came again into focus.

Betsy stood frozen in place. Her blue eyes bulged. Her hand covered her mouth. The doctor's face was pulled into a tight grimace that would admit no grins, nevermind that his eyes were streaming with tears and his shoulders shook with barely suppressed mirth.

Miranda dusted off her hands and tried to rip her skirt free from the chicken wire. "I think it's dead now."

Suddenly Betsy took off at a run toward the front of the house. "Wyatt! Wyatt! We need your help."

Miranda tottered to her feet. "Shh, Betsy. I don't need help." The chicken wire stubbornly refused to release her skirt. She yanked at it again. Wyatt jogged into sight just as she dropped the fencing and got her first look at the clumps of wet straw clinging to her gown.

Finally the doctor remembered his vocation. "Are you injured?" He took her arm and disentangled her from the frame and wire bunched about her knees.

How she wished she could faint and remain insensible until she arrived back in Boston!

Wyatt and the doctor continued to untangle the wire as Grandfather and Uncle Fred came around the back of the house. Uncle Fred pulled out a small tablet and began to scribble furiously. Betsy stood next to him on her tiptoes. She craned her nose over the tablet. "I witnessed the whole thing, if you need a source."

Miranda halted her repairs. "Did I break a law?"

Uncle Fred licked his pencil. "You performed wonderfully. This will sell more papers than Caesar Parrow's two-headed calf."

Now Dr. Hopkins smiled. "You mean my chicken coop will be in the journal? Why, the whole county will read of it. Isn't that something?"

"Why would you write about a chicken coop? Nothing important happened." Miranda's heart sank as he continued to jot his pencil across the paper. How many days would it take before the paper ran and could she be on the train by then?

Wyatt pulled the mangled gate aside. "Hopkins, you might want to get your birds in the henhouse until you have a chance to repair this fence."

"I don't know when I'll have time to fix it. Tomorrow I'm checking on patients. . . ."

"Property owner worried that damage will not be repaired. . . ." Fred mumbled as his pencil moved.

"Grandfather will have it fixed," Miranda said.

"I'm not responsible," Grandfather said.

"This just gets better and better," Fred cheered and his pencil moved again. *"Interloping business tycoon wreaks havoc on local residents. . . ."*

Betsy clapped her hands. "Be sure and mention that she was attacked by a headless chicken. That'll sell like hotcakes."

His head raised as he noticed the dead bird for the first time. He winked at Betsy and continued writing.

"I want to go home." Miranda pushed her bonnet back. Since the crash, it'd formed its own opinion of where it belonged and kept creeping over one eye. Now out of the way, she had a full view of the handsome man who was rising from the destruction she'd caused—the man who had the nerve to stare pointedly at her hat. His eyes traveled down to her shoulders, over her every curve—curves now adorned by clumps of chicken-coop confetti.

Wyatt stretched his arms before him and pretended to flick a spot of dust off his spotless elbow. "I understand now why your grandfather insists on keeping up appearances. Really, I'm shocked at your. . . . slovenliness?"

She humphed. "Bet you've never used that word before."

"Because it never fit the situation half so well." A shy smile teased at his lips. Miranda hoped that she'd remember how charming it looked at a time when she could appreciate it more.

"Let's go inside," Dr. Hopkins said. "Laurel will want to get this chicken ready for supper, and it's getting hot out here."

Still bending the newsman's ear, Grandfather followed the doctor and Betsy inside, leaving Miranda alone in Wyatt's company.

"Fred Murphy? Is he really the newspaper man? And will people really hear about this?" she asked.

"You're already big news around here. This story will guarantee people will talk about you for weeks."

"I don't seek attention. Of that you may be sure."

"No. You prefer to keep much hidden, don't you?"

She was still trying to remove the sundry articles clinging to her skirt, and now this? Not a safe topic, especially with the journalist just inside. "This mess is driving me to distraction," she said. "I'd love to discuss my personal attributes, but the dismal state of my wardrobe has me occupied at the moment."

Wyatt stepped in front of her. Her stomach tightened. Whatever she was trying to accomplish, this wasn't it. Slowly he took her chin in his hand and lifted her face to his. Standing there as he was, brown flecking in his green eyes, broad shoulders and perfect posture, he could've modeled for one of those risqué art classes the rich ladies so loved—if he'd only lose the beard. He tilted her head this way and that. At some point she'd stopped breathing, probably the moment the rough texture of his hands registered on her skin. Then with deliberation he wet his thumb on his tongue and applied it to her neck. With firm strokes he rubbed a path to her collarbone. The lack of oxygen was becoming a problem, especially as fast as her heart was beating.

"You had some blood splattered," he said.

She opened her eyes. When had they closed? She took a half-step to the side to reacquaint herself with the earth's tilt. He grasped her arm.

"Taking care of Grandfather," she said. "That's why I'm here. Not to stand around . . . with you."

Something ornery flashed in his green eyes. "Why else are you here, Miranda Wimplegate? Maybe I can help, if you'll come clean."

Coming clean was a big concern. Should she be feeling this way while her skirt was still adorned with dubious substances from the bottom of a chicken coop? But she couldn't tell him about the painting. Not without Grandfather's permission—even if it meant that she had to continue these fruitless searches. Even if she had to go out alone on dark nights to places much worse than the underside of the arena seating. Even then, she couldn't tell anyone what they were looking for. She'd take the secret to her grave.

Wyatt took her chin again. This time his eyes traveled down to her lips. "The answer is right there." His gaze softened. "Right there on your lips just begging you to share this burden—"

"A painting," Miranda blurted. "We're looking for a lost painting." So much for taking her secret to the grave. But she couldn't pull herself away, not until he'd stopped searching her soul with those green eyes. "It's very important to us. You wouldn't understand."

"Are you kidding? Isaac's always telling me I'm too sentimental about things. I can't seem to throw away anything that belonged to my parents—even Ma's broken churn. I think I understand perfectly."

It wasn't exactly the same, but this painting did mean a lot to her family.

Finally his hand fell to his side and he scanned the horizon. "I haven't seen a painting. That I can promise you."

A breeze cooled her skin as though she'd shrugged off a heavy coat. Miranda's shoulders drooped. "Please don't tell Grandfather. I wasn't supposed to say anything."

He brought his gaze back to hers. "Are you sure you're looking in the right place? What makes you think it's here?"

"I don't have time . . ." The door to the cabin opened.

Laurel waved. "Don't worry about your clothes," she called. "I put a towel on the sofa and I can sweep up after you leave."

Miranda swiped again at her ruined gown.

"You aren't going to find any fancy painting in there," Wyatt said. "But I'll be thinking on it. Anything I can do to help."

Guilt. After all the trouble they'd caused him, and he was still offering his best. "But why? We messed up your plans, so why are you helping us?"

Wyatt's throat jogged as he studied her. "I see how you care about your family. You must be a good person to love Elmer so much, and he must have been quite a man to earn it. Seeing you two just makes me want to help."

Miranda balanced on shaky knees. She'd held a grudge against him ever since she'd arrived, and she'd been horribly mistaken.

She smoothed her skirt, the fabric crinkling beneath her hands. "I haven't given you credit for all the help you've been to him . . . to me. Thank you."

Now he held her gaze—his face frank and unguarded. Her skin warmed. He really shouldn't stare like that. She might get the wrong impression.

"Just for this moment, for those words—it's all been worth it."

CHAPTER 16

Isaac had stolen the wagon again. As much as Wyatt hated to have him dawdling around town, he did wish he'd find a lady friend within walking distance instead of traveling up the mountain every time he wanted to go calling. Who was she, anyway? Couldn't be too particular if she was impressed by the mule-drawn feed wagon.

Wyatt slammed the barn door and stomped to the street, thinking on how he had nothing better to offer, either. Miranda's doctor-cousin probably had a shiny buggy pulled by ten white horses. Every day he probably wore suits like the one Elmer bought him. He probably had cooks who made oysters and lobster and all that strange coastal food that Wyatt would never get to eat. No, he couldn't impress Miranda. All he could offer her was protection while she was here, which wouldn't be for long. If it was up to her, she'd be on the next train and never look back.

Wyatt turned onto the town square and cut across the green. Too bad he was all grown up now and had to wear boots. He used to be partial to the feel of the grass on his bare feet, but those times were past. Most of the joys of his childhood were just memories now, memories that had faded with nothing new to replace them. What was it that kept him in Pine Gap, anyway? Since his parents died he had no reason to stay. The town needed the sale barn, but it didn't necessarily need him. Someone else could manage it, but could he leave behind the legacy his father had entrusted to him?

"Wyatt, I failed to get you your due," Pa had said one hot afternoon as he lay atop his sheets, ringed with sweat. "You should've had much more, but this is all I can leave you."

The wooden gavel wavered in his weakened grasp. Wyatt took it, still questioning his father's pride in the gift. Still not sure that he even wanted the responsibility. He didn't see a grand future working for Mr. Pritchard. Pa had always dreamed of buying the sale barn for himself and employing all his sons there, but as the years went by, Pete and Clifford grew tired of waiting, willing to leave for the promise of ready money. He'd expected Isaac to follow in their footsteps. Instead he seemed content to hang around and live off whatever meager wages Wyatt brought home. The both of them stuck, tied to their father's plans.

Not that Wyatt despised his life, but with the sale of the barn it seemed even more unlikely that he'd live up to his father's wishes. Why couldn't he pack up and go somewhere else? Maybe even Boston. He was a hard worker. He could make a name for himself wherever he went, and maybe once he found success Miranda would even consider . . .

Wyatt rubbed his neck as he passed beneath the hanging oak. He might leave someday, but he could never go to Boston. Not with the chance that someone would hear of his return. Someone would put two and two together and proclaim him for what he was—an interloper, an outcast, unwanted. And he couldn't let Miranda know. He'd better stay here where no one knew him as anything but the Ballentines' son.

He turned the corner to see Postmaster Finley driving up the road, all decked out in his striped fancy traveling clothes. As Wyatt approached, Mrs. Finley scolded the three tussling boys in the back of wagon, reminding him again of his childhood. The boys settled down, the little one sitting away from the others on a large flat crate.

"So where are you'uns headed?" Wyatt asked the postmaster.

The man stopped and swatted at a wasp. "We're going over Jasper way where Maude's family is. Going to see a new niece or nephew, whichever the stork brought."

"But Pine Gap is the long way around, isn't it?"

"I have a delivery, although I'm not sure it's going to do any good." He jabbed his thumb at the crate in the back of the wagon. "This was supposed to get off the train at Pine Gap, but the porter missed it, so they unloaded it at the Manes Depot weeks ago. I told them I'd never heard of anyone by the name of Yves, but I'd bring it here and let the stationmaster deal with it. He can ship it back if he don't have any more luck than I did."

Wyatt's skin puckered like he'd been hit with a bucket of ice. "How's that spelled?"

"Y-V-E-S. Yves Andres Thibault. Have you ever heard of such a ridiculous name?"

If he only knew. Wyatt hadn't heard that name pronounced since his mother died, but she'd taught him how to say it correctly. He studied the flat crate beneath the boy. What could it be? Flat and as large as a small tabletop. Who knew him by that name and what could they want?

"I'll take care of it." Wyatt dragged his eyes from the crate.

Rule number one of the auction—don't show your interest. Nonchalant. Was that a foreign word, too?

But this wasn't an auction. Why not just tell Finley? Wyatt's chest tightened. Illegitimate. Not belonging. Under the best circumstances he didn't like the reminder, didn't like the conversations that followed about how he was left, why he needed a family. Now, with Miranda and her grandfather reminding him minute by minute how lowly he was, he really didn't want any attention brought to his past. He felt like a fool for hoping, but neither could he let that delivery return on the train without knowing who was seeking him. Did he have some family after all?

The mother caught the shoulder of the boy's jacket and pulled him off the crate. Middle son scooted out of the way, and the boys helped push it to the tailgate. The crate spanned his arms from elbow to elbow. Not heavy, but awkward to maneuver.

"Do you need the boys to help?" Finley asked.

"No, sir. I've got it. Thank you."

Finley's brow lowered. "You sure about this? You don't mind seeing it to its rightful owner?"

"No trouble at all." Wyatt's damp collar stuck to his neck, but the rough wood of the crate barely registered in his calloused hands. As the postmaster rolled away, Wyatt looked up and down the road. He'd worried enough about Isaac taking the wagon, but he couldn't be sorry his brother wasn't there to mock him and whatever was held inside. And he didn't much want to run into anyone else, either.

Head down, he hurried up the hill to his house. Dr. Hopkins crossed his path, but he must've been in a hurry, for he didn't slow to say howdy. When Wyatt stepped off the road and onto the narrow overgrown path, he breathed a sigh of relief. What could it be? Half excited, half dreading, he didn't know what to expect. He propped the crate up with his knee and cranked on the doorknob. Once inside, he shut the door behind him and didn't slow down until he was in his room.

Easing the crate to the floor, he unsheathed his knife, knelt, and inserted the wide blade between the planks. Wyatt pried, but the nails were too tight. He jerked the knife free, then with sweaty palms, rubbed his hands against his pant leg. He needed a pinch bar. His father's was in the shed, but before he left he flipped the crate and smoothed his hand over the label pasted there.

Yves Andres Thibault—Hart County, Missouri.
Shipped from Boston, Massachusetts.

Boston. Location of his family—the ones who didn't want him anymore. This could be something significant. In a flash he ran down the stairs, busted through the back door, threw tools everywhere, and then returned to his room. Once Isaac came home he couldn't lock him out. He had to do what he could with the time he had.

Now with the added leverage, the fresh pine protested before splitting to reveal a framed . . . something . . . tightly wrapped in butcher paper. Heart pounding, Wyatt ripped the paper away. Long ribbons of the noisy tissue floated about the room as a gold corner emerged, an envelope fluttered to the floor, and vibrant colors burned through the haze to reveal a sneering aristocrat challenging him with a face that looked curiously familiar.

The powdered wig hid the man's age. A saber swung from his hip, and he stood with the ease of a man who knew how to use the weapon well.

Wyatt's fingers hovered over the oil painting, but he couldn't bring himself to touch it any more than he'd poke the president in the ribs. One didn't act familiar with a man like the one in this picture. He clearly enjoyed intimidating people. Or he had. Judging from his short britches and funny wig, he was from an earlier era.

Reverently, Wyatt lowered the frame to his bed. He squatted and ruffled through the brown paper until he found the envelope. For a moment he stared at it dumbly. Did he want to read it? Once before they'd contacted his family and the results had been devastating. Was he about to make the same mistake?

He picked at the corner. He already knew what he was, but that didn't affect who he was. Let the mysterious writer do his best; it didn't change Wyatt's heart or his character.

The delicate paper was as thin as a dried leaf. The letter crinkled as he spread it open and read the elegant, looping script.

Dear Yves,

I apologize for the unexpectedness of this missive and that there was no way to prepare you for its arrival. I don't know what you know of your birth family, or if you even care to know anything, but when I saw this portrait of your great-great grandfather, I wanted you to have it. I am your Aunt Corinne, your father's youngest sister, and I hope it doesn't discourage you to hear that I did not know of your existence until recently. Whether or not you'll take any comfort in this portrait, I cannot guess. I hope it does not bring you pain or regret, for that is not my purpose.

It may be that you have no desire to keep this painting—whether because your financial situation leaves you in want or because you have no desire to own anything

At Love's Bidding

pertaining to the family that has treated you like a stranger until now. If that is the case, your feelings will be honored, and I'd like to assist you.

Wyatt lowered the letter and looked again at the painting. The man sneering at him was his own grandfather? The real family that shared his blood?

Why now? Why after he'd already grown and suffered alone would they contact him? And wasn't there anyone who wanted to keep this portrait for himself? Even if it wasn't for sentimental reasons, it looked to be costly. Even the frame was a work of art.

He continued reading:

Should you decide to sell the portrait, and it is quite valuable as art, I insist that you contact me and me alone. Although I've never met you, I think this would be best in your care, and I pray I've not brought danger to you, but it is possible. There is some dispute over this piece, and there could be unscrupulous men searching for it even now. Please guard this painting until you decide whether to keep it or not. And should you sell it, which is your right, I'd be glad to broker the deal to see that you get what it's worth.

How I wish I could discuss this with you in person. Perhaps that day will come. In the meantime, God be with you, and may this unexpected gift only bring you blessings. Once you decide what you'd like to do with the painting, I'd appreciate the opportunity to learn of your plans.

Thank you and God bless.

Sincerely,
Your Aunt Corinne LeBlanc

LeBlanc. The bed creaked beneath him as he sank next to the golden frame. So LeBlanc was really his father's name, or was this a mistake? His ma, his adoptive ma, Mrs. Ballentine, had told him about his father and mother who'd set out in the wagon train with them. Mr. and Mrs. LeBlanc had joined the wagon train in Independence and when they'd died, the Ballentines had taken him to raise, or at least to keep until they could get him home to Boston.

But Boston didn't want him. His hand itched to crumble this letter into a wad. Instead he let it float to rest on the delicate brushstrokes of the painting. What did this Aunt Corinne know? Where was she when Ma had written and received the bitter reply?

And what about the unscrupulous men? There had been that redheaded man who'd surprised Miranda in the barn that day . . .

Miranda.

Had he not already been sitting, Wyatt would've crashed onto the bed. Miranda and Elmer. She'd told him they were after a missing painting, but this wasn't a missing painting. This had come directly to him from his aunt. Wyatt believed in coincidence like he believed in haints. This is what they sought, and they'd tried to keep it a secret from him.

The strings began to stick together like a spiderweb. A fancy auction house. Art collectors. So this painting was worth a pretty penny? Enough for them to travel all this way from Boston and buy a sale barn? They were systematically going through every house that could possibly own anything this fine. But they had never thought of his.

Wyatt rested the frame on his lap and met the old gent's arrogant gaze. They didn't give him any credit, did they? Thought it impossible that he'd have any connection with mighty Boston? Well, at one time he'd thought so, too, but Aunt Corinne must think differently. He didn't know what the appearance of the picture meant or what he'd do about it, but he knew one thing: He had to listen to Aunt Corinne's warning. Her prediction had already proven true.

"Wyatt?" Isaac's boots thudded on the first step. Wyatt jumped to his feet. The painting skittered against the floor as he slid it beneath the bed. His bed wasn't wide enough. He tugged the quilt until it hung cattywampus and covered the edge that refused to hide.

And there was nothing he could do with the splintered crate. Best intercept his brother.

"What do you want?" He squeezed through the opening and pulled the door closed behind him.

Isaac's eyes narrowed. "What are you doing? Are you hiding something?"

Wyatt crossed his arms. "Why? Are you?"

"I don't have to answer to you." Isaac smirked. "Besides, a gentleman doesn't kiss and tell."

"No one has ever mistaken you for a gentleman."

"That's where you're wrong. There is a certain lady . . ."

Wyatt's stomach twisted. The only race Isaac had ever beaten Wyatt in was chasing skirts, and the more Wyatt cared for Miranda, the more determined Isaac would be to win her. But was it possible that she was as big a fraud as Isaac?

"Good for you," Wyatt said. "At your age, it's about time you settled down."

"But when I marry you'll have to find another place to live. I can't ask my bride to put up with my little brother."

Wyatt didn't dare leave his room unguarded. Isaac was too

suspicious. "I'll leave whenever you ask me to, but the wife will expect you to provide for her, so your lack of employment will no longer be my problem."

Isaac lifted an eyebrow, looking ridiculously scholarly for one who hadn't cracked open a book since primer school.

"You're just jealous."

And dying to think through the implications of the letter. What did it mean to his future? What did it mean to Miranda and her grandfather? And could he trust them?

CHAPTER 17

Miranda gripped the picnic basket in one hand and tidied her hair with the other. She couldn't believe she was doing this. She, Miranda Wimplegate, was paying a visit to a man uninvited. But she couldn't allow the opportunity to pass without expressing her thanks. Her errand had nothing to do with his slow smile and green eyes; it was purely a matter of etiquette. She lightly rapped her knuckles on the frame of the door and tugged her bonnet into place.

The house was a neat clapboard two-story painted robin's-egg blue with white trim. A wide, low window displayed a collection of colored glass bottles. A far cry from the stained-glass windows she admired, but still an appreciation for light through glass. She knocked at the door again, but loud enough to be heard this time. The boards beneath her feet vibrated and the door eased open. Wyatt's eyes widened.

"Miranda. I wasn't expecting you."

"Who were you expecting?"

He didn't open the door any farther but looked over his shoulder as if assuring himself that his parlor was ready for company. "I . . . I . . . was just fixing to do something. Work, you know." He pulled the door closed behind him as he joined her on the porch. "Is your grandpa coming?"

"No. It's just me." She clutched the basket to her waist. "Is Isaac home?"

His face fell. "Just left. Did you want to see him? If so, we could take out—"

"Oh no. I came to talk to you. Not Isaac."

"I'm busy." He bit his lip, as if embarrassed by the speed of his reply.

"You're busy? Doing what?"

Wyatt looked straight ahead. His eyes followed the tree trunks heavenward. "Pruning. I really need to work on these fruit trees, but if you want to stay for a bit . . . just a minute." He motioned to a fallen log where she might sit near the grove.

Of course she wanted to stay. Why else would she have come? She made her way across the rocky yard as he darted inside the barn and emerged with a pruning hook. Already, Miranda regretted her decision, but she was determined to make the best of it. She wouldn't get another chance if she lost her courage now.

Wyatt stood before her and fished with a pruning hook above his head until he caught the decaying limb. The branches rustled and swayed as he jerked downward until the dead limb broke free.

"That's a fruit tree?" Miranda didn't know a lot about animals, but she had cultivated an appreciation for foliage. "It looks more like an oak.".

His neck turned red. "It *is* an oak. Did I say fruit trees? I meant it was the oak that warranted pruning." Picking up the limb, he threw it to the side and winced at the crash.

Why couldn't he slow down and talk to her? Miranda's news weighed heavily on her, but she didn't want to blurt it out to his back. She'd like for him to at least pretend to be attentive. Time to pull out the pièce de résistance.

With her foot she nudged her basket. "I brought you some pie."

The pruning hook lowered. He eyed the basket suspiciously. "I really don't want to go inside. Can we keep it out here?"

Miranda squirmed on the log. So she wasn't welcome in his house? "Maybe I should have warned you before coming over."

Wyatt dropped the pruning hook with a sigh. He squatted, meeting her at her eye level. "I'm glad you're here." The lines around his mouth eased. "Really." Then, with an exaggerated groan, he shifted himself to sit on the log next to her.

Finally assured of his attention, Miranda lifted the lid of the basket, prompting a tiny squawk from the hinges. Reaching down, she lifted out the pie, the pan still warm against her fingers. The violet syrup bubbled.

He stopped his squirming to stare at the pie pan. "Rhubarb. Of course it'd be rhubarb."

Miranda pulled out a thick table knife and lifted out a hefty slice, but then had nowhere to set it. With a shrug, she returned it to the pan and handed the whole tin to him, but instead of relishing the offering, he studied it from a bemused distance.

"Years ago Widow Sanders made a rhubarb pie for the auction," he said. "No one wanted it. Didn't bring a single bid. I felt sorry for her, so I bought it. The next week there was another pie. No one would bid on the second one, either, so I gave it my best shot. I talked it up, bragging on how delicious it was, but not a single nibble. I ended up buying the pie the second time, too. Now Widow Sanders is convinced I love her rhubarb pie. Every week I have to buy one." He pulled back the crust to expose the purple chunks.

Miranda jolted so thoroughly that she rocked the log. "You're tired of rhubarb pie?"

"I never liked it in the first place. Even my pigs are tired of it. But please don't tell her." He looked up with a conspiratorial smile that Miranda couldn't share.

"Widow Sanders didn't make this pie," she said. "I did."

His eyebrows raised. His Adam's apple bobbed. After a slight hesitation, he lifted a slice to his mouth and shoveled it in. "Mm . . . delicious."

Miranda slid forward, ready to dart to her feet. "But you don't like rhubarb pie." This had been a mistake. Why had she thought he'd be happy to see her?

"It's been years since I've tried it," he said. "And this doesn't taste at all like I remember."

"You're mocking me."

"No, I'm not. If I only had a warm glass of milk—"

Try to do something nice for the man and he pitied her. She stood, snatched the piece of pie from his hand, staining her fingers in the bargain. Grabbing the pie tin, she stalked to the burn pile and, with a plop, dumped the pie tin's contents on top of the recently added oak branch.

Wyatt studied his empty hands. Deliberately he licked the last of the remnants off his fingers. "I really did want that pie."

Miranda paced from the burn pile to the high grassy area at the edge of the clearing. "It was a thank-you for all you've done. How you've helped with Grandfather. I learned how to make it just for you."

"Why don't you have a seat?" He patted the log. "I can get some cold cobbler for us and bring it back out here."

Still not welcome inside the house? "I'm leaving." She turned to face him.

"But you just got here."

"Pine Gap. I'm leaving Pine Gap. I got a telegram from home. My father told me to give up. Bring Grandfather back." If this was the answer to her prayers, then why did her eyes sting? "I can't accept that we failed, but he's becoming too difficult to handle, so I came to say good-bye."

"You'll leave even without finding your . . . you know . . . ?"

"The painting?" How freeing to say those words aloud. "We have no choice. We can't jeopardize Grandfather's health. We'll just have to hope for a favorable ruling."

The log rolled forward as he rested one arm across his knee. "What's this about a ruling? Are you'uns in trouble?"

Miranda hesitated. She hadn't meant to discuss all the ins and outs of the case, but she'd held it in for so long. "We were selling part of an estate, and a certain picture made it to the block that was not supposed to sell. Now the family is blaming us."

His mouth twisted to the side. "Let's say you get home and the painting shows up. Someone up and gives it back. Would you be out of trouble then?"

"If the painting gets back to the family? That wouldn't happen."

"But say it did."

She dropped to her seat on the log. "If Monty King, their lawyer, could prove we were negligent, they might still press charges, but recovering the painting would help."

She lowered her eyes, uncomfortable with the urging she saw in his. He was begging her to say more, but what she'd shared was embarrassing enough.

"How about you? Are you going back to Cousin Cornelius?"

At his name, Miranda pulled her knees against her body. In his telegram Father hadn't mentioned any reprieve brought on by Cornelius. It sounded like the situation hadn't changed. She'd still be able to save them by marrying him.

"What else would I do? It's all planned out. Everyone would be horribly inconvenienced if I changed my mind."

"Hang them all." He rapped white knuckles against their log bench. "Are you that kind of person, Miranda? Someone who'd bind herself in marriage just to keep the peace?"

She dropped her head into her hands. "I don't know what kind of person I am. Until this trip, I agreed with all the decisions made for me. I didn't mind being kept safe, being protected from decisions and controversy. Now, I'm having to speak up and contradict Grandfather, and I hate it. It's not natural for me."

"But you're doing it, Miranda. You're strong. Don't give up. Your family needs you. The world needs you to be who God created you to be. And don't let some fool tell you who that is."

"But if we leave, we've failed. After that there's no point." Once she passed on deciding who to marry, there'd never be another decision as important.

He searched her face. "Don't worry about the painting. It'll take care of itself. But you can't let this determine your future. You'll find other quests. You'll face other challenges. All I'm asking is that you face them like a woman with a backbone, not the self-conscious woman who hid behind her grandfather the day she arrived. Making your own path will take courage, and you have that courage."

Could she stay strong, or would she sit passively by while Cornelius arranged her future? Having tasted freedom now, would she be content to let everyone else make her decisions? And would she ever see this man again?

"I could make you any number of promises," she said, "but I'm different here because I have to be. Once I go home I'll find it easy enough to do what they ask. With Grandfather cared for, there'll be no reason for me to fight like this." Except for that day with Franklin. Yes, she could speak up when forced, but that had been an accident. Embarrassing. She would never do that again.

"Then I'm going to pray that God sends a conundrum your way that you must solve and that you can only solve with His help."

Miranda straightened. "That's not very chivalrous."

His eyes were kind but firm. "I admire the woman I've come to know here, and while I can't promise I'll ever see her again, I refuse to let her disappear off the face of the earth. You have to keep her alive."

His eyelashes, so much darker than his hair, framed his green eyes. The woods were so silent that the cattle from the sale barn across town could be heard lowing. He stood. "Thanks for the pie. It looked delicious."

"I'm sorry you didn't like it."

"But I did. How about letting me finish a slice next time? Else how am I going to compare it to Widow Sanders's?"

"There won't be a next time. We're leaving tomorrow."

His forehead wrinkled. "Tomorrow? So soon?" He blew out a long breath. His hand went to his mouth, as if trying to hold back words. After a bit he spoke, his voice gruff. "Can I write you?"

She nodded her consent.

"And if I should ever find myself in Boston . . . ?" Miranda froze. Wyatt in Boston? She tried to evaluate the bearded mountaineer as if seeing him for the first time and was terrified by the thought of him appearing in front of their customers. She managed a weak smile.

"Please do. That would be . . . pleasant."

Something in the brush must have caught his attention, for he looked away.

Miranda waited, but clearly he had nothing left to say. What could he say beyond good-bye? That was all they had left.

And this would be the end. The end of her quest to help her family. The end of her freedom. And the end of sharing the company of this complex man. How had she thought that going home would solve all her problems?

CHAPTER 18

The stiff frame tilted gently in Wyatt's hands and the morning sun glinted off the knowing smile of his forebearer.

You know she wants me. That's what she's here for. Why don't you come clean and tell her instead of keeping me hidden under your bed? The dust tickles my nose.

"You are my kin," Wyatt said. "I can't give you up. Not yet. I have to think this through." How he'd hated not telling Miranda. It ate away at his gut like a cancer, especially since she had made a special trip to see him. But what if Miranda suspected the picture was coming to him all along? What if she'd been sweet-talking him just to get close?

You call that sweet talk? Boy, you need to get out more. Doesn't seem to me that she likes you much at all.

"She does," Wyatt answered. "She might not know it yet, but she does. And what if you can help me win her?"

Now you're talking. Sell me and buy that smelly auction house from her grandfather. It would be quite amusing to have one's image traded for an animal sale barn.

"I don't think the sale barn will win her. I've already written to Aunt Corinne. I need to see what else is at stake."

One eyebrow seemed to lift until it bumped the pony-tailed white wig. *That Corinne—always a troublemaker. Don't you wonder what all the secrecy is for? Why would she send you a family heirloom if you were illegitimate?*

"Heirloom? You think pretty highly of yourself."

And why would someone come all this way to take the painting from you? I mean, I've always been a catch as far as the ladies were concerned, but no one ever traveled to a wilderness for me.

The powder blue of Monsieur LeBlanc's fancy coat wouldn't match Ma's pretty wallpaper, but somehow Wyatt already knew that he wouldn't be hanging this picture in the parlor. He had turned a corner. Slowly God was prying what he'd once cherished out of his hands. The future he'd fought Isaac over didn't have the same allure it once had. Wyatt eased the painting beneath the wooden frame of his bed and pulled the quilt down low over the side.

What to do about Miranda? He couldn't imagine that she was a thief, but with her grandfather's confusion, who knew what he might have told her? The only thing Wyatt could be certain of was that it was no coincidence they'd come from Boston on the very same train as his painting.

Time to get them. With growing conviction, Wyatt knew he'd be in Boston soon, but not yet. Not until he heard more from Aunt Corinne and not until he could guarantee that his surprise gift was safe.

He dreaded saying good-bye to Miranda as much as he looked forward to seeing her on Widow Sanders' porch. And when he reached the Garden of the Year, there she was . . . with Isaac. Wyatt tugged his hat down low. He'd failed to ask his brother where he was headed to that morning. Should've known he'd spend every moment he could with Miranda, which is exactly

171

what Wyatt would've done if he wasn't afraid of slipping up and saying too much. The mules stopped in front of the house, already accustomed to his frequent visits.

Evidently Elmer had started the day in rare form. "In all my days I've never known your father to need me so desperately," he railed to Miranda. He held his crystal-topped cane beneath his arm while he tugged on his gloves. "Don't you worry, Wyatt. A quick trip home to straighten out this mess he's made, and I'll be back to resume business here. In less than a month we'll be rolling again."

"Until then you want me to keep the sale going?" Wyatt asked.

"Not completely. I don't trust your eye." Elmer's face crinkled in disapproval. "You can keep selling the animals, but leave the fine art to me." He cast a longing glance at Lady Godiva in the garden.

Wyatt released a breath he didn't know he was holding. In other words, he could run the sale barn just as he always had. Giving up Elmer's mad fascination with worthless doodads was no sacrifice. He darted a glance toward Lady Godiva and nearly choked. Her honey-colored torso had been draped in a modest kitchen apron. He grinned.

Miranda stepped next to him. "Widow Sanders insisted she be covered." Her low words were meant only for him. "Betsy helped me find something suitable."

"Lady Godiva isn't going with you?"

"Alas, no." Her mouth tipped up. "Grandfather didn't want her thrown into the luggage compartment, and I refuse to ride with her in the seat next to me. He said she can stay and greet him when he comes back."

"He's coming back?"

Her eyes lowered. "It's unlikely. Unless he recovers once we're home, I don't think he should leave again."

"What about you?" He blurted the question before he thought better of it. "Are you coming back?" Wyatt waited for a response, but she lifted her eyes, and the sorrow he saw there was her answer.

She didn't want to leave him. She cared about him, with or without a painting. He couldn't ask her to stay, and he had no part in her world, but he couldn't help but wonder what it'd take to earn his way.

He took Elmer's traveling case and scanned the empty porch. "Where's your trunk?"

"Josiah hauled it to the depot this morning, along with a crate of Laurel Hopkins' apple dolls and Arabella's rag rugs."

"And yet you leave Lady Godiva here."

"I'll take her," Isaac said. "She'd look good in Ma's vegetable garden."

"Ma would rise from the dead before she let you put that in her garden," Wyatt said. He lifted the traveling case into the back of the wagon. Maybe Widow Sanders could convince Mr. Rinehart's wife that the statue came from the Montgomery Ward catalog. That was their only hope.

He watched as Widow Sanders hugged both Miranda and Elmer. Betsy had been by the night before and said her good-byes, but a sick nephew was keeping her busy today.

"I can't go with you to the depot, so I'd best say good-bye here." Isaac pressed a gallant kiss on her hand.

Wyatt glared innumerable silent threats until Miranda reclaimed her hand. At least Isaac wasn't tagging along. He probably had another lady friend up the mountain fixing dinner for him.

Elmer climbed up onto the seat, obviously not pleased he was being forced to leave. Wyatt had to hand it to Miranda, she'd at least accomplished that much. Wyatt walked to his side of the wagon and turned to find Miranda following him. He held out his hand, unable to forget how she avoided him on their first ride together.

When she'd arrived she was the enemy, but now she was a friend—a friend who might want to steal his most treasured possession—but life was complicated.

She slid her hand into his and gripped firmly. Positioned before the wheel, she paused. Didn't look his direction, didn't give any sign beyond the tight grip that she knew he was there. Finally, she lifted the hem of her dark brown dress and climbed up into the wagon.

It was time to go.

Her eyes were as blurry as her posture was sharp. Wyatt told her to speak up for herself, to know what she wanted and to pursue it, and then he bundled her up into the wagon and sent her on her way. Either he wasn't following his own advice, or he didn't think as much of her as she wanted him to. The mules plodded slowly down the mountain to the depot in the valley.

Maybe Wyatt was more practical than he preached. Maybe he knew she had no choice but to accompany Grandfather home. If only he realized how badly she'd wanted to succeed here. How she hated returning home empty-handed. She who'd do anything to ease the suffering of a hungry shoeshine boy had failed in the biggest crusade of her life. Just when she was learning to assert herself, she had to give up and return defeated. Father's telegram had given her what she wanted—a way home—but already she wondered if she'd given up too easily.

A few wagons stood at the depot. Farming on the Sabbath

wasn't acceptable, so many made their trips to town under
the pretense of meeting the circuit-riding preacher, although
he'd only been through once a month. Horse tails swished in
rhythm as lazy flies looked for an unprotected spot of hide.
After the recent rain, the light had a crispness about it that
would be difficult to capture on canvas, but not impossible
for a master.

Wyatt threw the brake. His shoulder bounced against hers
as he took a deep breath. Staring straight ahead, he sighed and
then climbed down. Again, she took his hand. Again, she didn't
want to release it. But he pulled out of her grasp, and instead
of handing her down, he took her by the waist.

"My brother kissed your hand," he said. His fingers tightened around her waist as the train whistle echoed in the valley.

Miranda's heart did a flip-flop. "He's just a friend."

"What am I?"

A sudden attack of shyness overtook her. She had no answer.
Taking her hand, he lifted it to him. Her gloves covered all but
the pressure of his lips, but the gesture went to her heart.

"I'll miss you, Miranda Wimplegate."

How she wanted to stay with him. To have nothing else that
demanded her allegiance, no duty that lay a prior claim to her
conscience. Her throat constricted. "I'll miss you, too, Wyatt
Ballentine."

With a roaring shudder and squealing brakes, the train rolled
into the depot. Smoke chugged out from the stack atop the
black engine.

One last squeeze, then he released her and rearranged his
hat. "Looks like they're loading your trunk."

She lifted an eyebrow. "And the apple dolls."

Grandfather had found his bag. He waved at the train

standing ready. "If you insist on our departure, then we'd better go. They won't wait."

She knew what she was leaving, but what would she find at home? "Good-bye, then," Miranda said. "And thank you for everything."

He waved away her thanks. "Don't be surprised if I show up in Boston looking for that rhubarb pie you owe me." He escorted her to the train. Why hadn't he been this charming from the onset? Given more time, she could've grown even fonder of him. But what difference would it have made? Only caused more sorrow at their parting?

The porter reached down for her hand. With one last lingering caress, she relinquished Wyatt's arm and boarded the train. Grandfather stepped up behind her.

"Your father is making a mistake," Grandfather said. "What are we going to tell the LeBlanc family? How will we face them?"

"We did what we could, Grandfather. There was no trace of that painting. It disappeared into thin air."

He grunted and motioned to the nearest seats. "I don't like to lose, that's all. We've surrendered and now we're in full retreat. Shameful."

Miranda slid inside the row. She didn't like it, either. What would be the cost once they arrived home? Once the consequences of their failure began to manifest, would she wish that she'd tried harder? If the long hours on the road home gave her inspiration on how she could've handled Grandfather, it'd be too late. Her only chance would be lost. Would she regret giving up so easily?

She turned to the window. Wyatt leaned against the wagon, arms crossed over his chest. He wasn't leaving until they rolled out of sight. Slowly he straightened and lowered his arms as a rotund man approached, freshly off the passenger car behind her. His black derby hat marked him for a stranger just as surely as her layers of silk had. Wyatt frowned. He seemed to ripple with indignation. He shook his head and pointed at a buggy farther on. Was the man looking for a ride into town?

Grandfather propped his cane between his knees as the train whistle blew. "Two more weeks. That's all we needed. And I don't know what the rush to get back home is. Even if we didn't find the portrait, this is an untapped source of craftsmanship. Our investments here . . ."

The man marched toward the wagon Wyatt had suggested. As he passed, he turned toward the train. Reaching into his pocket, he pulled out a notepad and flipped through, looking for some information his triangular head hadn't been able to retain.

Miranda grabbed Grandfather's arm. "I made a mistake. Get off the train."

His face crumpled in confusion. His cane wobbled.

"Now." She rose and tugged at his sleeve. It wasn't too late. Not yet. "Get up and get off the train."

He grabbed his bag. "You don't have to convince me, but I'd like to know what changed your mind."

Miranda hopped from foot to foot, expecting the floor to begin swaying beneath her at any moment. *Hurry*, she prayed. *Let him hurry*. At quick glance through the glass, she saw the man climbing into the wagon. Well, he couldn't disappear. Wyatt would know whose wagon he rode in, and he'd be easy to find after that. She and Grandfather could do this. They could find the picture before this man could. She already knew the town. She had already earned their trust. What could a few more days hurt?

Grandfather fairly danced down the aisle. "Good for you,

Miranda. We'll stand together against your father. Who does he think he is telling me that I need to come home?"

If only she could send Grandfather back home without her. But she'd have to deal with him. She couldn't ignore the evidence right before her eyes. That man had accompanied Monty King to their warehouse after the painting had sold. He could be in Pine Gap for only one reason—Monty King had new information.

Grandfather teetered at the doorway as the train began to move. Wyatt was already running toward them.

"Ma'am, you must take your seat," the porter shouted from the other end of the car.

"Take him!" she yelled to Wyatt. "Get us down."

Clasping Grandfather's wrist, Wyatt helped the older gent spring forward. Then, jogging a few steps, he was able to offer Miranda the same assistance before the train picked up speed.

Barely pausing for her to gain her balance, he propelled her away from the platform and the mighty steel wheels clicking behind them. His grip pinched her arm through her sleeve. "What are you doing? You could've been killed."

She'd like to answer him and tell him she was fine, but she was having trouble catching her breath. Instead, she watched the wagon drawing away and up the hill toward town.

"I changed my mind," she gasped. "You said I shouldn't give up. You said I could win if I tried hard enough."

He looked dangerously close to walking away and leaving her standing at the depot just like the first time. "What about your grandpa?" His eyes darted to where Grandfather stood, meticulously dusting off his shoulders. He lowered his voice. "What are you going to do about him?"

"I gave up too soon. We still have time to accomplish our task. In fact, I'd say we just got reinforcements."

His brows lowered. "You know that fellow?"

Grandfather cleared his throat and called out in his loudest auction voice, "Wyatt, tomorrow is Monday! Sale day again! You thought you'd have to do it alone, but I'm back!"

Thankful for the interruption, Miranda eased out of Wyatt's grasp. Should she tell him that this was the man who threatened them back in Boston? Did that man know where the painting was? What story had he concocted to explain his appearance? And if he found it, would his success clear the reputation of the Wimplegate Auction House?

Standing at the depot baking in the sun wasn't accomplishing anything beyond blotching her complexion and irritating Wyatt's mules. As soon as they could get her trunk loaded . . .

Miranda spun. A hot summer breeze ruffled the puddles on the empty train platform, but no luggage awaited.

Her gaze followed the twin iron tracks stretching out until they disappeared into the narrow pass that split the mountains. "My trunk."

Wyatt held up his hand. Grandfather quieted his litany of tasks. "Excuse me, Mr. Wimplegate. Your granddaughter just said her trunk is on the train."

Grandfather's head snapped to where the train had been standing. "Most unfortunate, Miranda. Most unfortunate indeed. But look at the bright side. Our apple dolls will arrive in Boston before we do. By the time we get there, every respectable home will have one displayed with their other treasures."

Of course, Grandfather. Between the silver candelabra and Wedgwood's Jasperware, the fine ladies of Beacon Hill will proudly display their withered apple dolls. And if she didn't have a gown to change into, her wardrobe would look worse than the dolls' simple dresses.

"I can buy something, I suppose."

"Laurel Hopkins sews the dresses for the dolls," Grandfather said. "She could whip you up something in no time."

Just as she feared. Miranda caught the edge of a pleat in her skirt. It might be a boring coffee color, but it was heavily layered and silk. She didn't want to imagine what might be offered to replace it.

They made their way to the wagon. Miranda itched for a private word with Grandfather. Had he seen the man? She didn't think so, and his lack of curiosity over why she changed their course troubled her. What should she tell Wyatt? He wouldn't approve of her working with this ruffian, but this McSwain character might bring the help they needed.

Questions tumbled over one another as roughly as the old wagon rolled over the stony road. The thought of getting to be with Wyatt more delighted her. A tiny purr escaped her throat. Wyatt's arm tensed and his foot slid forward, bouncing against hers. The sudden contact startled her. She nearly topped forward, saved only by catching herself with a hand firmly grasping his knee.

Why did a hand on his knee make the mules take out crooked? With a grunted command, Wyatt reined the old jack and jenny into the center of the path and Miranda straightened. Somehow her decision to stay hadn't had the affect she'd hoped for on her stalwart companion. He'd spoken of coming to see her in Boston. Why wasn't he happy that she decided not to leave after all?

CHAPTER 19

It seemed to Wyatt that on occasion a man might ought to be allowed to speak his mind, compliment a lady, tell her how special she was, and then wait a bit before he decides exactly what to do with her. Had he been sweet-talking her out of a kiss or filling her head full of flattery to replace a rival, then he should be held accountable, but Wyatt had only said what he thought was decent, encouraging, and true . . . and it'd swung around and bit him on the backside.

Miranda was back, and she wasn't leaving until she got what she'd come for. Thanks to his encouragement, her determination had been propped up, and now she wouldn't quit until she took his great-grandpa LeBlanc away from him. Wyatt turned north toward Widow Sanders' house, nearly choking on the rising humidity. Sure he was happy to have Miranda around, but he didn't admire the circumstances.

Who was that man who had the power to spin Miranda's plans around? If anyone fit the description of the "unscrupulous man" that Aunt Corinne warned about, it was this fellow. And obviously he and Miranda were in cahoots. She could barely keep her hands to herself, she was so excited.

Maybe it wasn't all bad.

But what if the picture was stolen? He'd thought about that, but he knew he wasn't the thief. And perhaps he had a right to it. Perhaps more had been stolen from him than anyone knew.

Another hole in the road and Miranda bounced against him again. His mouth tightened. If only he'd known she wasn't leaving, he might've kept some of his sweet-talking to himself. How did Isaac manage women the way he did?

Speaking of Isaac . . .

Hands in his pockets, Isaac strolled down the hill from Widow Sanders'. Judging by his smile, he already knew the Wimplegates weren't leaving and already had thought of how to make Wyatt as miserable as possible. He stepped under the shade of a mimosa tree and fanned himself with his straw hat while he waited for them to reach him.

"Where are you going?"

"We're here to stay," Elmer announced. "Miranda hopped off the train at just the right moment."

"Is that so?" The obnoxious white teeth Isaac was so proud of fairly gleamed. "Well, we'll just have to make room for you."

Wyatt growled at the unexpected answer. "I'm taking them to Widow Sanders'."

"Then you might as well just turn this team around. Widow Sanders has a new guest. She doesn't have room for Mr. and Miss Wimplegate now. And that's why I insist on them boarding with us."

It was a good thing he wasn't a cursing man, because if he were, he'd be in the process of losing his job at that moment. "We ain't giving up that easily. That man can find a room somewhere else."

Isaac smirked. "You'd rather him bunk with us, I suppose?"

He narrowed his eyes. With the painting under his bed, he didn't need anyone poking around the house.

"Isaac, Wyatt doesn't want us to stay with you." Miranda's voice quavered. "We'll find someone who'll have us."

For crying aloud. He slapped the reins against the mules' backs. "You're staying with us. Let's go." Not only did he feel responsible for her, but he could hardly leave his boss in the elements, could he? He needed to just simmer down. The widow hadn't had any trouble with the old man. Maybe he was a more considerate guest than employer.

"Wait!" Elmer lurched over Miranda and grabbed the reins. "We have to go back to Widow Sanders'. I forgot something."

Wyatt shifted the reins to his left hand, out of Elmer's reach, and put his arm behind Miranda, giving her a little more room beneath his arm.

"What did you forget, Grandfather?" Miranda asked.

Maybe he was a little pleased that she leaned into him.

"Lady Godiva. We can't leave her behind. If that man sees her, he won't be able to help himself. He'll scour the countryside to find the artist and we'll lose our monopoly."

"We'll go visit tonight," Miranda said.

Wyatt shook his head. "For the last time, Lady Godiva is not coming to my house—wait a minute. How do you know that man?"

Miranda bumped against him, almost as if she'd shoved an elbow into Grandfather on her other side. He coughed and mumbled something in her ear. They both straightened and played mute. Miranda twisted her silver bracelet around in a motion that was becoming all too familiar.

He reckoned they all had their secrets, but it was a pity that their secrets were about the same thing.

He pulled up to his house and he'd never looked at it so critically before. Tidy, neat, except for Ma's old churn that he'd moved outside when they got a new one. How did it compare to her fancy place with maids and servants? Her barn was probably nicer than his house—if they even had a barn.

He helped Miranda down from the wagon, wishing he had an excuse to hug her. Wishing he could keep her in his arms and out of his house. Isaac's cheerful approach was signaled by a tune whistled with an overabundance of cheek. Wyatt went to the wagon bed to fetch her trunk, only then remembering that she didn't have one. A last look at her drab gown, he wondered what else she'd find to make her cheeks bloom.

"Where should we keep our guests?" Isaac said. "Ma and Pa's room?"

Miranda stood, head bowed, looking for somewhere to hide, no doubt. Wyatt tilted his head back and studied the green underside of the oak leaves above him. This was a trial, sure as shooting. How could he endure her living in his parents' house and not completely lose his mind, his painting . . . and his heart?

He had to hide the picture. Already carrying a stack of clean sheets, Wyatt took the stairs two at a time, trying to buy a few minutes before his unexpected guests came looking for him. If he didn't have the picture tucked away, he would've found it easy to welcome Miranda and Elmer. Already his step fell lighter just thinking about seeing Miranda morning, noon, and night, but his painting had to be a secret until he figured how to handle it—how to handle her.

On entering his room, he kicked the door closed and dumped

the sheets on his bed with a whoosh. Wyatt dropped to his knees and pulled the picture out from beneath his twin bed.

I hear we're entertaining company. Great-Grandpa LeBlanc seemed to stand a little straighter. His light blue coat stretched across his shoulders. *Go on and introduce us. It'll definitely change their opinion of you.*

"Yes, but not for the better." Not if they tried to force the painting from him and leave with it. Then he'd be robbed of both the family heirloom and Miranda's company. Wyatt cocked his head at the painting. "Where'd you get that accent? You aren't British, are you?"

He could almost hear the sniff. *We're French, imbecile.*

"Right. I'll have to remember when I hear your voice in my head, but I can't keep jawing. Got to find somewhere to put you."

Wyatt spun, searching every piece of furniture. Grandpa wouldn't fit behind the nightstand. The chest of drawers stood on four spindly legs. He'd show behind there.

"Wyatt?" It was Miranda. Footsteps on the stairs. "Wyatt, I'm coming up. Where are you?"

Heart pounding, he rushed to the space behind the door and leaned the picture against the wall, out of sight. Then, taking the doorknob, he opened it and draped himself across the entry.

"The room isn't ready yet."

"I came to help."

"Go back downstairs. We'll keep the upstairs for the men only."

Her head snapped back and her smile faded. "Grandfather and I decided to switch rooms. After a long day out doing . . . well, whatever it is he does, I don't want him to climb the stairs. Plus, this room is smaller, and with no trunks . . ." She shrugged.

She would be staying here? In his room? He glanced nervously at Great-Grandpa LeBlanc, who only wagged his eyebrows. Dirty Frenchman.

"What's a matter?" Miranda turned as if she could see through the door. "Don't worry if it's a mess. It can't be worse than the sale barn. Let me help you."

"No, no. Couldn't ask you to do that."

"Nonsense. I feel really bad about being here. You've been so kind, and now we're invading your residence."

Momentarily forgetting his forebearer, Wyatt felt his toes grow nice and toasty. "There's room. No worries."

"And to think I judged you so harshly in the beginning." Her lips parted in a sweet smile.

Wyatt stepped from behind the door to face her straight on. How had this Boston beauty come to be standing in his doorway? It was something so profound he couldn't get his mind around it. Hearing her words, knowing that she recognized something good in him despite Isaac's best efforts, filled him with some kind of unspeakable glory.

"Thank you," she whispered, and then with a skillful duck, wormed her way into the room. "This isn't dirty at all."

With the speed of a lead bullet, Wyatt shoved the door against the wall and angled his body in front of the doorknob. "You're not supposed to be in here."

"We're already imposing. If you don't allow me to see after Grandfather and myself, my conscience will trouble me."

Not nearly as much as his was at the moment. If only he could trust her. If only he was one hundred percent sure that she would understand about the painting.

"May I change the sheets?" She lifted his pillow off the bed.

"Absolutely not." But he was stuck to the door, too fearful to leave his post and stop her. When had she become so stubborn?

"They won't change themselves," she said. Her eyes flickered to the floor and she suppressed a shy smile. "But if you'd rather handle your dirty laundry, I understand. I'll stay behind and make up the clean bed once you're gone."

But he couldn't do that. He couldn't leave when the door might swing closed and there his painting would be, as exposed as Mayor Walters when Josiah tipped his outhouse over.

One more try. "Miranda, I need you to leave. I would much rather fix this room up by myself."

She bunched a fist to her hip and gave him a saucy look. "Give me one good reason you won't accept my help, Wyatt Ballentine."

How tiny her waist looked over the full skirts of her traveling costume. How nicely rounded she was everywhere else. His Adam's apple bounced. Lady Godiva had nothing on her. But was there a truth that would send her a running?

"You have to leave because I'm afraid . . ." His mind spun like a weather vane. What could he say? " . . . I'm afraid I might kiss you."

That did the trick. Her eyes widened. She stumbled away from the bed and didn't stop backing up until she bumped into his bureau. "And that . . . and that would be awful?"

Oh, heavens. She wasn't considering letting him kiss her, was she? Who would've thought? Wyatt could've sworn he heard Monsieur LeBlanc snicker behind him.

Maybe later, he promised himself, but not now. "Didn't want to embarrass you, but here you are in my room. You look mighty beautiful, and all I can think about . . ." *Shut up, Wyatt. What are you doing?* "We shouldn't be in here together. You best leave."

She crossed her arms over her chest, her chin tucked down. "Then I'll go. I'm . . . I'm terribly . . . I'll go."

Stepping forward, she hesitated at the door. Not daring to

leave his station, Wyatt turned away from her and breathed a sigh of relief when he heard her skirts swishing down the stairs.

Nice work, old boy. You insulted the lady. She'll never want to be alone with you again.

"And to think I did it to save you. What a mistake."

He didn't mean to slam the door hard enough to rattle the windows, but a man could only take so much. Ripping his blankets off the bed, he carried the whole mess to where Monsieur LeBlanc waited, and before the old gent could complain, Wyatt bundled him into them.

It wasn't enough. The sheets weren't thick enough. After reflection, he added his quilt to the bundle, but there was no disguising the large square of canvas. Well, what was he to do? He'd have to come up with another story if they caught him, but he hoped after his confession Miranda wouldn't be watching him too closely. Shoot, she'd probably never look at him again.

He made it halfway down the stairs, then bent to see what he was walking into. Elmer sat on Ma's red sofa. His cane rested against the inside of his knee, his eyes were unfocused. Wyatt eased down while bunching up the quilt even more. No sign of Miranda.

Elmer's eyes drifted toward him. "I thought I'd be on my way out of town," he said. "So glad I get to stay here longer."

His words were slurring. Sure sign of exhaustion.

"Miranda says you're staying downstairs?" Wyatt asked.

Elmer nodded. "She's in there now fixing it up. Practically flew past me."

Fleeing him, no doubt, but what to do with the painting? He eyed Elmer. "If you need something to drink, you'll find some milk in the kitchen. You should be able to find a mug easy enough."

188

"I know where they are," Grandfather said. "I've been here dozens of times before and I wouldn't forget a thing like that. You must think I'm losing my mind."

Exactly, because Elmer had never been to his house before, but now wasn't the time to contradict him. Wyatt shifted his bundle so the gilt frame didn't dig into his chest so. He could take the painting outside, but it looked like rain coming. Didn't want to leave it in the barn where the mice would gnaw on it. It had to be somewhere inside and somewhere that Isaac wouldn't look. If Isaac found it, he'd tell them in a heartbeat. Anything to make life more difficult for his younger brother. That left the parlor and the kitchen.

"I reckon Miranda should be done about now. Why don't you go check?"

The bags beneath Elmer's eyes looked as full as an unmilked udder. "She told me to wait out here."

"Yes, but now I'm here, so go on and see if she needs anything."

Elmer expelled a long chastising breath to share his opinion of Wyatt's idea, but as Wyatt didn't give him another option, he strained against his cane and majestically rose on creaky knees. "I'll be right back," he said.

As soon as he turned around, Wyatt headed to the piano. Laying his bundle on the ground, he shoved the piano away from the wall. Then, unwrapping his treasure while watching over his shoulder, he slid the painting into the back of the piano, balanced it in the frame, and shoved the heavy instrument so that the wall held it pinned inside and off the floor. Elmer returned as he was gathering his linens.

"She's coming."

With hands folded sedately before her, Miranda stepped into

the room. Moving slightly left, she pressed her back against the wall and came no closer.

"What do you want?" she nearly whispered.

What did he want? He'd only sent for her to get Elmer out of the room. One last glance at the piano to make sure it was flush against the wall, and he had to come up with an answer.

"I . . . I thought I'd see how Ma and Pa's room looked. I haven't been in there for years, and it could be dusty."

"It's fine."

"But it could be dusty."

"But it's not." She crossed her arms, letting him know that was the final word.

"I'll get dinner going directly. It's nearly noon," he said.

"Then I'll be sure and stay out of the kitchen."

That's right. Because he might attack her. Good grief, but she was moody. Thunder rumbled outside. The curtains whipped with extra vigor. "Do you have anything you want me to carry to the washhouse?" he asked.

"We did all our laundry before the trip." And she had no clothes here, either. Again he appreciated her fitted gown, and even the subtle color was growing on him, but how long could she wear the same getup?

"I'll be back." He crossed the parlor, strode through the kitchen, and delivered his sheets to the washhouse. By the time he reached the kitchen again, fat drops of rain had begun to fall. Not an auspicious beginning for his new boarders.

CHAPTER 20

He'd wanted to kiss her. With hands flying, Miranda tucked the corners of the sheet beneath the mattress and looked about for a quilt. She'd come back to Pine Gap determined to be brave, to speak her mind, and to act without fear. Yet within the hour she'd made a mess of everything. The back door creaked open. Miranda spun, expecting Wyatt at any moment, but from the clanging pans it sounded like he was staying in the kitchen. Her heart sped again at his words. He wanted to kiss her so badly that he questioned his ability to resist? She thought of his passionate outbursts, his determination, and she couldn't help but be a tiny bit awed. This was no cheek peck he was thinking of.

But maybe he didn't even like her. That would explain why he wanted her away from him. Or did he think she was being forward? Miranda twisted a dark lock of hair as she surveyed the tidy bed. He'd tried to get her to stay in his parents' room, but she'd insisted on staying in his. What if he mistook her intent? Knowing how he felt about Isaac, she really shouldn't be surprised at his disapproval.

After cleaning Grandfather's room, she tiptoed into the parlor. Grandfather was making use of a rocking chair and had propped his feet up on the sofa. Miranda nudged him out of his trance but remembered to keep her voice down. "You saw McSwain, didn't you? Monty King's man?" She kept nervous eyes on the kitchen.

"I'm hungry." He swung his feet to the floor. "Let's see what Widow Sanders has for dinner."

"We aren't paying guests there anymore. We need to eat here."

"We aren't paying guests here, either," he said.

"We are paying—"

"No, you're not." Wyatt stepped out of the kitchen, dishrag in hand. "Come get a bite to eat." He returned to the kitchen, opened the oven door, and bent to retrieve a tin.

Honestly, he looked attractive from every angle. And he'd wanted to kiss her.

"Bring me something, please." Grandfather patted her hand. "If I'm not getting Widow Sanders' rhubarb jelly and toast, it's not worth getting up."

Go into the kitchen with Wyatt? Alone?

Miranda slouched, ducked her chin, and dragged her feet. She wanted to look as unattractive as possible. Not really, but she definitely didn't want to look like someone trying to look attractive. She wasn't the type that wanted a man to kiss her against his better judgment.

A tin of cornbread clattered onto the table. Steam curled off it as Wyatt tossed the kitchen rag aside. He pushed his shirt sleeves up to his elbows, exposing tanned forearms. With his foot he pushed a chair out before sloshing milk into the mugs. Miranda clutched the back of the seat. "Are you sure you don't mind me being in here?"

"Sit down," he said.

Evidently he didn't find her quite as irresistible in the kitchen. "I'll eat standing, thank you."

He raised an eyebrow. "Suit yourself." He handed her a bowl of beans with a golden square of cornbread crumbled atop. She carried it in to Grandfather, and by the time she'd returned, Wyatt had prepared her a bowl. The cornbread melted in her mouth. She licked the butter off her finger before seeing the napkin he'd placed beneath her bowl. After a cool drink of milk to loosen her voice, Miranda spoke. "I'm sorry I didn't listen to you earlier. I thought I was being helpful by making the bed."

"Miranda—"

"I certainly don't want you to think I'm forward or brazen. Perhaps it'd be better for Grandfather to stay upstairs. Widow Sanders' upstairs didn't inconvenience him."

"No. You stay upstairs. It doesn't bother me none."

"It's probably not a good idea, especially if I might lead you into temptation too strong—"

"Miranda." He held her gaze, even as a slow red burn crept up his neck. "I'm sorry for what I said upstairs. You are in no danger around me."

"I know you wouldn't hurt me. That's not what you threatened." She lifted her spoon of beans, then lowered it back to the bowl, unsure that she could swallow with him looking at her like that.

A sudden bang on the kitchen door made them both jump. Wyatt leapt to his feet while Miranda steadied her nearly overturned bowl. A small bright face pressed against the glass pane in the door. Wyatt turned the knob and Betsy burst inside.

"Miss Miranda?" She wiped the rain off her face with her damp pinafore. "I thought you'd done left."

"Change of plans."

"Well, you ain't the only one. There's a man staying with Mrs. Sanders. City folk like you. Do you know him?"

Feeling the full weight of the question, Miranda smoothed her napkin. "It's possible my father sent him to help us. Help us run the auction house, that is."

"What do you need that for?" Betsy dropped into a chair and took a piece of cornbread from the tin. "Ain't Wyatt doing you right?"

"I was wondering the same thing," Wyatt said.

"Grandfather might need more help. He's involved in more than the sale barn."

Betsy nodded her blond head. "Like buying statues of naked women?" She blinked innocently until Wyatt bumped her chair and an ornery smile emerged.

Miranda had no answer and the beans were cooling. She shoveled in a savory mouthful, foregoing any pretension that she wasn't starving.

"Can I?" Betsy asked.

"Grab a bowl," Wyatt said, but before Miranda could take another bite, Grandfather called.

"Are we going somewhere, or not?"

"If you're ready." Miranda meant to take a delicate bite of the cornbread, but once it got to her mouth she couldn't help but shove it in.

"I'll take you." Wyatt stood, but Miranda stopped him with a hand on his arm.

"No, please. We'd rather go alone."

His gaze dropped to where her hand lay against his blue shirt. She was acting inappropriate again. She moved to snatch it away but he caught it. His warm hand covered hers and guided it back to his arm. "You don't know that man. You'd be safer with me."

So temptation no longer threatened him? Her eyes dropped to his lips and she couldn't help but feel disappointed.

"I told you so," Betsy said and raised her eyebrow in Wyatt's direction.

"Don't you have somewhere to be?" he asked Betsy. Miranda tried to pull away, but he held her tight.

"I'll leave with Miss Miranda and Grandpa," Betsy mumbled around a mouthful of beans.

"Might as well wait outside."

Betsy hummed as she sashayed past, leaving the two of them alone.

"Is this about the painting?" Wyatt asked.

"It has to be. That's the only reason that man would be here."

"Does he know where it is?"

Bless his heart, he sounded so concerned for her. "That's what we'll find out." She studied his dark hand on hers. "I wish you could go with me," Miranda said, "but Grandfather still wants to keep it a secret."

Slowly he slid his hand away. "I reckon I understand. We all have our secrets."

Her parasol caught the drops of rain, but once the fabric became saturated, she'd be as wet as the scraggly cat that darted across their path. Splashing through the puddles, Miranda pulled on Grandfather's arm.

"Let's walk faster. If that man was sent by the LeBlanc family, we want to be presentable."

"I'm not going," he said as he continued walking.

Betsy, who was hunched over to get her head beneath Miranda's ineffective parasol, twisted her mouth into a frown. "Looks like you're going to me."

"I know why that man is here. He wants to steal a share of

my apple doll business. They've seen how well Mrs. Hopkins' art has been received in Boston, and they've come to get a slice of the market."

"Grandfather," Miranda said, "the train left just this morning. Those dolls haven't made it to Boston yet. Besides, the LeBlancs are in the shipping industry. They don't deal in art and antiques."

His brow furrowed. "They have a spy, then. Someone told them what we were up to, Miranda. Someone has been watching us."

His fervor sent warning chills to the edge of her teeth. His misguided optimism was worrisome enough, but paranoia? This was something new. His eyes tightened as he turned to stare at Betsy. "Who have you been talking to, girl?"

Betsy straightened, meeting his accusation with the contempt it deserved. "That ain't none of your business."

"I knew it." Rain dripped off his hat brim. "She's a spy, Miranda."

Fear gripped Miranda. He'd never shown this hostility before. "No, she's not, Grandfather. A soft answer turns away wrath, Betsy. Tell him you haven't been reporting on him."

Betsy flung her braids behind her shoulder. "But Miss Miranda, sometimes Wyatt told me to see what you'uns were—"

"Achoo!" Even if the sneeze was obviously faked, it interrupted Betsy. Miranda shot her a warning glance. Both she and Wyatt had made use of the girl's ability to meander around town without any noticeable purpose. Grandfather wasn't mistaken that Betsy was watching him. He'd just failed to realize who she was reporting to. "The point is that you haven't been hired by any art dealers to report on Grandfather's stunning acquisitions."

Please don't mention Lady Godiva, Miranda prayed.

"Like Lady Godiva?" Betsy shuddered as a gust flung rain beneath the parasol. "I might have mentioned it to Uncle Fred because I thought he'd like to do another story, but he said he didn't want to raise community outrage."

"This child is a nuisance," Grandfather said. "She's led him to our treasure like the traitor she is. You can take her with you, if you'd like, but I'm leaving."

"You must come with me," Miranda said. "McSwain won't want to speak to me."

"Then don't talk to him. It doesn't matter to me because I'm looking for Leland Moore. It'll be nice to be with someone who has my best interest at heart."

They stood at the intersection before Widow Sanders' house. One road led to town—the other to the sale barn. "Watch yourself, Miranda," Grandfather said. "Don't trust anyone." And with a last glare at Betsy, he walked into the rain in his stern black suit and his tall stovepipe hat.

Betsy watched him a few paces, then turned, shielding her eyes from the rain. "You want me to follow after him?"

Miranda drew a strong breath in through her nostrils. "No. Keep your distance, Betsy. Grandfather would never have accused you like that if he still had his wits. I just don't know what he's capable of in this condition."

Betsy splashed through a puddle. Water gushed out of the toe in her boot. "Seeing how it's only raining heavier and heavier and how you don't seem likely to let me listen in on your conversation with these strangers——"

"I'm afraid I can't do that."

"Then I might as well be getting back home to see if Eddie's fever has dropped. He was sleeping when I left."

"I'm sorry, Betsy."

"That's all right, Miss Miranda. You know, everyone about these parts talks about how mean and nasty Yankees are; even the people who fought for the Union don't cotton to them any. But you and Miss Abigail have both been right nice to me."

Miranda gave her a tired grin. "I'm glad you think so." But being nice wouldn't get her through the upcoming interview. She waved good-bye as Betsy trotted away. Miranda stepped onto the familiar walkway through the widow's competitive garden, still unsure of what she'd say or do. Just the thought of speaking to this stranger twisted her stomach into knots. How much simpler would it have been for her to have spoken up at the auction house that day when Grandfather sold the wrong painting. Her cowardice had led to this dilemma. She wouldn't let it get in the way again.

She'd turned the knob on the door before she remembered that she no longer resided at this house. With a shake of her head, she knocked and listened as the occupant of the cabin had to move from his seat to allow Mrs. Sanders through the room.

The woman's calico shirt hadn't changed, and neither had her efficient grin. "Miranda, I didn't think to see you again so soon. Did you miss the train?"

McSwain inspected her as if trying to place her. She didn't blame him if he didn't recognize her. The month since Boston hadn't been kind to her.

"Grandfather and I decided to extend our stay."

"Oh no." Mrs. Sanders covered her mouth. "I only have one room empty. If only I'd known—"

"We're fine," Miranda assured her. "In fact, it's most beneficial that we decided to stay. I believe I might have some acquaintances in common with this gentleman."

Widow Sanders' eyebrows hopped and she turned to glance over her shoulder at McSwain. "All right, then. Since you already know Miss Wimplegate . . ."

"Wimplegate?" He pulled a notepad from his pocket.

"W-I-M-P-L-E-G-A-T-E?" Then with a nod he said, "We thought you'd given up already."

He scratched at his large jaw and stared at her through dull eyes. Miranda would've backed away from the inspection, but to do so would deposit her on the front porch. Forced to stand her ground, she hardened her face into an expression that would have impressed her father and horrified her mother. "We have not given up in our quest to help your client, but before I answer any other questions, I'd like to know what you are doing here."

The man carefully closed the notepad and returned it to his shirt pocket. "Monty King sent me. According to your father, you had failed and were returning home. Tough break for you, but it's not too late for us to find the painting, which we would've by now if you would've told us where it went instead of trying to go it alone."

The rebuke stung because it was true. She had wasted their time. She and Grandfather were no closer to finding the painting than they'd been in Boston. It probably wasn't even in the state anymore. Miranda rubbed her forehead, the exact spot that denoted her abundance of apologies. She might be sorry, but if he knew something, she needed to find out.

"If you have more information, we'd be glad to help. The people here don't much like outsiders, and they might not trust you, but I could speak for you if you already know where to look——"

"Not likely, boss . . . er . . . ma'am. You'd be the last one we'd tell. Your mishandling of the family's heirlooms is why I'm here in the first place. I don't need a list of your friends. I know who I'm looking for." McSwain motioned to the door. "I've got to review my notes before I start investigating tomorrow. I'm going to be like a real detective and all." His eyebrows wagged on his crowded forehead. "So enough chatting. Go on home to your lunatic Gramps and don't expect me to keep you informed."

So that was it? After all that she had done—all the fear of the journey, the trials with Grandfather, the awkwardness of the sale barn, the headless chicken—after all of that, this stranger was going to march into Pine Gap, pluck up the painting, and return the victor? How did he find out where it was sent when there was no record?

Shaking in frustration, Miranda glared, but he didn't care—no more concerned about her anger than a bear frets over the bees. Where had that saying come from? Not only had she lost all her nice clothes, now she was even thinking like a mountaineer.

Miranda spun around and marched out of the house. No sooner had she reached the peony bush than she heard a whistle behind her. Holding an opened raincoat over her head, Widow Sanders motioned her over to where she crouched by Lady Godiva.

"I heard what he said to you, Miranda. I don't know what you are looking for, but you can beat that man. I really don't think he's that clever." The widow's eyes narrowed with tight focus. "Before you got here, he asked me right particular if I knew anyone named Eves."

"Eves? Is that a last name?"

"Not one I've heard of. Sorry I can't help you, but I thought you ought to know."

Miranda nodded. "I appreciate the hint. If that name is all he has, he might not be as close to solving the mystery as he thinks." Widow Sanders blinked as a gust threw water beneath her shelter. "You'd better go inside," Miranda said. "And be careful with that man. I don't trust him."

"I can handle him," Widow Sanders said. "I'll sleep with a

knife under my pillow, and heaven help him if he crosses me." Then she hustled back to the house.

Miranda bunched her shoulders up around her neck and then pushed them low. The dreaded interview was over. Sometimes you might not accomplish anything from an encounter beyond surviving it. She'd faced McSwain and she was still standing.

But she didn't know an Eves, or an Eve for that matter. First or last name. It sounded like Monty King's research had been more thorough. He probably even knew that the Pine Gap sale barn sold animals, not antiques. Inadequate—her efforts, her intelligence, her persuasion. She'd given everything she could, and still she came up short.

The rain dumped out by the cupful, and her saturated parasol finally admitted defeat. Sludging through the slick mud, Miranda made her way back to Wyatt's house, heavy with disappointment. If the LeBlancs had new information, why hadn't they wired it to her? Why send someone else to get the job done? Obviously Father hadn't been able to convince them that she was capable. And why should he? He must've had his doubts, too. As hard as she tried, she'd failed and no one believed in her.

Only Wyatt. Wyatt, who worked so patiently with Grandfather, despite Grandfather's eccentricities. Wyatt, who escorted them through the hills in search of their treasure. Wyatt, who occasionally wanted to kiss her against his better judgment—okay, maybe only once. Sure, he believed in her, but as much as he tried, he couldn't help her. He had no more influence than her young friends hawking papers on the corners of Boston. In the end, if you weren't a rich man with an office full of lawyers and detectives at your disposal, you were going to lose. Wyatt was just a simple country boy with a big heart, and in the LeBlancs' world that didn't count for much.

CHAPTER 21

With a grunt, Wyatt hefted the collars for the mules. Already in place in the steamy stable, they waited for the weight on their necks, but it never fell. Instead, through the wall of rain coursing off the side of the barn, he watched Miranda trudging toward the house. She was alone, so maybe they didn't know about the painting after all. The bottom of Miranda's dress carried an extra five pounds of mud, dragging it down until it met the original source. Shoulders hunched, she trampled across the sodden grass. He hung the collars on the wall and checked once to see the mules were tethered, then ducked into the fray and trotted to her side.

"I was on my way to fetch you." He flipped up the collar of his coat to keep the rain from running down his neck. She didn't even spare him a glance.

"Has Grandfather made it back?"

"No. Betsy told me he took out, so I sent Isaac to Leland Moore's to look for him." Moore wouldn't be happy to see Isaac, but he had to know that if he was messing with Elmer that the Ballentines would come looking for him. And Isaac didn't seem to mind the chore one bit.

He reached in front of her to push the door open, but she stopped at the threshold. Lifting her messy skirt, she twisted her foot this way and that, examining the boot slick with mud. With a sigh she tossed her frilly umbrella on the porch and knelt to tug at her boot fasteners. Wyatt let the door close and leaned against the wall to keep her company. "Don't seem right going inside without you."

"I need to get out of these wet clothes and—" Miranda lifted her head. Her mouth quirked to the side in adorable frustration. "I have no clothes, do I?"

He scratched his wrist. "I can find something. I mean, we have to have something . . ." His mother's clothes were the only things he'd given away. Never had any sisters.

"I don't want to dirty your clean rug. I could change in the kitchen." Giving up on her balance, Miranda flopped onto her backside and yanked off a boot.

A glimpse of a smooth, thin stocking—wet enough to see every delicate curve of her ankle—and Wyatt swallowed air. "The kitchen. Go around to the back door and I'll bring you something to wear." He rushed into the closed door, outpacing his ability to turn the knob, and slammed full force into solid oak. Bouncing back, he nearly toppled over Miranda. She steadied him with a hand to the back of his calf.

"Don't forget me down here."

No fear of that. Finding that his wrist still worked, Wyatt opened the door and took the stairs two at a time. As the youngest of four brothers, his childhood clothes had been handed down until there was nothing left to pass. The only clothing in the house was his and Isaac's, and although Isaac was smaller, you could bet your last cotton-picking dollar he wouldn't let Miranda wear Isaac's clothes.

He busted into his room, his eyes naturally drawn to the space beneath his bed before he remembered that Monsieur LeBlanc no longer hid there. The drawer to his bureau rasped open and he pulled out two pairs of trousers. Holding them at arm's length, he weighed his choice. The smaller ones were nearly worn through. The fabric had softened till it was liable to rip with one snag. The newer britches were stiffer, offered more protection, but they were also bigger. Throwing the old trousers over his shoulder, he swiped a worn white shirt. Somehow he thought softness suited her right well, and he wanted her to be comfortable. She wasn't going to be impressed with his clothing, anyway. He heard the door creak open below. A grab for his best leather belt and Wyatt lost no time sprinting to the kitchen.

She'd already removed her silk jacket, leaving her white blouse clinging to her generous figure. Beneath his pile of clothes his hands flexed, knowing instinctively that nothing would feel so good as gathering her up and pressing that softness against himself. He'd been behind horses that couldn't pull as strong as the desire that was working him over.

She lowered the jacket to the sink, moving the dinner dishes to make room. "This skirt is impossible," she said. "I can't drag it up the stairs without scraping mud everywhere."

"I brought you clothes." How had his arm grown so heavy? He lifted the wadded clothing. "This is all I have. When it stops raining we can buy something at the mercantile."

Her hair sparkled with droplets that had managed to make it beneath the brim of her hat. She took the clothes from him. "There isn't a door, you know."

Yeah, he'd been thinking about that. Quite a lot. "I'll wait by the front door to make sure no one comes in."

Already reaching behind her to her waistband, she nodded. "I'll be quick. After the chicken incident I don't want you to accuse me of slovenliness again."

He no longer noticed the mud. Her impossible curves were bewildering compared to the flat plains of his own body.

Enough. Wyatt spun on his heel and marched to the front door. Keeping his back to the kitchen, he hummed "She'll Be Coming Round the Mountain" to cover the soft grunt of accomplishment that proceeded the sigh of silk slipping to the floor.

"Oh my. These clothes . . ." She stopped. "I don't know whether to laugh or cry."

"They're dry and clean. I can't promise you anything more." Had he already made too many promises? He'd promised to help her get back home, but she'd returned. Now what? What if she flat out asked him about the painting? He had to make a decision. He wouldn't lie to her, but he couldn't predict how she would respond if he told her the truth. It had all the makings of a disaster.

From behind the piano he could hear Monsieur LeBlanc. *I can't believe any grandson of mine would let a painting come between him and the woman he loves. Forget about me. She's what you want.*

But what if that painting was the key to winning her? And what if he gave Miranda the painting, only to find out she never did care about him? He didn't have much experience with women. Quite possibly one could hornswoggle him and he'd be none the wiser.

Wyatt closed his eyes. He couldn't give it away until he knew more. It all boiled down to trust. Did Miranda trust him enough to let him keep Monsieur LeBlanc, or would she insist on possessing it herself? He was afraid he knew the answer to that question and it didn't favor him.

"I think I'm ready," she said.

Wyatt spun to see her rolling up the sleeve of the roomy white shirt while her other hand held her trousers up. The belt he'd given her hung around her waist as loose as a barrel hoop.

"It's too big," she said. "It won't buckle small enough to hold these pants."

Wyatt stepped toward her. He'd better figure out something quick or he was in danger of blurting everything to her.

----•◦◦⟨∞⟩◦•----

When Wyatt darkened the kitchen doorway, "darkened" described his expression, as well. Not angry, though. More pained. Determined. He stood frozen while his gaze traveled from the shirt sliding off her shoulder to the unfamiliar trousers bunching around her waist, then back to her face. He was breathing like he'd just scaled Bunker Hill. The way his chest moved, the way he'd now become fixated on her, if she didn't know better she'd think . . .

His warning from the bedroom came to mind. Miranda backed away from him. She raised her hand, keeping it between them. "My visit did not go well. You said you wanted to talk about it."

His face lightened. "Absolutely."

"You won't think ill of me dressed like this?"

"Not if you can keep your trousers up."

Miranda scrunched her nose. That was a problem.

Wyatt reached for her waist. Miranda's heart leapt when he caught her by the belt and tugged her toward him, but instead of touching her person, he cinched up the belt, then looped it back through itself twice. His hands dropped away and hung by his side. Miranda kept her chin ducked and studied the wet toes of his boots. She swayed. He lifted his hand and, with the slightest nudge at her waist, brought her forward.

Her forehead rested against his chest. Wyatt gathered her closer, enveloping her in his clean, rainy scent. Confronting McSwain alone had felt like walking into battle, and from the way Wyatt was sheltering her, he understood.

"I'm proud of you for going by yourself," he said. "When Betsy told me that Elmer had lit out without you, I wasn't sure you'd go through with it."

"Bravery isn't in my character," Miranda said. "It's going against nature. Given the same challenge again, nine times out of ten I'd fail."

"Horsefeathers." Now his arms shifted and fitted her against him in a way that felt both soothing and dangerous. "All this is from that crazy doctor-cousin who feels the lumps on your head and tells you what you can do?"

Normally, she'd never allow this, but standing in his kitchen wearing his clothes made anything seem possible. "Phrenology is a proven science. . . ." Her words failed as his hands slid up her back. "What are you doing?" She tried to look up, but he cupped the back of her head and threaded his fingers through her hair. With a gentle tug, he removed a hair pin, loosening her coiffure.

"Surely Cornelius couldn't tell anything about you as long as you have your hair up."

"Cornelius is a doctor. You really shouldn't . . ." But at his touch on the back of her neck, Miranda couldn't continue. Her hands rested on his narrow hips as the last of the pins were removed and her damp hair tumbled down her shoulders. His fingers stroked up her neck to her hairline and buried themselves into her thick tresses. Her eyes closed as he followed the contours behind her ears.

The clock in the parlor chimed, each gong marking time that felt impossibly slow compared to her racing heart. A button on his shirt pressed into her forehead, but she didn't mind.

"You tell me that you're a coward, but so far I only find evidence of courage and loyalty." His husky voice sent goose bumps up her arms.

"Maybe you don't know where to search."

"Then I'll be very thorough." He massaged a slow circle near her temple. "I may have found something. . . . No, wait. I know what this is. It's a spot of longing. That's what it is."

Her eyes felt heavy, her head light. She couldn't deny it, not the way she was holding on to him. Somewhere between her worry and the luxurious feeling of his hands on her, she wanted him to know her, because the lady he claimed to see was so much better than the one who faced her in the mirror.

"I wish everyone believed in me the way you do," she said.

"Then show everyone the spirit you show me. Although, I don't really want you letting them touch you like this."

No. No one could touch her like that.

He disentangled his hands and smoothed her hair with slow strokes. Besides the rain pattering against the roof, nothing disturbed the calm grayness inside. And when she finally raised her head, Wyatt flicked her on the nose. Not what she was expecting or hoping for, but she noticed that the lightness of the gesture was at odds with the intensity of his eyes. With an arm around her shoulders, he escorted her to the sofa in the living room. Chilled by her damp underclothes, Miranda accepted a colorful afghan from him, tucked her bare feet beneath her on the sofa, and draped it over her lap.

The walls of the main room were covered with a deep red fleur-de-lis paper. A brave choice that spoke of confidence. A circular rag rug covered the smooth wooden floor, and against the wall a roughly crafted parlor table held an odd assortment of keys, tools, and work gloves. A restful room, if Wyatt wasn't so busy trying to rearrange the clutter.

He finally settled on the piano stool opposite her. Leaning forward, elbows on his knees, he asked, "What did you find out?"

She'd learned that if Wyatt decided to be a phrenologist, he'd have no shortage of ladies coming to him to perform that particular inspection, but then she remembered the nature of his inquiry.

"I'd hoped the man might be helpful, but he sees himself as our rival." Miranda picked at the yarn of the blanket. "When I saw him get off the train, I thought we'd finally solved our problem, but we're no closer. In fact, it might be worse if he beats us to the painting." She pulled the blanket up to her chest.

Seeing her shiver, Wyatt unfurled another blanket from the stack he'd carried in from his parents' room. Miranda leaned forward as he draped it over her shoulders and tucked the length of it behind her back, but he seemed too agitated to sit down again.

"How did you lose this painting?" he asked.

Miranda threaded her finger through the loops in the yarn blanket. "It sold at our auction, but our customer had no intention of selling it. It's a family heirloom. If we don't get it back for them, our reputation will be ruined. You, of all people, understand how bad it'll be if word gets out that we mishandled property."

"Was it your fault?"

Here Miranda tugged on her ear. Her eyes flickered to the floor. "In part. Grandfather was the auctioneer. Normally he would've noticed that the item didn't match the sale catalog, but recently—"

"Grandfather hasn't been himself."

"Exactly. I didn't realize how strongly affected he was, though. I couldn't correct him and take a chance that I was mistaken."

Wyatt's head tilted. "You were there. You saw it on the table?"

Miranda's chin trembled. "I was there. I knew it wasn't the Copley. I knew I should speak up, but there were so many people in the room. To question Grandfather's judgment before an audience—" Wyatt came to her side. The sofa cushion tilted under his weight. He gathered her hand into his. "And I couldn't predict how Grandfather would react. I was a coward. But you see why it's been so important to me to recover the painting. It's the only way I can make retribution for my mistake."

"Who bought it? You should have a record." He fairly crackled with excitement. Unable to sit, he bounded to his feet again.

"The information that was left was false. Our only clue was an associate who overheard the name of Hart County, Missouri, at the shipping dock. We didn't know where it was sent, but we assumed that the sale barn dealt in art, as did ours. By offering us such a bargain, Mr. Pritchard made the decision an easy one, but we didn't want to announce our intention when we arrived."

Wyatt seemed to mull over this explanation as he took a seat at the piano. Leaning back, he stretched his arms out across the piano keyboard behind him, then with a lurch he righted himself and crossed his arms, hiding his hands against his chest. Miranda's eyes narrowed. Why the sudden agitation? He didn't have it, did he? Cautiously, she scanned the simple house once again. Nothing to denote luxury or riches. The LeBlanc painting would be as out of place here as . . . well, as Wyatt would be back in Boston. She sighed. If only he did have it, but it was impossible.

"What will you do when you find it?" he asked.

"Give it back to the rightful owner."

"Who's that?"

"Why, Mr. Frederic LeBlanc, of course. He's the one who organized the sale—at least his lawyer did."

With a sudden jolt, Wyatt took to the floor and paced before the piano again. "And what does this Frederic LeBlanc do? Why is he selling his family's paintings?"

"He doesn't do anything. They have a solicitor to manage their estate and provide them with income."

"Then the solicitor must not be doing a good job. Else they wouldn't need to sell out."

"You never know. Sometimes the family decides to move to a smaller home, or they want some funds to invest. It doesn't always mean they are liquidating."

Wyatt's steps padded as he crossed the rug, then echoed hollowly as he hit the wooden floor again. "I just wonder what kind of man he is. Would he resort to violence to get his painting back?"

What a strange question. "They don't need violence. The LeBlanc family is powerful enough to ruin us without lifting a finger. Just a whiff of their displeasure and no one in society will give us their patronage."

"They sound like bullies to me."

She nodded her affirmation. Odd how his interest had piqued so suddenly. And odd that his questions were about the family back in the Boston. He hadn't even asked what it was a painting of, for goodness' sake.

The clean cotton shirt she wore carried his scent. Miranda breathed in woodsy aroma as she studied the man before her. Either Wyatt Ballentine was very curious, or his interest ran deeper than he was admitting.

<hr />

He couldn't keep from pacing before the painting hidden behind the piano as he cogitated on the new information. She knew the LeBlancs? She'd spoken to the family that'd rejected him? Did she know the mysterious Aunt Corinne? Had the woman acted against her own family? Who were they to him?

Sometimes the people in Boston felt like make-believe. The stories Ma told him about his birth and his parents' death— fairy tales. But from his family he'd received something concrete. Something to hold on to that tied him to his past. And Miranda was another link.

Or was she an obstacle?

Outside, the rain had let up, and along with the sun peeking through the dripping leaves, Isaac appeared with Grandfather in tow.

"You wouldn't believe it, Miranda." Elmer tilted his hat, draining the rainwater from the brim before entering the open door. "Leland Moore has betrayed me."

Isaac met Wyatt's gaze over Elmer's head. "You owe me," he mouthed as he struggled out of his wet coat.

Miranda slid her bare feet to the floor. "What happened?" she asked.

Wyatt got a glimpse of slender ankles before she arranged the blanket over her unusual clothing.

"Leland and I were at the bank securing a loan when Isaac happened in, and it's a good thing he did. Not long after he entered, the bank president informed me that he couldn't loan any more money to me or my partner. Isaac happened to be nearby and he suggested that Leland put up a piece of property he owns as collateral."

Leland invest? Wyatt got a tickle in his throat that had to be booted out with a forceful cough.

"You'll be just as amazed as I was," Isaac said, "but Mr. Moore wasn't willing to help Mr. Wimplegate out. At the suggestion that he risk his own sorry homestead, he took out of that bank like a miner with a dead canary."

Wyatt wasn't the least bit surprised by Moore's desertion, but what did amaze him was that Isaac had taken the effort to protect Elmer. "I'm glad you happened by," he said.

Isaac shrugged. "Leland Moore has much to answer for. You don't know the half of it." And then his gaze wandered again to Miranda. His eyes widened. "What are you wearing?"

With a blanket across her lap and shoulders, all that was visible was the white shirt billowing around her in cloud of cotton. An unfamiliar crease stretched horizontally where her corset began. Wyatt touched the second button of his own shirt. He'd never realized how impossibly high her bosom was until he could compare it in reference to his own body. There were a lot of comparisons he'd like to make, come to think of it.

"Stand up and let me get a look at you," Isaac said.

Wyatt's gratitude to Isaac stretched only so far, but before he could intervene, Miranda spoke up.

"My clothes are drying in front of the kitchen stove. Until then, I'd prefer to remain covered by this blanket."

When not asking him to tighten her belt. Wyatt couldn't keep from stretching his chest at the thought that she trusted him, that she willingly went into his arms. But didn't he trust her the same way? The piano drew his gaze, and the secret behind it gnawed on him. No, he didn't.

"You look tired," Miranda said to her grandpa. She patted the empty spot on the sofa, and he sank into the cushions. "My visit with McSwain didn't go as I'd hoped. He is indeed here for the picture, but—"

"Miranda!" Elmer coughed and jerked his head in Wyatt's direction.

"Oh, Grandfather, what's it matter? What's to keep McSwain from telling the world? Besides, Wyatt might be able to help us. We've already tried doing it secretly and we accomplished nothing."

"What's this?" Isaac smiled his winning smile. "There's a picture missing?"

A chill ran through Wyatt. Isaac knew his story. One mention of the LeBlanc name and Wyatt's secret would be furled out for all to see.

"You haven't seen a fancy painting around here, have you?" Wyatt asked. He forced a guffaw. "Imagine, someone accidentally shipping art to Pine Gap."

"I never knew why you came here," Isaac said to Miranda, "but it was clear as day you weren't auction people."

Miranda straightened. "You are mistaken. We are auction people. We run an auction house in Boston, actually."

Isaac wrinkled his nose. "Really? I thought that was just a story you'd concocted. Well, you fooled me. I never would've thought you'd handled livestock before. But now that everyone's home safe and the rain's let up, I might as well go about my business. You'll excuse me, I hope." He picked up his coat and stopped at the threshold. "Wyatt, keep the bed warm for me."

And this time his sass didn't bother Wyatt at all. As long as he had no further interest in the painting, then Wyatt would allow for all the attitude he could dish out.

CHAPTER 22

"I can't waste my time at the auction, Miranda." Grandfather straightened his cuffs and pulled his walking stick from behind the door. "My efforts would be better utilized pursuing other opportunities."

Her heart sank, but she kept up a good front. "What efforts would those be?"

"I hate to speak of it, because you never know who might overhear." His eyes shifted to Wyatt. "But I suppose since he's not in position to take financial advantage, it doesn't signify. I'm considering purchasing a gold mine."

Wyatt spewed his coffee back into his mug. "A gold mine? For crying aloud, there isn't any gold here."

"That's exactly what my partner wants everyone to think." Grandfather winked at her.

"Is Moore involved in this mess?" Miranda peered out the window expecting to see the ne'er-do-well on the road but instead saw the pristine world beyond the glass. The leaves hung heavy, still dripping with the overflow. But at least her one dress was dry and ready for the day.

"Moore is worthless," Grandfather said. "Miles Bullard is my contact now."

"Who is that?" Miranda asked.

Wyatt's coffee cup clunked as he placed it on the back of the piano. "Miles Bullard makes Leland Moore look like one of the disciples."

"Which one?" Miranda asked. "Judas?"

Grandfather pointed his cane at Wyatt. "Miles is going to get that banker set straight. They shouldn't need any more collateral than the sale barn."

Miranda and Wyatt had already obtained the bank's cooperation. There'd be no further loans made to Grandfather, but still the threat of losing the sale barn was enough to worry Wyatt. Miranda shot him a sympathetic smile.

He brightened. "If Mr. Wimplegate is busy, then I'll need help at the sale. Can you come?"

She never felt more useful than on auction day, or more exposed. "I'm willing as long as I won't be in the way," she said. True, Grandfather would be roaming the hills unrestrained, but even when she'd tried, she'd been unable to keep the prodigal out of the swine pit.

"I'm looking forward to it."

He pulled on his dress coat over his satin waistcoat. Miranda had to bite her tongue before she found herself offering to button the jacket for him. His tie rested crooked. Maybe he wouldn't mind a little help. Miranda stepped close. Wyatt's hands stilled on his buttons as she reached up and tugged it horizontal. His lashes lowered. "Thank you."

Grandfather opened the front door, stopped on the threshold, and then announced. "I declare, every time I turn around, that girl is there." And then he bellowed out across the yard, "Don't think I don't see you. You may think you've got me fooled, but I know when I'm being followed."

Floating among a tattered mob of young boys, Betsy maneuvered them toward the house.

"I ain't following you, Mr. Wimplegate. I'm just coming by to see if Wyatt has left for the sale already. Thought me and the boys might walk over with you'uns."

But instead of greeting his former friend, Grandfather huffed past her. "You stay away, young lady. I don't know what you're up to, but I will find out."

For the twentieth time that morning Miranda readjusted the crumpled collar of her gown that hadn't dried just right. "She isn't doing any harm, Grandfather. She's a little girl."

But Betsy's cocky tilt of the head showed her willingness to argue that assessment.

"So are all the boys coming with us?" Wyatt scooped up a little fellow with hair just as blond as Betsy's.

"Yes, sir. Their pa said they could come along if'n they behave themselves and don't bother him while he works in the office."

With that they gathered their hats and made their way toward the angular structure. The boys ran forward and behind, darting between their legs, bumping against the adults, tossing rocks off into the thick growth on both sides of the road. "They will have traveled three times the distance by the time we get there," Miranda observed.

Wyatt tugged at his collar. "And if I'd known your Grandfather wasn't coming to the sale, I could've worn my usual clothes."

She opened her mouth. Closed it. Opened it again and, with burning face, choked out, "I think you look nice."

His chin went up. His lips twitched. Suddenly he broke out

217

in the biggest grin she'd ever seen. "Then maybe I'll wear this more often."

It felt nice to make him smile like that, but all Miranda could do in reply was nod.

Betsy whistled. "Listen to you, Wyatt. As vain as a banty rooster in the henhouse at the county fair."

"I just want to be clear exactly what she's admiring. If it's the waistcoat, I could throw it on over my work shirt and keep her happy at the same time."

Finally finding her voice, Miranda spoke up. "It's the impression you give in general. The coat civilizes you. You look refined."

His eyes sparked with interest and he leaned closer as they walked. "Tell me honestly, Miranda. Do you think I could pass as a member of one of those rich families you're so fond of? Do I have the look?"

Miranda bit her lip. He could never pass for the elite class. Not with that honest, earnest expression. People like the Le-Blancs never cared half as much as Wyatt appeared to care at this moment. Besides, they didn't have the robust good health, the skin tanned by labor instead of sun-kissed in leisure. The fluid movements and joints made smooth by nonstop motion. The direct mouth that only said what was required instead of dancing around the niceties of vapid conversation.

"You're dangling me over a barrel," he said.

Miranda was already fanning herself before she realized how warm it'd become. "You'd never be mistaken for one of them," she said. She hadn't meant to hurt his feelings, but her answer didn't please him. If only she had the courage to tell him that she preferred him the way he was.

Now within the confines of the barn, Betsy's charges scattered to the four winds. "Stay out of the pens!" she yelled as they raced toward the gates, and then she clapped her hands together and squealed. "Mr. Jeremiah . . . Miss Abigail! Over here!"

At the sound of their names, Wyatt lifted his head and waved. With a frank, determined air, Abigail strode toward them.

"How's our little Betsy faring in the big city?" Her eyes danced, obviously adoring the girl as much as Wyatt did.

"I'm staying out of trouble mostly," Betsy said. "Having those cousins of mine to tend is surely a trial."

"And how about you, Miranda? Are these, er . . . mountains . . . winning your heart?"

Why did her eyes dart to Wyatt? "We won't be in Pine Gap much longer," Miranda said.

"Not unless Wyatt can give her a reason to stay," Betsy quipped.

Mr. Calhoun whistled. "You might have your work cut out for you, Wyatt."

He gifted Miranda with a slow, warm smile. "Miss Miranda can't abide all these animals. I'm just lucky she tolerates me." Then, seeing a man smiling at Jeremiah's shoulder, Wyatt extended his hand. "Wyatt Ballentine, sir. Don't reckon I've ever seen you around here."

The man's scraggly blond hair fuzzed past his ears. He smiled pleasantly. "I'm up from Arkansas, aiming to buy a horse off the Calhouns." And despite his friendly tone, Miranda's blood ran cold. She'd seen this man somewhere before. But where?

"The Calhouns have the best horses around," Wyatt said.

Still standing with an arm wrapped around Abigail's waist, Betsy scratched beneath her slat bonnet. She opened her mouth, then with a quick look at Miranda and a shake of the head, popped it closed.

Whatever memory niggled at Miranda seemed to fluster

Betsy, too. The girl's eyes narrowed and she watched him as closely as a mouse watches a sleeping cat.

In answer to Wyatt's observation, the man said, "When Mr. Calhoun described the breadth of animals being offered today, I thought I'd better come have a look-see. I might pick up some cattle or sheep while I'm at it. I do love an auction."

And that's when she knew. She'd seen him here, in the dark, beneath the stairs. She shrank closer to Wyatt, wondering what excuse the man would make if she exposed him. He hadn't just arrived, and why was his hair blond now instead of red?

"We'd best get the sale started." With a touch to the small of her back, Wyatt leaned close. "Are you ready?"

Ready to do what? Several options presented themselves. She waited for the chills to fade before she spoke.

"That's the same man, isn't he?"

Wyatt turned to face her. "The same man that what?"

"The same man I saw beneath the seats. The same man that Mr. Fowler caught at the Rineharts'. His hair is different, but it's the same face."

Wyatt watched closely as the man took his seat with the Calhouns. "Any chance you're mistaken?"

Unlikely. Once Miranda made an identification, she was never in doubt, and yet she'd choke before she insisted. "I could be wrong," she said finally.

Judging from the way his chin hardened, Wyatt didn't like that answer. "Stay close today."

And judging from the way her pulse quickened, Miranda didn't mind his response.

As the two of them took the stage, she couldn't help but wonder how it happened that Wyatt was dressed finer than she. To look at the two of them, one would think that he had all the breeding and culture, if it weren't for his untrimmed beard. Her throat constricted. Better not to think of anyone looking at her on the stage. She'd just keep her chin down and focus on being accurate. Wyatt pushed her chair in as she took her seat on the raised platform. Widow Sanders nodded and held up her rhubarb pie, but even that notice twisted Miranda's stomach. She tidied the stack of buyer's tickets before her and grasped the pen with stiff fingers while Wyatt greeted the crowd and called for Josiah to send in the first animals.

"What you see here are five steers. Five Angus steers from Holbrook's farm. They weigh . . ." He slid the metal sleeve over the arm of the scale, tapping it until it swung balanced. "They weigh 9,275 pounds. That'd be 1,855 each. Ready for butcher or to ship out on the next train north. What do I hear for them?" And then started that song peculiar to the mountain auctioneer until it came to the conclusion, "Going . . . going . . . gone."

It took Miranda a moment to locate the space for head count and weight. She'd already written the farmer's name, and all that was left to add would be the buyer's name and the price they sold for. Then off to Fred Murphy in the office where he'd figure the payout amount and the money would exchange hands. Not so different from her auction house after all.

The first hour flew by. Laughter, then a contentious argument over who had won the fifteen-cent bid with neither side willing to bid fifteen and two bits. Wyatt handled it firmly, and they were off again. Miranda craned her neck up, scrunched her shoulders to stretch, and saw the blond man leave. Wyatt's knee bounced into hers. His cadence faltered.

"Keep going," he said as he stood.

A fat drop of ink dripped off her pen and soaked through the ticket. "What do you mean?"

With the back of his hand, Wyatt pushed the gavel toward her. "Sell the animals. I've got to see about something."

"I can't do this. I don't know the first thing about these animals."

"You'll do just fine." And he stepped down off the platform and around the arena, leaving her to face one hundred or so skeptical farmers. She didn't blame them. This was a disaster waiting to happen.

Josiah led in a cow and had to take second look at Miranda sitting alone at the table. She took a deep breath. The metal band on the gavel's handle cooled her fingers. Her job at the Wimplegate Auction House was to write the descriptions for the catalog. Making each piece of furniture sound unique and irreplaceable was her specialty. Surely her powers of description could be used here, as well.

The sun filtered through the high windows to illuminate the arena. The beast snorted at her, its spray sending the dust motes spinning in the sunbeam. She cleared her throat and those in the room grew deathly quiet, with only the cheers of the cowboys outside to distract them.

"What we have here is a cow. A multi-colored cow with a blazing gaze."

Josiah grinned crookedly. Two men in front looked amused. Widow Sanders set her pie on the seat next to her and hid her hands between her knees. Jeremiah Calhoun was making his way to the corner where Wyatt had disappeared.

"We can't hear you," Mr. Rinehart called out.

"Very well," Miranda said. Her voice bounced thin and fragile in the room. "I'll start again."

By now the cow had stalked forward, its tail slashing through the air with every prod of Josiah's cane.

"We have a cow here. . . ." Was she yelling? She felt like she was. "But not just any cow. This cow exhibits a remarkably unique pattern. You'll notice that besides an aura of ivory around its muzzle and eyebrows, it has an ebony face. This dark motif is carried on across the fur on its shoulders where it slowly begins to fade into a coffee tone, and as it reaches the median of the beast, it turns caramel."

She dared a look around the room. Just like Mr. Wakefield when she was detailing the Chippendale bureau, they hung on her words. Father had always said she had the ability to enhance any item with her descriptions. Warming up to the powerful animal before her, she continued.

"And while you might be tempted to purchase this cow for its aesthetics alone, please don't overlook the powerful build of the beast. Crafted by the finest . . ." She covered her gaffe with a cough. Was she getting as bad as Grandfather? "Beneath this sturdy, velvet covering lie supports solid enough for the most discriminating . . . cow person. This cow has stood the test of time and will be reliable for many years to come."

A bearded woodsman stood on the third tier, cupped his hand to his mouth, and belted out, "What we want to know is how good a milker is she?"

Afraid she'd made a mistake, Miranda raised out of her seat for a better look. Then with a shake of her head she corrected her antagonist.

"There's no milk coming from that animal, as you well know. It's a male cow, not a female."

<hr>

Wyatt jerked the door open but didn't have to wait for his eyes to adjust to the darkness before plunging ahead. He'd played behind the seats since he was shorter than a billy goat, swinging around the two-by-four braces, stepping between the supports that stretched up to cradle the seats above. Evidently the newcomer wasn't as confident.

"What are you doing in here?" But instead of finding the Calhouns' suspicious guest, Wyatt ran into Widow Sanders' new boarder, McSwain.

"I think that was a rat," the fat man gasped, but even for his scare he stayed out of Wyatt's reach.

"You aren't who I expected to find," Wyatt said.

"You have something that belongs to my boss."

"And what would that be?" Wyatt's gut tightened. He knew this day would come. Hadn't Aunt Corinne warned him? But if he decided to hand the painting over, it'd be going into Miranda's hands—not to this smarmy man.

The man held his hands up between them. "There'll be no charges filed. In fact, if everything works out all right we might be able to give you a little something for your trouble."

"I don't want anything of yours."

"Then give it back. It's that simple, Yves."

Wyatt's head spun a bit at the use of the name.

The man laughed. "I've done my research, and I'm not as slow as everyone says. Of course I'd check at the auction house, but I know something Wimplegate didn't. I know that a sniveling family called Ballentine tried to con the LeBlancs out of the fortune years ago. Luckily, Mr. LeBlanc's solicitor kept the letter. Working on a whim, he sent me directly to you."

No longer did his head feel light. Now it felt near to bursting. "My parents are gone," Wyatt said. "And you won't say aught against them." Heavy boot steps thudded just outside the door. Wyatt flattened himself against the wall just in time to see Jeremiah Calhoun enter.

"Everything okay?" His eyes darted from Wyatt to the stranger.

"Just fixing to tell this fellow that he ain't welcome on the barn property," Wyatt said.

"This isn't your place," McSwain replied.

"I said leave." Wyatt motioned behind him as Jeremiah backed out to make room.

"I know you have it, and I will get it. Might as well cooperate. It'd be worth your time."

"I'll keep an eye on him." Jeremiah didn't look mad, but Wyatt wouldn't want to tangle with him, and neither did the ruffian from the city. With a last unconvincing glare, he obeyed when Jeremiah pointed ahead and then followed him out.

Wyatt ducked his head passing beneath the last support beam to exit and nearly ran into Isaac as he stepped into the storage space. Sweating like he'd been locked in the smokehouse, Isaac blocked his way. "Wyatt, I need to talk to you."

Isaac at the sale barn? Not a good sign. "If it can wait, the auction is going on without me."

"It's important." Isaac's hair stuck to his neck. It was possibly the first time he'd ever seen Isaac sweat. If this was just another stunt to disrupt him and keep him from his work . . .

"She's pregnant." Isaac gripped the seams of his trousers just like he used to when Ma was chewing him out.

Wyatt's jaw dropped. "Who is?"

"Alice Moore." With an effort, he raised his eyes to Wyatt's. "I'm going to be a pa."

Wyatt had to hug the support beam to keep the room from weaving. Confusion, outrage, and yes, even a touch of jealousy flooded over him.

"What have you done, Isaac? Moore will kill you."

"It's not like that."

Of all the emotions, anger was outpacing the others. "Then how exactly is it?"

"We're married."

"You're what?!" Wyatt stomped to the door, but one look at Miranda, head tilted as she tried to examine a ram, stopped him cold. Had Isaac told Miranda, or had he continued to toy with her? Seething, he turned around and marched right upon Isaac's toes. "You have some explaining to do, big brother."

"We wanted to get married—she's a good girl, Wyatt, you'd like her—but her pa wouldn't let us on account of me not having a job or house or anything. So when the circuit rider came through he hitched us, but we decided to keep it secret."

"Why get married if you're going to keep it a secret?" But at Isaac's raised eyebrow, Wyatt sighed. "Fine. Go on."

"We were going to tell everyone. I just needed to get some things straight first, but it's too late now. We have to tell her folks and after that . . . well, I'm bringing her home. Her pa doesn't go none too lightly on her anyway, and the longer we wait, the more people are going to talk when the baby comes."

Through the screeching banshee going off in his head, Wyatt could hear Miranda's patient but firm voice. "With ears shaped like tulip petals . . ."

And here he'd thought Isaac was after Miranda. He closed his eyes. Isaac would need some way to support a family, and wasn't this Isaac's sale barn as much as it was his?

In his prideful quest to show his parents that he belonged, Wyatt made sure to outdo Isaac in every endeavor. If Isaac worked hard, Wyatt would work twice as hard. If Isaac helped Pa all day, Wyatt would stay up at night. Anything to earn his place in the family. After a while, Isaac stopped trying. Maybe if Wyatt left, then Isaac could live up to their pa's expectations. Suddenly, all he'd fought for in Hart County seemed puny compared to the importance of giving Isaac his chance at being a man.

And without the sale barn, that painting became even more valuable to him.

"We'll make room for her, Isaac. Just tell me what you need me to do."

"Thanks, Wyatt. And I intend to do my part from here out. I'm going to prove her pa wrong. You'll see. And I have to say, I'm surprised it isn't you first. I thought for sure you would settle down before me."

And it was high time that he did. When he boiled it all down, Wyatt would rather have Miranda than the family in Boston and the painting. If she loved him as he loved her, they'd figure out what to do to make it right. He'd write Aunt Corinne and explain his change of plans. He couldn't let fear keep him from acting. He couldn't dwell on what could go wrong.

He'd made his choice. Now if she would only make hers.

CHAPTER 23

"Going . . . going . . . gone." Wyatt dropped the gavel on the last bid of the day. Miranda jotted down the winning amount and gathered the slips of paper that identified the owners.

"You'd better watch her, Wyatt, or you'll be out of a job." Jeremiah didn't crack a smile, but his wife's grin told Miranda that he was jesting.

"Maybe I could learn a few pointers from her," Wyatt jabbed back, but his gaze lingered gently on her.

Abigail cleared her throat. "We need to get back to the farm, husband." Then turning to Miranda, she said, "We left the children with Dr. Hopkins and Laurel, so they've had a houseful all day. Please tell Betsy good-bye for us. I hate that she left already."

Had she? Miranda had been so focused on her task that she'd missed the disappearance of Betsy and her nephews. "I most certainly will."

"And if you leave for home before we're back in town, safe travels and God be with you," Abigail added as they strolled off.

"Did you ask about their visitor?" Wyatt said.

Miranda shuddered. She'd be watching around every corner for him. "I thought you talked to him beneath the stairs."

"I only found McSwain under there, looking for a painting." Wyatt offered her his arm. "We still have a long day ahead of us. Let's see if Fred needs any help."

She threaded her arm inside his. She didn't need an escort to walk down the hall to the office, but she felt something special had transpired, as if she should celebrate the day's accomplishments. And this feeling of satisfaction wouldn't have been possible without Wyatt. "Never did I think I'd run a sale myself," Miranda said, "And definitely never imagined it'd be animals."

"Today has been full of surprises, and that's a fact."

Miranda leaned against his side and whispered, "But no fear of us going hungry. We'll be well-fortified by Widow Sanders' rhubarb pie."

She giggled at his grimace. Here he was, dressed so sharp, looking so dapper, she could almost forget they were walking through a sale barn. Actually, she couldn't forget, but she didn't mind it so much. Contentment had never been so real.

"Miss Miranda! Mr. Wyatt!" The voice behind a stack of feed sacks whispered urgently.

Wyatt stopped. Leaning forward, he peered into the dark space. "Betsy? What are you doing there?"

"Is he gone? That man with Captain Jeremiah? Have they left?"

Releasing Miranda's arm, Wyatt caught Betsy by the shoulder and pulled her out of her hiding place.

"Did that man bother you?"

"No. He didn't say a word to me, but he didn't have to. He's an impostor. He's lying, and he's up to no good."

"What'd he do?" Miranda asked. If that man as much as

spoke a word to Betsy, Miranda would find Fowler and help hunt him down. No one better interfere with her little friend.

Betsy looked both ways and, seeing no one too near in the breezeway, motioned them closer. "His beard and hair—he changed the color. Real close to his face you could see it growing dark. Once I noticed that, I started watching closely—little things, like he had them scuffed-up old boots, but the soles and the shoestrings were brand-spanking-new. Looked closer, and they looked like he'd deliberately roughed up the tops and stomped through some puddles, but they were new, no mistake."

Wyatt turned to Miranda. "Could he be sent from your friends in Boston?"

Miranda shook her head. "This man was here before McSwain, remember? But he's hiding something." The skin on her arm puckered. "Where's Grandfather? Has he been around at all today?" Her feeling of accomplishment was fading fast.

"I haven't seen him," Betsy said.

Wyatt shot a glance into the office where two dozen impatient men stomped and spat. "Isaac is on the way up the mountain right now. He's as likely to see him as anyone."

And that had to suffice. As much as Grandfather's antics concerned her, she couldn't allow them to disrupt this good man's life any further. When had her loyalty changed?

Having made a decision and, to her surprise, feeling confident that it was the right one, Miranda clapped her hands together. "Then I'm staying to help close up shop. On auction days it's all hands on deck. Betsy, if you see Grandfather, you'll come tell us, won't you?"

Betsy grinned. "You bet. And I think I know just the place to look for him. Mrs. Rankin made a satchel out of a dead armadillo. The outside of it looks just like the armor the knights wore. Anyway, I wouldn't be surprised if Mr. Wimplegate wants a trunkful of them."

Miranda shuddered. Suddenly the wrinkled apple dolls felt sophisticated. "Thank you, Betsy. You are a young woman of many talents."

Betsy winked and skipped away.

"She's not the only one," Wyatt murmured.

An hour of shuffling through her sale tickets and matching them to the farmers' bills, Miranda finally felt that she'd earned his praise. This time she hadn't sat idle looking over Mr. Murphy's shoulder. She'd contributed, and nothing felt better.

"That's it." Fred Murphy swept his notebook and pen into his hand. "Until the next sale . . . or the next chicken attack, whichever comes first."

As the man departed, Miranda smiled in spite of herself. Despite his threats, the chicken coop had never made it into his newspaper—a mercy that hadn't escaped Miranda's notice. Wyatt's chair creaked. He stood and pulled down the faded curtain over the lone window.

"You never know what's going to happen on a sale day." She wanted to stretch this period of camaraderie out as long as possible. Remind him of who'd been at his side today, but Wyatt's eyes kept flickering to the door.

"Did you happen to see Isaac come in during the sale?" he asked.

Miranda plucked on her sleeve that hadn't quite survived the rainstorm from the night before. "Now that you mention it, yes. I'm surprised he'd come near the sale on auction day."

Wyatt took a gunnysack off a nail in the wall and, with one hand, scooped up the cash box and tucked it inside. Slinging the sack over his shoulder, he cocked his head toward the door. "Let's go home."

A lot of questions, but no answers. Miranda opened the desk drawer, took out her reticule, and walked past as he held the door open. Down the hall they traveled, stopping only to lock the double doors of the building behind them. A gorgeous sunset bathed the hills in rose while skipping over the dark valleys. The locusts screeched their rhythmic song.

"I hadn't realized the sun had gone down already. I do hope Betsy and Grandfather are home waiting for us." Grandfather. Miranda sighed. Proof that life was more than sunsets and insects chirping. She rubbed her arms.

"Are you cold?"

"The breeze feels delicious after a day inside the dusty barn," she said. "Tonight I'll have to bathe or your poor bed will pay the consequences." Warmth flooded her face at the inappropriateness of her comment. "I didn't mean anything by that," she said, but Wyatt seemed absorbed in his own ruminations.

The short distance to Widow Sanders' wasn't far enough for her to get over her embarrassment. As they passed the house, a wavering light from the porch caught their attention. A glowing cheroot stub, smoked by no other than McSwain.

He called out from the dark, "Hey, Yves. Have you found our picture yet?"

Miranda shrank toward Wyatt. Yves? Did he think Wyatt was the man he was looking for?

But Wyatt didn't even bother to correct him. "You're on your own. No help coming from us."

"Oh, you've been more help than you know." The man chuckled in the darkness, and the ember burned brighter as he took another draw.

Wyatt kept an eye on the man until they were safely down the hill.

"What did that man mean by calling you Yves?" Miranda asked.

"It's been a busy day." They'd reached the path to his house. He held a branch aloft to clear the narrow trail upward.

Miranda twisted her silver bracelet on her wrist. Had she said something wrong? Wyatt's conversation skills had certainly vanished. "Is everything all right?" she asked.

The gunnysack still swinging against his back, Wyatt walked with even strides. His black suit blended into the shadows thrown by the dark trees.

"Just thinking." His hand clenched and then stretched wide at his side. He hoisted the sack higher.

"About?"

The gravel flew as he skidded to a stop. The suddenness of his movement startled her. She clutched at her heart as he spun to face her, his eyes intense.

"I'm thinking about how Isaac is married, has a baby on the way," he said, "and here I am pretending that I wouldn't give anything to make you my wife."

Miranda's eyes widened. Wyatt couldn't mean what he'd just said, could he? Marry her? Was this a legitimate proposal? He wasn't on one knee, but from the determined set of his jaw she knew he was in earnest. She stuttered even as warmth radiated through her body.

Avoiding an immediate answer, she finally squeaked, "Isaac's married? You aren't making any sense. I don't think you know what you're saying."

But Wyatt wasn't deterred. Miranda jumped as the gunnysack and money box crashed to the ground. "I know exactly what

I'm saying, and it isn't easy. I've let things come between us, one thing in particular. There might be a million reasons why we couldn't be together, but we can make it work. I'll make it work."

And maybe they could. "If I could stay here," she said, "then perhaps we'd find a way, but my family—"

"I'm not asking you to leave your family. I'd come to you."

"You'd come to Boston? To live?"

He stepped forward. "To live. With you."

She tried to swallow the lump in her throat. He obviously didn't understand Boston.

"I love you, Miranda, and I'm willing to prove it to you. Our life might be more humble than you're used to, but no queen could be treated better."

A step backwards and limbs brushed her head. Why was she running? She'd determined to know her own mind, but her feet weren't in agreement. The memory of their time in the kitchen, of his hands buried in her hair, had her taking another step backwards. It had been too good—*he* was too good—to be true, and he wasn't keeping a safe distance from her. Not tonight. She ducked her head beneath the limb and soon the sycamore's trunk pressed against her back.

"One question," he said. "One question and from there the rest will be easy." His chest swelled as he stepped closer and planted his feet wide. "Do you love me?"

Her gaze dropped to his new tie, now loosened. With shaking hands she undid the knot, then slowly retied it. The way he made her feel, the way she missed him when they were apart, the alarming power of her affection for him—what else could that be but love?

"Miranda," he said. "I'm willing to give up everything. More than you know. I understand how scary it is. . . ."

No, really he didn't. Wyatt was never as uncertain as she was.

"But I believe I can make you happy. I'll spend the rest of my life trying."

He stepped even closer until his boots were inches from her toes. She released his tie. Her fingers rested lightly on his chest. Wyatt slid his hand along her jaw and tilted her head up. His thumb caught the corner of her lip. "Trust me, please. This is painful for me. Painful, but I've made my decision."

What was painful? Giving up his dream of owning the sale barn? Finally finding her voice she said, "I don't want to make you do anything—"

"That I don't want to do?" His eyes softened, as if he pitied her for her lack of understanding. "Miranda, I've never wanted anything more."

Slowly and deliberately, he bent toward her. Of its own accord, her head tilted back, giving him full access to her lips. He smiled. "Maybe this won't be as painful as I thought." She wished she had a smart retort, but even if she did, there was no time for it. He wrapped her in his arms and kissed her so thoroughly, so confidently, there was nothing to do except hold on to his new suit and enjoy the moment she'd been longing for. His beard tickled her face, but it was his hot, smooth lips that made her head spin. Reckless, passionate, without reserve— never before had his wild upbringing been so evident.

He drew back, leaving a hint of tangy sweetness behind. "Give me your answer, Miranda. My future, my life, is in your hands."

The thundering she felt against her chest was his heart. She couldn't break it. She reached for a better hold on his shoulder, and although she didn't mean to do it, she pressed herself tighter against his hard body. It felt delightful. She ran her tongue over her upper lip and breathlessly answered, "You ate the rhubarb pie. I can taste it."

"Wrong answer," he groaned as his mouth covered hers again. She couldn't be sorry. It felt so good to give him what he wanted. What she wanted, too. His hands skimmed the length of her brown silk bodice to her waist and held her there. The tree was at her back, holding her firm as she got all the rhubarb she'd ever need.

Wyatt loved her. He was putting everything at her feet, and with her giving nature, no gesture could mean more, but was it enough? Could she ever be at peace knowing that she'd gone against society? Knowing that he would live with the disapproval of her class for the rest of his life?

His kisses slowed. With a long sigh, he stepped back. "You didn't say *yes*." Wyatt hadn't yet learned how to hide his raw emotions. Deep lines furrowed between his eyebrows. Fighting for control, he brushed her bangs down so that they again lay in a neat fringe across her forehead.

Miranda gripped the tree to steady herself as she cried for divine guidance. She'd spent her whole life living somewhere else, being a different person. What if this adventure had affected her as much as it had Grandfather? Could she be certain?

Her heart tightened as she realized what her answer must be. Not yet. It was too soon. Too soon to know forever. The heady feelings he evoked were not enough to carry them through the storms they would encounter. He would be an outcast, ridiculed and rejected, and she loved him too much to expose him to that.

She reached for him, catching his hand in both of hers, hoping that he understood. "All my life," she said, "I've been taught that I'm supposed to follow a certain path." His grip loosened, but she held on, refusing to let him turn away. "It's too early,

Wyatt. I've only known you for a few weeks. I can't ask you to give up everything to follow me. Not yet. Not until I know."

His eyes tightened. With his free hand he tugged on her bonnet ribbon and tried to smile. "I understand. I reckon it's not fair that I figured it out before you." As he helped her away from the tree, she noted a tremor in his hand. "I needed an answer, and that's what you gave me. I've just got to decide where I go from here."

He'd laid open his heart and now Miranda heard it clang shut. She squeezed his hand. "But it's not a final answer. It's just the best I can do for now."

"Please," he said. "I understand. You don't need to say anymore."

He'd told her to speak her mind, to be courageous, so that's what she was doing. Not letting others choose for her, but she felt like she'd just made the worst decision in the history of the world.

After brushing off her shoulders, he turned her away from him and picked off all the remaining debris from their secret arbor. He picked up the money box and tried to smile. "No hard feelings," he said. "Nothing's changed betwixt us."

But they both wished it had.

When they reached the house, the front door stood wide open with light flooding out. The porch looked like a Christmas tree lit up with packages and trunks gathered on it. "Isaac must be back," Wyatt said, "with my new sister-in-law."

He'd mentioned Isaac being married, hadn't he? Miranda touched her cheek and wondered if she looked as ravished as she felt.

Isaac met them at the door, but he acted nothing like a happy bridegroom. The pretty brunette from the church raising stood behind him, looking unsure if she should approach or not. "You got trouble, Miranda," Isaac said. "Sheriff Taney is looking for you."

Her stomach turned into a chunk of granite as she stumbled onto the porch. "What have I done? Where's Grandfather?"

"He's at the jailhouse. Evidently he had a run-in with Betsy. Accused her of spying on him and stealing from him. Got real nasty toward her."

Isaac was lying. He had to be. Miranda clenched her teeth.

"What did Elmer do?" Wyatt asked. "The sheriff doesn't put people in jail for having an argument. He doesn't put people in jail for murder, either, come to think of it."

"You don't believe Isaac, do you?" Miranda cried. "Grandfather wouldn't hurt Betsy. He's probably just ranting about his rights."

"I'm telling the truth," Isaac interrupted. "Betsy's scraped up a bit, but she'll be fine. She's with her uncle now, more frightened than anything."

Betsy hurt? Miranda's hands went cold and she began to tremble. "No, it can't be. Grandfather would never lift a hand against a woman. He's the most gentle . . . I have to go see him." She spun on her heel.

"You can't," Isaac said. "The sheriff's pretty hot about it. Everyone here dotes on Betsy, and to see her mistreated riled him up. Anyway, he said to tell you that Mr. Wimplegate needs to learn a lesson. He's not getting any sympathy from you tonight. He said that a night in the pokey will make him more patient with women."

Miranda covered her mouth as desperate tears appeared. The shame of it. Why would God remove Grandfather's reasoning and then leave him to the consequences? Was this the reward for all his years of service advocating for street children? To become their oppressor? How he'd despair if he fully understood what he'd done.

Next thing she knew she was in Wyatt's arms, crying on his black suit. Isaac discreetly closed the front door, leaving them alone on the dark porch.

"He's safe, Miranda. Sheriff won't hurt him. You can see him in the morning."

"But Wyatt, the humiliation. Why? Why would God let him do this? It's a cruel turn when he's been so good his whole life. Why would God destroy his reputation for wisdom and good sense now?"

"I don't pretend to know God's purpose, but just look at how dealing with him has made you stronger. Look how you've changed. If he hadn't needed help, you would have never come to Missouri. You would've stayed in Boston and lived the life you'd always lived, and I would've never met you." He cupped the back of her head and held her against him. "God is still at work. He hasn't forgotten you, or your grandpa."

Rocking slowly, he murmured until her sobs quieted. If she hadn't loved him before, she surely did now. Wiping tears away with the back of her hand, Miranda sniffled. "Will you go see him, please? I won't rest until someone can tell me how he's doing. If I could go—"

But he didn't wait for her to finish. "I'll go, as long as you promise to stay here. No running off to check on Betsy. Not with that man lurking about."

"He isn't interested in me. He works for LeBlanc."

The mention of the name made Wyatt cringe. There was still something he wasn't telling her. If she wasn't so worried about

Grandfather, she would've demanded to know why McSwain called him Yves, but that would wait until morning.

"Don't forget the man who came to town with Jeremiah today. And besides, these hills aren't safe. You stay here with Isaac and . . . what's-her-name. You'll be safe as long as they're around."

"How can I thank you?"

He caught one tardy tear that glistened on her cheek, and then taking her by the chin, Wyatt leaned in until his lips met hers. How warm. How gentle. "It's not your thanks I want," he said.

Another kiss pressed to her forehead and he hurried away toward the jail.

CHAPTER 24

Miranda stood on the porch until Wyatt disappeared into the trees. In all her life she'd never felt so alone. How she wished Father was here to deal with the sheriff. How she missed Mother's calming voice and reassurance. She sat on the porch and hugged her arms tightly as a whole mountainside of trees rustled in the night breeze.

God had crafted this wild land, formed it, and covered it in unrivaled beauty. His creation demonstrated His power and His perfection. But it wasn't perfect, was it? If so, her grandfather wouldn't be in jail right now. He wouldn't be viewing the world through the distorted fog of paranoia. How much of God's power would it take to heal Grandfather? A mere drop from the ocean of His ability? A brief thought from His infinite mind? If He had such power, such goodness, why didn't he heal her grandfather? Why had Grandfather's wisdom faded out of his healthy body?

But then there was Grandmother. The rough porch beam scratched Miranda's face as she leaned into it. Grandmother had been the opposite. Her body had wasted away and she'd been alert for every painful breath. Was that better? Would Miranda ask God to do that to Grandfather?

She didn't like her choices, but it really wasn't her choice, was it? The persistent, comforting voice of reason could finally be heard over her hurt. She might not be able to choose her circumstances, but she still had a choice. She could still choose to show patience and love to Grandfather no matter how he misconstrued her actions. And she could still choose to trust God. She had to believe that God could make the destination worthy, even if the journey was painful.

Just like this journey. So many things she wished she could've done differently, but could she be sorry for the opportunity to know a man like Wyatt?

Inside the house, the piano began to play—heavy, halting chords that denoted a beginner. Pushing off her knees, Miranda rose and gathered her reticule and the money box. Wyatt should be to the jail by now—Grandfather wasn't alone—but time would pass more quickly inside than out here staring into deep shadows watching for Wyatt to reappear.

When she entered the house, the tentative notes on the piano stopped. The young woman on the piano stool turned and pushed up sleeves that were already rolled up to her elbows. "Hello, there."

Composure, even when her heart was broken . . . especially when her heart was broken. Although Miranda couldn't quell the image of Grandfather sitting on a grimy cot behind bars, she didn't want to sit and cry all evening. She removed her hat and gloves. "I'm Miranda Wimplegate. What's your name?"

"Alice Moore . . . Ballentine, I mean. My goodness, this is the first time I've introduced myself with my married name." She smiled prettily, her freckles lost in the blush that tinted her cheeks.

Moore? Inwardly Miranda groaned, but she couldn't hold a family connection against the girl. Not while her own grandfather sat in a cell.

Still holding her gloves and hat, Miranda looked for an empty place to set them. Every available surface was covered with boxes, piles of quilts, and crates of household goods. She pushed the doily on the back of the upright piano over until the bowl of imitation fruit crowded the candlesticks, and balanced her items on the small clearing there. Recognizing Grandfather's suitcase, Miranda lifted it from the couch. "Why is this here?"

Isaac rushed out from the adjoining bedroom, appearing more ruffled than Miranda had ever seen him. "I don't want to be disrespectful to your grandfather . . . especially tonight of all nights . . . but I'd already started moving our rooms around before his trouble. He and Wyatt can share a room, and Alice and I will stay down here."

Immediately the piano burst into a lively jig. If Miranda thought Alice had a blush before, she was blooming scarlet now. Her hands danced enthusiastically over the keys, her eyes wide and her mouth a firm line.

"I understand," Miranda said. It was his house, after all. She looked again at Alice, dressed in a common work dress. Nothing as fine as she'd seen in town, definitely not wedding attire. "Congratulations on your nuptials. When . . . where was the ceremony?"

The music slowed. "We've been married for well-nigh two months now. We just weren't ready to tell Pa yet."

Of all the monkeyshine. How like Isaac to secretly marry a woman and expect her to deceive her parents. How unlike his brother.

"But now you're ready to tell the world?"

"Well, we'd better be. Our little one will be arriving this winter, and we don't want any questionable talk." Alice beamed at Isaac, but it was all Miranda could do not to glare. Isaac had not conducted himself as a married man. Now that she better understood the brothers, she could imagine his gallantries were performed more to irritate Wyatt than to please her. And furthermore, how did the man who ridiculed his brother, shamed him throughout his childhood for being illegitimate, come so near to putting the same stigma on his own child? Suddenly tired, Miranda wanted no more of the day. She'd wait in her room until Wyatt returned home. The newlyweds surely wouldn't mourn her absence.

"If you'll excuse me, it's been a difficult day. I'd like to retire." Miranda gathered her hat and gloves, but as she swept forward, one of the gloves slipped between her fingers and disappeared behind the piano.

Alice hopped up and moved the stool away. "Here, let me help you." Bending to take the thick leg of the piano, she tugged with a grunt. Seeing that it wasn't going to budge without help, Miranda braced herself against the wall, dug her fingers into the top, and pushed while Alice pulled. With the combined effort, the piano rolled across the wood floor, giving Miranda about six inches of room to fish out her glove.

Something was in the way. A large frame was wedged between the back of the piano and the wall. She turned for the lamp, but anticipating her move, Isaac brought it to her.

"I've never seen that before," he said. With a grunt he rolled the piano another foot and grabbed the gilt corner. Slowly, so as to not scrape it, he lifted the portrait out.

By the lamplight, the colors gleamed. Vibrant, decadent, and oh so familiar. The room spun and darkened. Miranda

244

couldn't breathe. Vaguely she felt gentle hands leading her to the sofa. The spinning slowed and the light returned enough to see Alice fanning her with sheet music.

"What's a-matter with her?" she asked. "I'm the one expecting."

Miranda pushed away the flapping music to see Isaac still holding the portrait out at arm's length. Curious, but wary.

"Where did you get that?" Miranda gasped.

He gave her a sardonic grin. "Like I said, I've never seen it before. You need to talk to my brother."

"Wyatt didn't hide it. He would've told me if he knew about it."

Bracing his thigh against the piano, Isaac shoved it against the wall. Then he propped the portrait on the back of the piano, right behind the bowl of imitation fruit. Stepping back to admire his work, he crossed his arms and whistled. "That's an arrogant boss if I ever saw one. Where in the world would Wyatt find a painting like that?"

In Boston. In her family's auction house.

"It'd been sent to the sale barn after all," she said. But that meant Wyatt did know. Her anger battled with her fear. What right did Wyatt have to take it and hide it? She pressed her hand against her stomach, trying to quiet the growing fear that suddenly threw all his proclamations into question. Just minutes ago, when he'd offered to give up everything for her, what was that? What kind of game was he playing?

Miranda gripped the arm of the sofa and pulled herself to her feet. Isaac and Alice jumped out of her way as she forged ahead to the painting. How well the artist had captured the character of this man—the practiced slouch that denoted disinterest, the slight smirk that betrayed his awareness of his audience, as well as his disregard for them. Miranda noted the soft white hands adorned by a thick signet ring. She leaned closer to inspect it. The ring had never been cataloged—Miranda would've remembered. Either way, the almost feminine hands and the sloped shoulders were probably portrayed more in keeping with fashion than an actual representation. As far as she'd noticed, the LeBlancs yoked up as straight as the horizon, but the sneer, the condescension had surged forth undiluted through the generations.

And Wyatt's dishonesty had nearly ruined both the LeBlancs and her family.

One last look at the soft folds of his periwinkle coat and the lace at his wrist—lace that she'd never be able to afford—and she could stand it no longer.

"I'm going upstairs," she said.

"Do you feel well enough?" Alice followed her with quick steps.

"Tell me when Wyatt arrives." Miranda stopped at the stairs and turned to Isaac, who couldn't take his eyes off the canvas. "Don't let anything happen to this painting, Isaac. Please. It's valuable."

But she'd didn't need to tell him that. Already he seemed strangely affected by the portrait. He couldn't take his eyes off it, even to notice his new bride . . . or not-so-new, as the case might be.

"How fine!" Alice fluttered. "Where in the world did he get it?"

The decisive footsteps coming up the porch steps could only be one man's. The door swung open. Wyatt's careworn expression almost roused her pity, but then he saw the painting, and worry was erased by something much more definitive.

Guilt.

His eyes lowered. There was no room for doubt. He knew he was caught. Miranda wanted to run away. She wanted to hide from whatever insincere excuse he offered, but she couldn't. She had to face this. To retreat would be to lose ground, and she and Grandfather had already lost too much.

Tears had already broken through once that night. With no dam to hold them, they coursed freely now. "You knew." She sobbed the words that couldn't be blocked. "You didn't tell me."

"I was going to tell you. . . ." He took a step forward, then thought again. He rubbed his chest. "Your grandpa is fine for the night. He's angry, but as far as jail cells go—"

"Stop!" Miranda cried. "Leave my grandfather out of this. If it weren't for you he wouldn't be in jail—we'd be home. In fact, we could've turned around and gotten back on the train the next day. I wouldn't be stuck here missing home, missing my mother . . ." Miranda choked. She had to regain her composure, but he should answer for his betrayal. He'd known what his secret would cost her. He knew her family could lose their business, but even worse, he knew that she might have to marry Cornelius.

And he didn't care.

Her breath jerked into her lungs in painful gulps. He didn't care. He didn't care about her, or Grandfather, evidently. No use making a spectacle of herself. Hadn't she spent her whole life hiding her opinions? Swallowing her emotions? She could do this one last time. Survive it, that's all she had to do. Survive . . . and get the painting. It wasn't too late.

"It doesn't matter how you got it." She wiped her cheeks and sniffed. "We'll return it to its rightful owners. They'll have to honor the effort we put into reclaiming their property."

Wyatt walked past her to stand before the painting. Seconds ticked by as he stood with his hands on his hips, his foot tapping. Then he turned. "You aren't taking it."

247

Miranda's stomach heaved. She couldn't be hearing him right. Wyatt, her Wyatt, couldn't mean that.

But he didn't look like a man about to change his mind. "It's mine," he said, "and I'm not giving it up."

Wyatt had been willing to sacrifice for her, to give up every-thing for Miranda, but she wasn't interested. She claimed that she needed more time to decide, or maybe she was there for one purpose, to get the portrait, and didn't want the complica-tion. Either way, Wyatt knew he couldn't give Miranda what she wanted, and at this moment she wanted that painting more than she wanted him. As much as her earlier denial had hurt, now he knew where he stood. Maybe he'd been hasty in what he offered her, but he had another chance, and it was possible that something more was at stake. He couldn't close the door on the only family member who'd ever come looking for him.

With a last look at Monsieur LeBlanc, Isaac slapped Wyatt on the back. "Here's a mystery I'd like to see solved, but I think I have more interesting pursuits for the evening."

"Isaac!" Alice's nervous giggle pitched higher. "Don't say such things. And shouldn't we stay up and chaperone them?"

Funny, her seeing the benefit of a chaperone now.

"Don't think they'll be getting into any trouble tonight," Isaac said. "But if you get into a brawl, please don't damage the house. I want my bride kept in style."

The bedroom door closed. Miranda stood at the foot of the staircase with tearstained eyes. His timing couldn't be worse.

"Miranda, more than anything I want to help you and your grandfather. Ever since you arrived I've done all I could—"

"Everything besides turning over our property."

He tilted his head. "Is it really your property? According to your story, it was bought at the auction fair and square."

She pushed back her hair. "You're using my words against me? That painting was not supposed to be sold. It made it to the block by mistake."

"But if the buyer paid real money for it, then it wasn't stolen."

"You didn't buy it. You have no right to that painting. If I was speaking to its rightful owner, I might have to make an offer for it, but as you have no claim to it, I'm wasting my time."

"I might have more claim than you imagine."

He cringed at the way her eyebrow soared to new heights. Her wet lashes fluttered. "The sale barn does not belong to you. If this was sent to the auction—"

"It was sent to me. Addressed to me, from my family."

She hiccupped a sob. "Isaac told me, but I thought he was being cruel."

"What did Isaac tell you?" He hated the way his voice strained. Why did he fear Isaac's opinion?

"He told me you were from some disgraceful family, but I never dreamed that you were in league with them. What is their plan? Did they send this to you for blackmail? Are you holding the painting for a ransom?"

And he'd once worried that this woman lacked courage? Well, she certainly had imagination in abundance.

"I couldn't vouch for the character of my family, especially after what you've told me, but this painting is my only tie to them, and I can't give that up. I made a mistake by offering it to you earlier, but you declined my offer, and I'm not making it again. I'm standing my ground and doing what my Aunt LeBlanc requested."

Miranda didn't breathe. Her eyes blinked rapidly. "Your Aunt

LeBlanc?" Her nose twitched. "The LeBlancs do not know you. They don't acknowledge *us* socially, much less send family heirlooms out to country boys in the mountains."

He'd been patient with her, but she was getting downright insulting. "You claim to know my story. Did you know that my father, Stephan LeBlanc, and my mother, Tarisa, came out west in a wagon train and both died?"

Chin up, her eyes narrowed. "I had not heard that these claims were made against the LeBlanc family, but it doesn't signify. I understand your ma contacted them and they denied any connection."

"I don't know why they'd do that, but it seems that someone has had a change of heart."

She gazed long at Monsieur LeBlanc, but the man didn't speak a word to her. Finally, with a sigh, Miranda turned to him. Her face wasn't quite as red, her demeanor calm. "I'm not as angry as I was. I see what this means to you. You've always held out hope that your family would accept you. You always thought they had made a mistake, and now this . . . of course this looks like a sign of inclusion, but Wyatt, you don't know these people." She tilted her head up to him, her face softened by pity. "I don't mean to insult you—I'm not a LeBlanc, either— but everyone is born to their station."

His hands balled into fists. "Just like everyone is born with lumps on their heads that tell them what they can and can't do?" She could be right. Perhaps his parents weren't married after all. Perhaps his father only worked for the LeBlancs and took their name when he started west, hoping to profit from the association. There really was no link besides what his ma had been told before his parents died and this painting. Forget what it might be worth to a collector, the connection to his family was what he valued. The chance was slim, but he refused to give up. Not yet. "It's my painting and I'm not giving it away."

Tension gathered in her like a river about to burst a dam. "That's your final word? Knowing what it'll cost me, that's your final word?"

Alice's irritating giggle drifted through his parents' bedroom door. Wyatt refocused. "I didn't say I couldn't help you. I've written Miss LeBlanc and I'll see what she suggests. I don't know what the situation is between her brother and her, but they can't blame you."

"Her brother wants the painting back."

"Well, my aunt wants me to have it, and she bought it. I'm not letting Mr. LeBlanc take it until I understand what my aunt wants me to do."

Miranda held his gaze, the challenge clear, until a throaty chuckle from behind the closed door made them both look away.

Her shoulders slumped. "I'm worried about Grandfather. Worried about Betsy. I can't believe you aren't more sympathetic."

"Me? I offered to give up everything for you, didn't I? All I needed to know was that you loved me. But you couldn't say it, so don't lecture me on how I should feel." The words came out of his own mouth, and still they pained him. She hadn't been the only one hurt tonight.

Miranda's eyes blazed. "So all I have to do now is say that I love you, and you'll give it to me? Somehow I find it hard to believe."

Wyatt's throat tightened. "Because if you said it now, it'd be a lie." Miranda didn't argue. With a shaking hand, Wyatt smoothed the doily on top of the piano. "It's getting late, and frankly I'd rather not stay down here any longer with Isaac and his bride. I'll sit outside or at the top of the landing and argue with you all night long, but a better plan might be for both of us to get some shut-eye and see how things lie in the morning."

"How you can sleep when Grandfather is in jail. . . ." Red splotches returned to her eyes faster than raindrops fall. She wavered on her feet.

"Listen to me, Miranda Wimplegate. You're upset and exhausted, but I can't stand here and watch you cry. Either go to bed, or I'll snatch you up, carry you to the rocking chair upstairs, and hold you like a baby. It's your choice."

He watched closely for any sign that she'd welcome his comforting. Silently, he begged her to come to him, but she'd have none of it.

With a last tired flicker of rebellion, she spun around and clumped up the stairs.

Wyatt locked the front door, but before he could snuff out the lamp, Monsieur LeBlanc caught his eye.

So that was the lady in question? Ah, belle. *Now I understand.*

"Then I wish you'd explain it to her," Wyatt answered.

CHAPTER 25

The light from the window assaulted her sore eyes. The darkness hadn't lasted long enough for them to recover from the tears she'd shed last night, but that was behind her. Today would be a day of action. She must make amends to Betsy, secure Grandfather's release, and then persuade Wyatt to let them have the painting. Perhaps Grandfather could talk some sense into him, if Grandfather had any sense left. She rolled onto her back and clenched the sheets in anxious fists. Would she involve the persistent McSwain? No. Not even with Wyatt's betrayal could she trust his secret to King's men. Once in Boston they could try to unravel the mystery of Aunt LeBlanc, but it would be the Wimplegates who restored the painting. Monty King would have to acknowledge that they'd found the mistake and that a disgruntled member of the LeBlanc family was the instigator. Nothing they could've done to prevent it.

The door across the way creaked open. Wyatt's boots thumped into the hall, then stopped outside her door.

"Miranda?" he whispered.

She froze. Her fingers knotted as her grip on the sheets

tightened. A moment of silence, then his sleeve rasped against the door before he clomped down the stairs.

It never would've worked. Although the ruggedness of the hills, the haunting savage beauty fascinated her, it could never be her home. She wasn't like Abigail Calhoun, ready to roll up her sleeves and work in a barn. No, Miranda would miss the gentle civility of Boston. And even if Wyatt were to move to Boston, he wouldn't be accepted. He'd be only a few steps above the paperboys, with his rough manners and unpolished speech. He'd be a detriment to their auction house, offensive to their aristocratic customers.

Besides, she couldn't forgive him for the hurt he'd caused her family. How long had he had the picture? How many times had he lied to her, laughed at them, when he could've helped them all along?

The breeze tossed the curtains and teased her unbound hair. From below she heard the barn door groan. Cautiously, Miranda rolled to her side and raised an inch at a time, until only her eyes peered over the windowsill. A flash of a blue shirt, and she knew Wyatt was in the barn harnessing the mules.

The sale was yesterday. No livestock in the empty barn, but he had found something else to do while Grandfather waited. Her jaw clenched. Well, she didn't need his help, and now that he was gone, she was free to go about her business without him spying on her.

Unsure of what the day would bring, Miranda pulled the curtains closed and reached for her only dress. No one wanted them here; it was time to leave for good. She tightened her stays, tied her petticoat around her waist, and wiggled into her skirt. She fumbled with the buttons in her rush. Grandfather would already be awake. She didn't want him to wait any longer.

On sudden impulse she pushed aside the curtain one last time. There was Wyatt, driving the wagon out of the barn. He lifted his face to the window. Miranda stepped away. He continued to watch, probably waiting for more movement, but when he didn't find what he was looking for, he hawed to the mules and continued down the path to the road.

She bustled to the hall, the scent of fresh rye bread floating up from below. Miranda smoothed the lace on her collar. She'd almost forgotten about Alice and Isaac. At the doorway to the kitchen, she paused. Isaac had his arms wrapped around Alice at the stove, pretending to help her stir the pot. Miranda backed into the parlor, embarrassed. No wonder Wyatt headed out. This wouldn't seem like his home anymore.

The morning sun illuminated the contentious painting still propped on the back of the piano. The oil colors fairly glowed in the light, making the blooms on the tree behind the gentleman visible for the first time. It was a simple painting, really. Its uniqueness lay not in the skill of the painter, but in the character of the subject. A playful arrogance, a man at the apex of his strength who knew he was as yet untested, but who welcomed the challenge. Those who knew the man would appreciate the likeness and the telling, but besides that it wasn't collectible. Not worth the value that'd been placed on it. Not worth losing her family's living. Not worth losing Wyatt. But evidently he thought it worth more than her.

For a moment she could almost imagine the man was Wyatt, turning away from her need with arrogant aloofness. For a moment the proud features resembled the man who'd betrayed her. Drawing near, she trailed her finger over the gilt frame. Opulent scroll work twisted and turned the wood into something moving and alive. Dare she take it? What if Wyatt's story were true? But did it matter? Frederic LeBlanc was the elder child, and the male. He would be the rightful owner and he wanted it back.

First things first. Grandfather. She looked again at the face, already growing familiar, and wondered . . .

"Does he remind you of anyone?"

Miranda startled. She dropped her hand and stepped back guiltily at Isaac's approach. "I know the family, and there is a resemblance. I just can't believe Wyatt had it the whole time."

"Had you mentioned you were looking for something of the LeBlancs, I could've told you that was the family Wyatt thought he belonged to, and after seeing this painting . . ." Isaac's eyes traveled up the artwork.

"You don't think it's true, do you?" Miranda asked.

Isaac shrugged. "For Wyatt's sake, I hope it is. He's been disappointed by them once already. Why would they send this if they were only going to reject him again?"

"Wyatt LeBlanc?" Miranda bit her lip. "He just doesn't belong in their world. If you knew them—"

"It's not Wyatt. It's Yves Andres Thibault LeBlanc. Quite a mouthful for us simple folks, so Ma and Pa took to calling him by his initials which quickly ran together. Y. A. T., you understand. Anyway, his pa was from somewhere back East. He left his family and got holed up in St. Louis for a spell, where he met Wyatt's ma. They claimed that's where they got married—even left a fancy certificate with my ma when they died—but when she sent it to the LeBlancs, they said it wasn't valid. No marriage had taken place."

"Why didn't you tell me this at first? Why act like he was delusional?" Miranda asked.

"I didn't know what town they were from, and you never

mentioned the LeBlancs." Isaac stopped when Alice appeared in the doorway to the kitchen.

"Breakfast is ready, Isaac. Won't you join us, Miranda?"

This morning, everything about Alice spoke of a freshly scrubbed keeper of the home. Clean as a shiny apple. Clean and not wanting to be dirtied by her husband's petty rivalry.

"No, thank you, Alice. I've got to go to Grandfather."

Alice flapped the kitchen towel over her arm. "Well, as soon as I clean up breakfast, we're going to town for shopping. I could use your help in ordering some new linens. It's so hard to judge by the pictures in the store's catalog."

"Do you know Mrs. Rinehart?" Miranda asked.

"I know who she is, but she probably wouldn't know me."

"Have Isaac take you to her house before you order. It'd be worth your time."

"What do you think, Isaac? Would she receive us? I've heard her house is the finest in the county."

Isaac still studied Miranda. Her questions hung between them. "I'll take you as soon as we finish breakfast. Be there in a second."

Still smiling, Alice twirled her towel and waltzed into the kitchen. Isaac waited for her to exit, then he leaned against the piano. "Did you know it's possible to tell yourself a story about how you were wronged, about how your friend is your enemy . . . to tell yourself this story so often that it grows until the weed little resembles the shoot it began as? Then when you meet someone new, you show them the ugly thistle instead of the innocent seeds that began the whole thing." Isaac and his sad poet eyes. "You were just someone passing through, or I would've been more careful with what I said. I didn't think it'd make much difference one way or another."

But it did. Had she taken the story of Wyatt's parents seriously, she wouldn't have wasted her time looking all over creation for that painting. No, she would've found it sooner, he would've refused to give it to her, and she could've rushed home and married Cornelius before she realized how much she'd be missing.

She sighed. "Maybe I was too eager to believe you, but it really doesn't matter what I think. The truth will come out. I just hope my family doesn't lose everything when it does."

If Isaac looked chastised, Miranda had no doubt he'd recover before she reached the jail. Especially with Alice cooking eggs and gravy for him. She set out and immediately wished she'd brought her parasol for the heat. The sun warmed through her dark hat, making her scalp tingle. The day promised to be scorching. She'd better get Grandfather somewhere safe while it was still early. But where? Perhaps it was time to go home.

She'd just reached the corner of the square when to her wonderment she saw Betsy approaching. Forgetting who might be watching, Miranda nearly trotted to join her outside the sheriff's office.

"Oh, Miss Miranda," Betsy snuffled. "I feel so sorry for what happened."

Miranda threw her arms around Betsy and hugged her tight. "I'm the one who needs to apologize. You didn't deserve Grandfather's anger." She stepped back and took Betsy's chin in her hand. "Now, show me where he hurt you."

"That's just it. I'm not really hurt. He shoved me down, but my skirt padded my fall. If he were Josiah, I would've torn into him and held my own, but it being your grandpa and all, I didn't think it'd be proper. Then he was hollering at me and carrying on, so I didn't know what to do. I just sat there as dumb as a rain barrel and started crying. Those men who pulled him away thought I was crying cause he'd done me harm, but mostly I was just surprised and feeling sorry. I didn't mean for him to be in trouble with the law."

Her straightforward account wrung Miranda's heart. Betsy didn't deserve that treatment, and the sheriff was right to punish anyone who treated the dear girl so harshly. If only it weren't her grandfather.

"Is he in here?" Miranda motioned to the brick building.

"Yes, ma'am. Mr. Wyatt came by already to check on him, but the sheriff was gone, so he couldn't get him out."

Wyatt had been there already? "Well, I'm glad to see you well. I would've visited you last night, but Wyatt wouldn't let me."

"It was for the best. My uncle might have been unkind. He had to send a letter with Postmaster Finley to my folks to tell them before they read about it in the paper."

The paper? This was much worse than the chicken attack, but Mr. Murphy couldn't spare them this time. Grandfather's shocking behavior deserved censure. The mangy dog running across the street blurred before her eyes. People already resented him. Now he'd be even further exposed to abuse. With her shoulders feeling like they supported Samson's pillars, Miranda trudged toward the jail.

"You don't need to come any farther, Betsy. I don't know what temper I'll find Grandfather in, and I can't allow you to endure his vitriol again."

"That's what Wyatt said, too, in plainer words. I'm awfully sorry, Miss Miranda. If I'd known he was going make a fuss—" She bit her lip as her blond eyelashes bounced back tears.

Walking inside the stone building, Miranda felt the air cool, but the dampness from the rock walls could be tasted. Slowly her eyes adjusted to the shadowy room. Grandfather was lying crumpled on a narrow bunk that stretched the length of his cell. His rough blanket reached no farther than his knees, and his mouth hung slightly agape in the slackness of deep slumber. Miranda clutched her waist and rushed to press herself against the bars. "Grandfather?"

He blinked drowsily, stretched his legs to the ground, and pulled himself up to sit. "It's about time you came. I've been detained since last night, and it's inexcusable that Wyatt didn't tell you. I knew he couldn't be trusted." He tried to smooth his white hair that popped up like the lid on a tin can.

The cold bars dug into her body. If it weren't for her hat, she would've had her face wedged between the iron bars. He moved slowly, resigned, and perhaps that was for the better. The last thing she wanted was for him to be excitable. "When is the sheriff coming back?" she asked.

Grandfather ran his hand over the cot beneath him. "Oddly enough, the man didn't feel compelled to report his whereabouts to me."

Sensing his acceptance, she stepped back and scanned the rest of the room. Bookshelves of law books, a desk, a gun rack, and coat hangers. Next to the back door, a sweating bucket sat with a ladle handle hung on its side. "Are you thirsty?" Not waiting for him to answer, she sloshed a cupful of water to him, grateful that at last she could do something to help.

And that was about all she could do for the next hour. Although Grandfather had calmed, he remained convinced that Betsy had opposed him in some vile manner and that she was conspiring against him to cause his business dealings to fail. The longer they spoke, the more Miranda's unease grew. Clearly, Grandfather could not be convinced of Betsy's innocence, and because of that the girl wasn't safe. And neither was Grandfather. One more incident and some of Betsy's rough defenders might take justice into their own hands. She'd seen what they'd intended to do with the man who lurked about. What kind of punishment would be handed out for laying a hand on one of their children? Miranda shivered at the sight of the empty gun rack.

The clip-clop of hooves sounded. Dust floated through the barred window as the sheriff tethered his horse and waddled inside. Seeing Miranda, he sighed and tossed his gun on his desk. His weathered face had seen more years than she could guess, and although his movements were slow, they were deliberate and steady. "This here's your grandpappy, I'd guess."

Miranda stood, glad to see Grandfather had, as well. "Yes, sir. I don't know precisely what occurred last night, but I can assure you that he's never—"

The sheriff held up his hand, stopping her. He removed his hat, releasing a flood of pure white hair. "Miss Wimplegate, if you'd accompany me outside, please." His wide palm extended toward the door.

Grandfather grasped the bars. "Now wait a minute. Whatever you have to say needs to be said right here. I'm the boss here. She's not my guardian."

"We can stay here," Miranda said. "I don't want to upset him."

"Too late. Outside?" Even though he was the sheriff, he looked uncertain as to whether she'd comply.

She stepped into the sun, then followed the sheriff to the green of town square, away, she presumed, from earshot. Sheriff Taney stopped under an oak tree.

"Miss Wimplegate, there's a train coming through today just after noon, and it's my suggestion that you and your grandfather be on it."

261

Miranda cast an anxious glance to the jail. "Today? We can't leave today."

"Then it's quite possible that your grandfather won't be able to leave for quite some time, because if he continues to gallivant around town, throwing accusations against our children, trying to borrow money from our citizens, and harassing our local businesses, he will be facing charges of disorderly conduct. Did you know that I've had to personally escort him from the bank on almost a daily basis?"

She could feel her face reddening. "I . . . we . . . we tried to stop him, but we never knew where he was going."

"Well, they wouldn't loan him money, and he took offense at their refusal. Every morning he marched in there and disrupted their business while insisting that they fund his latest scheme. Now with Miles Bullard at his side, people are getting tetchy. He's even more of a threat."

How had she not known? But it wasn't fair to let others deal with her responsibility.

The sheriff slid his hands into his pockets and scuffed a knot of clover with his toe. "Miss Wimplegate, I don't hold you accountable for Elmer's behavior. I've seen the years play out on many a fine man just like this, and there's no shame in what's happening, but we can't allow him to wreak havoc on everyone else. Do you have any family back home?"

"Oh yes," Miranda stammered. "My family would never allow him to act this way, but he worsened when we left home. My father would know what to do."

He nodded with satisfaction. "I'm glad to hear it. Then the sooner you get back to your father, the better. Can you have your things together by noon?"

What things? Miranda didn't have anything besides the

clothes on her back and her reticule. Grandfather's bag had been packed by Isaac. But what about the painting? She needed to talk to Wyatt. Perhaps after having time to think it over, he might decide to let them buy it from him.

"I need to go to the sale barn first. It belongs to Grandfather, and I need to speak to the manager before we leave."

The sheriff wasn't fooled. "I'm sure Wyatt would appreciate that. I'll take Elmer to the house to gather his things. I really don't think he should go about unsupervised."

"Thank you, sir." She couldn't say anything else, still numbed by the sudden news of her departure.

"You come back anytime, Miss Wimplegate. You and your family are welcome here. Like I said, we won't hold this incident against you'uns."

That was one person who'd forgiven them, but how many others had Grandfather offended?

CHAPTER 26

Wyatt tossed an armful of hay over the fence to the goat, who stared with dull eyes, clearly unimpressed. Chores at the barn went much faster now that they sold out every week. If it weren't for this lone billy who'd gotten away from his new owner, the pens would be empty. He could be thankful for that. The clean scent of the hay was one smell Wyatt could appreciate about the place. He didn't admire it quite as much as the smell of rhubarb pie, but it was close. Dusting the straw off his shirt, he smiled ruefully at the memory of Miranda's pie. He'd enjoyed it. Honest. But what he'd enjoyed even more was that she'd baked it for him. Who would've thought she'd go through the trouble?

But that was before she knew about the painting. Now she wouldn't toss him a rope if he was neck deep in quicksand. Wyatt hadn't expected something so frivolous as a fancy painting of a man dressed like a sissy coming between him and the woman he loved, but without the painting he'd never have a chance at her, either. If only she believed in him.

He caught the mules' harness and led them to the shade to wait while he dusted up inside. Over the years, Wyatt had always seen this place as the pinnacle of his ambition. His pa always wanted to have an honest-to-goodness sale barn. Traveling the mountains, from settlement to settlement, auctioning whatever people brought on market day was no way to support a family. Pa wanted the people to come to him. He wanted to play host to the commerce and the camaraderie that took place during a sale day. And that was his dream for his sons. But his sons left, one by one, until only Wyatt and Isaac remained. Isaac always hanging back, never willing to outright compete against Wyatt. Never brave enough to challenge his little brother, but always there to pop his bubble, to criticize his attempts, to try to remind Pa that he didn't belong. And Pa had done his best to even the score. Wyatt was showered with love to make up for his brothers' lack of acceptance, which only widened the gap.

When the wide door swung shut behind him, the hallway darkened, but the arena, lit by the high windows, drew him forward. Maybe it was time to go. If he didn't see Aunt Corinne and the other LeBlancs with his own eyes, he'd always wonder. He had to know. If his parents were married, it meant that they hadn't lied to the Ballentines, and it meant that for some reason, someone in Boston had wanted to discredit him.

He climbed the steps to the platform and took the gavel in his hands. His pa had been so adamant that he cherish the sale barn—he'd almost made the handing over of the gavel a ceremony—but was that who Wyatt was born to be? Was he a man who'd be content here hidden in the hills, or was he willing to risk everything he knew for an uncertain life in a busy, crowded city?

That night, pruning the trees after Miranda had left got him to thinking. What did you do with a dead branch? You lopped it off. When something stopped growing, it started decaying and would soon affect the health of the whole tree. That's how he felt about this auction. He'd given it time and it'd borne fruit for its season, but autumn had come. It was time to cut loose and look for growth elsewhere. Like Boston.

One thing—the only thing—he knew for sure about his natural parents was that they were adventurers. Hadn't they started out for a new life? Hadn't they set out for the great unknown? Whether or not he had any LeBlanc blood, whether he was a poor relation or no relation at all, he knew this about his parents—they hadn't been paralyzed by security. They'd longed for a new start, so it should be no surprise that he wished for the same.

And that wasn't all he wished for.

The big door squawked. Wyatt swung the gavel into his palm and waited. The ray of light widened as the door swung open. Wyatt's blood pulsed as the outline of a very familiar female darkened the doorway and proceeded to the arena.

She had hidden from him this morning, but here she was. Had something changed? Wyatt stepped around the table on the platform. "Did you visit your grandpa?"

She shivered, her eyes burning brightly. "Yes. He's with the sheriff at the house now, getting ready for our journey." She hesitated by the first row of seats.

"You've no call to be upset with me," Wyatt said. "I've done everything in my power to ease your way. I've given you everything I could—"

"Everything except for the very item I must have." Her voice trembled. "You had it all along—"

"That's not true," he said. "I only got it Saturday. You were just coming to tell me that you and Elmer were leaving town."

"So that's why you wouldn't let me in your house when I brought the pie?" She covered her mouth, before gaining control and hiding her hand behind her again. "I didn't come to argue. I wanted us to part as friends."

If only she knew how this was tearing him in two. Wyatt stepped down from the platform and rested his hand on the arena fence.

"Let's be honest, Miranda. What if I'd given you that painting? What then?"

Her head lifted. "Then Grandfather and I could return it to the LeBlancs, and our auction house would be cleared."

He felt like he was fixing to grab ahold of a wasps' nest, but he had to know. "And what about us? Once I hand over that picture, who am I to you?"

Miranda rubbed her nose as her eyes darted to the ground. "If you ever come to Boston, you are welcome to call on us— Grandfather and me, that is. We've found work for several of the young men who live around our auction house. Maybe we could help you."

His shoulders melted. Not the answer he was hoping for, but he'd known the risks. And Wyatt was not a quitter. This painting wouldn't always come between them. If she was willing to see him again, then there was hope. But he needed to give her something to show his intent—some piece of him that would remind her of his love when Cousin Cornelius came calling. With a grunt, Wyatt extended the gavel to Miranda. It wasn't fancy, but until she'd arrived, it was his most treasured possession.

"Keep this," he said. Probably not a fitting gift for a lady, but Miranda covered her surprise and accepted it just the same.

"It's not what I was hoping for. . . ."

The massive barn door swung open again. Hands in his pockets, completely unaware of the tension he was wading into, Isaac moseyed up past the first row of seats and leaned against the arena bars. "Miranda, Wyatt . . . seeing how you're both here, I'm going to guess you don't know." He looked from one to the other, drawing out the suspense until Wyatt was ready to wring his neck. "You know that painting? It's gone."

Wyatt's mouth went dry. "What do you mean?"

"Alice and I went to town, and when we came back it was gone. I thought maybe you'd put it behind the piano or upstairs, but I didn't find it. Even Elmer and the sheriff helped me look."

And here she was pretending to know nothing about it.

"Came to say good-bye, did you?" Wyatt hated the bitterness in his voice, but he couldn't help himself. Not since his brothers had jeered at the letter from the LeBlancs had he felt so disrespected. Inconsequential. "You're just here covering for McSwain—making sure I didn't go home and catch him in the act."

"If he has it, it's your fault," she sputtered. "You left it unguarded."

His fault? Wyatt had trouble seeing straight. Just like that his gift, his hopes, were gone. Aunt Corinne would never trust him now, and Miranda was blaming him?

"Now, Miranda," Isaac stepped forward and took her hand. "According to Sheriff Taney, you're leaving today. You don't want to leave like this."

Her face was tight. Her brows knit together, nearly meeting. As the gentleman, Wyatt knew he should be the one to offer peace, but she hadn't apologized. Instead, she'd blamed him. How could he forgive her when she wasn't repentant? When she'd used their relationship to conspire against him?

Slowly, she allowed her indignation to subside. She looked bored now that her act was over. No use in pretending to be hurt any longer. She'd got what she'd come for. No wonder she was in a hurry to get back home.

"Have a good trip," he finally managed.

Her thick black lashes fluttered as she lowered her eyes to the gavel. "Thank you for the souvenir. It wasn't what I wanted from you, but maybe someday I'll understand."

He was spent. Too bruised to decipher her meaning. She'd played him and won.

"Do you want me to walk you home?" Isaac asked. "Maybe Alice can make you a dinner basket for the train."

They walked into the bright light streaming in through the open barn door. Wyatt pounded his fist against the auction table. For once Isaac was right. He didn't want to part under such sorry circumstances.

"Wait!" He marched to catch them at the door. Miranda turned to him, the sunlight lifting a deep red shade from her dark hair. She stood her ground as he approached. "I'm still coming to Boston. I intend to come up there and get this painting back, so be watching for me."

"You're still not willing to let this go?" To look at her exhausted face you'd think she was the one who'd spent the night in the slammer—which is exactly where she belonged. "You don't know the power of the people you're up against."

"They don't know about me," he said.

"C'mon, Miranda," Isaac said. "You'd best hurry if you're going to catch the train."

With her proud back just as straight as ever, she stepped outside and let the massive door crash closed behind her. The noise echoed through the empty barn, the sound quaking against his chest, but he'd made up his mind.

The barn was Isaac's. True, it still belonged to the Wimplegates, but Isaac could manage it. As far as Wyatt's future, well, he'd start out in Boston just as he'd planned, although he couldn't be too excited about what awaited him there. He'd done gone and lost the painting, just as Aunt Corinne had warned him against. Thanks to Miranda and McSwain, he'd failed. But Aunt Corinne knew something, and learning from her was the best he could hope for.

There wasn't much trash left to gather. He changed the saw-dust covering inside the pen and raked it out smooth while wondering over Miranda's departure. Did she pause in his room to look it over one last time? Did she linger in the kitchen remembering their time together? Did she duck beneath the sycamore tree?

By now she was standing on the platform at the depot, where he first saw her. Somehow his painting was crated up and wait-ing to ship, although whether the finagling was done by her or through McSwain, he didn't know. Well, he'd ask her once he got to Boston. If Corinne LeBlanc wanted it back, he'd know where to look for it.

Now finished, Wyatt locked up the barn. He jangled the keys one last time. After this, it'd be Isaac's. Once he'd decided to change his life, he wouldn't look back. Morosely, he walked home, trying not to let the recent events taint all his fond memo-ries of this place. Once in the city, he knew he'd miss it.

Near Widow Sanders' house, Wyatt heard a grunt. He turned in at her gate and followed his ears to her garden. There he saw the infamous Lady Godiva, still wearing the apron, laying on her side in the rocky soil. The widow knelt beside her.

"Are you okay?" Wyatt couldn't tell who had fallen first, but Widow Sanders didn't seem to be pinned.

"I finally toppled her! Now if I can just wrestle her to the burn pile."

After some consideration, Wyatt grabbed the statue by the

bare shoulder and the base and hefted it as Widow Sanders directed him. Dropping it so he could finally take a breath, Wyatt brushed off his hands.

"I reckon your visitor is gone."

"Him?" She waved her hand. "He took out after breakfast, didn't say where he was going. And then he ran back here lickety-split, snatched his bags, and lit out."

Of course he'd left with the Wimplegates. Just as he'd suspected. Wyatt thanked her and continued down the hill, then back up the mountain to his house. If Isaac and Alice had escorted the Wimplegates to the train station, they wouldn't be back yet.

So why was his front door standing open?

CHAPTER 27

Miranda stood on the last step of the railroad car, peering out of the train to the platform. The road that curled up the hill to Pine Gap yawned open in the trees like the mouth of an empty cave. The train whistle blew. For the third time, the porter told her to have a seat, but not yet. Wyatt might still come.

It wasn't too late. Surely he didn't want her to leave both empty-handed and brokenhearted. Given some time, he'd realize how hurt she was, how he'd wronged her, and knowing Wyatt, he'd feel awful about it. Beneath her feet the floor swayed. Wheels clanked. Again the whistle screeched. Her hand formed an iron claw around the brass rail. The thick forest swallowed them, blotting out the chance for any last-minute apology from him.

Miranda weaved her way to the seat beside Grandfather. His eyelids sagged, his chin dipped. Still exhausted from his ordeal in the jail, Grandfather had been taciturn all morning. Miranda understood. She too had much to consider.

They shouldn't have parted like that. She'd come to the barn to tell him that although they were on opposing sides, it didn't affect her opinion of him.

At first he'd played along—given her his gavel, reflected her wistfulness back at her—but as soon as the painting disappeared, how quickly he'd turned the tables and tried to blame her. But she had nothing to do with McSwain's theft. Miranda had been completely honest. . . . Well, maybe she'd hid some things in the beginning, but now Wyatt was the one refusing to cooperate.

Grandfather slept on, leaving Miranda alone with her regrets. What would become of them? Would Monty King keep his word and use all the means at his disposal to ruin them? Would Cornelius speak for them, even if she wouldn't marry him? And she wouldn't. She knew now that it wouldn't be fair—not to Cornelius and not to herself.

And what about Wyatt? What did he hope to accomplish in Boston? Whatever misinformation the LeBlanc lady had would be corrected soon enough. Wyatt would be exposed as a fraud, but this would be much worse than just his brothers mocking him. He shouldn't have accused her, the one friend he had on the coast. Had he refrained from that last threat, she and Grandfather would've helped him. They might even be able to get him a job at the docks.

The car door opened and McSwain stepped inside. Could this day get any worse? Miranda had hoped that the snub she gave him at the station would've kept him at bay, but it'd only lasted five miles. His salt-and-pepper walrus whiskers curtained each side of his mouth, which was puckered into a whistle. Grandfather stretched. Miranda frowned. The tune stopped.

"No hard feelings, I hope." He dropped into the seat across from her and pulled at his too-tight collar.

"I have nothing to say to you." She laid a hand over her wrist, covering her bracelet.

"Sure you do. You have lots to say, but you're too scared to tell me how mad you are. You've been here a month, and I marched in and took the prize."

Miranda's ears prickled with heat. "I found it first."

The fat on McSwain's pointed forehead formed rolls. "But you weren't clever enough to get it. All that time flirting with that chawbacon, and it got you nowhere. I was quite afraid he'd give in to your charms, but at the end that yokel turned out to be smarter than you thought."

Suddenly the swaying of the train soured her stomach. Is that what Wyatt thought? That she'd been trying to manipulate him ever since she arrived in Pine Gap? Did he wonder if she'd been feigning her regard for him just to get the painting?

Of course he did. Miranda's heart felt covered with grime. When he'd refused to give her the painting, how her manner toward him had changed! The only decision she'd made that might clear her name had been when she refused to marry him. If she was truly playing with his affections, she would've promised him anything, but she could hardly boast of a rejection to prove her loyalty.

No wonder he didn't trust her. It hurt to be misunderstood by someone she loved. Yes, she could say she loved him. She loved him enough to know that marrying her would only cause him heartache in the long run, but could it be worse than the agony she felt at their hateful parting?

Miranda missed her mother. She missed the comfort of her house and family. In her world she was a saint reaching down to help the unfortunate, not a thief who expected friends to hand over their treasures. She didn't like this depiction of herself. It was unfair. Mostly unfair.

Time to put this awful experience behind her and immerse herself back into the orderly, staid existence she'd always known. Time to go home.

Wyatt approached the house with caution. Maybe those dirty skunks hadn't left town just yet. Wishing he had a gun, he eased onto the porch. He passed quickly by the windows and listened beside the door before rounding the corner.

Piano music.

Something fancy. Dainty. Miranda?

Even though he didn't know what to expect, seeing the Arky was still a shock.

Hearing his entrance, the blond shaggy man turned on the piano stool, his hands staying in plain sight on the keyboard. His wardrobe hadn't improved since sale day, but his beard was gone, revealing a closely barbered jaw.

"Mr. LeBlanc, I apologize for trespassing, but as you might not want our meeting to be public, I didn't want to wait on the front porch."

Mr. LeBlanc? Wyatt tensed. "We don't cotton to people sniffing around uninvited."

"I know." Slowly he completed his turn and deliberately rested his hands on his knees. "Rarely are people eager to see me in my line of work, but I hope you may be the exception."

This man didn't know the danger he was in. Miranda had left Wyatt with a barrel of anger ready to be dumped on the first person to cross him.

"What are you? A doctor?"

The man's plain face remained smooth. "I'm a private investigator hired by Miss Corinne LeBlanc."

Wyatt closed the door behind him. "You're working with McSwain?"

"Not hardly. He was hired by Monty King. He's the one desperate to recover the painting . . . and to silence you."

Why should Wyatt trust a man who made his hair a different

color than God intended? He wasn't a large man, but he was compact. Looked like he could move quickly in a tussle. Wyatt sat on the side of the sofa nearest the door. "I guess I'll shut up and let you do the talking."

"First, let me introduce myself. I'm William Sears. I've been retained by Miss Corinne LeBlanc to look after the family's interest."

"Does Miss LeBlanc often need the use of spies?"

William's face grew deathly still. "If it weren't for Miss Le-Blanc, you would be left out in the cold." A second passed before he could continue. "She hired me when she became convinced that Monty King was taking advantage of her older brother. Frederic LeBlanc has few talents, and managing a large estate isn't one of them. As the third son, he never expected to have resources at hand, so he allowed the solicitors to continue as they had for his oldest brother, Armand. Only Armand kept his eye on the accounts. I'm afraid Frederic has allowed Monty to dispose of their property unchecked."

Wyatt leaned forward. "So Armand died, leaving his little brother in charge? What does their sister want with me?"

"This is where it gets interesting. When going through the family's books, looking for evidence of Monty King's misdeeds, I found a letter from Hart County, Missouri. A family by the name of Ballentine had written asking once again for any information on a child that had been orphaned on the Santa Fe Trail out of Independence. According to the letter, they'd written the family before, but they didn't accept the answer they'd received."

Wyatt felt as if he'd just swallowed a cupful of baking soda. He knew the answer, but William had guessed, as well.

"Judging from the letter, it sounded like the attorney had

claimed that the child was unknown and possibly illegitimate. I thought it odd that the family wouldn't make further inquiries about a child, so I presented the discovery to Miss LeBlanc. The information she had was startling."

"My parents were married?"

"Your father was Stephan LeBlanc, the second son. He had the heart of an adventurer and struck out on his own, determined to seek his fortune. Of course, his older brother Armand granted him a hefty amount to invest once he got settled and started in whatever industry he discovered, but then word came back that his wagon train was attacked by Comanches with no survivors. On hearing the news, all of Boston mourned."

"I know about the attack. But my real ma and pa died of scarlet fever before that. They left me with Ma and Pa Ballentine, who abandoned the wagon train and headed back to Missouri before the Comanches attacked."

"Fortunate decision, but the LeBlancs had no knowledge of a child, and with the whole wagon train massacred, you see why they would've been suspicious."

"Didn't they care to search it out? Why just ignore my claim?"

"In regards to your legitimacy, the letter from the Ballentines spoke of a marriage certificate that they had naïvely mailed to Boston. Of course, Monty King denied receiving it, but I did my own investigation and found them on the registry in St. Louis. They were married months before they set out on the trail. Perhaps Stephan wrote home and told the family, but Monty hid the letter? All we know for sure is that it was kept quiet, even from his younger sister, Miss Corinne."

It had been true, what Ma had told him. His parents had been a respectable, loving couple looking for a new life together.

Slowly the knot in his chest began to soften. "But why does she believe now?"

William stood up. "She doesn't. That's where I come in. She sent me to see what kind of man you were, and I'm pleased to report that you are well-respected here. Sending you the portrait was another test. You might be family, you might not, but if you were a scheming money-grubber, then you would have sold that painting to the first bidder."

"But I failed the test, didn't I?" Wyatt gripped his knees. "The portrait is gone."

"I sat in your barn and watched McSwain carry it out of the house."

He grimaced. "While the Wimplegates egged him on."

William shook his head. "McSwain isn't working with the Wimplegates. They're just the unlucky victims to the whole affair. Had Miss Corinne any idea they were going to be blamed, she would've considered another method. Hopefully once the LeBlancs get the portrait back they'll release the Wimplegates from their obligation."

Wyatt looked to the clock. Had the train left already? It had. Miranda had left town with his accusations ringing in her ears. She hadn't deserved his anger.

"The painting is on its way back to Boston," William said. "But as for you, it would be helpful if you had something . . . anything from your parents. A baby blanket? A pocket watch?"

Wyatt held out empty hands. "Nothing. When my parents died, the rest of the wagon train burned their possessions to keep the illness from spreading. Nothing was left behind. Ma never told me about anything special." He scanned the room, hoping something would jog a memory, but no.

William threaded his fingers together. "Well, we'll do the

best we can. Are you willing to return to Boston with me? It might not be easy, but I suspect it'll be ultimately rewarding."

This was real. He was going to meet the people he'd dreamed of for years. "But what will they think of me? This family wanted nothing to do with me. And if this solicitor went through all the trouble of sending McSwain out to stop me, they aren't going to welcome me with open arms."

"Like all families, they have their successes and their less-than-exemplary members. Your uncle Frederic gets by, but he has no head for business. He's allowed the trust to be mismanaged by Monty King and doesn't even know what he's squandered. On the other hand, Miss Corinne is a lady of rare intelligence and grace." His eyes softened. "She's entirely undervalued. They don't know her worth."

Wyatt raised an eyebrow. "But you do?"

William cleared his throat. "Miss LeBlanc is a lady of very high social standing. She is unattainable for a man like me."

"I know the feeling."

"Are you referring to Miss Wimplegate?" William laughed. "I don't think you understand. When the oldest brother, Armand, died, the fortune passed to Frederic only because your father, the second son, was presumed dead. That's why Monty King had to keep your claim a secret. You see, as your father's son, you outrank your uncle Frederic. A lady such as Miss Wimplegate is completely below your notice, because you, Mr. Yves LeBlanc, are the heir to the entire LeBlanc family fortune."

Chapter 28

All the way from the train station, Miranda had rested her forehead against the glass window of the hired hack and tried to filter out Grandfather's railing. Father hadn't released her from his welcome embrace before Grandfather began his list of grievances that he'd perfected on the eternal train ride home. By the time they reached her family's three-story townhouse, Miranda didn't wait to be handed down, but bolted out and raced up the walk. Bursting through the doors, she didn't stop running until she fell into her mother's arms. Laying her head on her shoulder, Miranda clung while her mother swayed and cooed, just as she had when Miranda was a child and had suffered some boo-boo.

"Here you are, my girl. Home safe. What a journey you've taken. What tales you must have for us." She smoothed Miranda's hair and shooed the maid out of the study.

Safely tucked away, inhaling the comforting lavender scent of her mother, Miranda didn't want to raise her head. All she wanted was to be pampered and protected after her horrible ordeal.

"It's good to be home. You have no idea—"

"Well, when we saw the odd assortment of items Grandfather shipped back, it confirmed what you'd said in the telegrams. And then when your trunks arrived without you . . ."

"Thank you for shipping my clothes to Cincinnati. I never want to wear that gown again."

"I'd think not." With a last squeeze, Mother took her by the shoulders and straightened. "But I mustn't monopolize your time. Others are expecting you." Her narrow face crunched into an amusing grimace as she tilted her head toward the high-backed chair in front of the fireplace.

Cornelius, patiently waiting his turn.

Standing in her home, Miranda could almost imagine that the place called Pine Gap was a figment of her imagination. That it only existed in some oil painting or between the pages of a book. She was Miranda Wimplegate, citizen of Boston. The portrait had been recovered, and although she couldn't take credit for the discovery, at least the name of the Wimplegate Auction House had been cleared. On Monday she'd be at the warehouse working on the catalog for the next sale. Nothing had changed.

But it had. She had changed.

"You've returned, after all." Despite his light summer suit and straw hat, Miranda couldn't stop marveling at how he'd aged. Then again, she wouldn't be surprised to find a few gray strands of her own after all she'd been through. Cornelius stood with a newspaper in one hand and his portfolio at his feet. "I was on my way to a patient and thought I'd stop by to see how my favorite cousin is doing."

Funny how spotless he looked. Untried, untouched. Had any emotion ever ruffled him?

Mother politely withdrew, much to Miranda's dismay. Miranda

held her reticule in her palm and felt the gavel through the brocade fabric.

"How was your trip?"

"Miserable . . ."

"I can only imagine."

"But exhilarating at the same time. But mostly miserable." Or at least that's how she felt now. Whatever euphoria she'd experienced had vanished now that Wyatt believed her a thief.

Gently she spun the world globe that stood by the bookshelf. "You'll want to see Grandfather, won't you?"

Cornelius tucked his chin into his chest. "Of course, but first I'd like to have a word with you, if you don't mind. You've been gone for two months, and it just reminded me that we have waited long enough. We are of age, of means, and it's time to set the date for the wedding, Miranda. There's no reason to wait any longer."

"I can think of several." Her fingers skimmed over country after country as they spun on the axis. "The most obvious reason is that I'm not in love with you. As it stands now, I don't see how I benefit from this arrangement. If love isn't what you're offering me, then you must present your case more clearly."

"I must?" He smirked as he tossed the newspaper onto the table. "Listen to you. I never thought to hear my Miranda tell me what I must do. It's charming, truly."

Charming like a child who stomps her foot to get her way? "Father was right. This journey taught me much. It taught me that occasionally I have to act on my own behalf. I have to decide what I want and be willing to accept the consequences."

"You figured this out on your own, or did someone help you?" Cornelius walked to the world globe and halted it in its orbit. Startled, Miranda lifted her eyes. His mouth twisted and he shook his head. "Don't forget, Miranda, I know you. I know what you're capable of and what's beyond you. It's my professional opinion that this determination is not your own idea. You didn't independently make this decision. Instead, you were influenced. That is a failing of yours, you know. You are easily influenced by more choleric personalities."

Was he right, or was he the choleric personality influencing her now? She rubbed her forehead, worried about the tension building there. Either way, Miranda was certain that she did not want to spend the rest of her life with this man. But footsteps in the hallway alerted her to another man making his appearance.

"Where's my girl?" Father bellowed. "You left me in the carriage with Grandfather without as much as a by-your-leave."

Pressing her palms together in thanks, Miranda skipped across the study to meet Father halfway. Another hug, just as heartfelt as her mother's, although accompanied by more cracking joints.

"I am so proud of you," he said. "Handling Grandfather and keeping up with King's man out there all by yourself. I don't know how you managed."

"I don't know that I managed well, but now Grandfather can get the care he needs. I'm just glad it's all behind me now."

"But is it?" Cornelius crossed his arms over his chest. "Uncle Charles, I'm afraid that trouble may have followed our dear Miranda home."

Father rolled his eyes. "First my father, and now you. Go on and tell us your news, Nelly," he said as he fell into a deep chair. "Let's see if your sneer is warranted."

Cornelius rattled open his newspaper and searched for his spot, reminding Miranda of her newsies and shoeshine boys. She'd see them tomorrow. Surely she could get some treats together by then. Ralphie had probably grown while she was gone.

Cornelius cleared his throat,

"All society is agog at the news that the shipping titans in the LeBlanc family have potentially rediscovered a long-lost heir. As to be expected, the possibility has thrown the house into disarray, setting family members at odds over whether the uneducated backwoodsman is indeed the son of Stephan LeBlanc, and if so, what exactly his role in the family should be. Will the debutantes of Boston have another worthy bachelor to practice their charms upon this season?"

Miranda's throat tightened. "That's enough." She snatched the paper out of Cornelius's hand and crumpled it up. Wyatt, the catch of the season? If he was truly a LeBlanc, every cash-conscious papa would shove his daughter in his direction. And with one look at his broad shoulders and piercing eyes, the ladies would jump in his path even without Papa's insistence.

But what if he wasn't? Would they want him then? Did they know how he always bid on Widow Sanders' rhubarb pie to save her pride? Had they seen how kind he was to little Betsy? Had they watched him as he humbly took the unreasonable abuse of an old man who—if he knew better—would have begged Wyatt to marry his only granddaughter and join the family?

The newspaper sailed into the trash bin.

"My, my," Father said. "What does Cousin Cornelius think of your newfound opinions?"

Cornelius adjusted his spectacles. "I think Miranda needs a doctor as much as Uncle Elmer does. Her association with a verifiable fraud has affected her sense."

Miranda's jaw tightened as she glared at the smug man.

"So you think the LeBlanc heir is a fraud?" Father asked.

The courage lump on her skull seemed to shrivel up, but she spoke her mind before Cornelius could answer. "He is not. Whether or not his family's claims prove true, I know Mr. Ballentine, and he wouldn't be here if he didn't believe them. Cornelius is just out of sorts because I've made it clear that I want no wedding plans with him."

Now Father sat up. His eyes twinkled. "Truly? Well, Cornelius, I don't know what to say."

"Save your condolences. Once this Ballentine fellow is exposed, Miranda will see things more clearly."

Why was it she only now found his translucent skin so repulsive? "Perhaps I'm seeing clearly for the first time."

Father roared with laughter. "Well, well. All those phrenological exams, and it took a trip to the backwoods for you to finally know your mind. Now don't sulk at me, Cornelius. If Miranda wants to marry you, I'll give my consent, but I can't say I'm sorry to see her show some spunk."

But Miranda saw nothing to be happy about. She turned her charm bracelet around her wrist and listened to the sounds of the traffic on the street below their window. She had what she didn't want, and what she wanted, she'd let get away.

At the end of his endurance, Cornelius rose, made a curt bow, and left her and Father alone.

Her father leaned back in his chair and, having no charm bracelet to fiddle with, twisted the end of his mustache instead. "Grandfather doesn't have a good opinion of the dashing Mr. Ballentine-LeBlanc, but from what I've read in that paper you're trying to hide, he's quite the catch."

"Don't be absurd. The whole situation is ridiculous. He's nothing more than a mountain man." She erupted with a short harsh laugh. "He drives a homemade wagon with a team of mules. That's the sort of person we're talking about."

"And Cornelius rubs on people's heads, but it never bothered you before."

She turned to the window and watched the maple branches sway in the wind. "I tried to imagine myself living there. Tried to think how I'd fit in, what my life would be like, but I couldn't see it. Then to hear that he's going to live here, why, he'll be as lost as I was there. The whole idea of it is . . . ludicrous."

The chair groaned as Father kicked back. "Your candor is refreshing, daughter. And the way you handled Cornelius—this trip seems to have accomplished exactly what your mother and I had hoped it would. We're proud of you."

She smiled, grateful for the encouragement but certain his praise was unmerited. She'd let fear master her and rejected Wyatt when he was poor. Although her love for him had only grown since their separation, how could she express it now when he could be a very wealthy man? The very idea reeked of hypocrisy.

Making a decision meant living with the consequences—for better or worse. And because she'd denied him during the worst, she had no right to any of his better.

CHAPTER 29

One Week Later

So this was Boston? As Wyatt stepped out of the noisy train depot, all that met his eyes were buildings stacked up against each other like fence staves with no space in between. Wagons crowded the road so closely that a man could've crossed the street by hopping from carriage to carriage without ever once touching his feet to the ground. A boy, heavy laden by a canvas bag strapped around his chest, stepped in front of him and waved a newspaper before his eyes. With just a glimpse of the flaying headline, Wyatt read: *MYSTERIOUS LEBLANC ARRIVING . . .*

"What's that say?" he asked.

William snatched the paper, crumpled it under his arm, and tossed the boy a coin. "Just a bit of insurance. Miss LeBlanc notified the papers so everyone would anticipate your arrival and you couldn't mysteriously disappear on your journey."

"Why would I want to do that?" Wyatt asked.

"I didn't mean to imply you'd die willingly."

Oh. Wyatt's teeth clenched. Maybe he should've been more vigilant on the train.

But they had reached town safely, and now Wyatt followed William across the street, swinging his head from right to left, watching for a stray runaway carriage. Once they were back on the sidewalk, the way was no easier. He caught himself peering into each and every face they passed. Used to knowing everyone he encountered, Wyatt couldn't understand why the Bostonians acted so snippy from the attention. Glares and oaths resulted left and right. He reckoned he'd have to learn to walk like William, head held high, ignoring everyone, but Wyatt couldn't stretch his legs out without trampling over a child peddling something.

"Do we have far to go?"

"It's uphill to the Common and then from there only a few blocks. If you get tired I'll hail a cab, but I thought you might appreciate getting a sense for the city. Especially after the long ride we've had."

He couldn't see enough of the city. At every corner he looked for Miranda or Elmer in the off chance that they'd happen to be outside among the crowds of people.

As they walked they passed through a section of the city where the smell of smoke hung thick on the buildings under construction. "Is this part new?" Wyatt asked.

"Yes and no," William answered. "Last November the business district had a blaze that got out of control. It burned sixty-five acres of buildings to the ground."

"Sixty-five acres?" Wyatt couldn't get his mind around a town that big, much less it burning. "And that happened here?"

"Yes, sir, but the Bostonians didn't sit in the ashes and wring their hands. As you can see, the streets are filling back up."

Wyatt would prefer they'd leave some of those roads empty so a man could breathe. "Did the Wimplegates lose anything in the fire?" he asked.

288

"They were south of the blaze, not far from here. If we continue our course a block over, we'll walk past their auction house—if you approve."

William was acting all fancy, as if Wyatt were someone important. "I reckon I'd like that." He had to see Miranda. He owed her an apology after accusing her of being in cahoots with McSwain. As soon as he was settled here in town . . .

They turned down a smaller alley, thrown into deep sweltering shade. The heat bounced off the white stone building they were passing on his left.

"This is their business." William threw a nod toward the building. "Looks quiet today. Maybe they don't have a sale."

The building was one of those fancy Greek structures that politicians seemed to favor for their offices. The second and third floors didn't quite match the base, but when it came to style it was definitely more planned out than his angular barn at home.

They turned the corner to see the front doors. "Doesn't look like they're open." The twelve-paned windows displayed only the backside of rich blue drapes. Pillars as thick as hundred-year oaks flanked the double doors at the entrance. Too easily he could imagine Miranda here. Too easily he could remember her shock when she arrived at his barn. No wonder.

A buggy had stopped at the entrance. One look to see if he recognized the passengers—when would he stop looking people in the face?—but seeing only a stranger, he turned away.

"Wait." William tugged at his own cravat and dusted off his sleeves before stepping to the street and grasping the handle on the carriage door. Wyatt couldn't see past him but knew it must be a lady from the way he bowed and then straightened with his chest puffed out. Evidently a pretty lady had the same effect on a man no matter what part of the country he was from. One hand on the door, he motioned to Wyatt. "Please."

It went against Wyatt's instincts to climb into the little cage on wheels, but his instincts wouldn't always serve him through these new experiences. He ducked inside and slid onto a velvet-covered bench opposite the lady. Before William could join him, he'd taken in the rich interior—the fringe hanging over the windows, the flower-filled glass vases bracketed to the wall. Something, either the flowers or the woman, smelled good.

"Had our paths crossed in the street, I would have known you," she said. She held his gaze with eyes as green as his own. "I congratulate you on your success, William. It'd be impossible for even Frederic to miss the resemblance."

He'd expected her to be older—more like Ma's age—but then again, she was his father's youngest sibling. Already her youthful fleeting beauty had matured into something that promised to endure.

"Aunt Corinne?" He tucked his long legs in tighter to his bench. "I didn't think we'd meet here."

"You and William did stray from the path, but I had a good idea where you might wander. Forgive me for my impatience. I had to see for myself before Monty King put you through the test."

Of course. He hadn't thought it'd be that easy, had he? After years of denying Ma and Pa's letters, they wouldn't just roll over and show their throats because he'd bought a train ticket. The carriage dipped. Wyatt looked out beneath the fringed curtains at the busy street, amazed that after all their walking they were still in town.

"So what do we call you?" she asked. "I fear we've disrupted your life and don't want it to be more painful than necessary."

"Wyatt is my name . . . and so is LeBlanc. I see no reason to pretend otherwise."

"I was never fond of Yves anyway." Her gaze stole to William, who was obviously mooning over her. "I wish we had more time to become acquainted before this interview," she said, "but the painting and its story made it back before you. Frederic and Mr. King are awaiting your arrival and are none too pleased with me."

William gripped the edge of his seat. "Just say the word and I'll make Monty King sorry."

"Dear William, ready to take on the world for me." She smiled fondly, but clearly the gesture was received with more thought than it was given. "When I heard how they were trying to ruin the Wimplegate family, I had to disclose my actions. I confessed that I'd been the one who arranged for the painting to be sold and shipped west. I didn't tell them where initially, because I wanted to give Yves . . . er, Wyatt . . . time to think through his decision, as well as time for us to determine what sort of man this Wyatt Ballentine was. The attorney must have had a guilty conscience, because he's the one who deduced that I'd learned of their old secret."

"Why did you do it?" Wyatt asked. "Don't you trust your brother more than a stranger?"

"My brother, maybe, but not Mr. King. As you're probably too chivalrous to mention, I'm a young lady no longer. All my life I've wanted adventure, to travel, to meet people. When I present my plans to Frederic, he worries so much he can't make any decisions whatsoever and passes it on to Mr. King. For years he's claimed that I couldn't afford any expenses, and then he gives me some extra pocket money—as if that takes the place of freedom. Eventually, I refused to take his excuses and began to investigate our finances for myself, but it hasn't been easy. Mr. King opposes my every request, and Frederic doesn't want to cause any problems. He's content to stay at home as long as his dinner is cooked and he has enough credit at the clubs."

"So you hired a detective?"

Her eyes slanted in fondness. "Dear William. He's been my salvation throughout this, my contact with the outside world. At first, I lived vicariously through William's adventures—his dangerous cases—but then we realized that the biggest mystery of all might be in my own family. And so we started looking for you."

She ducked her head, her earrings swinging with the rocking of the coach. "But enough about my trials. How are you feeling, Wyatt? I can't imagine the questions you must have."

He wondered how much his aunt and his father had favored each other. His own green eyes were all he recognized from her, but such things were difficult to judge for oneself. "I knew my father claimed to be from a fine Boston family, but then the LeBlancs told Ma that they didn't know me, that my father was a liar. I tried to forget what I'd been told, but even if that picture hadn't come, I would've made my way here someday. I always wondered what I'd find."

"Prepare for a difficult start," Corinne said. "I'm sure there'll be many adjustments, but there's no denying your paternity. You have your father's eyes and his bearing."

William leaned against the seat. "The testimony of your adopted brother helps, too. Although he was just a child, his memory of the wagon train and your abandonment verifies what we already know."

Thank you, Isaac. He couldn't do the calling for the auction like Wyatt could, but he'd been anxious to jump in and learn the ropes. Wyatt had been surprised by how much he did know. Evidently he'd been paying more attention to Pa than Wyatt gave him credit for.

The curtains swayed, revealing swaths of a bright green spread. Men swung wooden mallets at a ball to roll it from hoop to hoop. Women strolled with parasols overhead, their dresses reminding him of Miranda, but none of them walked as graceful as she. What was she doing now? Had she heard that he'd followed her home? He'd prayed over this meeting ever since he'd learned it was going to happen. Now that the significance of the painting was understood, surely Miranda would forgive him for keeping it.

The carriage stopped. William descended, then turned to help Corinne down. Wyatt ducked through the opening, nearly tripping as he tried to take in the massive redbrick building before him. It was two, three, four stories high, with small round windows popping out above that. He stumbled backward a step trying to count all the white-framed, black-shuttered windows on the face of the home. And yet for all the windows, there was no porch. The front of the house was flat up against the walkway, just like every other building pressing in on both sides.

"Do you live here?" he asked Corinne.

"I prefer spending my time at our Cape Cod home, but this townhouse works well enough for when I must come to the city."

"And my father?"

"He grew up here. Loved to fly kites with me on the Common."

William forged ahead, his steps made brisk by the importance of his task. He seemed to challenge the curious stares of the man, dressed in a fancy suit, who opened the door.

"Is that my uncle?" Wyatt whispered.

Corinne squeezed his arm. "It's the butler. Perhaps you should hold your questions until we're alone again."

The noises from outside blurred as they entered. Then the door swung shut behind them and the boom echoed through the vast room.

Not the least intimidated, Corinne released his arm and swept forward. With quick tugs, she removed her gloves and deposited them, along with her hat, in the hands of the butler.

"Jeffrey, tell Frederic we've arrived."

"He's waiting in the library, ma'am," and then in an undertone, "and Mr. King has done his best to trouble him over the matter."

"No doubt." But she seemed to relish the coming confrontation. William stepped to her side, prepared to go into battle for his lady. Wyatt just hoped he was worth all the fuss. She took one last appraising glance at him and nodded. "Let's go, shall we?"

Wyatt's first impression of the library was of an endless cavern of books. Towers of leather spines reached for the ceiling. He almost didn't notice the man dwarfed by the shelving around them.

Frederic LeBlanc stood in much the same pose as the monsieur in the painting, but with none of the arrogance. His chin trembled. The arm of the chair creased beneath his fingers. "My goodness, it's Stephan back from the dead." He looked like he was fixing to cry.

Only then did a stout man rise from beside the fireplace. Frederic shrank from him, curling in as the man wrapped an arm around his shoulders. "But Frederic," the man said, "your sister has worked so hard to disinherit you, of course she kept at it until she found a believable impostor."

Wyatt watched with a strange feeling of distance. They were

speaking about him, but he'd had no control over who'd birthed him. He hadn't worked for whatever goods they claimed belonged to him. If they decided to send him on his way, he was prepared to be content. And yet his first need, the only need he had at the time, was to better understand where he belonged and whose he was.

"He isn't an impostor." Corinne's voice was as smooth as a puppy's fur. "He's here to help Frederic manage the estate."

"A backwoodsman from the mountains? He's going to be the salvation of your fortune? Corinne, you've been misinformed. Frederic doesn't need help. This is just your plot to take everything away from him."

Frederic couldn't take his eyes off Wyatt. No matter how this played out legally, Wyatt had the satisfaction of knowing that as far as his aunt and uncle were concerned, he was their blood. The son of their brother. Maybe that was all he'd get, but it was the most important.

"I never wanted to be in control," Frederic said. His chin quivered. His age-speckled cheeks bloomed. "Armand was the oldest, and Stephan should have taken the reins after him, but they both died. Ever since then my life has been a nightmare. A nightmare of knowing that I should be doing something, but not being strong enough or smart enough." His thin lashes flickered up. "I'm sorry, Corinne. I let you down. You deserved better than what I've provided, so I think it'd be best to acknowledge this man as my brother's heir."

Wyatt wanted to hug the fellow but could tell any sudden movement would scare the living daylights out of him. Besides, Monty King beat him to it.

"Let's not be hasty, Frederic." Once again he had him under his arm. "There are safer, legal ways to settle this question.

Let's allow Mr. Ballentine to have his say. Take this case before a judge and see what should be done legally."

"What will a judge do?" Corinne asked. "He's going to look at the same evidence we have before us and make the same call. Why put Wyatt through the ordeal?"

"A hearing is called for." Monty twisted a ring on his chubby pinkie. "If he's legitimate, he has nothing to fear, but it's in the best interest of the family to test his claims."

Wyatt made his way to the sideboard as they deliberated. The pitcher sparkled like a bubbling spring as he poured himself a glass and munched on a fancy cookie of sorts from a nearby silver tray.

Monty stood on one side of Frederic and Corinne on the other—an angel and demon battling for his soul. Wyatt drained his glass and pushed it on the table. Surprising, really, that behind all the fancy manners and expensive clothes, these were just people. Somehow in his imagination he'd built his family up to be something grander, people who were by nature heroic, wise, and intuitive. Instead, he was faced with a derelict uncle, no better than Isaac really, and with a bully lawyer who'd taken advantage of them for so long he felt it was his right. Wyatt had faced bullies before, but maybe there were laws in Boston against cracking a skull and sending him on his way. He'd have to do his best without using his fists.

"If that's your decision," Monty said, "I have to agree it's the wisest course."

"And he should stay here with us," Frederic was saying. "Have the court case, but there's no reason he can't live here until it's official."

"I'll get it on a docket immediately." King gathered some papers off of Frederic's desk. "And I know just the judge who can help us."

Wyatt had seen less vile grins on rabid dogs, but he didn't look away. If this was his new home, he'd have to deal with that man sooner or later. Wyatt wasn't Frederic.

As Monty passed out the door, Wyatt took another cookie. Judging from Aunt Corinne's wrinkled brow, she wasn't too pleased about a hearing. Uncle Frederic and Aunt Corinne? It was beyond believing.

"You haven't eaten, have you?" Corinne went to the wall and pulled a thick ribbon that hung from above. Wyatt leaned backward, visually following the silken rope up to the soaring ceiling and half expected something to fall down from above.

"I am hungry, no fooling."

"Well, Monty will get this straightened out soon enough." Frederic rubbed a gouty knee. "I can't tell you how truly sorry I am that we didn't know about you sooner. You must believe it wasn't me who answered those inquiries from the Ballentines."

"The Ballentines did a fine job with my raising. I was where God wanted me to be."

A solid maid waltzed in carrying a silver tray covered in thin strips of rolled up meat, fruits, and tiny squares of cheese. Wyatt dearly hoped this wasn't what they called supper. He moved a decent-sized pile into his hand before he realized that Corinne was holding a plate out to him. With a wrinkle of his nose he dumped his hoard onto the plate. Corinne smiled.

Frederic took the plate Corinne offered him. "What would I do without my little sister?"

"Now you have a nephew to take care of you, too. Although, Wyatt, I don't want you to feel rushed. Take your time getting settled, and after that we'll see what information we need to prepare for the hearing. And in case you're concerned, as far as I can tell, our accounts aren't completely empty, and we still have all our assets. We might even have enough to buy back some of the heirlooms that were auctioned." She winked.

"Now that you mention it . . ." he stacked the cheese squares onto each other, because his hands wanted to be busy. "I would like to smooth things over with the Wimplegates. I feel bad for all the trouble this brought on them."

Corinne scratched at the back of her hand. "I regret involving them like I did. Nothing would please me more than a chance to offer my heartfelt apologies to Mr. Wimplegate and his granddaughter. I understand she traveled with him to Missouri in search of the portrait?"

"Yes, she did." So much more he could say, but he didn't.

"Poor child. From what I've heard she's very timid. Such a trip must have been a trial on her."

From her shocked outrage when he pummeled Isaac at the train station to her deep sorrow when he accused her of stealing the portrait from him, he'd been nothing but a hardship, but he wanted to make it up to her.

In fact, he wanted much more than that.

CHAPTER 30

Although Miranda hadn't been allowed to visit the doctor with Grandfather, she had insisted on meeting Father immediately after the appointment. She wouldn't rest until she learned what the doctor prescribed.

Now that the LeBlancs had cleared their name, the Wimplegates were inundated with discreet inquiries that more often than not led to Miranda and Father waiting in the bountiful kitchens of the upperclass. So far their activity had not brought them in contact with Wyatt. Miranda both longed for and dreaded it. Evidently all of Boston believed what Miranda found incredible—that Wyatt was the heir to the LeBlanc fortune. If it was true—and how long could she deny it when the family accepted him?—then she owed him an apology. But not yet. Only when the longing for his company became too great, because after that she had nothing. One last interaction and she'd have no excuse to contact him again. Their acquaintance would come to an end. So no matter how guilty she felt, she wasn't ready to correct the situation. Not yet.

From behind her, Miranda heard the enormous oven creaking open at the hands of one of the Stuyvesant's cooks. Her concern over Grandfather had prevented her from eating lunch, but now the hearty aroma of roast and onions made her stomach grumble.

Father lifted an eyebrow. "None of that in front of Lady Stuyvesant."

A kitchen maid hurried by, but not without pausing to toss Miranda a cold muffin. Barely making the catch, Miranda smiled her thanks and consumed the muffin before she could be caught refreshing herself without her hostess's permission.

The butler entered, head aloft, arms held bent at his side as if he carried an invisible tray. "Mrs. Stuyvesant will be with you shortly."

Father acknowledged the news, and soon the lady of the house entered.

The pearls on Mrs. Stuyvesant's morning gown warmed to a pink glow beneath the outstretched candelabra. She had the arms of a longshoreman or she wouldn't have been able to heft the silver monstrosity as she led the way to the butler's pantry. Father kept the conversation at a perfect balance, respectful enough to show he was aware of the gulf between their stations, and yet casual enough to show himself worthy of her trust for this most delicate transaction.

"Our shelves are so crowded, you see." Mrs. Stuyvesant set the candlestick on the worktable and motioned grandly around the pantry designed for the storage of valuables. "I'll probably want a new silver service soon, so we might as well make room."

She directed them to a punch bowl that was as big as a hip bath and adorned with dryads and nymphs. For the silver alone it'd bring a fortune, but the craftsmanship was divine.

"It's a lovely set," Father said. He lifted one of the cups, delicate despite its weight.

"I wouldn't want anyone to know where it came from." Mrs. Stuyvesant brushed her fingers to her temple. "You can act with discretion, can't you? Maintain the seller's anonymity but still ensure that we get the funds? Delphia must have her season, and with what the dressmakers are charging"—her hands fluttered skyward—"well, you know."

"Yes, ma'am." But Miranda only knew what her clever seamstress charged to imitate the fashions.

"Do you want us to crate this up and take it now?" Father asked.

The woman's eyes lingered on the kneeling nymph trailing a flower into the basin. "Just as well. There are crates in the corner, and the groom brought some fresh straw to pack with. Take the punch bowl set, the clock, and the silver beakers. If I think of anything else, I'll return."

Father lifted the mantle clock and set it on the worktable. With a flick of his finger, he set the pendulum to swaying and filled the room with the mellow tick-tock as Mrs. Stuyvesant made her departure. Finally Miranda could sate her curiosity.

"What did the doctor say about Grandfather?"

Father turned from the clock, but his finger continued to mete out the rhythm against the tabletop. "He examined your grandfather, and I gave him an account of his recent behavior—the forgetfulness, the poor judgment, the belligerence. The doctor has concluded that his decline is permanent." His hand closed around a beaker. "There's nothing that can be done to slow the progression."

Miranda shook her head. Why hadn't they let her go to the appointment? She knew more about his condition. "It wasn't until we arrived in Pine Gap that he really declined. He invented elaborate schemes that could never be profitable. He trusted people who were taking advantage of him while calling into question the loyalty of the only man there who had his best interest at heart."

Her throat tightened. Hadn't she done the same thing? Through every setback, every trial, Wyatt had stayed by her side.

"But it was the trip that exhausted him," Miranda continued. "Once he gets rested he'll respond better. Give him time—"

"Miranda," her father turned to her. "Time is not his friend. After you left for Missouri, I had a chance to look over our books. They were a mess. I had no idea Father had been loaning people money. This has been going on for longer than either of us cares to admit."

The ticking of the clock took on a more sinister tone. Miranda spun away and paced the room, feeling how dark and stuffy it was.

"It just isn't right. The Bible talks about wisdom as something you gain, something that can't be taken away from you. Self-control, perseverance, the fruits of the spirit—they are supposed to accumulate." She gripped the walnut cabinetry, the shining cylinders and bowls blurring before her eyes. "It was awful to see Grandfather humiliated. He was in jail—a mean, shabby jail. And why? Because he was cruel to a little girl. How does that happen? How does God allow a wise man to become so foolish?"

The beaker clinked against the worktable. "I don't guess it's any different from any other disease."

Miranda spun to face him. "But you don't get thrown in jail for having the whooping cough. It doesn't turn one into a laughingstock. It just doesn't seem fair that Grandfather could live his whole life serving God and then humiliate himself in the end and do things he'd never do if he could think straight." She clutched her stomach. "I don't mean to be cruel, but it seems that if God is leaving him here just to make a fool of himself and be ridiculed, then he'd . . . he'd be better off . . ."

"Don't, Miranda." Her father leaned against the shelving and took her hand. "We still have your grandfather. He still loves us, he still enjoys life, and he's still part of this world. And even if he loses that, even if he no longer recognizes any of us or is unaware, he still has a purpose. We've learned many lessons from your grandfather over the years, lessons that he enjoyed passing down. Caring for him will be the last lesson he has to teach us. It's up to us to learn it well."

Hadn't Wyatt said the same? Grandfather had changed, and she was sorry for that, but she couldn't be sorry for the changes she'd made—changes that would embolden her to get the care Grandfather needed.

I have a choice, she reminded herself. She couldn't choose her circumstances, but she could choose her response.

Hard heels thudded dully on the brick floor of the kitchen. Mrs. Stuyvesant appeared. Miranda hurried to the crate of hay and bent over it, giving herself time to compose herself.

"I have a few pieces of jewelry that haven't been used for several seasons," Mrs. Stuyvesant said. "Does your establishment handle jewels?"

"Yes, ma'am," Father said. "We have a strong market for jewels. At an auction, we cannot guarantee what they will bring, but I'd be honored to appraise them for you."

Grandfather should be there with them. When would his absence feel normal? Still shaky, Miranda straightened as the butler entered.

"Mrs. Stuyvesant, you have guests. Mr. Wyatt LeBlanc and Miss LeBlanc have asked if you are accepting callers."

Wyatt? She was just thinking of him. Then again, Miranda was always thinking of him.

"Wyatt LeBlanc is here?" Mrs. Stuyvesant's eyes widened. "And Delphia isn't even awake yet. Go, go. See them to the parlor. I'll send Mabel to prepare her. No, I need to greet them. You see to Mabel and Delphia. Oh, I don't know."

Miranda's throat ached. He was here. In this house. Her mind was racing. Wyatt hadn't called on her. She'd hoped he wasn't angry, hoped he was so busy with the ongoing hearings and other adjustments that he couldn't get free for a visit, but evidently he had time to call on Delphia Stuyvesant.

"Don't worry about us." But Father's gaze was fixed on Miranda. "We'll finish up here and see ourselves out."

"No, no. You must come back another time." Mrs. Stuyvesant crushed Miranda's leg of mutton sleeve in desperate hands and pulled her toward the door of the pantry. "Mr. LeBlanc cannot find out that we were considering selling off . . . well, you know . . ." She pried her hands free, gave a little shiver of anticipation as she tidied her hair, and then with regal posture intoned, "Balford, see the Wimplegates to the back door. I'll find Mabel and greet our guests."

They parted ways at the kitchen. As Balford and Father made arrangements for the transport of the silver service, Miranda dallied. She had to see him. If there was anyone who would comfort her over the doctor's news, it was Wyatt. One glimpse. She'd be content with that. One glimpse of the man she'd rejected. One glimpse before Delphia Stuyvesant or another debutante got her neatly manicured claws into him.

Stepping to the side, Miranda fell behind a maid carrying a tray of tiny circular sandwiches. *Hurry,* she begged. *Hurry before Father realizes I'm gone.* The maid turned the same direction Mrs. Stuyvesant had gone. When she came to the swinging door, she spun to push it open with her back. Seeing Miranda, she paused.

"Can I help you, miss?"

"I just got turned around. Is the servants' exit the other way?"

"Yes, ma'am. Back through the kitchen."

Miranda nodded but didn't move. With a saucy shrug, the maid continued on her way.

The door swung wide as the maid passed through . . . and there stood Wyatt. Hands behind his back, he was leaning forward slightly as Mrs. Stuyvesant flapped on about something. Miranda feasted on the sight of him. His powerful body was finally clad in a perfectly tailored suit. His hair . . . land sake's alive! Where was his beard? Instead, she saw a well-defined jaw and slightly rough cheeks. She expected him to look different, but mercy. Her heart sped, but the door was closing, narrower, narrower . . .

He looked up, saw the servant with the food. The gap was narrowing. His eyes lifted, met hers, and then the door closed.

Miranda waited as the door rocked to a halt, then settled closed against her. Had he really seen her? From behind she could hear her father calling for her, but no one else said her name.

She spun and made her way through the bustling kitchen and through the servants' entrance, picking up speed until she fairly ran. Her knees felt weak, drained by yet another disappointment. Doors were flying open for Wyatt, the same doors that had always been shut in her face.

--------◄◦►--------

Miranda. Wyatt couldn't care less what the gossipy woman was saying. He'd seen Miranda. Time to put an end to this visiting nonsense of Corinne's.

"What's behind that door?" He pointed at the door that the maid had just passed through.

Mrs. Stuyvesant stopped midsentence and had to think, as if her house was so big she couldn't remember—and maybe it was.

"That leads to the kitchen. Are the sandwiches not to your liking?"

"Are the Wimplegates here?"

Aunt Corinne made a funny noise. Mrs. Stuyvesant's mouth got small and bunched up.

"The Wimplegates? Absolutely not. While I don't condemn those who've been forced by circumstances to employ those sort of people, Mr. Stuyvesant and I would never need their services."

Aunt Corinne's eyes widened. "Like my brother did?" Whew, her voice could freeze salt water in August.

Mrs. Stuyvesant sputtered. "As I said, there are times . . ."

But Wyatt was done. He'd been done from the time he introduced himself to the butler and shook his hand. Evidently, that was taboo in these parts, as if you're supposed to ignore the only other man in the room.

Mrs. Stuyvesant might be high society, but she was as sorry a liar as Leland Moore. Aunt Corinne should be proud that he remembered to say "Excuse me" before racing through the kitchen door, but it wasn't the kitchen. It was another hallway full of uniformed help that stood around with their mouths hanging open and eyes bugging out.

"May I help you, sir?" an aproned girl asked.

"Where'd that lady go? The one who was just standing here?"

The girl looked over her shoulder for permission from that Balford fellow, but they were wasting precious time.

"I'm not sure of whom you speak," the butler said, "but I do believe someone exited the building recently."

306

Wyatt narrowed his eyes.

"Follow me," Balford wisely amended.

After a quick pass through an enormous kitchen—did his own house have one this big?—he burst through a door and found himself in an alley. He looked both ways. No one.

Wyatt scratched his head, only then realizing he'd left his hat inside. No matter. He wasn't going back. He had to find out what Miranda was doing in the kitchen. Were the Wimplegates in money trouble?

Wyatt started out for the main road. Although still waiting for the judge's ruling, he had been able to send some discreet help to the Wimplegates. At his insistence, Frederic had Monty buy the sale barn in Pine Gap from them. If it hadn't been for Monty's threats, they would've never bought it in the first place. He'd paid the Wimplegates twice what they'd paid Pritchard, but were they still running short?

He turned toward the sun, hoping he remembered his way through the maze. He'd wanted to have everything ready when he went to Miranda again. He wanted to know for sure what he could offer. He wanted to have his city manners down and be a man she could be proud of here, but now, after seeing her, that didn't matter as much. Being with her was all he wanted. He was who he was—and he missed her.

CHAPTER 31

Miranda stood before her mirror with the daring blue silk blouse reflecting back at her. Why had she allowed Mother to talk her into this? She'd thought the black overskirt would help to sober the effect, but nothing could tame the wild blue of the bodice and the cascading underskirt. It begged to be noticed.

As she reached for a somber jacket to cover the color, her eyes fell on the newspaper—one of many that had been thrown in the trash bin. She couldn't read it from that distance, but the words had permanently burned themselves into her memory.

Is it any wonder the debutantes of Boston begged to be noticed by the young Mr. LeBlanc, whose swashbuckling countenance and thick portfolio make him one of the most desirable . . .

Miranda lifted a hand to her temple, and then, with slow deliberation, ran her fingers into her thick dark hair, remembering the gentle hands that'd caressed her. No one else here had ever had Wyatt Ballentine LeBlanc run his fingers through their hair while whispering sweet words of love.

Or had they?

With a start, Miranda flung the jacket against the wall. The buttons slapped into the wood paneling, and it slid to the floor in a heap. She'd spent too much time playing it safe. What if she made a mistake? What if everyone thought she was stupid? She couldn't fall back into her old pattern. She had to stop worrying about what people thought of her.

Although it'd only been a few days since seeing Wyatt at the Stuyvesants', Miranda had all but given up hope of hearing from him. Obviously he had time to make visits, but she wasn't a priority. She should've taken her chance while she had it. She sulked out of her bedroom, pulling snug the fitted polonaise bodice that emphasized the figure she usually kept hidden.

"We thought we'd have to leave you." Mother balanced a tray of delectables against her hip. "The gentlemen have gone on without us."

"Even Grandfather?" Miranda took her bonnet from the entryway hooks.

"Even Grandfather. Remember, if you see him acting erratically, tell your father. You don't have to do it alone anymore." She started to the door, but Miranda stepped in her way.

"Isn't there another tray?"

"Certainly, but those are for later tonight. We'll need something, since dinner will be so late."

"But Essie can make another, right?" Miranda swished past her mother and trotted to the kitchen. Before the cook could protest, she snatched the tray and called over her shoulder, "Sorry, Essie. You have until nightfall to make more."

"We don't need those. Let Essie bring them by later. They'll be picked over before we get a chance to stop and eat."

"No, they'll be gone by then. I'm going to share them with the paper boys." The sapphire of her shirt reflected in the silver tray.

Her spirits rose at the thought of giving a treat to her friends. "Those boys appreciate a tidy snack more than all the old goats in the auction combined."

Her mother raised her eyebrow. "You're going to feed our hors d'oeuvres to the paper boys?" She tried not to smile. "What about the shoeshine boys?"

"They'll get the petit fours." Miranda said it matter-of-factly, as if it were her decision.

Mother studied her, then seeming to have found what she was looking for, said, "Just keep an eye on the trays. Earlier this summer, one of them suffered substantial damage. We still haven't figured out how it happened." She pushed open the front door and motioned Miranda toward the waiting public carriage.

Miranda wanted to laugh aloud. That's all it took? Why had she been so afraid to ask for anything before? And even if Mother said no, there was no great shame in having an idea. She hadn't lost anything.

When they disembarked before the thick stone pillars, the excited gathering of the newsboys across the street told Miranda that they had marked her return. Newspapers lowered as they greedily watched the extra tray. She spotted Ralphie, who braved a small wave. Connor jerked his chin in the air by way of greeting. A flash of blond hair caught her eye, bringing happy memories of Betsy, always underfoot with a song, a joke, or some news. Taking time for a quick prayer for the girl, that she'd find another confidante now that both Miranda and Wyatt had left Pine Gap, Miranda summoned the boys with a toss of her head. They didn't move immediately, instead looking at each other nervously and consulting behind gritty fingers.

Her mother stepped up next to her. "Are they afraid of me?"

Miranda nodded, remembering the number of times she

hid from her mother while serving her friends. No wonder they were waiting. Miranda stepped back to stand side-by-side with her mother, and when Miranda lifted her tray, so did the older woman. Finally convinced, the boys streamed through the street, dodging around carriages and stopping traffic. Once they reached the ladies, they hesitated.

"I'm Mrs. Wimplegate. Pleased to meet you."

Neither lady could keep from laughing at their wide eyes, but it only took a heartbeat for them to recover and to demolish the pretty offerings on the trays.

"Oh, Miranda. This is much more fun than serving the buyers," Mother said as the boys elbowed each other for the last of the crumbs.

Miranda smiled. She wasn't the only one who'd changed over the summer.

<hr />

She'd never looked more beautiful. Wyatt waited in the carriage across the street, enjoying the sight of Miranda surrounded by the grimy, enthusiastic kids. Her bonnet shaded her face, but nothing could dim her radiant smile. She belonged here, spanning the gap between those who were comfortable and those who were needy. Always thinking of others, always willing to give. And while she might not like to stand on a stage in front of bidders, she had no qualms about rubbing elbows with rough and tumble guttersnipes. They didn't intimidate her at all.

Maybe that's why she was willing to stand up to him.

Seeing her now made him realize how much he'd missed her. The crowd around her thinned. She leaned in as her mother wrapped a proud arm around her waist and they sashayed inside the auction house with empty trays dangling from their hands. What would she think of him? Would she find his sudden citification ridiculous, or would he remain the dirty laborer in her eyes?

No use standing around a'wondering. Wyatt hopped down, adjusted his new hat, and headed toward the auction house, brimming with enthusiasm. So much he wanted to accomplish today—apologize to Miranda, meet her parents, and make plans for their next encounter, if she wasn't willing to run off with him immediately. And he might make that offer. Wyatt hadn't figured on being so lonely in the big city. He missed everyone from back home, but even though he'd spent his life with those people, he missed Miranda even more.

He entered the roomy building. The marble walls raced to the sky, holding the lacy expanse above his head on solid columns. The thick carpet cushioned each step toward the registration table. Miranda's mother cruised behind the table to look over the shoulders of the young clerks as they helped the bidders.

"Cornelius, don't forget to record the bidder's bank in the blank here. If you don't know it already, you must ask them."

Cornelius? Next thing he knew he was standing at the front of the line, staring down at the uptight man.

"Can I help you?" Disdain and cold recognition. So Cousin Cornelius had figured out his identity? Wyatt sized the man up and made his decision.

"Yes, my buggy is outside and my horse has been acting up. I wondered if you could come rub its skull and tell me if it's got a bad case of stubborn, or if it might be indigestion?"

Cornelius's lips whitened. "I take it you're not a man of science."

Wyatt leaned close. "I've got no bone to pick with science, but first off I'm a man of faith. If you're using science to put limits on what God can accomplish with a person, that's where we part ways."

"Mr. LeBlanc?" Mrs. Wimplegate rested a gentle hand on the back of Cornelius's chair. "I'm Mrs. Wimplegate. We're honored you've decided to visit. Can we help you find anything in particular?"

"Your daughter."

Mrs. Wimplegate's eyes widened. Maybe he should've thought before answering. But her kind face eased into a smile. "And you'd want to meet Mr. Wimplegate, as well. If you'll follow me."

As he followed Mrs. Wimplegate, the whispered comments were hard to ignore.

"That's the LeBlanc heir."

"Didn't they blame the Wimplegates for the whole mess?"

"My wife insists we throw a party for him. I suppose I might as well introduce myself—"

The room they entered had red cushioned chairs arranged in rows facing an elaborate desk. The auction arena. No wonder they didn't sell animals. The rugs would be ruined in minutes. Wyatt snatched a folded pamphlet from a pile on a brass stand as he passed by. With the stage empty, every eye was trained on him and the man he was approaching, but still no sign of Miranda.

What was he doing here? She had expected . . . well, hoped really . . . for a letter, a card, maybe even a polite social call . . . some token to acknowledge their acquaintance so he could tie up the loose ends and move on with his new life. But why would he come here?

Miranda had promised that she'd never hide again, but she

found herself standing in the storage area behind the stage. It wasn't her fault that it was dark, that no one could see her. And Mother was looking for her—her back never straighter as she presented Wyatt to Father. Father drew back. His handshake offered only conditional approval, and then with some quip from Wyatt, he beamed. Next thing she knew, Father had slapped Wyatt on the back as if they were old friends.

One by one the men left their seats to be presented to the recent oddity. As Father introduced Wyatt around, Miranda watched proudly as their attitudes went from condescension to marked approval upon a few short exchanges. Certainly there'd be those who would refuse to be impressed, but Wyatt had no flaw that would keep him from taking his place in society—a place far above hers.

Three sharp raps rang out. Miranda spun to the stage and there was Grandfather with the gavel, gripping the podium and calling the sale into order, and in his hand . . . a wrinkled, dried up apple doll.

"Good morning, gentlemen. It's time to open the bidding on our offerings today. Our first item for sale is this one-of-a-kind, handmade statuette from a gifted artist in the Ozarks."

Heads spun. Puzzlement turned to amusement as people found their seats. Miranda squeezed the rolled up catalog in her hands until it collapsed upon itself. It was happening again. Would she take the coward's way out, or would she try to save Grandfather's dignity?

"You'll notice the fine stitching on the gown that delineates this work from other less established artists. . . ."

She couldn't let this go on. Her heart pounded, her stomach floated, but her feet carried her out of the shadows and onto the stage.

"So what do I hear for this fine piece? We'll start the bidding at five dollars. Five dollars just to get us started."

Miranda reached his side. Moving slowly as to not startle him, she stretched a hand to the podium and pulled herself next to him.

"Grandfather, let's wait a bit before starting the sale. Let's wait for Father."

He shook his head. "Miranda," he whispered, "I'm busy. You're causing a scene."

She might not have caused it, but she was a part of it, and that was bad enough.

"Here comes Father. Let's talk to him."

"Five dollars!" Grandfather cried. "Will no one give me five dollars?"

The vibration beneath her feet told her that her father had stepped onto the wooden platform. Grandfather's cry was weaker this time. "Will no one give me five dollars?"

"Twenty, right here."

Miranda's head jerked, but she knew the voice even before she located the tall man in the crowd.

"I'll give you twenty dollars for that beautiful doll, Mr. Wimplegate." Wyatt weaved his way through the crowd toward the front. "I've never seen anything finer."

Was he mocking them? Miranda turned pale.

Grandfather snorted. "You might be able to buy pigs and goats, Wyatt, but you can't afford pieces like this."

The room went deathly silent. Her father groaned. After all they'd done to pacify the LeBlancs, Grandfather was insulting them again. Just think how the buyers would repeat this story.

"Mr. LeBlanc." Her faithful customer Mr. Wakefield stepped forward. "Mr. Wimplegate hasn't been himself recently. He doesn't mean any offense."

Wyatt shook the man's hand. "Mr. Wimplegate and I are old friends. No offense taken."

"Grandfather," she whispered. "He doesn't want the doll. Let's go get a drink of water and—"

"I do want it." Wyatt had reached the stage. "Twenty-five dollars. Twenty-five dollars for the doll as long as it is delivered to my house . . . with a rhubarb pie."

Miranda had to clutch the podium to keep from swaying. The excited comments blurred into a roar, and every eye was on her.

"You don't have to humor him—"

"Wyatt is my employee," Grandfather belted. "He feeds the pigs and cows. He needs to get back to work and stop interrupting this sale."

Wyatt kept calm amid the horrified gasps. "No truer words were ever spoken. And I do have to say that you have a right nice sale barn here. Maybe not as clean as my own—"

"Clean?" Grandfather snorted and turned to her father. "You should see his place. It smells worse than the fish market."

"I can't wait to hear about it." Father took his arm and motioned Cornelius over. "You haven't had a chance to tell Cornelius about your trip, either. . . ." As the two men led him away, Miranda snatched the gavel from his hand and picked up the doll from the stand. Now would be a good time to direct the buyers to the refreshments, if she hadn't given them all away. She wanted to look up but she couldn't without seeing the handsome man waiting at the foot of the stage. She drew a shaky breath and then announced, "Forgive us the interruption. The sale will begin shortly."

But no one moved. She hugged the apple doll over her sapphire bosom and turned to exit at the back, but before she could make it to the curtain, Wyatt was there.

"Thirty dollars," he said. "Thirty dollars for the doll and the pie as long as it's delivered by you."

She hurried out of the salon and into the warehouse area. "Are you mocking me?"

With quick steps, he followed. "Not at all. But you haven't accepted my bid. Aren't you supposed to bang on the stand and say something? Going . . . going . . . gone?"

"This isn't funny," she whispered.

"Miranda . . ."

A warm thrill ran up her spine at the sound of her name on his lips. The squares of marble spun beneath her feet. Every snub she'd made in Missouri, every insult played back to her. How she'd put on airs, and now Wyatt was in Boston and could see for himself what her true condition was. Just another working girl dependent on the upperclass for her wages.

"I apologize for Grandfather. If you want a more formal apology . . ."

"Your dress looks nice."

Slowly she lowered the apple doll. She'd decided to stop hiding, after all. "Since I've been back, I've tried to wear colors besides brown," she said. "And maybe I've had more courage for other things, too."

Although how she could talk to him standing there in a perfectly tailored suit, looking every bit of the dashing catch the *Herald* proclaimed him to be, she couldn't fathom. Then the dread returned. "How are you finding Boston?"

"It ain't like home," he chuckled. "I got chewed out something fierce by the driver for giving the newspaper boys rides in the buggy."

Miranda blurted out a laugh. "You did?"

"It was raining. I had empty seats."

Despite her nervousness, she couldn't stop the smile from breaking out. She'd rather hear about that than the fine parties he was attending. And just maybe this was one wealthy man who would understand the barriers the poor boys faced.

"You do have a lot of treasures," he said. "Almost as many as Mrs. Rinehart."

"But none from Montgomery Wards." She found herself gazing up at him as a warm contentment covered her. They hadn't changed him. Even if she didn't see him again, there was satisfaction in knowing that he was every bit the man she'd thought he was.

Miranda walked Wyatt through the warehouse and back toward the front entry. Along the way, they strolled between the tall rows of shelves. Clocks, lamps, candlesticks, paintings—the treasure from one hundred homes, and she could only think of the man at her side.

"You don't mind if I keep this catalog, do you?" He slowed before a Boucher of a couple embracing on the banks of a creek. "When I read it, I'll hear your voice."

Why did he need something to remember her by? Was this a farewell? "Take it," she said. Then on impulse she shoved the doll toward him. "And this, too. It's something to remind you of home." And then, just in case he thought she was being sentimental, "We have crates of them."

Gently he took the doll out of her hand. He turned it over, as if inspecting the work. "Seeing you here, I realize how dumb I was to think . . ." He rubbed his thumb against the wrinkled apple face.

To think? To think . . . what? Miranda searched his face, but with his tailored clothes and clean-shaven jaw, he once again felt unfamiliar.

318

"I should go. Corinne is taking me to dinner . . . I mean lunch . . . But before I go, I wanted to apologize to you." He lifted his eyes to hers. "I shouldn't have accused you of stealing the painting from me. I had no reason to think you'd do that."

"You had plenty of reasons to suspect me. But I accept your apology." She heard Father take the stage and knock the gavel against the podium. The sale was recommencing.

"I have an apology to make, too," Miranda said. "I was so focused on the consequences to my family that I didn't consider how that painting could change your life. If I'd understood, I wouldn't have expected you to hand it over."

"Thank you," Wyatt said. "I didn't want to leave any misunderstanding between us. It's nice to have that settled."

But nothing was settled, least of all her heart.

CHAPTER 32

She understood why he had to have the painting, but did she understand why he needed her? Wyatt wasn't sure. She hadn't agreed to marry him in Pine Gap, and now that she was home with her family—and that uptight doctor, Cornelius—she might never take him seriously.

Wyatt spotted the door he'd entered and followed the long corridor of furniture to the front. Seeing her again, the first familiar face in this strange land, was too much for him. If he wasn't careful, he'd blurt out another proposal here in the storeroom.

A man didn't go begging a woman. If she turned him down flat, he ought not bring it up again, but she'd asked for time. How long was enough? Besides, there were a million reasons Miranda would turn down a poor sale-barn manager in Missouri. He only hoped the reasons that mattered didn't apply to a millionaire in Boston.

But he wouldn't waste his only chance here and now. Wait until one of them fancy dance parties they kept promising him. That would be a good place. Ladies were supposed to get all sentimental about such events.

They came to the end of the warehouse portion of the building, and who should be waiting for them but Cornelius. You could roast a duck over the steam coming off his ears.

"You're leaving?" he asked.

"I'll call on you soon, Miranda." Wyatt wasn't going to ask for permission, especially in front of that tonic-swiggling fool.

"I'll walk you out," she said.

"That's hardly necessary," Cornelius said.

"But extremely pleasant," Wyatt answered, then leaned toward Cornelius and whispered, "By the way, I did my own examination of her skull and found her to be remarkable in every way."

Then before he could respond, they scuttled past and into the salon. Directly into the path of a strangely agitated Mr. Stuyvesant.

Compulsively wiping his hands on his suitcoat, Mr. Stuyvesant's cheeks glowed an angry red.

"You should be ashamed of yourself."

Wyatt shot a glance at Miranda, but she looked as puzzled as he felt.

"Mr. Stuyvesant," Wyatt said. "How can I help you?"

"You can board the next train out of Boston and never return. To think my own precious daughter entertained a charlatan like you. I hope the LeBlancs prosecute you to the full extent of the law." His voice had gathered strength until it echoed off the high ceiling in the salon.

"I don't know what you're talking about," but he understood it to be an insult. "You'd better have a good reason for your accusations or be ready to eat your words with a fist-fork."

"Wyatt," Miranda pled, "I'm sure Mr. Stuyvesant doesn't mean to cause an incident on our premises. Once his meaning is clear—"

"My meaning is this," Mr. Stuyvesant said. "The hearing has concluded, and the LeBlancs have prevailed. The judge has decided that this man has no evidence to support his claim. We don't know who he is, but he is not a LeBlanc."

The sight of the furious man blurred before Wyatt's eyes. It couldn't be right. Hadn't Frederic recognized him immediately? Hadn't Corinne found his parents' marriage certificate? Suddenly his new collar felt like it was strangling him. His stiff new shirt chafed his skin.

Who do you think you are? Who do you think you are?

Those words had haunted him his entire life. In his stronger moments he could combat the uncertainty, but not now. Not in this room full of rich men, raising their monocles to inspect him, murmuring behind their sales catalogs, shaking their heads in disapproval.

Ignoring Miranda's pleas, Wyatt marched out of the building.

He didn't know who he was, but evidently he wasn't the man for her.

"Wyatt, where are you going?" Miranda trotted two steps before Cornelius grabbed her by the arm.

"Didn't you hear? He's an imposter. You knew they'd find out soon enough."

"Let go," Miranda said as Cornelius dragged her back into the warehouse and away from prying eyes. "He needs me."

Cornelius spun her around and grasped her shoulders. "What he needs is a stern lecture about the impertinence of impersonating a gentleman. And I won't have you making a fool of yourself chasing after him. . . ."

Pulling backwards, Miranda earned a foot of space between

them before lunging forward and using all her momentum to crash her thick, submissive skull right into Cornelius's nose.

"Oww!" He released her and shielded his nose, which was spouting blood profusely. "You broke my nose."

"With my lump of cautiousness," she called over her shoulder as she raced through the crowd of startled bidders.

She hit the doors at full steam, nearly plowing over a rotund man who'd been in the unfortunate position of opening one of them. Bounding to the street, she stopped and looked both ways but didn't see Wyatt anywhere.

Frantically she waved Connor and Ralphie over to her. They dodged carriages as they scurried across the busy road.

"Did you see a man leave just now?" she asked. "A tall man with blond hair?"

Connor adjusted his cap. "Large man, walks like an admiral?"

How long would he keep his swagger? Gulping, she nodded. "That's him."

"We know him," Ralphie said. "He gives us rides sometimes. He jumped in his buggy and took off. You can't catch him now."

Again, she looked down the crowded street, but the traffic was rolling too quickly. She couldn't get ahead of him, even if she knew where he was going.

But another buggy pulled up to the front of the auction house. The jet black buggy, the horses, the swaying velvet curtain could only be one family's. Expecting to see the elegant woman who'd commissioned the purchase of the LeBlancs' painting, Miranda had to do a second look when the man disembarked.

"I know you." Miranda narrowed her eyes and followed his path back to the carriage. It'd been a few months, but she remembered. "You were the one who bought the LeBlanc painting for that lady, weren't you?"

He dipped his head in shy acknowledgment. "William Sears, also known as the horse buyer from Arkansas who came to observe the two of you, but I'm afraid my efforts were in vain."

"The Calhouns' friend?" Miranda gasped. "And the man in the barn? You look so different here."

William shrugged. "You didn't look beyond my ragged clothes to see the person."

Evidently Miranda made that mistake more than she'd care to admit. "Where's Wyatt?" she asked.

"I had hopes that you would know."

"He was here, but someone ran in and said something about a hearing, then he left."

William frowned. "I wanted to reach him with the news first. Frederic should've never let King take it before his hand-picked judge. We believe Wyatt's claim is true, but a court needs hard evidence—evidence we didn't have. The judge threw his case out."

They didn't believe him? As much as she'd ridiculed Wyatt, she was surprised to realize that she had every confidence in his story now. "So what happens? What will become of him?"

"His prospects aren't promising. Mr. King is allowing him enough money for a train ticket to his home and, ironically, the judge ruled that the painting was his, as it was given to him by a member of the family."

"After all the hullaballoo, the court decided the painting was his after all?" Miranda's eyes stung. "But acknowledgement from the family was really what he was after. This aunt of his, she'll be able to help, won't she?"

"I'm afraid not. Her funds are limited to her allowance, which after this fiasco will be curtailed by the financial manager."

"Monty King?" Miranda asked.

"Yes, ma'am."

Again her eyes traveled the street. He was going back to Missouri? At least while he was being courted by Boston society, she knew he was being looked after. What about now? Would Isaac welcome him back after he'd given up his place at the sale barn? Did he even have a home any longer?

The giant oak door thudded closed behind him. Wyatt shifted the awkward gilt frame into his left arm and pulled his hat on. Stupid bowler. He shouldn't have let them get rid of his slouch hat in the first place. He was who he was—a LeBlanc who had the benefit of growing up a Ballentine. Because of that he knew how to take care of himself—something poor Uncle Frederic had never learned.

Uncle Frederic hadn't realized that Monty could manipulate the law just as he manipulated those account books. Now, seeing no end in sight for his mismanagement and the exploitation of his weakness, Frederic was nearly having an apoplectic fit.

Two ladies decked out like parade horses slowed as they passed him still standing on the LeBlancs' steps. Out of habit he tipped his hat. They giggled and hurried on past, throwing a second glance over their shoulders. They hadn't heard. By morning it'd be in those papers his young friends on auction house corner were hawking.

The auction.

Miranda.

What was he going to do? He was a stranger in a strange land. His train fare would buy him a few weeks of lodging, maybe meals to last half that long if he didn't go home . . . and he wasn't going.

He didn't have the foggiest notion of where to stay, but he knew this neighborhood wouldn't shelter him. Instinctively he headed north toward the rougher areas he'd passed through. He didn't know why God had led him to Boston, but he'd said good-bye to Missouri. It was the past. His future was here.

He strode down the sidewalk, drawing amused looks. How could he forget the painting tucked beneath his arm? Yes, he probably did look crazy, but Grandpère LeBlanc was staying with him. He'd keep him until he had his own home where he could hang him proudly.

Tilting the frame so he could get a look at the man, he muttered, "It's just you and me now. But you're a good reminder that if anyone can make something of themselves here, I can. Just wait and see."

I didn't come here penniless. You have some catching up to do.

"Well I'm not wearing silky short pants, either, and that's one factor in my favor."

"Hey, mister."

Wyatt skidded to a stop and pulled the picture around to face him. Had he just heard that aloud?

"Excuse me?"

He turned to find two of the newspaper boys who frequented the Wimplegates' corner, watching him warily.

"Sorry, mister. We wouldn't have bothered you, but we're walking home and thought if you had a buggy available, you might want to share a ride."

Wyatt studied their scuffed shoes and tattered woolen britches with renewed interest. He needed to get some work clothes and put his fancy clothes away for the time being—just as soon as he had a room to keep clothes.

"Sorry, fellas. I'm down on my luck. Kicked out with nothing but the clothes on my back and this humdinger of a painting."

The tall one whistled. "Tough break. Well, you might as well walk along with us. Where you staying?"

"I wish I knew."

The boys exchanged glances as they fell in together. "If you'll be needing a place, we can show you where to lease a room. We'd let you stay with us but there's not an empty space on the floor."

Wyatt had come from humble people, but he'd always had space, even if he had to sleep outside. "I think I can pay for a room, but not for long. I need to find work."

The little one piped up. "You're too big to sell papers."

"Big enough to do a lot of work, though," the tall boy said. "Anything you're good at?"

He'd given up his gavel, but he still knew a thing or two about animals. "I can handle livestock, horses, that sort of thing. I don't know how much call you have for that in the city, though."

The two boys stepped aside. Wyatt stopped and watched as they consulted each other. The smaller one chewed his fingernails, then with a grin made a suggestion the older boy approved of. A slap on the back and they returned to him.

"You helped us out when you could, now it's our turn." The kid's face widened in a confident grin. "You just stick with Connor and Franklin, and we'll take care of you."

CHAPTER 33

One week later

"It's about time someone acknowledges the years I've spent honing my taste." Grandfather held the door open for Father before entering the warehouse. "The curators at the Athenaeum know art when they see it."

Miranda looked up from her notes on a man's leather and gold nécessaire traveling kit to watch the men enter.

"Once again you've proven yourself a connoisseur of the first rate." Father winked at her.

"What's this about the curators?"

Grandfather fiddled with his cufflink. "I was just telling your father that the Athenaeum, the pinnacle of style and taste, is going to display my apple dolls in an exhibit on American craftsmanship. Miranda, you must prepare for another trip. Everyone will want one of those dolls, and the only way to ensure their production is to oversee it ourselves. If we take the morning train to New York tomorrow . . ." He stopped to frown at her notebook. "Aren't you finished yet? Your mother sent us to bring you home for dinner."

"Just this one last item." She drew a deep breath over the

gold-fitted jars and bottles for a last whiff of the colognes they formerly carried.

"Well, I'll meet you at the house." Grandfather reversed course. "I have to get Patrick to pack my bags if we're going to be ready in time." He exited as if he were trying to get out of the way of an oncoming train.

She'd just put the finishing touches to the catalog description and closed the notebook when Father spoke.

"Don't you want to accompany Grandfather back to Pine Gap, Missouri?"

Miranda's fingers turned as numb as ice cubes. The lid to the nécessaire fell shut.

"Are you really letting him go?"

"Careful there, Miranda, let's not destroy a Betjemann case over a joke. No, Grandfather isn't going anywhere, but I thought you might miss your friends."

One friend in particular. Somehow knowing that he was no longer in Boston made her lonelier than ever.

"He'll write once he gets settled," she said. "Getting over the court's decision will take him some time."

She pushed the drawers of the nécessaire closed. They slid like they were floating on air. The drawer for the shaving tools was the last she closed as she wondered if Wyatt had allowed his beard to grow back. Her fingers traced the smooth knobs on the nécessaire. He should have a case this nice, with pomander and cologne and . . .

Her father cleared his throat. Miranda looked up, startled to find him watching her.

Her mouth popped open. "But, but the gallery . . . are they really displaying the dolls?"

He raised an eyebrow before answering, but she couldn't

read his thoughts. "They are. Those dolls aren't as worthless as we'd assumed."

"Aren't you afraid that's going to encourage him?"

"Your grandfather needs some encouragement. The road ahead isn't going to be easy. Much like another, much younger fella you're worried about."

Silently she moved the nécessaire to its place with the other auction items. If only she'd hear from Wyatt, but when he was a poor man before, she hadn't been much help to him. When he'd asked for her love back in Pine Gap, she'd rejected him. He had no reason to think she'd do differently now.

But would she if he asked?

They left the building together. Miranda tied her bonnet ribbons into a half-hearted bow and took her father's arm. Ralphie saw her from across the street, but instead of merely waving, he dashed through the traffic.

"Miss Wimplegate! Miss Wimplegate!"

"I do wish he'd be careful," she gasped as he darted around a fire wagon.

Ralphie doffed his hat as he skidded to a stop before her. "Miss Wimplegate, I saw your friend."

"My friend?" She looked at her father, whose eyes twinkled like Grandfather's used to with Betsy.

"Mr. Wyatt—the rich bloke who got kicked out of his family. You told me he'd gone back home, but he's here. He found himself a job around the corner from me in West End. Got himself a room there, too, but he doesn't have that fancy carriage anymore."

"He's here? In Boston?" The air tasted like dust. She couldn't catch her breath. She knew Father was leading her to the steps, but until she felt the cold of the concrete seeping through her skirt, she didn't realize she was sitting down.

Father sat next to her, patting her hand as her view cleared. Her eyes fell on Ralphie, twisting his hat as his chin trembled.

"Now, now," Father said. "No use in getting upset, young man. Miss Wimplegate is recovering quickly. You did her no harm."

Wyatt hadn't left and he was living in the tenements? So many emotions—relief that he was near, sorrow that his circumstances had been so reduced, disappointment that he hadn't called on her.

"What's he doing?" she asked. "Why is he here?"

"He's working at the livery stable," Ralphie answered, "taking care of the horses. Mr. Fillmore even took him to the country when he went to buy new stock. Said Mr. Wyatt was a good judge of horses and a fair barterer."

Wyatt, who threw the Stuyvesant parlor into a tizzy, was back to dirtying his hands at the livery stables?

"Fillmore's Livery?" Father said. "I know it well."

While Father asked for more particular information, Miranda's thoughts reeled. No longer an Ozark auctioneer, no longer a Boston heir, Wyatt was still who he'd been all along—an honest, hard-working, and loyal man. Miranda never could imagine living in Missouri, and she would've felt like a hypocrite seeking him when he was wealthy. But now she could appreciate him for the man he was—and that man was wonderful.

"Thank you for the information," Father said.

Ralphie slapped his hat against his thigh before pulling it back over his head. "I didn't mean to scare her. Just thought she'd like to know." His young eyes were still filled with concern. Miranda reached up and grasped his grimy hand.

"Thank you, Ralphie. Your news means more than you can know."

331

He beamed at her before skipping away, his newspaper bag bouncing against his hip.

Wyatt was here. She could find him.

A calm determination settled over her. What would her parents think?

Her father cleared his throat. Miranda's eyes lowered as she waited for his pronouncement.

"I've never seen you quite so overcome," he said. "I take it that the news holds more significance than one might suspect?"

Miranda pressed her lips tightly together. Would Wyatt want to see her? She realized it didn't matter, he was going to. She would find him and see if there was any way she could . . . help him. And maybe his little room wasn't so bad. Maybe she'd find a simple charm about the tenements. Maybe she'd learn that it was possible to keep a level of civility even in those dark alleys.

"I've watched you grow up, Miranda," Father said, "always wishing that you felt more confident expressing yourself. Yet here you are, and I'm afraid the next words out of your mouth are going to mean that I've lost my little girl."

Miranda laid her head on his shoulder, unconcerned about the questioning glances of the pedestrians streaming by. "I'm always your girl, Father, but I think I'm done being little. It's time for me to grow up. If it means facing heartbreak, then that's just the cost of being brave."

He nodded, his chin sagging against his chest. Then, with a sigh, his head popped up. "Taking care of your grandfather is growing more and more taxing. I don't know how I'll manage him in addition to all my duties at the auction house. I've been thinking about hiring a new partner." He squeezed her hand and his face broke into a grin. "You wouldn't have any out-of-work auctioneers among your acquaintances, would you?"

Miranda smiled so big her cheeks hurt. She threw her arms around her father's neck and squealed.

"Easy there, child. Don't assume he'll want to work for us—the man has his pride—but as for the matter of your heart, if I'm not mistaken, he'll take any opportunity to settle that issue as soon as he's able."

"But, Father, what about the LeBlancs? Won't they be furious if you hire a man they've publically denounced?"

He shook his head. "They've done no such thing. Cornelius reports that Frederic himself bemoans the fact that the court couldn't reach a satisfactory conclusion. The way is still clear should he uncover any evidence. No, I'm not concerned about the LeBlancs learning of his employment—I'm more worried about what your grandfather will say."

Passing through the stalls, Wyatt did a last tally of the horses. Only the bay and the dun were left. The rest had been rented out, but it was time for him to grab a bite to eat before the carriages began returning.

More thirsty than hungry, he took a long pull from the dipper that rested in the bucket outside his room. Inside this barn, he felt at home. The teeming streets outside were as foreign to him as the bottom of the ocean, but the smell of hay and horses comforted him. The dipper landed in the bucket with a splash, then he pushed through the rough wooden door beneath the hayloft. As always, his eyes landed on Grandpère LeBlanc first, hanging over the head of his metal-framed cot. The bright colors of old Grandpa's fancy clothes glowed like a lantern in the simple room, but he didn't seem to mind.

I do hope your employer doesn't see me in here. He won't appreciate you consorting with unsavory characters.

"Unsavory? You flatter yourself. There are men on the other side of this wall that'd sooner kill me than say *Gesundheit* when I sneeze." He smeared a thin pat of butter over his day-old bread. That and some jerky would have to tide him over. He was saving every penny he could for a better future.

Wyatt sat on his bed, leaned against the wall, and hung his heels off the side. This wasn't so bad. He'd made friends, was appreciated by his boss, and saw new opportunities for advancement every day. No longer tied to his father's dreams for him, he was free to try his hand at any task that caught his eye—any job that brought him closer to winning Miranda.

The strict discipline it took to only buy the cheapest vittles was nothing compared to the struggle of staying away from her. Every time he stepped out of the barn, his boots seemed to carry him away, often getting him as far as the State House before he caught himself and turned back to his new home. She would be fine without him for a little longer, but he was wasting away from longing. If only he could see her, talk to her, without having to explain his situation. How tempting to don his fancy duds and act as if nothing had changed. Just march into her auction house and pick up where they'd left off, but that would be dishonest. And to present himself in his ratty work clothes wasn't an option. She didn't want to see him like that. He couldn't offer her enough.

The knock on his door came completely unexpected. His boots thudded to the ground, and the metal frame creaked as he rose. As far as he knew, Mr. Fillmore had never entered the room since he'd moved in. What would his boss think of the bewigged gentleman hanging from his wall?

He slid the door fastener over, swung the door open, and came face-to-face with Miranda. His slice of bread tumbled out of his fingers. He tried to catch it, but only succeeded in getting butter all over his hand before it landed face down in the dirt. He wiped his hand on his pants and lifted his eyes to see if he'd made a mistake. But no, she was still there, just as fetching as ever. His eyes traveled up her poofy emerald skirt, hungry for the rich color that reminded him of his mountains in the spring. With her closed parasol she tapped the door.

"May I come in?" Her face sported the dearest blush, but even if she was made uncomfortable by the request, he was proud that she'd dared.

He looked over his shoulder, already knowing how pitiful the room was. He should've gone to her. Anything would've been better than her seeing him like this. But he wouldn't send her away.

He pulled the door open wide, then bent to smooth out the blanket covering his bed. "Sorry. I don't have a decent place to visit. If you want I can ask if Fillmore will cover for me and we could take a walk to the river."

But she didn't seem to notice the room. She sat on the cot and took to studying her folded hands. "This is fine. I don't mind."

He nodded. Then, having nowhere else to rest his sorry hide, he sat on the cot, but as far away from her as possible.

Her scented rose powder tickled his nose. He hadn't realized how he'd missed it. How her calm attitude soothed him. Then again, she didn't act very calm. Her hands trembled, her chest rose in quick, short breaths. He wanted to encourage her, to assure her that he wasn't down, that he could make this work, but he didn't want to rush her. He'd rather wait until he had proven himself.

"I'm so sorry, Wyatt." She wrapped her reticule with both hands. "I know how much coming here meant to you." Her lashes dusted her cheeks.

"I'm still here, aren't I? Maybe it's not what I was hoping, but I'm no stranger to hard work. Don't worry about me."

"But—" she bit her lip. Her gloved hands tensed. "When I didn't hear from you, I thought you'd gone back to Missouri."

"I told you Isaac is running the sale barn now. There's nothing for me in Missouri."

She picked at the ties to her reticule. "If you'd been on the train, I'd understand why I went so long without a letter, but you were here, not five miles away. It wouldn't have been difficult to post a note."

Wyatt raised his eyebrow. If he didn't know better, it sounded like she'd hunted him down, traveled into the slums, and interrupted him at dinner to scold him for not writing. Her behavior was downright shocking. And Wyatt couldn't be happier.

"Why are you here?" he asked. "Surely you didn't come all this way just to school me about my manners."

Her hat bobbed. "I do have a purpose." With her finger, she outlined a strangely shaped bulk in her reticule. "As you know from your visit to our auction house, Grandfather hasn't improved. He won't be able to help Father any longer." As she spoke, her words came faster. "Father needs assistance running the sale. I know you aren't very educated about art, furniture, and jewels, but you do know how to call an auction."

Only after Wyatt had reached the pinnacle of Boston society had he understood Miranda's fears for him. He'd leapt and crashed as spectacularly as any mountain climber, just as she'd warned. And yet . . .

"We'd provide you with the wardrobe and housing in the beginning, but Father is convinced you'll soon be earning enough to live quite comfortably."

"He said that?" Her skirt had spread across the blanket, and Wyatt couldn't help but run his finger lightly over the satin edge that almost reached his leg.

"I told him about your sale barn—how you knew your customers, how you cared that they got the best price for their items, and that everyone was treated fairly. I told him how you were well-respected, treated Grandfather with patience, and took care of me. He believes that those are the most important qualities for a partner—"

"Wait." Wyatt leaned forward. "Your pa is offering to make me his business partner?"

Miranda stood. She turned so only her profile was visible. "Not specifically a business partner, just a partner in general. You know, someone you can trust for a . . . permanent relationship."

Wyatt stood. Ever so slowly he took her hand, pulling it away from the handbag she'd been twisting since she'd arrived.

"About this partnership . . ." He ran his thumb over her knuckles. "Does this primarily involve your father, or might you be the main party?"

Slowly she pulled out of his grasp. Fumbling with her reticule, she loosened the tie, fished in its depths, and presented him with his gavel, the one he'd given her the day they'd parted.

"I know you thought you'd given up on auctioneering, and if you don't want to go back to it, we'll try to carry on without you, but I thought you might want this. I even cleaned it up a bit, oiled the wood, and polished up that gold band."

Instead of taking it from her, he wrapped his fingers around hers, growing more and more confident that her visit meant exactly what he hoped it did.

"Miranda, do you believe that I can make it on my own?"

Finally, finally, her brown eyes met his, and how they shined. "Absolutely. Even if you keep working here at the livery stable, I have no doubt you'll be managing the place before Christmas." Then the warmth faded into doubt. "But does that mean you won't accept our offer?"

"And give up the chance to see you every day? Are you crazy?" Then he sobered. "But you are crazy. Before we go any further, Miranda, I have to remind you that I have less than when you rejected me the first time. If there's no hope for us, tell me now. I can't accept a position that would mean watching you and Cousin Cornelius . . ."

"I would say there's hope." She touched her collar, and her next words were more than a little breathless. "About as much hope as Widow Sanders has rhubarb."

Wyatt's heart filled. He felt like falling to his knees and kissing her hand, but there really wasn't room. Instead, he grinned like a lovesick fool until they both giggled. Miranda released the gavel into his care. Wyatt couldn't help but notice that it looked completely different all scrubbed up. The wood was richer, the metal band shone with a swirly design etched into it that he'd never seen before.

Miranda had turned and was studying Grandpère LeBlanc.

"It's good for him to be in these humble surroundings," she said. "Maybe he'll appreciate your new rooms after this."

The gavel had represented so much to Wyatt. His future, his father's expectations, his one bit of legacy that'd been handed down to him, but it was something more. Something that danced just past the lantern light and couldn't be grasped. Much like the painting, it was all he had of his family, and it seemed fitting now that they should be in the room together.

"Such a snooty Frenchman," she said. "He needs to sleep in a livery stable, him with his powdered wig, satin breeches, and signet ring."

Wyatt's heart skipped a beat. His eyes narrowed as he stepped closer to inspect the painting.

There it was. A gold band on Grandpère's finger. The same gold band that was warming in his grasp that moment.

He stumbled backwards. On his deathbed, Pa had placed this gavel in his hand and told him never to lose it. It was his legacy.

Miranda took his arm in both hands. "Careful there," she said. "If you knock yourself out, I won't be able to get the door open for help."

It was here—the missing proof that Aunt Corinne had been searching for all along. Unbelievable. All Wyatt could do was take Miranda by the shoulder and hold her firmly before him.

"Are you sure about this? Even knowing how everyone has ridiculed me? How people have called me a fraud? Even knowing that everything I own wouldn't fill a slop bucket?"

She grinned. "I've been sure for longer than you know."

He gestured to the room around him. "My life might not always be this fine. What if things get worse?"

She surveyed the tiny space with a twinkle in her eyes. "As long as you don't change, I won't complain."

"Oh, I've changed," he said. "I always had to prove myself. I had to prove I was above my shameful birth, but now I know the truth. Instead of dreaming about my birth family, I met them and found that they have their own struggles. And while I'd still be proud to join them, I've changed. I'm free now. Free to make new commitments."

Of course he'd changed, but what was important hadn't. He'd always been responsible and fair, determined and trustworthy, but he no longer had the fear of undisclosed shame hanging over him. Wyatt had been through the worst—she dearly hoped he didn't read the papers—and he'd come out the stronger for it. And so had she.

"I shouldn't stay," she said. "Father is waiting on me outside. What should I tell him? You never gave me an answer."

Wyatt turned the gavel over in his hands as if seeing it for the first time. "I'm afraid I can't guarantee that I'll auctioneer for you. There's a situation that isn't quite settled yet that could tie me up for some time." Wyatt stuffed the gavel through his belt. She couldn't help but notice that his trim waist had perhaps gotten a little leaner. With a touch to her chin, he raised her face to his. With eyes that kind, that sweet, how had she ever thought him fearsome? "I don't know about the job offer," he said, "but I'm certain on that other issue. As soon as I'm finished with work today, I'm coming to find you, and I'll keep pestering you every evening until I can snatch you away from there and make you my own."

"Even if Grandfather makes a nuisance of himself?"

He smiled. "Even Lady Godiva couldn't change my mind."

"How about a headless chicken?"

"Not even a rhubarb pie, or a hundred."

"How about—"

"Enough." His jaw hardened with a warning. "I got the final bid on this property, and I intend to claim it. If I have your permission, nothing else will get in my way."

Stepping into his embrace, she smiled as he drew her close, and didn't even mind that he wasn't wearing a cravat and waistcoat. What did the future hold for Wyatt and her? For Grandfather, Isaac and Alice, Betsy, and for even the LeBlancs? Miranda didn't know, but God did, and she'd leave all the details in His hands.

As Wyatt bent to claim their first Boston kiss, Miranda realized this was one bid she didn't mind losing. And if she wasn't mistaken, from somewhere above them she heard a voice with a French accent exclaim . . .

"Going . . . going . . . gone!"

EPILOGUE

The woodsmoke burned her nostrils the moment Betsy stepped foot on Widow Sanders' property. As agile as a fawn, she bounded through the yard, dodging the rosebushes that were wont to drop branches. Even with feet as tough as hers, a thorny twig hidden beneath a pile of autumn leaves wasn't no benefit.

Miss Abigail stood by the smoldering pile with her handkerchief pressed to her nose. Widow Sanders herself was too busy playing tug-o-war with her rake to mark Betsy's arrival through the thick smoke.

Betsy squinted into the heap. "What you burning, Widow Sanders?" She took the newspaper from under her arm and fanned her face. "That ain't just leaves."

"It's that lewd statue straight from the pit of Hades that's been dishonoring my perfect lawn. Must be spawned by the devil, cause it won't burn for nothing."

The wind shifted and sure enough, Betsy could clearly see the blackened form of Lady Godiva in the midst of the conflagration. The flames swirled around her but didn't seem to do anything but tan her hide.

"I think she likes it," Betsy said. "Looks like she's dancing."

Did Abigail wink at Betsy? It was hard to tell with her eyes watering and her mouth covered. Widow Sanders' rake broke free from the log it'd been caught in and she stumbled back a step. She righted herself, then stood with one hand on her hip. "I'll give it some time, but if it doesn't burn through soon, I'm for burying it."

What a pity. Someone spent so much time working on that statute that it seemed a waste to destroy it. Well, if Widow Sanders did bury it, Betsy would find where, dig it up, and put it somewhere so that everyone could appreciate it. Like on the new church grounds. Wouldn't that be a fine surprise for a Sunday morning?

From the road Josiah called to them as he and Isaac came down from the sale barn.

"Are you done already?" Widow Sanders asked as they made their way around to the front porch and out of the sun.

Isaac wiped his eyes. He sure acted different now that he had a wife, a baby on the way, a job, and whatnot. "Yes, ma'am. Headed home now."

"Well, don't be counting on my pies come sale day," she said. "Wyatt sure knew how to sell them. Now that he's gone, they haven't brought squat." She tucked a graying strand behind her ear.

Isaac rubbed his chest. "That's my fault. It took me a while to learn how to take bids, especially on pies. You bring your pie, and I guarantee it'll sell."

Oh no! Did he have any idea how Wyatt had gotten sucked into the same trap? "Isaac . . ." Betsy began, but Miss Abigail stepped on her foot. And she had boots on.

Her brother didn't miss the dirty look she shot their older, much more mature friend, but Miss Abigail kept that maddeningly calm smile. "It looks like Betsy brought us a paper. What's the news, Betsy-girl?"

The news was that Miss Abigail was up to some mischief, but Betsy didn't know what. She hated not being in on the joke. She'd have to pester Josiah until he explained it to her. "I have here a newspaper all the way from Boston." Betsy unfolded the paper, which was already opened to the fourth page and took a seat on the porch. "You won't believe who got married."

Josiah rolled his eyes. "Since there's only one person we know in Boston—"

"Three, counting Mr. Wimplegate and Miranda," Isaac corrected.

Widow Sanders clapped her hands together. "Wyatt and Miranda got married? Well, butter me up and call me a biscuit."

Still enthralled over the beautiful descriptions in the big-city paper, Betsy cleared her throat and began reading over their exclamations.

"The bride was given in marriage by her father, Mr. Charles Wimplegate. She wore a gown of ivory satin draped with Brussels lace and trimmed with orange blossoms. Her train was gathered twice to form two bouffant puffs, also topped with orange blossoms. The gown, while breathtaking, was modest, considering her new position in society, and well-reflected the spirit of her groom, who, although possessing ample funds at his disposal, opted for a humble venue, much to the disappointment of those who wished for a spectacle."

"Bah." Widow Sanders smoothed her apron. "My wedding gown was every bit as nice. I don't care what that Yankee paper says."

"Keep reading," Abigail urged.

So Betsy did, until the article concluded with,

" . . . despite floundering upon his arrival, Mr. Wyatt Le-
Blanc has put to shame the naysayers who shunned him
after the initial unfavorable ruling in the courts. Now who
could object to the generous man who has come to take
his place among us? It is wished that Mr. and Mrs. Wyatt
LeBlanc will enjoy the greatest happiness and a brilliant
future in our fair city."

"I'm not sure what all that's about." Josiah balanced on
one foot, sixteen years old and still as fidgety as a grasshopper.

"It means that poor Wyatt has faced his share of disappoint-
ments and should've stayed here, after all." Isaac stretched his
belly forward like a cat lying in the sunshine. "I'm surprised
that fancy gal stuck with him."

"That's not what it says." Betsy lowered her newspaper.

"Sure it does," Isaac said. "Didn't it say how everyone was
disappointed? That means he doesn't have the funds to afford
a proper church wedding."

"It means that he has the funds, but he chose—" For the
second time that day Miss Abigail stepped on Betsy's bare foot.
"Oww . . ."

Widow Sanders picked at her fingernail. "If we would've had
a church nearby, I would've had the grandest wedding around.
Slicker than any ol' Boston wedding, guaranteed."

"I wonder who'll be the first to get married in the new church
building," Miss Abigail said.

Isaac smirked. "My money is on Josiah. Ever since I caught
him smooching Katie Ellen—"

"Josiah!" Betsy gasped. Since when had her brother started

caring about girls? "You kissed a girl? And Katie Ellen, of all people! Pa is gonna wear you out."

Josiah's brows lowered. "He already did." He shifted like he could still feel the willow switch stinging his backside. "I ain't coming near her again. Not for a long spell. But I declare, if you say a word about it, Betsy, I'll whoop you so bad—"

"Now, children." Miss Abigail stepped between them. Even though the lady had to look up at Josiah, Betsy knew there'd be no back-talking. Between Pa and Mr. Jeremiah, Miss Abigail had plenty of defenders.

"I'd best get home." Josiah glared at Betsy one last time before turning to Miss Abigail with a more respectful expression. "Do you want me to walk with you?"

"That would be splendid. Jeremiah and Bobby are both at Walters' Dry Goods. Tell Jeremiah that I recommended he buy you both a stick of candy to keep you out of trouble until I get there."

"It's time I be going, too," Isaac said. They made their farewells and sauntered away, Josiah scuffing his worn boots against the gravel road.

"Pork drippings." Widow Sanders rushed up the porch steps. Betsy had to scoot to keep from being trampled.

"What are you talking about?" Miss Abigail asked.

"Pork drippings." Widow Sanders pulled her front door open. "I'm going to throw my pork drippings on that woman. Maybe then she'll ignite."

Betsy guffawed at the shocked look on Miss Abigail's face. "You thought she was talking about someone else, didn't you?"

Miss Abigail pressed her hand to her forehead. "I couldn't imagine who she was going to douse with bacon grease." She took a seat next to Betsy and picked up the clipping that had fallen out of the folded papers.

"That's a page from last week about a king who went to jail and about some museum that's got a display of apple dolls. You don't reckon those would be Miss Laurel's dolls, do you?"

Miss Abigail scanned the article quickly, her eyes flickering even faster than Betsy could read—but Betsy was getting better every day. "Looks like the man's name is King, and those dolls may very well be Laurel's. Wouldn't she be pleased?"

"I thought you might could take this to her on your way home." Betsy tossed a blond braid over her shoulder.

"Be glad to. You know, Betsy, your nephews aren't going to need you much longer. Are you planning to come back to the farm? I know your parents miss you."

That question had been gnawing at her for a while. Betsy ran her finger down a narrow column of text. "I don't rightly know. Uncle Fred has been helping me write better. Says I'm about ready to do some articles for him, as long as he can read them over and fix them up." She gazed at the paper in her lap and tried to put words to the longing she felt. "Wouldn't it be something, though, to write up a story and it be shared all over the country?" She scooted forward and leaned closer, hoping Miss Abigail would share her enthusiasm. "Just imagine, someone went to Wyatt and Miranda's wedding. They watched it with their own eyes, and now because of the words they wrote, I can see it. Isn't that something?"

Miss Abigail tugged on her braid. "You would be an incredible journalist, Betsy. You are verbose, curious, and have a knack for being in the thick of things."

"But there's nothing famous going on here. Nothing that people outside the mountains would care about."

"I'm afraid you're wrong." Abigail's eyes tightened. "There's trouble brewing, and if our lawmen don't get ahead of it, we're all going to pay the price."

"I'd rather write about weddings," Betsy said. "Isn't it something how Miranda and Wyatt are married now? When Miss Miranda first got here, it seemed that Wyatt would've been the last person she'd want to marry." She smiled up at Abigail. "It's just like you and Mr. Jeremiah. You'uns couldn't stand the sight of each other, and look at you now. I've got to wonder who God wants me to marry . . . and if I'll hate his guts when I first meet him."

Abigail chuckled. "You have a few years before you need to worry about that, Betsy Huckabee. Keep whooping up on those boys for as long as you can." She stood and fanned the smoke that had returned with vigor. "Speaking of menfolk, I'd better go meet mine and head home. We don't want to be caught in the woods after dark."

Standing, Betsy got a strong hug from Abigail, along with promises to carry Betsy's love home to her family. One last wave and Abigail strode purposely down the road.

Betsy gathered her paper and folded it carefully, not wanting to mess up the spectacular report that she would read over and over until the print smudged. Instead of heading to the road, though, she cut through the woods, preferring the winding shortcut to the wider path. The leafy green branches curtained every view with color as rich as Mrs. Rinehart's curtains. Betsy split them without thought, following the footpaths that were as familiar to her as the lines of her own signature.

She missed Wyatt and Miss Miranda, but she was tickled pink that they'd found their happily ever after. And while she wasn't sure she wanted to get married—she had enough of caring for snotty-nosed kids and doing laundry and cooking—she was downright curious to see what kind of man God would send her way, if that was in His plans.

With a sigh, she hopped a little spring and turned up the bank to the newspaper office. She'd try her hand again at a short news piece with the hopes that soon Uncle Fred would find it fitting to be printed in his paper.

And if she was lucky, maybe another paper from a big city would be delivered—one with stories of regal weddings, horrific crimes, and political intrigues. And maybe she'd find a story or two to feed her imagination until she was grown up and it was her turn to be the heroine.

Regina Jennings graduated from Oklahoma Baptist University with a degree in English and a minor in history, and has been reading historicals ever since. She is the author of *A Most Inconvenient Marriage*, which won the National Readers' Choice Award for Best Inspirational Novel of 2014, as well as *Sixty Acres and a Bride* and *Caught in the Middle*, and contributed a novella to *A Match Made in Texas*. Regina has worked at the *Mustang News* and First Baptist Church of Mustang, along with time at the Oklahoma National Stockyards and various livestock shows. She makes her home outside Oklahoma City, Oklahoma, with her husband and four children. She can be found online at www.reginajennings.com.

More From Regina Jennings

Visit www.reginajennings.com for a full list of her books.

To fulfill a soldier's dying wish, nurse Abigail Stuart marries him and promises to look after his sister. But when the *real* Jeremiah Calhoun appears alive, can she provide the healing his entire family needs?

A Most Inconvenient Marriage

When an abandoned child brings Nick Lovelace and Anne Tillerton together, is Nick prepared to risk his future plans for an unexpected chance at love?

Caught in the Middle

Forced to choose between a handsome cowboy and a debonair railway tycoon, will Molly Lovelace find love in the balance?

Love in the Balance

◊ BETHANYHOUSE

Stay up-to-date on your favorite books and authors with our free e-newsletters. Sign up today at bethanyhouse.com.

f Find us on Facebook. facebook.com/bethanyhousepublishers

anopenbook

Free exclusive resources for your book group! bethanyhouse.com/anopenbook

You May Also Enjoy...

When a map librarian and a young congressman join forces to solve a mystery, they become entangled in secrets more perilous than they could have imagined.

Beyond All Dreams by Elizabeth Camden
elizabethcamden.com

At Irish Meadows horse farm, two sisters struggle to reconcile their dreams with their father's demanding marriage expectations. Brianna longs to attend college, while Colleen is happy to marry, as long as the man meets *her* standards. Will they find the courage to follow their hearts?

Irish Meadows by Susan Anne Mason
COURAGE TO DREAM #1
susanannemason.com

⬥BETHANYHOUSE